This book is a saga of the early forties that takes us on a roller coaster ride with some of the leading figures of that time: Charles Lindbergh, Hitler, Hess, Henry Ford, Thomas Edison, Josephine Baker (The Black Pearl), Klaus Barbie, Ernest Hemingway, and Edvard Heinz (Hitler's hit man). The story takes us on a fast train from Fort Myers to Brazil, to France, Berlin , and Key West in rapid succession. And the conductor is Emmet MacWain, a retired and colorful Scotland Yard detective, trying to solve the mystery of who was behind the attempted murder of Henry Ford as well as several related murders. A Dickensian epic!"

Richard Conrath,
author of the *Cooper Mysteries*

International Standard Book Number 13:
Hardback 978-1-60452-202-0
Softback 978-1-60452- 203-7
eBook 978-1-60452-204-4

International Standard Book Number 10:
Hardback 1-60452-202-X
Softback 1-60452-203-8
eBook 1-60452-204-6

Library of Congress Control Number: 2024940543

BluewaterPress LLC
1218 Willow Oak Dr
Edgewater, Florida 32132

http://www.bluewaterpress.com

Other Titles by Patrick Kendrick

Papa's Problem, A MacWain Mystery

American Ripper: The Enigma of America's Serial Killer Cop

Extended Family

The Savants

Witness Protection

Edison's Last Breath

A MacWain Mystery

Patrick Kendrick

This book is dedicated with love to Dorothy "Dottie" MacMillan,

and

for Ardis Clark. Thank you for believing in my work.

PROLOGUE

WEST ORANGE, NEW JERSEY, 1931

Thomas Edison's hand trembled as he reached for yet another glass vial. "For...Hen...ry...," he said. Edison's son, Charles, looked up from dozing and stood quickly to assist his father.

"I know," said Charles, "for Mr. Ford." Charles took the glass tube from his father's trembling hand and held it to his mouth as he'd done so many times before.

Edison slowly exhaled into the vial and then sank back into his pillow. A sheen of perspiration covered his pale face as his mouth went slack.

Charles sealed the tube with a cork and found a candle with which to melt sealing wax onto the vial. He finished the project efficiently, having become quite adept at the practice over the past few weeks since his father had been bedridden. He went to the chifforobe in the bedroom and pulled open its door. Inside, the box containing the other sealed vials was there and he placed this vial into it along with the others. When he turned back to his father, he saw his eyes had not fully closed. Charles initially thought his father was watching him perform the usual ritual. Then, he saw the old man's chest was neither rising nor falling. It was as still as a hill. His father, Thomas Edison, the world's greatest inventor, was dead.

ONE

FORT MYERS, FLORIDA, 1940

The rabbi watched the mail carrier through a small telescope as he approached the auto magnate's house and brushed back the payot braids that framed his face. It was a face filled with despair and desperation. But his years of diligence might finally pay off. He held his breath as the postman reached into his leather satchel and withdrew the mail. *Was there a package among those many letters?*

"*Yes!*" hissed the rabbi, as the postman pulled a cylindrical cardboard tube from his bag and placed it in the mailbox of Henry Ford's winter home, then turned to resume his route. The telescope's lens flashed as it moved back and forth, now peering through the Ford home's windows to see if anyone was there. Ford usually came to the Fort Myers residence this time of year but had not yet arrived this season. There was a groundskeeper who came and went in his black Ford pickup, but that truck was not there currently. It was now or never.

The rabbi pulled a wide-brimmed hat over this head, assured his braided payots were exposed, and peeked outside. Dark clouds passed quickly overhead as if the world had accelerated on its axis. The watcher exited the small house he rented on Larchmont Avenue and walked quickly toward the combined estates of two of the country's most famous captains of industry: Ford, of course, and the inventor Thomas Edison, dead now, these many years. Once there, the rabbi looked around quickly, then reached into the mailbox and withdrew the cardboard tube addressed to Mr. Henry Ford.

He'd seen tubes like this arrive every year around this same time and he'd watched Ford scurry into his study to open the package and withdraw a glass tube sealed with a cork and wax. Each time, Ford would crack the seal and immediately inhale the air in the tube. The rabbi had made inquiries, discretely of course—Ford's antisemitic views as well known to him as anyone—and discovered a story that was as unbelievable and fascinating as that of the lost Ark of the Covenant. The tubes contained the last breaths of Ford's friend and mentor, Thomas Edison. They were rumored to give strength and increased mental capacity to the automotive industrialist and, having observed him for so many years, the rabbi knew this to be true. Ford still walked like a man twenty years his junior and his mind was as sharp as a soldier's saber.

The rabbi did not waste time, pulling the glass tube from the package, he carefully picked the sealed wax away with an overgrown thumbnail. Then he put the mouth of the bottle near his nose as he'd seen Ford do previously, plucked the cork out, and inhaled deeply.

Immediately, it felt like a cord wrapped tightly around his throat. He began foaming from his mouth and blood trickled out of his nose. His eyes bulged as he choked and clawed at his throat, veins swelled in his neck like enormous roots. Then, he fell forward, dead before he hit the ground, his last breath leaving his body like air from a deflated automobile tire.

TWO

KEY WEST, FLORIDA

Gregory Hemingway ran past the phalanx of lazy cats sprawled across the porch and into the house on Whitehead Street only to find his mother, Pauline, on the phone, her face a mask of concern.

"Yes," she said. "I understand Agent Serey." Pauline looked at her son and held up her pointer finger, indicating that Gregory needed to wait a minute. "Of course," she said into the phone. "I'll locate Mr. MacWain as soon as possible and have him call you. Yes. I'll tell him it is extremely urgent."

"Was that FBI Agent Serey, Mama?" asked Gregory, excited, hopping from one foot to the next as if he were walking on hot coals.

Pauline went to him and bent over to peer into his huge dark eyes. "Yes, it was. He..."

"Is he coming back here? Is there another murder? Or another spy?"

Pauline shook her head. "No, there aren't any more murders, or spies, thank the Lord. I don't know all the details, Gregory, but Agent Serey said he must talk to Mr. MacWain right away. Do you think you can find him for me? Quickly, no dawdling about?"

"I think so," said Gregory. "I think he keeps his boat offshore near Fort Zachary Taylor most of the time now. Ever since the hurricane took the roof off his house last year and..."

Pauline put her index finger across the boy's mouth. "Ssshh, this is extremely important. Take your bike son, and go fetch Mr. MacWain, and bring him here. Tell him he must come back to our house right away. Don't make him stop to buy you ice cream or another comic book. Just bring him back as fast as you can. Do you understand?"

Gregory nodded his head then turned and burst out of the house as if it were on fire. He grabbed his bike and ran with it, placed one foot onto a peddle like he was mounting a horse on the run, then stood and pumped his legs like pistons as he raced away. He hadn't seen Mr. MacWain for a few weeks, and he missed him. He was his buddy. Gregory wished he was more. A quiet, but strong man who always shared a smile and a kind word, Gregory wished Mr. MacWain was his father.

Pauline watched him go and sighed. He was growing up so fast. Ernest was missing so much but it was his choice, his loss. She inhaled as a pang stabbed her heart as it always did when she thought of him. Their divorce was still new and still painful.

Gregory sped down Angela Street, past shops and around cars that were beginning to fill the streets. He zoomed past the sundry shop where the owner was putting newspapers in a bin on the sidewalk, next to some fresh fruits, flowers, and vegetables.

"Where's the fire, Gigi?" yelled the shop owner as the boy flashed by.

"Can't tell you now, Mr. Turner," hollered the boy, "but, I'll be back later for ice cream."

"Got some new Superman comic books, too!"

Gregory glanced back with a grin and a thumbs-up gesture then peddled away even faster, speeding past coconut palms, royal poincianas, and gumbo limbo trees.

Mr. Turner smiled and continued stacking the newspapers, pausing to read the headlines: "PARISIAN STUDENTS DEMONSTRATE AGAINST NAZI OCCUPATION." Mr. Turner shook his head and muttered to himself. "It's only a matter of time."

THREE

DEARBORN, MICHIGAN

Ernest Liebold, secretary to Henry Ford, squirmed in his office chair at the Ford Motor Company in Dearborn, Michigan. *What was taking so long?* He got up and went to the window, pacing back and forth, looking through the glass like an expectant father. He overlooked the vast expanse of The River Rouge plant, an enormous industrial monstrosity that spread out over some thousand acres and contained its own steel mill, docks for access to the river for bringing in supplies and sending out the product, an electrical plant, and some sixteen million feet of factory space. It was the largest factory in the world and employed some one hundred thousand assembly line workers.

Watching it function was like observing a world being built. Raw materials would come into the docks and thirty-three hours later, a new car would emerge. They weren't just building cars, mused Liebold staring through the ghost of his reflection in the window, they were building a world. When the phone rang, Liebold almost jumped through the glass. Racing back to his desk, he grabbed the phone before it rang a second time.

"He...hello," he said, forgetting to announce who he was and where he worked.

"Fail," said a voice on the other end. Then silence.

Ice water ran through Liebold's veins as acid filled his stomach. He had barely put the phone back in its cradle when it rang again, the vibration innervating his hand like the tail of a rattlesnake. "Liebold," he said.

"Ernest, it's Ford."

"Well, hello, sir," he said, a drop of sweat raced down his neck and soaked into his collar. "How are you, sir? I wasn't expecting your call. I...thought you'd be enjoying the warmth of Florida, maybe doing some fishing or camping."

"Maybe I would be," said Ford, with his midwestern twang. "If someone wasn't trying to kill me."

"Good Lord, sir. What are you talking about?"

"I'll tell you about it when you get here. I need you to be here, with me, taking notes, helping out. Get on a plane, or train, whatever will get you here the fastest. I need a man I can trust by my side."

"Yessir, and may I say, you've called the right man."

"I know I have," said Ford, then the line went dead.

Liebold pulled a silk handkerchief from his coat pocket and swiped at his damp forehead. He found a cup of coffee he'd been drinking earlier and drank it down cold, just to wet his throat. Then Ford's secretary called his secretary and asked her to book him a flight to Tampa, Florida.

FOUR

Emmet MacWain awoke early that morning, netted some mullet for bait, and set out a few lines hoping to catch an elusive snook or a mutton snapper for dinner. If nothing else, he'd catch a few more z's while the morning was still cool and the sea gentle. The burly Scotsman assured that his rods were deep in their holders before he sat in a reclining canvas chair, arms crossed, his tanned, muscled legs propped up on the boat's gunnel. Then, compelled by the warm, morning sun and the gentle rocking rhythm of the sea, he nodded off.

Images flickered through his head like motion pictures in a dark cinema. His wife, Solana in bed, her once sienna-colored skin, now ochre, the sheets enveloping her emaciated body stained with his tears. The fog of dismal London waiting outside their bedroom window, waiting for her final breath to join it, and finally, it did, taking a part of Emmet's soul with it.

A tap, like bony fingers against the pane. Emmet stirred, and looked at the fog, curling, swirling, but revealing nothing. Another tap, like a raven's beak. Emmet stood and opened the window in his dream, and he heard a faint call, summoning him. "MacWain," it said from far away. Then closer, "Mr. MacWain!" Emmet peered deeper into the fog that began to thin. "Behind you, on the shore."

Emmet blinked open his eyes to the bright glare of the sun, as another tap sounded on the hull, and he saw where the sound came from: coconut seeds were bouncing off the cabin of his boat. He sat up and looked toward the shore, his eyes refocusing to see a boy on the beach. He stood up and shaded his eyes and finally made out his young friend, Gregory Hemingway, his arm drawn back ready to throw another coconut seed, when he realized he didn't need it anymore.

"Good morning, Master Hemingway," said Emmet, his Scottish brogue heavy with mischief. "What brings you here this fine morning to launch an attack on my peaceful vessel?"

"I'm sorry to bother you, sir," yelled Gregory, "but my mother got an important phone call and said she needs you to come right away."

Emmet's heart fluttered like a grade-school boy with a crush. Maybe she was ready to welcome him into her arms again. Then, fondness turned to worry, and he felt like a fool. Something was amiss.

"Is she okay?" Emmet hollered back. "Your mother. Is she okay?"

"She's fine," said Gregory. "Can you come, right now? She said it was very important."

Just then, Emmet heard the reel on one of his fishing poles scream out as something hit the bait and ran with it. He ran back, grabbed the bent pole, and tugged back on it. He saw a silver streak cut through the water, a distinctive black stripe running down its side. A snook! Emmet fought it for a moment but realized it would take some time to haul the fish in. If Pauline had sent for him, it had to be something important. He relaxed his shoulders, exhaled with defeat, and cut the line. He saw the snook race off to one side of the boat, then dart into deeper water.

"I'll get back to you, later," he mumbled, then reeled in his other lines.

Emmet checked the anchors to assure they were holding, then grabbed the rope that secured the dinghy and pulled it close enough for him to jump in. He rowed quickly to the shore, then stepped out into the shallows and tugged the small skiff onto the beach. He strode over to Gregory and blanketed him with his tall shadow as he proffered his hand. Gregory took it and gave an exaggerated shake.

"How have you been, lad?"

"Fine and dandy, sir. How's about you?"

Emmet smiled down at the boy and his sun-leathered face softened with a wide grin. "Never better. It always raises my spirits to see you, son."

"You grew a beard!"

"Did I?" said Emmet, feeling his face, his brown eyes full of mischief.

"It's got more gray in it than your head," noted Gregory.

Emmet laughed, running his hand over his scalp. "It's got more hair in it than my head, too."

Gregory giggled as if he'd been tickled.

"Now let's go see what your Mum needs. I see you brought your bike. Okay if we share this gallant stallion?"

"Sure," said Gregory.

Emmet straddled the bike and with one swoop of his arms, grabbed the boy and sat him on the handlebars. "Hang on, Gregory!"

The bike spun gravel from its back tire as it took off. The former Scotland Yard Inspector with the son of the world's most famous author sped toward Whitehead Street and Pauline Hemingway. Emmet and Gregory sped past clapboard houses—old sea captains' homes—with their ornate wood rails around their porte-cochère, and the fancy arched attic vents of their gable-styled architecture. The boy felt like a superhero speeding through the air, his arms extended like Superman, while the aging Scot felt his heart swell with the prospect of seeing Pauline again.

FIVE

THE PERIGORD REGION OF FRANCE

At the *Chateau Des Milandes*, Josephine Baker lay prone on a gold satin couch like a lithe, ebony panther and gazed languidly out a window overlooking the Dordogne River from the window of her Renaissance castle. She was naked except for the other nude woman—a young, local, blonde she'd picked up at a nearby café the night before—whose pale-as-bone arms and legs crisscrossed her dark backside like a fleshy chess board.

Empty bottles of champagne were scattered like dead soldiers on the coffee table and fallen onto the dense, red carpet. Lacy panties and brassieres were strewn around the huge room like confetti and an ardor scent permeated the room.

Josephine's servant, Claude, entered without a sound as if he were floating. "May I bring you some-zing, Mizz Baker?" he asked with his work-in-progress English, his face expressionless, ignoring the amorous scene as if it were commonplace, which it was.

"*Oui*, Claude," said Josephine, "A robe would be swell."

"Very well, madam. Will Monsieur Lion be returning home soon?" he asked, timidly, not wanting to upset *La Baker*, but considering the possible discontent if her husband showed up.

"No, Claude. Jean and I were divorced last week."

"Ah, pardon me, madam. I just..."

"Oh, don't fret over it, Claude. He was a nice gent but couldn't keep up with...my, eh, *mode de vie.*"

Claude smiled knowingly at her. "Eet is his loss, if I may be so bold."

The pretty blonde began to stir, then sat up and looked around, lost, hungover, and rubbed her eyes, which were sky blue, probably very pretty when they were not bloodshot.

"Better bring her a robe, too, Claude. And maybe some café and juice."

"Right away, madam. I'll bring some croissants as well," said Claude and walked away quickly, his steps making no sounds.

"Attaboy, *merci,*" said Josephine softly.

She had come a long way from the slums of St. Louis to become the most popular entertainer in France and beyond. Dubbed "the Black Pearl," "The Bronze Venus," "the Creole Goddess," and now, "La Baker," by her adopted France, she could never get over the fact that she had been a street urchin *mulatto* who dropped out of school by the time she was twelve, lived in alleys in cardboard boxes, and survived on scraps of food from garbage cans.

Now, she'd been painted by Pablo Picasso, and famed author, Ernest Hemingway, had called her "the most sensational woman I'd ever seen."

The blonde began to tip-toe around the room trying to locate her clothing, picking up panties here, a bra there.

Josephine watched her as if she were prey. "You're cute...," she said. She couldn't remember the woman's name.

The blonde turned to her, slipped her panties on, and located her skirt and sweater. Her cheeks flushed pink as she said, "*Merci, Madame.* My name is Pasqual."

"Of course, it is," said Josephine.

Pasqual continued to get dressed and was looking for her shoes when the enormous cheetah entered the room, a growl rumbling in its throat. Pasqual saw the animal and let out a shriek.

Josephine chuckled. "Chiquita, baby, come here." The cat strolled over to her and placed its head on her lap. She ran her fingers through its fur and scratched under its diamond-studded collar. "This is my baby," she said, looking at the terrified woman. "He won't hurt you." The huge carnivore had dark, tear-shaped streaks coming from its eyes that made it appear to be crying.

Pasqual swallowed a dry gulp and shuttled sideways like a crab toward the door leading out of the room. She turned and whispered, "*Au revoir, madame,*" then hurried down the stairs.

Josephine smiled after her and said, "*Adieu.*"

Claude re-entered the room, a slight smile on his lips. "I saw your guest departing."

"Yea. Guess we won't need that other robe." She stood up and stretched, then took the robe that Claude had brought her and covered up as he placed a silver tray, laden with croissants, hot coffee, and jam on the table by the couch. "Better catch her before she finds her way out. Make sure she gets home okay."

"Of course," said Claude, then whispered, "*Monsieur* Abtey, called. He said he would be by this evening after sunset."

Josephine nodded. "Very well. I haven't seen Jacques for a while. How did he sound?"

Claude tried to find the right word, then whispered. "Eh, nervous, I think. You know how he is. He mentioned we might get another um, *visite* from the Gestapo."

"Oh, did he say when that might happen, or whom we might expect for the *inspection*?"

"He wasn't sure of an exact date, but he thought it might be a man named Barbie. Klaus Barbie. He was giving us, how do you say, a head up?"

"Heads up," Josephine corrected. "Barbie. I've heard he is a monster. We've heard he might be coming to France. Did he say anything else?"

"*Oui,* madame. He said this man is very dangerous. Unpredictable."

"*Merci, beaucoup,* Claude," said Josephine, then looked out the window, a slight smile on her lips as she watched the river below eternally pushing along. As Claude left the room, she said to herself, "I like it like that."

SIX

Emmet slowed the bike as he entered the Hemingway compound and maneuvered it over the lawn. Gregory jumped from the handlebars before they stopped. The olive-green shutters surrounded the open windows of the two-story house like welcoming open arms. Running up the steps to the front door and slinging it open, Gregory yelled, "Mom, Mr. MacWain's here!"

Cats of all colors and shapes dotted the porch, all with too many toes from inbreeding. They scattered from Gregory's ruckus, darting like furry ghosts up trees or under bushes.

The big Scot lumbered up the steps and was almost to the door when Pauline appeared, like an apparition in the opening, wiping her hands with a dishtowel, a benevolent smile on her lips.

Emmet stopped and inadvertently took a deep breath, a slight pang in his heart. He swallowed, always at a loss for words upon seeing her after a few weeks, or had it been a couple of months?

"Mornin', Mum," he said. He wished he'd bathed before coming, but the boy had said it was urgent.

Pauline nodded, "Good morning, Emmet. Have you been well?"

"Peachy keen, Mum. And yourself?"

Pauline dipped her chin ever so slightly. "I'm doing better now that the divorce is over..."

"I'm sorry to hear about that..."

Pauline's eyes hardened. "Don't be."

The two of them locked eyes for a time that was too long, and then Pauline broke the silence. "Agent Serey called. He needs you to call him right away. He said he needs you, uh...your services, perhaps."

Emmet emitted a small laugh. "My services these days are occasionally catching a fish, or two, and trying to remove my hook without getting it caught in my thumb."

Pauline smiled, her eyes brightening a little then going dark again, like a cloud passing overhead, as if being happy was a gift she felt she did not yet deserve. "Don't be so modest, Emmet. Or so formal. Now, come in. I've made some iced tea. I wrote Mr. Serey's number down and you can use the phone in the kitchen."

"Thank you...Pauline," he said, as he stepped into the house and followed her into the kitchen where she poured him some tea. After all these years Emmet still found it odd that Americans sweetened, then poured, the tannin-colored liquid over ice. He enjoyed it all the same, particularly with fond company. Pauline handed him the tea with one hand and with the other, handed Emmet a slip of paper with a phone number scrawled across it.

Emmet fumbled with the phone—a device he still did not use much—until the operator came on and he gave her the number. He listened to some connections being made, plugs pulled out and pushed back in until, finally, the ringing started. It didn't last long before a familiar voice answered, "FBI, Chief Serey speaking."

"Ah, hello," John," said Emmet. "It's MacWain, returning your call."

"Hello, Emmet, how are you faring?"

"As fine as frog's hair, as they say around here. Just lazing about, doin' some fishing and the like."

"Very good. Wish I could grab some time to do that, too, but work has kept me as busy as a one-legged man in a butt-kicking contest. There's another colloquialism we use around here."

Emmet laughed. "Are you still in Miami chasing men who keep the brim of their hats down over their faces?"

"I am and, sad to say, there's no shortage of them around here. Almost two hundred thousand people are living here now—can you believe it—and I think half of them are crooks."

"Sounds like you have your hands full."

"I do, for sure. Listen, Emmet, I'll get to the point. I apologize for the abruptness of the request, but an incident has occurred that I feel could have national, perhaps international consequences. I could use your help."

"I'm not sure what an old, retired flatfoot could do for you..."

"Ah, cut it out, man. You're still sharper than most of the guys we employ here. I'm serious Emmet. I could use you on this."

"All right, tell me what you need."

"I'm sure you know who Henry Ford is, yes?"

"The carmaker?"

"The same. And, uh...well, it seems there's been a murder at his house in Ft. Myers. It may have been an attempt on his life."

"Okay. That's unfortunate, I suppose, but that's not a *federal* crime in itself. Why aren't the local police handling the matter?"

"We can make it federal in that the weapon used came through the U.S. postal service. It seems someone sent Ford a vial of...some sort of poison, or gas. Another man, a thief we believe, was going through Ford's mail, opened it, and inhaled whatever was in one of the packages. It seems there was a test tube, or beaker, that had something poisonous in it. And here is the weird part. Evidently, Ford receives a package like this yearly. They come from different places each time, but the beakers are supposedly the breath of his long dead friend and mentor, Thomas Edison."

Now, Emmet was interested. How odd, he thought. He did not want to get into another investigation, but he felt the irresistible draw of this bit of oddness. He had to ask, "Who sends them?"

"That, we don't know. They have different addresses each time. This one came from France. Which is another reason we can't get into an investigation that might lead to Europe. We have no jurisdiction there, and with what's going on with the Nazi invasion, if we were to get involved, it might be considered an act of war if we go over and start sticking our noses into...whatever is going on." Serey paused for a moment, before adding in a whisper, "Look, the truth is we don't want the FBI attached to this, right now. The newspapers will be all over it if we step in and it could upset some other investigations we're looking into."

"May I ask what those investigations might be?"

"I'd rather you didn't. The less you know about what we're doing, the safer you'll be. Listen, Ford doesn't want us involved either, but we can't very well ignore the fact that someone is trying to kill one of America's most recognized and biggest manufacturers, and by that, I mean employers, too."

"You left out one of the country's biggest antisemitic bastards, too."

"I know, Emmet and I know you have strong feelings against that. I get that, but you would be helping us out as well as doing a big favor for your adopted homeland. Ford's company is helping pull this country out of the economic depression we've been in for the last decade. We need him to keep doing that."

"I don't know, John. It's not something that I'd care to get involved in..."

"I'm sure it's not," said Serey. "And it's something the FBI *can't* get involved in at this time. I can't tell you all the reasons why, but I hope you'll just trust me. We *need* someone like you and there aren't many around. A man who knows investigative rules and how to look beyond the obvious. Listen, Ford has a man who works for him named Harry Bennett. He's head of Ford's security and sort of his ad hoc bodyguard. He reached out to us to look into this matter, and we think it is imperative we do, but not in an openly public way, if you know what I mean. I told him about you and your background with Scotland Yard and..."

"Sir, with all due respect, I know of Bennett, too. He's a Union buster and a murderer..."

"Emmet, please, I *need* your help on this," Serey said, his voice so urgent it made the hair stand up on Emmet's neck. "We need an inside man, and I know I can trust you to be discreet. I'll fill you in more as soon as I can, but Ford is sending a car to pick you up..."

"What? When?"

"Today. In fact, they should be there any minute. I told them you could be found at the Hemingway house..."

"You shouldn't have done that, sir," grumbled Emmet, surprised by the heat in his own voice.

"I'm sorry Emmet but you *have* to do this. The bureau will be right behind you all the way, but we just can't appear to be the lead on this. Understand?"

"No, John, I'm afraid I don't."

"Emmet, I can tell you...it's a matter of national security..."

"All the more reason a retired Scotsman with the ink barely dry on my citizenship card, should not be involved."

There was a pause, and Emmet thought Serey might have hung up the phone.

"Forgive me for being blunt, but maybe the ink isn't dry..."

Anger spread through Emmet's body, boiling up to his head which felt as if it might explode. A vein pulsed in his temple. "You son of a...I fought a war for this country," he whispered.

"Emmet, I understand you're upset but buck it up and just make sure you get into that car when it comes for you." Then, the phone went dead.

Emmet hung the phone up slowly as if it were made of glass. His throat felt parched, and he turned to retrieve the iced tea he was enjoying before the phone call. Pauline was standing behind him, dough stretched out across the counter in preparation for a pie, her flour-dusted hands near her mouth, lips parted.

"Well, that didn't seem to go well," she said.

"No, it did not," said Emmet.

"Why? I heard something about Henry Ford. What did Serey want?"

Emmet gnashed his teeth, grinding his jaw, his fists clenching, opening, then clenching them again. "I can't say," he murmured, then turned toward the door.

SEVEN

Pauline had just finished cleaning up the kitchen, the baking biscuits yielding a yeasty scent when there was a loud knock on the door. Pauline wiped her hands with a dishcloth and went to see who it was. Before she could get there, the knocking began again, harder and faster. Irritated, Pauline waited for the knocking to stop so she wouldn't get hit by the visitor's impatient, knocking fist. Then, she pulled the door open wide and quickly.

Frowning, Pauline said, "To whom shall I request a cease of the assault on my front door?"

A short man stood on the porch, wearing a white suit and a brimmed, wide-banded fedora that sloped down over one eye, like a big-city mobster. A bow tie that looked too big for the man's neck hung askew, like a crooked, polka dot smile. His eyes were dark, piercing, expressionlessly cold, and aimed like a scope at Pauline's eyes.

"Hello, ma'am," the short man said, his voice bigger than him. "You must be Mrs. Hemingway. I'm Harry Bennett. Mr. Henry Ford's man." He stuck out his hand. Pauline took it and was unnerved at the strong grip and vigorous shake he proffered to a lady. "I believe Director Serey may have contacted you about my arrival?"

"He did."

Bennett nodded. "Very well. Is Mr. Emmet MacWain around?"

"You just missed him. I think he went to pack some things."

Bennett appeared disappointed and impatient. "Well, if you tell me where I can find him, I'll go hurry him along."

Pauline couldn't help but smile. Emmet was the gentlest man she'd ever known but he was not a man to be ordered around. "I wouldn't do that if I were you."

"Oh? Is MacWain some sort of tough guy, or somethin'? I used to be a boxer and can hold my own, you know."

"Mr. MacWain used to box, too. Occasionally and spontaneously. Still does I believe."

Bennett smiled and put out his hands which he shook as if he were trembling. "Ooohh, look at me, I'm shakin' in my shoes."

Pauline stared at him expressionless. "He's not to be trifled with Mr. Bennett, I assure you. He killed a man trying to harm me once."

Bennett sniffed and shrugged, then scuffed his shoes against the porch like a scolded schoolboy. "Guess I'll wait for him to come back then," he said.

"You're welcome to wait inside," said Pauline. "I've made some fresh tea and biscuits."

Bennett displayed a crooked smile and removed his hat. "Well, that would be swell, Mrs. Hemingway," he said. "Thank you."

Inside, Bennett gazed around the house looking more like an interested student than a Detroit thug. He noted the taxidermized animal heads displayed about the room as well as some of Hemingway's various collections of weapons, memorabilia, and photographs of his various travels and trophies.

Pauline emerged from the kitchen holding a tray of biscuits and tea with condiments, including local honey and mango jam. She set the treats on a small table by a peacock chair in which Bennett had made himself comfortable and poured some tea into a glass with ice.

Bennett accepted the tea with a thank you, then added. "I think I met your husband one time, you know, at a gathering of some big wigs and fancy people. He was quite the storyteller."

Pauline nodded. "Yes, he is that, and now he is my ex-husband."

"Oh, I'm sorry to hear that..."

"Don't be. I'm not," said Pauline, then turned her face toward the upstairs quarters. "Gregory, would you come down, please? I have another errand I need you to run."

Within seconds, Gregory flew down the stairs, stopping abruptly when he saw the man in the suit, nibbling a biscuit.

"This is Mr. Bennett," said Pauline. "He's here to meet Emmett." Turning to Bennett, she said, "This is my son Gregory."

Gregory eyed the man suspiciously. He reminded the boy of men he saw at railroad stations and airports in the big cities up north. Men who were always in a hurry, briefcase in hand, a newspaper rolled up under the arm, who didn't fish in the ocean, or put you on the handlebars of a bike and make you feel like you're flying, or buy you superhero comic books, or fill in a spot that a father used to fill.

"Pleased to meet you, son, I'm Mr. Bennett. I work for Mr. Henry Ford, the biggest carmaker in the world. You ever hear of him?" He did not stand to greet the spindly boy and thought the kid appeared ill or undernourished.

Gregory nodded. "Chevrolets are better."

Bennett's face twisted like an angry vise. "The hell you say?" he snapped.

"Excuse me, Mr. Bennett," said Pauline, "I won't have you cursing in my home."

Bennett stood, face flushed, "I'm sorry, Ma'am. Just didn't want the boy to be confused about the cars..."

"I understand," said Pauline, "Now, let's not prolong this intrusion any more than necessary. Gregory, please go tell Mr. MacWain that Mr. Bennett has arrived and wants to expedite their departure."

"That means, speed it up, sonny," Bennett added.

Pauline glared at Bennett and Gregory stood his ground, frowning, but when Pauline tilted her chin toward Gregory indicating he should go now, the boy ran, grabbing his trusty Schwinn steed and mounting it on the run.

As she had Bennett ill at ease, Pauline thought it might be a good time for inquiries. "What is it that Mr. Ford believes requires the services of Mr. MacWain?"

Bennett removed his jacket and hung it over the porch railing, then crouched down on his haunches and answered reluctantly, like a boy who has been scolded. He shrugged. "Beats me. I coulda handled it."

"Handled what, exactly, Mr. Bennett?" said Pauline and continued to stare at him.

Bennett felt compelled to answer. "There was a guy. He got into Mr. Ford's mail. There was something in one of the packages, must've been some poison or something. The guy—he was a goddam kike, by the way, looking for something to steal—got a whiff of it and was dead on the spot. If it woulda been Mr. Ford, well...he woulda been dead. So, someone is out to get my boss...," he paused before adding, "My friend."

Pauline ignored the epithet. She'd been a writer, too, and was particularly adept at recognizing all the slang words and euphemisms people overused in their conversations. She knew where the word "kike" had come from. While it was now a derogatory term for Jews, it came from Ellis Island when Jews who could not sign their name, refused to sign with an acceptable "X," as it looked too much like the Christian symbol of a cross, so they signed with a circle, an "O," the Yiddish word for circle, or "*Kikel.*" After a while, immigration officials began calling those that signed with an "O," *kikels*, initially, and that evolved into "kike," thus the origin of a racial slur. There would be many more to come. Pauline pondered this as they waited on the porch in the steamy Key West heat.

Bennett removed his hat and wiped his brow with a handkerchief. "*Damn*, it's hot down here," he said but quickly apologized. "Sorry, it was a long drive here. Took me all night. Guess I'm a bit tired."

Pauline did not reply but looked down the road and saw Emmet and Gregory returning on the bike, traveling slowly up Olivia Street. Emmet had not changed clothes but had a small travel case with him. She did not see the gleam of the oversized smile he seemed to always wear around Gregory. She saw a crease between his brows, the edges of his full lips turned down.

Still keeping her gaze on Emmet and Gregory approaching, Pauline pondered aloud, "Perhaps, it was some sort of chemical Mr. Ford ordered. He's somewhat of an inventor, isn't he?"

"What, uh, yeah, well he was. He used to tinker with things like that when Mr. Edison—you know, the inventor—was around. They had a lab built. They were trying to make rubber for car tires, so they didn't have to pay out their nose to import it, but that never worked out too well. But, since Mr. Edison died some, gosh, has it been 10 years? Yeah, about that, I think. Anyway, Mr. Ford, doesn't mess with things in the lab so much anymore. Too busy."

Pauline thought she noted remorse in Bennett's tone and felt some pity for him, but the moment didn't last long.

Bennett stood up and began pacing back and forth across the porch, impatient. As Emmet and Gregory approached, he said, "About time." He stepped off the porch and walked briskly toward Emmet. "You must be MacWain. I'm Harry Bennett, Mr. Ford's assistant." He held out his hand, looking like an eager boy as he approached Emmet's tall figure. They shook hands, then Bennett took a handkerchief from his pocket and wiped his hand.

"I understand you used to be some sort of law investigator in England?"

"Yes," said Emmet cautiously, ignoring the rude gesture with the handkerchief. "I was an inspector with Scotland Yard."

"Well, how about that," said Bennett, a sarcastic lilt to his words. "I guess that makes you special. You might have cleaned up before we drove back. Now I get to sniff goddamn fish for three hundred miles."

Pauline saw Emmet's jaw muscles tighten and thought, *uh-oh.*

"Look, errand boy, it wouldn't take much for me to drop this request," said Emmet. "Don't try my patience."

Bennett sprang to his feet as quickly as a panther. In a truly dramatic moment, he tore off his jacket and hat and tossed them on the porch railing. Grinning like a shark he said, "Okay, wise guy, let's see what Mr. Ford is getting for his money," then rushed at Emmet like a dog off its chain, fists swirling.

Emmet, suitcase still in one hand, sidestepped Bennett and threw a short jab with his free hand. The punch caught Bennett squarely in the forehead and his feet shot up as if he'd slipped on ice as he fell flat, and unmoving, on his back, a lump growing like an egg on his brow.

Pauline had seen Emmet fight before but the abruptness of the assault and how quickly Bennett had fallen took her by surprise. "Oh, my word," she said. "I do hope you haven't killed him."

EIGHT

FORT MYERS

Henry Ford paced through his home as restless as a gambler waiting for the right card to drop. His hawklike face was stern, his gait long and quick, his patience unborn.

"Henry, if you don't sit down or get out of the house, you'll wear our carpet down," said Clara.

She'd been his wife since she turned twenty-two and Henry was only twenty-four when they married. They'd known each other since the days when both of them grew up on farms near each other and he'd met her at a New Year's Eve dance in 1885. He wanted to marry her right away, but her parents made them wait until she was a little older and he had something more to offer than a swollen heart and incessant hand-holding.

Ford's father gave him some farmland and they made a go of it for a few years, but Henry wanted more and they moved to Detroit and lived in ten different rental homes while he worked at the Edison Illuminating Company. Working on his idea for an automobile at nights and weekends, after five years he had made a self-propelled, gas-powered, four-wheel vehicle he called the Quadricycle. A few years later he fine-tuned that creation into the Model T and their life changed dramatically.

Ford stopped pacing and looked out the window. "I'm sorry, dear. I just thought that Harry would be back by now. I wonder if he had some trouble on the road."

"I'm sure he's fine," said Clara. "He probably stopped along the way. Maybe slept in a hotel. It is a long drive to Key West and there is only one way to get there. I'm sure he would've called if there was a problem."

Ford nodded but continued to peer out the window. Clara, whom he'd given the nickname of "The Believer," as she'd always believed he would succeed in making his automobile, approached her husband and placed a reassuring hand on his shoulder. Though they were in their home, Ford still wore his tailored, three-piece wool suit, his high-collared shirt tight around his throat and cinched off with an ornate silk tie, fluffed up for increased opulence, with a matching silk flower pinned to the jacket lapel. He always dressed as the dapper gent, even when he went camping.

Ford smelled Clara's reassuring scent—that of fresh-cut hay—as she slid her arms around him, and it brought back memories of their youth that made him smile. And Clara still enjoyed his scent, too, which she'd told him was much like that of motor oil as he was always working on one of the farm's many machines, tractors, pumps, and oil-fed furnaces.

"You're not being accused of murder, Henry," she whispered. "I don't know why you felt you had to hire an investigator. The poor man was stealing your mail..."

"I know, darling, but he died doing it. On *our* property. A damn Jew, no less. I don't need this kind of negative publicity. You know how the board is now. Things are strained with those people as it is."

"Oh, hon, Edsel is running things now and..."

"Running things into the ground, I'd say. He's always fancied the fancy, I say. More trim, more chrome, more costs!"

"How can you say that? Edsel is doing a great job for the company. For *you.* You're still the highest-selling car maker in America..."

"Doesn't matter if we lose the profit margins due to his extravagant contrivances."

"I wish you could just relax and let Edsel run the company. Isn't that why we bought this house? So, we could spend the winters here and enjoy our lives?"

"I'll relax when I'm dead."

Clara shrugged. "Okay, you seem content to be discontent. Mina asked me if I wanted to go shopping today and I'd like to get out of the house."

"Mina's here?"

"Yes, Henry. I told you that already. I've asked her over for dinner, too, just so you know. We need to get caught up on things. I like her and we just haven't seen her as much since Thomas died." She watched her husband turn back toward the window and swallow to ease the lump that swelled in his throat every time she mentioned Thomas Edison.

"I still miss him. He was everything to me. Employer, advisor, and always cheering me on as a...friend," said Ford, his voice breaking.

Clara stood behind him, wrapped her arms around her husband's chest, and leaned her face into his back. He was still the tall, solid man she'd fallen in love with nearly a half-century ago. He could be hard-willed, stubborn, and often angered her, but he was always in her heart. Some people thought his cornflower-blue eyes were icy-cold, but when she looked at them, she thought she saw portals to heaven.

"I know, darling," she whispered. "I know how much he meant to you." She felt a tear drop on her hand but knew how hard it was for her husband to share his emotions. So, she slowly eased her embrace and quietly left the house, leaving Ford to grieve his friend as he had for the past decade.

Ford looked out the window at Edison's lab, a growth of Queen's Wreath stretching its vines upward on the wall, its leaves like sandpaper to the touch, its blossoms bursting purple. The inventor had taught Ford much about plants as he searched for one that could grow well in Florida and produce the rubber that was so needed for the car industry, yet so cost-prohibitive to import. That memory provoked more thoughts for Ford.

Thoughts that took him back to Brazil where he'd tried to produce his rubber in his own Fordlandia, the factory and surrounding town he'd endeavored to create, only to discover one of the few failures in his life. Fordlandia, where people he'd tried to employ turned against him. Heathens he'd tried to turn into a civilized, productive workforce but who'd fought him every step of the way. Primitives who still lived in the past, who still believed in and practiced voodoo. Voodoo, the godless, pagan practice that used potions and practices that would render its followers into mindless zombies. A thought occurred to him.

If anyone could make a gas that could kill a man with but one whiff, it would be them, the pagans, the rebels who caused his biggest failure in business to date. That thought brought Ford out of his dour, sad mood. It gave him something to think about and a plan began to form.

NINE

A s Pauline tried to revive Bennett with a wet dishtowel, Emmet patted him down, found a snub-nose .38 in an ankle holster, and removed it. Then he stood and walked to the pool in the back of the Hemingway house and threw Bennett's gun into it. Spying a bucket, he grabbed it and filled it with the pool's saltwater. He returned to Pauline and the still unconscious Bennett.

"Get back, Pauline...please," said Emmett, and poured the bucket onto Bennett's face.

Bennett sputtered as if drowning, coughed, and rolled over. He stayed on the ground in a fetal position trying to regain his breath and consciousness. He pushed himself up on his arms which were visibly shaking, while the world still spun in front of his eyes. Looking around he saw the giant Scotsman who'd turned out his lights and focused on him, the memory of what happened coming back.

"You son of a bitch," he said, slurring his words like a drunk. Suddenly he reached toward his ankle, fumbling for the gun that was no longer there.

"It's in the pool around back," said Emmet. "The *saltwater* pool. Might need a bit of cleaning and a little oil before it's operational again."

"Damn you!" said Bennett and pushed himself up trying to resume a fighting stance then fell to his knees, his world still spinning out of his control.

"May I use your restroom to freshen up, Pauline?" Emmet asked.

Pauline nodded. "Of course."

"Perhaps you can offer Mr. Bennett some refreshment and put some ice on that horn coming out of his head," said Emmet referring to the doorknob-sized knot on Bennett's head. "I'll go with you to meet your master, ya whelp, if you can mind your manners while I clean up." Then he shook his head in disbelief, turned, and went into the house.

"I'd say I'm sorry, Mr. Bennett," said Pauline, "but I warned you." She put her hand out to steady him and he pulled away from her.

"I'm fine...been a little under the weather lately or your friend would never have landed that lucky punch."

"Of course," said Pauline, turning away to hide a smile. "I can see you're a tough guy. I'm going into my home if you care to rejoin us."

"I'll sit on the porch if it's all the same to you, Mrs. Hemingway," said Bennett.

Pauline paused, started to turn, and reminded him she was no longer Mrs. Anything but let it pass. "Suit yourself, *Larry*," she said and walked back into her home, chuckling.

"It's Harry," Bennett yelled after her.

Pauline hid a grin as she turned away.

Bennett looked around as if he'd lost something besides his pride. He noticed Gregory standing a few feet away, his hand over his brow to shade his eyes from the sun.

"What are you lookin' at kid?" said Bennett, his ego bruised, like an overhandled banana.

"That was really stupid," said Gregory, then turned to pick up his bike and strolled back to his home.

Bennett made his way to the porch, his legs weak beneath him, and sat in a wicker chair, his ear ringing like the bell between rounds of a boxing match.

Emmet showered quickly, dried off, and fastened the towel around his waist. He was trimming his beard when Pauline came up and saw him through the open door. Her heart swelled like it did when she first met Emmet, and heat spread through her abdomen. She felt a light sweat break out on her neck and brow, gulped some much-needed air, and swallowed, dryly.

Emmet saw her from the corner of his eye and turned to her. "Excuse me," he said, "I should've closed the door."

"No...that's...all right," said Pauline. "I should've, uh, stayed downstairs while you freshened up."

"Nonsense, my lady. It's your house and I appreciate your hospitality." He smiled at her and added, "You're welcome to join me in here if you care to."

Pauline's face flushed red and she averted her gaze which had been wandering over Emmet's muscled chest. He was probably twenty years older than Hemingway but was in superior physical shape. "I...I...can't," she said, trying not to lock eyes with him.

Emmet stared at the side of her face, once again noticing the beauty, even in her profile. He felt his heart beat harder and could hold back no longer.

"Why," he said, almost in a whisper. "What happened to us?"

Pauline lowered her head. "There wasn't really...an us," she said, unable to look into his eyes.

"Was I imaging it then?" asked Emmet. "Was I imagining us in each other's arms?"

"Stop," Pauline whispered, "Gregory is in the house."

"I don't care. He knows how I feel about you." Emmet stepped from the bathroom and went into the bedroom where he'd left his travel case, his clothes already laid out.

Pauline watched as he dressed while maintaining vigilance on the stairs in case Gregory should come up. She saw Emmet drop his towel and pull on some briefs and his pants. Before he could put his shirt on, she came up behind him and laced her arms around his chest.

"I'm sorry," she said.

Emmet stood, looking out the window as he'd done many times after they'd made love. His jaw muscles flexed and he shrugged her off and put on his shirt. He turned to Pauline as he buttoned up.

"I don't know if, or how, I might have offended you, Pauline, but you know how I've felt since the first time we met. I thought you felt that, too."

Pauline stared up into his eyes, her mind reeling. It wasn't him and she should be honest enough to tell him, but she could not. "I... can't, she said, a tear welling in her eye and spilling over her soft cheek. "I don't...I *won't*...be hurt again." She stood statue-still as she said this, her arms stiff at her sides, body trembling, fists balled up, her fingernails dug into her own palms. A vein visibly throbbed on her temple. She closed her eyes and held a hand on the vein as if to push the pulsing mass back into her head.

Emmet turned, closed his bag, and grabbed it like a club. He started to walk past her but stopped. "I won't be either. You might be good to remember, that I lost my wife, too."

"That's not like you to say something unkind," said Pauline, her brow furrowed as she rubbed the side of her head as if she'd bumped into something.

"And it's unkind of you not to say anything after what we've been to each other, after...," said Emmet, but he noticed Gregory standing at the foot of the stairs and stopped himself.

He turned to look at Pauline, heat evident in his eyes. "Thank you, once again, for your hospitality. I'd better be going," he said and began down the stairs. He stopped and looked up at her one last time. "So long, Pauline. Stay well." Then added, "I've asked Charles Thompson to put my boat in dry dock until I return."

"I'll be sure that he does," Pauline offered.

At the bottom of the stairs, Emmet put his hand on Gregory's hair and mussed it, then leaned down to kiss his head. "You take care of your mother, Master Gregory. You are her Superman, aye, lad?"

Gregory looked up into Emmet's eyes, his own filling with tears. "I'm going to miss you, Emmet. When will you be back?"

Emmet swallowed hard. "I'm not sure, Gregory. But you be safe." He started to walk out the front door and turned. "I never told you, young man, but if I ever would've had a son, I would hope he would've been just like you."

Then the tall Scotsman turned and found Bennett sitting like a lapdog on the porch. "Are you okay to drive Mr. Bennett, or shall I take the wheel?"

Bennett stood up, obviously humbled from his trouncing. "I can drive MacWain. Let's go. Mr. Ford is many things but patient ain't one of them."

The car, a once shining, maroon, 1940 Ford Deluxe Tudor sedan, now covered with a film of dust, sat idling, smoke puffing from its tailpipe. Emmet tossed his bag in the backseat while Bennett got behind the wheel. As they shut the doors and pulled away, Gregory stood on the porch waving until the car vanished from sight, his lip trembling with loss. It had been unusually dry lately and his face wore the same dust from the dirt roads he'd cycled all morning. A tear ran down his cheek like a stubborn, clear stream in a desert.

Pauline glided over to him and placed her hand on his shoulder. Gregory looked up at her, his lips trembling now as he said, "He's not coming back, is he?"

"I don't know," she said, lowering her head and pinching her eyes shut, the pain in her head throbbing.

TEN

For the first few hours, neither Bennett nor Emmet spoke. Emmet was in a dour mood, thinking of the fading romance with Pauline. Bennett was trying to stay conscious. His head throbbed and he was nauseous from the buffeting Emmet had given him.

As they drove north on U.S. 1, they passed through Big Pine Key and saw small herds of diminutive Key deer working their way through mangroves off the side of the road. Bennett had retrieved his pistol from the pool at Pauline's house and suddenly pulled it out and aimed at one of the small animals and pulled the trigger. There was a metal thud, and the gun didn't fire.

Emmet said, "What the hell are you doing?"

Bennett glared at him while trying to keep one eye on the road. "Was gonna tag one of those tiny deer but some Limey ruined my gun tossing it into a pool!"

"You enjoy killing things just to pass the time?" said Emmet. "I should've stuck that gun up your arse, you damn fool."

Emmet thought Bennett would pull over and have another go at him but he didn't. The little thug seemed to be thinking for a moment, then laughed out loud, though doing so caused him to grasp his head and groan. "You're gonna get payback for this lump one day," said Bennett. "I can promise you that."

"And I can promise you if I have to do it again, you won't get back up...ever."

"We'll see," said Bennett, his jaw muscles flexing.

The conversation ended and they drove the rest of the way through the Keys without words, passing through Marathon, Long Key, Islamorada, Tavernier, and Key Largo before angling slightly to the northwest through Homestead.

Along the way, Emmet noticed the ravages of the longest economic depression in history, still evident after a decade. Homeless people ambling down the road, occasionally sticking their thumbs up to try to hitch a ride. Rail-thin men hanging out at docks, their skin sunbaked into brown leather, the bones of their spines sticking out like those of ancient reptiles. Desperate men waiting for boats to come in so they could offer to wash the decks down or help unload the catch of the day for whatever pocket change they could earn or accept the carcass of a fileted fish to make some hobo stew. Families living in makeshift tents along the road, their eyes wide with fear and hunger, barefoot kids with dirt-smeared faces dotted with flies. Open-air bars with women heavily perfumed in place of bathing, dressed in swimsuits, and flirting with fishermen, whose hands were still stained with blood from the day's catch.

It reminded Emmet of the street urchins and homeless denizens of London, though instead of being enshrouded and hidden by dense fog, these people were ablaze in the sunshine, and, in that bright light, there was no place to hide their poverty, their "ignorance and want," as Dickens would write. From a beat copper to skilled inspector, Emmet had seen it all, the cruelty of people who lived day to day, the horrid things they would do to themselves including selling their bodies, or their children, to rosy-cheeked Pickwickian men whose tongues slipped over their veracious mouths like tentacles as they led their sacrificed victims into dark alleys.

A flock of pelicans flying in formation like an allied aircraft attack drew Emmet out from his dark thoughts and lightened his mood as they dove, one by one, into the ocean, slammed into its surface, and came up gargling down a fish.

Bennett stopped for fuel in western Miami. It was the last place to get gas and refreshments before heading across the state on the thin stretch of road known as the Tamiami Trail. There was an ice chest in the backseat of the car and Bennett filled it with bottles of soda, beer, and chunks of ice. He bought some beef jerky, smoked fish and pork rinds, and some apples to nibble on, then filled an extra gas can he had in the trunk of the car.

"Can you drive a car MacWain?" asked Bennett.

"Of course, we traded in the horse and buggies some time ago."

"Good," said Bennett. "I could use some shut-eye. You just head out west on this road. There are no turns or any way to get lost. Nothing but a straight road with nothing to see. When it starts to turn north, you'll see the Gulf of Mexico and you just stay on it heading north until you see signs for Ft. Myers. I'm sure I'll be awake before then but just so you know. Okay?"

"Got it," said Emmet. As he slid in behind the wheel of the car, it occurred to him that it had been several years since he had driven one. But as soon as he started the engine and heard its rumble, he felt like a boy at the county fair, trying out a new ride, butterflies aflutter in his stomach, aching for adventure. He mashed the accelerator down and the car lurched forward.

"Whoa, man, you don't have to push it so hard," said Bennett. "This baby has an eighty-five horsepower, V-8 engine. It'll fly. Keep to a nice even speed so we don't overheat the motor and the gas will last longer, too."

Emmet nodded understanding but as soon as Bennett fell asleep, he pushed the pedal down a little more, like a child with a new toy, and watched the red needle of the speedometer arch to the right, surprised at how fast the car could go. He drove for over an hour, occasionally glancing at Bennett, who was slumped over to one side sleeping with his mouth open, emitting a slight snore.

Bennett had been wrong about "nothing to see," on this road. Emmet saw pink roseate spoonbills and flamingoes scouring through the mud for morsels, and great blue herons, standing as still as flagpoles, patiently stalking fish with their spear-like beaks. Ospreys dove into the canals and scooped out fish with their talons, while red-tailed hawks flitted through cypress tree branches on the hunt. Alligators—some of them longer than the car—warmed themselves on canal banks, their huge jaws wide open as if calling out silent warnings. Anhinga birds emerged from the water and dramatically spread their wings out wide to dry. Redwing blackbirds flitted through bushes that lined the dark water banks. Occasionally a deer would run across the road, often followed by a couple more that seemed as if they were waiting to see if it was safe to take their turn. Huge gopher tortoises and tiny box turtles followed suit but lumbered along, impervious to the few cars that would zoom past them, narrowly missing them as they sped by.

Emmet had seen some of the creatures in and around Key West but not in the numbers there were along this barren stretch of the Everglades. He was enjoying this plethora of colorful wildlife when he spotted something far ahead. As he drew closer to it, he could see it was a car, its hood raised to indicate it was broken down. Emmet slowed, then stopped to look inside to see if anyone was still there. The car, a late model Plymouth, was empty and as far as Emmet could see down the road, there was no one nearby. Emmet's instinct was to wonder where the occupant was. Out here on this lonely stretch of road, with the heat and the abundant wildlife, no one would last for long.

ELEVEN

E mmet continued along the Tamiami Trail, squinting his eyes against the bright sun, and pulling the visor down to help him see ahead. For at least ten miles he saw nothing, then way ahead a tiny figure came into view. Emmet assumed it was the driver of the Plymouth because no one in their right mind would be so far out on this desolate road for a casual walk. He slowed the car as he drew closer and saw it was a man in a suit, his coat slung over one arm, his white shirt soaked with perspiration. He didn't stick out his thumb to hitch a ride or even turn to look at the car he had to have heard approaching him.

Closer now, Emmet could see he was a black man and it occurred to him that was why he wasn't trying to hitch a ride—he'd probably tried at first, then gave up when no one stopped. His tie was loosened, and his shirt collar open to help cool himself. There was nothing in sight, no service stations, homes, or sign of human life other than the occasional car, and none of them were stopping.

Emmet eased off the accelerator, slowed the car, and pulled off the road in front of the man. He got out of the car and the black man stopped walking. His face glistened like wet coal. A tongue eked out of his full lips, dry, searching for some wetness but finding nothing but salty sweat along his upper lip.

"Sir," said the man, "I don't have much money with me nor a weapon to defend myself if you're stopping to rob me." His voice was melodious, not that of a farm worker or common laborer. He sounded more like the black men Emmet had known and worked with in London.

Emmet grinned. "I'm not here to rob you, sir. I stopped to offer you a ride."

The man stood for a moment staring at Emmet as if he thought it was a mean joke, then his lips trembled, and he wiped his eyes with one hand. If he had enough moisture left in his body, he might have shed a tear. Emmet reached into the back of the car, into the cooler to extract a soda pop for the man.

Bennett woke up and looked around as if he was lost. "What're you doing?" he asked, his words slurred from sleep.

"I'm stopping to help this man," said Emmet. "His car broke down some miles back."

Bennett craned his neck around and his eyes popped wide open. "Whu-what?" he stammered. "You're stopping to help a nigger?"

"I'm stopping to help another man, you dullard. And that will be enough of that," Emmet warned. Emmet saw Bennett inch over on the seat, so he pulled the key from the ignition. Then he placed the edge of the key against the knuckle of his hand and under the cap of the bottle. With a flick of his wrist, he popped off the cap. He walked back to the black man and handed him the soda. The man put the bottle to his lips and downed the contents in seconds.

"The Lord must have sent you, sir," said the man. "To whom may I offer my gratitude?"

"Name's Emmet MacWain. And who are you, sir?"

The man grinned widely. "My name is Victor Hugo Green."

"Named after the French author?"

"That's right. You'd be surprised how many people don't catch that. And I'm a writer, too. I write travel guides. Specifically, to give people like myself, advice on places where they can stay and eat."

"That's fascinating," said Emmet.

Green grinned. "You're not from around here, are you sir?"

Emmet smiled back. "I've taken up here the past few years, down in Key West. But, no, not from around here. Scotland was my homeland, though I worked most of my life in London. Now, what can I do to lend you a hand? I assume that was your car some miles back."

"That's right, I'm afraid. I borrowed it from a friend. The fuel gauge is broken and stuck on Full, so you never know what you have in the tank. I usually fill it up anytime I get a chance but I couldn't find anyone to sell me gas in Miami, so I said a prayer and hoped I could get across the state to Naples. There's an Esso station over there that will sell Negroes fuel but it sure is a long way on foot. You're the first people to stop out of about 30 cars that's gone by."

"Well, you're in luck, Mr. Green. We have some extra fuel. We'll take you back to your car and you follow us to make sure we all make it across this swamp."

"I'd be beholden to you, good sir. I was praying I wouldn't have to run past that monster over there." Green pointed at an alligator—well over twelve feet long—sunning itself on the bank near the road. Its mouth was open giving it the impression it was smiling. As if on cue, it emitted a guttural growl.

Emmet nodded. "That's a brute for sure. So, what say we get you back to your car."

Bennett had emerged from the car. "Way a minute, boys. There ain't no way a nigger is going to get into my car."

The ever-present smile on Green's face disappeared like one of the mirages of water on the hot road.

A feeling like lava erupting from inside him, Emmet's temper rose, and he turned slowly and began walking toward Bennett.

"Hold it there, Limey," said Bennett, raising his arm, his fist filled with the pistol. "I don't know if this thing will fire or not, but you can find out if you take one more step."

Emmet didn't hesitate but continued toward the car and Bennett.

Bennett pulled the trigger. Once again, the hammer fell with a thudding sound.

Emmet was in a full, running charge now, his teeth bared in anger like a wolf. Bennett tried to make it back into the car, but his hand slipped off the door handle and Emmet was upon him. He grabbed the hand with the pistol and crushed it until Bennett squealed. Emmet wrenched the weapon free and slung it into the nearby canal. The motion scared the alligator, and he clambered down the bank and splashed into the water. Then, Emmet slapped Bennett across the face, then again, with the back of his hand. Bennett's lips and nose burst open, and blood flew with each smack until his head seemed like it would detach from his neck. Emmet dragged him over to the canal and slung him into the water.

The shock of the cool water and the grumble of the gator that had just slid into it snapped Bennett out of his shocked encounter. He tried scrambling out of the canal, but his feet slipped repeatedly on the slick mud bottom.

"He...help," Bennett pleaded but Emmet just crossed his arms and leaned against the car. To everyone's surprise, Victor Green strode across the bank, reached down, grabbed one of Bennett's flailing arms, and pulled him from the dark water.

Bennett's gratitude was to shout, "I don't need no help from a darkie." Then crawled on his hands and knees closer to the car and collapsed into a silent, sobbing heap.

Emmet stepped over him and opened the passenger door for Green. "Let's go fuel your car, Victor."

Green reluctantly edged around Bennett and got into the car. Emmet cranked the motor and turned the car around.

Ignoring the encounter with Bennett, Emmet said to Green, "Tell me more about your travel guides Victor."

"The guides let colored people know where they can stay, or where they can get fuel or food, you know, where we are welcome."

Emmet stared ahead, a slow burn inside him. When he didn't say anything, Green added, "There's a lot of places that won't sell Negroes food, nor fuel. A lot of them won't let us use their restrooms. Some of them are downright hostile toward people like me. I saw a need for a guide like this because people, like me, enjoy traveling, too. We have families that like to vacation and see the country, even if the country doesn't want to see us."

They sped down the road until they spied the Plymouth then pulled over and parked behind it. Emmet got out and took the gas can from the trunk of the car. He opened the cap on the tank and poured the contents into it.

"That's very generous of you, Mr. MacWain," said Green. "Are you sure you've got enough gas in your car to spare all that?"

"I think so," said Emmet. We fueled up before we left Miami. But, let's stick together until we get across the state and hope we can find another filling station."

"There's that Esso station I know of and they sell to Negros. I was going to drop off some of my books to them, so if we can make it there, I'll be fine."

Emmet nodded and said," See if your car will start."

The Plymouth struggled to start initially but finally got a sip of the new fuel and the motor cranked up with a hefty roar. Green held a thumb-up hand gesture out the window as Emmet got back into the Ford and pulled back onto the road.

After a few minutes, Emmet spied Bennett, still sitting where he'd left him. He thought about speeding past him but realized if he wanted to finish this business with Henry Ford, he might as well bring his servant dog back to him. He slowed and pulled up next to him. The passenger window was open, so he leaned toward it and said, "You've tried to assault me, and you've tried to shoot me. You're lucky to be alive little man. Now, if you behave yourself, we'll get to your boss's house, and I'll try to help him with his problem. But, if you cross me one more time, it'll be the last thing you do. Understand?"

Bennett nodded, utterly defeated, and got into the car like a boy who was caught skipping school.

They drove on, Emmet keeping an eye on the Plymouth in the rearview mirror. In a few hours, they'd made the trek across the peninsula of Florida and passed the sparsely populated area of Ten Thousand Islands, where Calusa Indians used to dwell until they were slowly exterminated to make room for the pale-skinned invaders who wanted to live on every inch of *Florido*, which meant "full of many flowers," and decimated everything in their path like a pestilence.

The gas tank needle on the Ford was nearing "E" when they pulled into Naples and Emmet spied the Esso filling station that Green had mentioned. His Plymouth pulled in behind him and they topped off their cars. Emmet and Bennett used the restrooms and waited while Green dropped off a box of his guidebooks to the owner of the station.

"Would you fellows like to join me for a late lunch at the diner next door?" asked Green. "The food is as good as homemade, and it would be my treat to show my gratitude for your kind help."

"Thank you, Victor, but that's not necessary," said Emmet. "Mr. Bennett's boss is expecting us, and I'd like to get there with enough time to find some sleeping quarters myself."

Green held up a finger, "Just a minute," he said and darted to his car. When he returned, he had one of his books and handed it to Emmet. It was green in color and Emmet looked at the title: *The Negro Motorist Green Book.* He thumbed through it and noted places—very few in Florida—that were open to doing business with people of color.

"There are some nice places in there with good people running them," said Green. "They even allow white people into their businesses'," he joked, giving Emmet a wink.

Emmet smiled and stuck out his hand. "Thank you, Mr. Green," said Emmet. "I hope we meet again."

"Thank you, sir. I hope we will, too. It's a small world, so who knows? So long and good luck with *your* business," he said, never inquiring what their business even was. "I hope if we do meet again, Mr. MacWain, your spirit is lifted because I can see sadness sitting on your shoulder like an uneven load and you're too good a man to bear that weight." With that, he turned and walked toward the diner as Bennett took over behind the wheel. Emmet looked back one more time and saw Green, one hand on the door to the diner, the other waving to them as they pulled away.

TWELVE

FT. MYERS

A fter a little over an hour of a non-conversational drive, Emmet and Bennett pulled into the Winter Estate of Henry Ford in Fort Myers. It was a lovely two-story home, with clapboard sides that showed the work of a skilled New Englander shipbuilder's carpentry. There were a few outbuildings, a garage and workshop, and another house near it—Thomas Edison's former home—not far away that appeared to be of the same architect if not the same builder. Huge Royal Palms lined the street on the way in. Smaller palms and various other trees and flowering plants surrounded the home.

As the Ford crunched through the gravel driveway approaching the car's namesake home, Emmet spotted a figure in the window staring out at them. The man was tall, his silver hair coifed around a face that was as still and emotionless as a tobacco store's wooden Indian. He was dressed in a suit and tie as if he were heading to work or just got home from a day at the office. A wide upper nose separated colorless eyes that peered at the men like those of a raptor searching for something to kill. Even through the reflective window, Emmet could see Henry Ford peering at him, assessing him, like prey.

Bennett hopped out of the car and ran into Ford's home without knocking, nor closing the door behind him, like a little boy beaten up by the neighborhood bully who hurries home to share his tears of misfortune with his mum. Emmet sat in the car and watched as Bennett silently gesticulated, his arms flailing as he told his tale, his mouth moving soundlessly from where Emmet sat and watched, surprised at how much he was enjoying the scenario. He wasn't worried about what Bennett told Ford, nor what the automotive magnate thought of him.

Typically, when Emmet began an investigation, he felt the thrill of the unknown and what it might reveal to him. It energized him. But this new thing he felt forced into did not sit well with him at any level. It fatigued him.

Emmet watched the two men talk and saw Ford occasionally look out the window several times before finally gesturing to him, waving him into his house with an impatient come-hither motion of his hand. Emmet slowly got out of the car, sauntered up to the home, and up the steps to the shaded porte-cochere that led into Ford's home. His hips hurt from riding in the car for so long and his legs felt heavy as he entered the still-open door of the residence. Emmet looked around the living room, a piano against one wall, and tasteful, over-stuffed couches and chairs, upholstered in fine silk, hugged the other walls. Rich tapestries lined open windows, like decorative sentries. Plaques with engraved accolades, framed photographs, and magazine covers picturing Ford glad-handing other captains of industry, or political figures, dotted the walls.

Ford came into the room but rather than greeting Emmet with a handshake, he opened his jacket and placed his fists on his hips like an angry schoolteacher ready to give a sharp oral discipline to a naughty student. He was taller than Emmet initially thought now that they were face to face. Meticulously dressed in a pale-grey herring-bone linen suit—the pressed pleats so severe they looked as if they might incise flesh—and included a vest with a gold watchchain draped stylishly from one pocket to the next. With his wing-tipped shoes shining like black mirrors, Ford was the picture of sartorial elegance. His long neck was enveloped with tall shirt collars that were pinched together with an elaborately styled maroon tie that matched the car that Bennett had driven to pick up Emmet.

"Well," he said, "You know who I am, and I know who you are. My colleague, Mr. Bennett, has informed me of your shenanigans along the way. I can't believe he didn't kill you. Maybe he still will. I should dismiss you right away."

"Dismiss me?" said Emmet, his brow furrowed. "I'll gladly dismiss myself if you'll give me the keys to that car or a ride back home."

"Well, I'll certainly not do that, sir. I'd just like an explanation from you on your behavior. You were recommended by FBI Director John Serey, whom I've come to know as a good man. I wonder how he could've been so wrong about you."

"Did your little bulldog tell you what happened—the truth—or do you just take the word of such a common lout?"

"You're insulting...," Ford began.

"Your henchman was rude to me when he came to fetch me, tried to pick a fight the moment we met, and was felled with one blow. Later, when I tried to help a disabled motorist, he tried to shoot me, but his gun misfired, and he had to be spanked again. He's lucky I didn't feed him to the alligators."

Ford pursed his lips, then sucked them in as if chewing on them. "Okay," he said. "I know Harry can be a bit persuasive..."

"Pushy," said Emmet. "And dangerous."

Ford allowed that with a slight nod. "Okay. But you need to know, I have no closer friend than Mr. Bennett and you'd do well to remember that."

"Then you need to make more friends, sir."

Ford seemed to relax, his shoulders softened, and he took his hands off his hips. "I have many acquaintances as you might imagine with the industry I built, but none closer than Harry. I'll talk with him. Maybe we can get past this," said Ford in something as close to a conciliatory remark as he could muster.

"I'm here," said Emmet. "Mr. Serey called me shortly before your man showed up and shared some brief details with me. That's why I came. Serey and I worked together on another matter a year or so ago that involved a murder, in fact several..."

"Yes," Ford interrupted, "He mentioned that, but wouldn't go into details. He has high praise for your...talents, shall I say?"

"I'm either the luckiest, or unluckiest, man alive, sir," said Emmet, his temper subsiding for the time being. "I was a Metropolitan bobby in London for a spell but managed to move up with the Scotland Yard to an inspector position."

"An admirable vocation, sir," said Ford, utilizing a charm Emmet was surprised to discover. "Then you retired and moved to Key West?"

"Yes," said Emmet, wondering how much else Ford knew about him.

"But men like us never retire, do we, sir?"

Again, with the charm, thought Emmet and shrugged. "I try to help where I can."

"As do we all, Mr. MacWain," said Ford, smiling slightly, then let it fade. "Did Director Serey explain to you my need for discretion?"

Emmet hesitated before answering, then chose his words carefully. "He did and I understand your need for privacy but I'm not sure how much help I can lend you. I'm no longer licensed as an investigator...."

"And I'm no longer in charge of the company I built, but that doesn't mean I don't still run it. I don't need a licensed man, Mr. MacWain, I need a smart one."

"Why don't you tell me what your expectations are, sir, and I can better tell you what I may, or may not be able to do."

Ford grinned, his stern countenance disappearing, "I want you to find out who tried to murder me by sending a sealed bottle that I receive every year, only this time it was filled with something deadly," he exclaimed, then hesitated. "But you have come a long way and I do have some business I need to tend to. Allow me to share my needs with you over dinner, say six o'clock? I have some sleeping quarters arranged for you at a nearby hotel. It's that first big building with the spires and all the palm trees surrounding it," Ford said with a wave of his arm. "It's appropriately named the Royal Palm Hotel. It is not the grand place it used to be—the casino and pool are still closed—but the lobby and rooms are quite nice, and I think with this economic depression beginning to subside, the old palace might find some new life. You can take Bennett's car unless you care to walk."

Emmet considered for a moment. Ford was right, he didn't want to turn around and drive back to Key West today. He could stay for dinner, he supposed. Maybe find some answers to this odd case as well. The manner of the crime was fascinating to Emmet, and he was personally curious about why someone would steal mail from Ford and having found a sealed tube, why would that person open it and breathe its contents?

"Well, I do enjoy driving that car," said Emmet.

Ford beamed even more, and he approached Emmet as if they were old friends, sliding his hand onto Emmet's shoulder.

"It's nice, isn't it? I love every one of my cars like they were my own children," he said, then grew serious as he led Emmet back to the car and opened the door. "Here, the car is yours, sir, with my appreciation just for coming over upon my ungracious summons."

"Are you serious, man?" said Emmet, astounded. "I couldn't accept such a gift. What about your man, Bennett?"

Ford didn't hesitate. "Oh, don't worry about Harry. I am loyal to him because he is loyal to me. I'll let him pick out another," he said, running his hand over the rounded fender of the car. "I do like this color, don't you?" Then, without waiting for an answer, he added, "I used to believe black was the only color I'd ever use on my automobiles but isn't this color magnificent?"

THIRTEEN

E dvard Heinz sat in a bar at the seaport in Tampa killing time before he was to board a ship—the SS Brazilian— that would take him far out of this country and the farther he went, the better. The ship was bound for South America, Brazil specifically, where it would load up its cargo of coffee, then sail on to France to unload the precious roasted beans for the popular libation.

Heinz looked at the telegram he'd picked up at the dockmaster's office, along with his urgent "orders" and his passage. He already had his official papers and passport that declared he was a Swiss citizen in the U.S. on business that had allowed him into the country. Officially, he was there to purchase automobiles, new and used, for a car dealership in Geneva. The dealership did not exist but held a real corporate name that could be verified if anyone took the time to try to investigate its existence. No one did.

The American government was either oblivious to the war in Europe or simply did not care. That was a good thing for the Germans who were moving through Europe like termites through soft wood. They already occupied France, Belgium, Luxembourg, and The Netherlands. This time, it appeared the Deutschland forces might actually take the world.

Heinz saw his reflection staring back at him between bottles of booze lining the saloon's mirror. He couldn't help but admire his reflection. He was blonde with blue-grey eyes set into a long face with a strong jawline. His lips were full, and his nose was like a Luger's barrel, long and straight with a small nub, like the gun's sight at the end. It was the face of a true Aryan, the chosen race to whom all others were inferior, and they were now on the brink of the world recognition—possibly, domination—they deserved.

Heinz thought of trying the American Whiskey, Kentucky Bourbon, but thought it would not be good enough for him. He considered *Jagermeister*—which meant "master of the hunt" in German—but didn't want to draw attention to himself and thought it better to stay with common beer out of the tap. When people asked him about his accent, he simply said he was Swiss and most of the dumb Americans, who'd never been farther than 10 miles out of their dreary little towns, didn't know the difference.

He sat sipping the frothy, tasteless American Beer called *Schlitz*— at least it sounded German—though it did not have the rich, wheat taste and fine bubbles of his favored Hefeweizen. As he waited for his ship to begin boarding, Heinz wondered what was in that tube. The one he'd placed in the mailbox at the home of the American automobile magnate, Henry Ford, in Ft. Myers. It didn't appear to be anything and yes, of course, he had taken a look at it. He felt he had the right to do so after having had to kill the postman to obtain his uniform and his mailbag. He wondered if it was some sort of new, ingenious bomb Hitler's famed scientists had made. He also wondered if anyone had found the postman's body.

Recalling the evening two nights before in Ft. Myers, Heinz thought about how he'd caught the eye of the postman as he ended his rounds and invited him for a drink at Bert's Bar in the waterfront building that housed a variety of businesses: seafood markets, sandwich shops, fishing tackle, and a dock where that gear could be used. There were also several small bars filled with sailors and some low-class women looking to make a few dollars by attracting seamen who had been away from land and ladies too long.

After a few drinks and some flirting, Heinz had whispered in the postman's ear, offering him some carnal activity if they could find a place nearby. They made it to an alley behind the building before they began groping each other.

Heinz had taken off his belt as if he were going to drop his pants, then asked the postman to turn around. As the postman began to drop his pants, Heinz quickly looped his belt around the mail carrier's neck and cinched it tight. He heard a pop and while he was unsure if the sound was that of the man's windpipe bursting or a vertebra jerked loose from its place in his neck, he was sure of what followed: an instant and quiet death.

Heinz quickly removed the postman's clothing and stuffed it into the mailbag. Then he took the man's naked body and slung it over his shoulder with ease. If stopped, he would say his pal was drunk and he was carrying him out to their ship. Once Heinz made his way to one of the darkened docks, he found an unattended sailboat, nonchalantly removed its anchor and tied it around the postman's neck before slinging the body into the dark water.

The next day, wearing the postman's uniform, Heinz took over the postman's route, at least as far as Henry Ford's house. There he placed the package with the beaker in the oversized mailbox along with dozens of other letters.

Now, as he watched his ship come in, literally and figuratively—he'd been paid a lot of money to place the mysterious package—he felt he was more than a hired hitman. He was part of history, part of a plan that would change the world forever. Once he got back to Germany, he would resume his place in the Third Reich and continue his path to world domination.

"*Sieg Heil,*" he whispered to himself, then stood up and wiped the stinky American brew from his lips. He threw a dime on the sticky bar, pulled a cap over his head, and marched toward the ship that would take him back home.

FOURTEEN

After driving *his* car—he'd never owned one—to the Royal Palm Hotel, Emmet parked near the entrance of the building and gazed up at the structure. He'd seen bigger, grander hotels but this one, with its wrap-around porch and peaked rooftops and tall bay windows, had a splendid mix of southern charm and New England carpentry. It had its own water tower and coal-driven generator that, it turned out, supplied power for the all-electric building. Not surprising in 1940, but the hotel had been built before the turn of the century and it was "the cat's ass," as was a common expression Emmet heard American people say when something was supposed to be impressive in its opulence.

Emmet checked into the hotel and was told by the front desk clerk that he was Mr. Ford's guest. Anything he wanted, just put it on the tab. If he had a car, they would park it for him. Emmet was hesitant to give up the keys to his new car but the clerk assured him they would take very special care of the vehicle. He was given a premium room with lush furnishings, and a spectacular view of the water, and told to help himself to the bar in the lobby.

After taking his bag to his room, washing up, and putting on fresh clothes, Emmet went back down to the ornate bar where he was surprised to see a female bartender. He'd never seen a woman in that line of work before. She was an attractive lady, too, with hair the color of a chestnut horse he had when he rode with Roosevelt's Rough Riders in the Cuban battles. The red hair reminded him of an American movie star whose name he could not recall.

She greeted Emmet with a smile surrounded by bright, red lipstick, "What'll ya have, sir?"

Emmet, surprised by the lady's accent, returned the smile and said, "What is the likelihood of meeting an Irish lass here?"

The bartender beamed, "About the same as meeting a Scottish gentleman, I suppose," she quipped. "I'm Bessie Murphy, sir, and whom have I the pleasure to be talkin' to?"

"Emmet MacWain."

"Pleased to meet you, sir," said Bessie, and gave a little nod.

"The pleasure's mine, Mum," said Emmet, returning the nod. "Where are you from?"

"*Baile Atha Cliath*. You know it as Dublin," said Bessie.

"You speak the old language?"

"My father insisted we know it. He spoke it all the time. I do it out of respect for him, God rest his soul. Where ya from?"

"I grew up on a farm east of the small coastal town of Ayr, but I lived a good part of my life in London as a copper."

"Well, you traded heaven for hell, didn't ya?"

"I think you're right, Mum. I'll drink to that." Emmet ordered a scotch, a water back, and a couple of pickled eggs they had behind the bar in a giant jar filled with beets and brine. He'd missed lunch and was starving.

Bessie brought Emmet his order and made some small talk.

"You're a tall drink of water, aren't ya?" she said. "I bet you're as tall as Gary Cooper."

"Who?" asked Emmet.

"Why, the movie star. You don't know who he is?" said Bessie.

"I think I've heard the name. I don't get to the moving pictures much."

Another customer sat at the bar and Bessie excused herself and went to serve him.

As he sat there, Emmet pondered why Ford, a man with innumerable resources, who had his own trusted men, would allow a stranger, such as himself, to come in and pursue something so... personal? But, after meeting Bennett, who seemed as close to Ford as anyone, Emmet answered his own question. Bennett was as uncouth, brash, and impulsive as any man he'd met—a total opposite of Ford— but he was obviously loyal to Ford, and Emmet suspected loyalty was more important to the captain of industry than competence.

Numerous other questions began to emerge for Emmet. First: why would Ford stay in Ft. Myers if he thought someone was trying to kill him? He had homes in several places and could retreat to any one of them, some much more private and inaccessible than the one here. Anyone could walk up to the home if they wanted to harm him. Second: Why would someone mail him something intended to harm him? As Emmet pondered his own questions, he forgot about the time. Looking up he noted the clock above the bar showed it was 5:45 PM. Emmet stood to leave and when Bessie saw him stand, she came over.

"Leaving so soon, Mr. MacWain?"

"I'm afraid so. Can you put my bill on my hotel tab? I have a dinner date, but I'll be back for the night."

"Sure thing," said Bessie.

Emmet added, "If you're still working, I'll stop by for a nightcap."

"That would be swell, Mr. MacWain."

"Call me Emmet, please."

Bessie gave a wink and a nod as Emmet turned to leave but stopped, contemplating for a moment. He turned back, "It was a pleasure to meet you, Bessie."

"And you," said Bessie, her cheeks flushed, as she turned to wash beer mugs and cocktail glasses.

Emmet asked the front desk man to have his "automobile" brought around. He watched nervously as the car was retrieved and was pleased to see it had been washed and polished. He gave the valet a half-dollar and slid into the driver's seat. He had barely gone a half block when he glanced at the rearview mirror just as a man's disembodied voice came from the backseat and said, "Keep driving."

FIFTEEN

E mmet drove a short distance and having spied an alley between some of the downtown buildings, pulled in and slowed the car as he idled through the dank corridor where cats leaped from overfilled garbage cans. A few homeless and drunken men slept against the wall or scurried away believing the police must be coming for them. Emmet stopped the car. He got out and acted like he was checking the car's tires in case someone was watching. He got back in the car and glanced in the mirror but didn't turn around.

"What are you doing here, John? Come to check on my U.S. citizenship documents?" asked Emmet, with a sarcastic lilt.

Serey edged up to peer around and checked to see if anyone was following or watching them. He was wearing a large fedora hat and sunglasses. He'd grown a beard since Emmet had seen him last, but his skin was still spotty and as flaky as an onion, perpetually peeling. The man was always sweating, profusely, but now he appeared to be *melting* from the heat. "C'mon, man. You were being hesitant about doing this for me and I didn't have time to elaborate," he said, then stopped as if he was not sure what else to say or was waiting for another rebuttal from Emmet.

"You still don't have time," said Emmet. "I'm almost late now for dinner at Ford's house."

"Ah, very good, it seems you're already making some progress."

"Well, I haven't found out much of anything yet. We had to... how should I say this, establish our common ground. So, whatever you've got to say to me, you should do it quickly before I lose that ground."

"Okay," said Serey. "Okay. I'll be quick. Here's the deal. The agency, of course, wants us to find out who tried to kill him if that is the case here, but realistically that's peripheral to what we *need*. And what we *need* you to do is get close to him. He's been doing business with the Nazis for about twenty years and now has huge military contracts with the Germans and we want to find out the extent of those contracts. We know he's building troop transport trucks for them but legally, we can't do anything about that. Ford has had a company in Cologne for years making work trucks. But if we can find out he's making war machines for them, that's a different matter. He's published articles about his disdain for Jews and recently a poem in one of his business magazines entitled, "The Fuhrer." When he was considering a run for president in the '20s, Hitler offered to send his shock troops into the streets of Chicago for him. Collectively, we—those in government I'll say—just don't understand this little romance he has with a maniac and butcher, the likes of which we've never seen before. Put simply, if you can find out who tried to murder him—if that is the case—it might endear you enough to him so you can dig for some other information that we really need."

"Ah, Jesus, Mary, and Joseph, John," said Emmet, staring straight ahead. "I am, or was, an inspector of crimes. I am not a spy..."

"I knew you would say that, but I also know you did some intelligence gathering for the Queen while you were under her employ, so it is not an unprecedented act for you, Emmet."

"I wish I never would've shared that with you..."

"I would've found out anyway."

Emmet sat silently for a moment. "I'd like to punch you in the face for pulling me into this."

"I know, but I hope you won't. As I recall you threw a pretty good left hook."

Emmet shook his head, exasperated. "I've got to be going now that I've been shoved into this thing by a man I used to consider a friend."

"We *are* friends, Emmet. Well, not close friends but good acquaintances. I hope you still feel that way, but in any case, we have an opportunity to get close to a man who does not allow anyone to get close to him. We need to learn more about his association with the Nazis. We believe he already has a spy working for him and we want you to try to confirm that for us. Does he have an inside man working for the Krauts or is Ford, himself, working for them? Do they have something on him or why would he work for them? And, before you say you positively won't do it, keep in mind that these bastards will stop at nothing to take over the world. They've got most of Europe now and it's only a matter of time before they move into your home soil in the United Kingdom."

Serey had been talking like a man who had drank too much coffee, now he paused and waited, hoping to hear Emmet say.

"All right then," said Emmet. "I'll see what I can find out. But there has been a murder here and that will be my first order of business," Emmet grumbled. "Now, I've got to go."

Serey put his hand on Emmet's shoulder and gave it a squeeze. "Thank you, Emmet. I'm sorry about..."

"I know, John. We'll talk later. I'm staying at..."

Serey cut him off. "I know where you're staying. I'll be in touch." Before he got out of the car, he added, "Ford's charming. I know the man. But he's slick. Watch out for him and above all, find out if he has a spy working with him and if so, who it is."

Then, Serey was out of the car, walking with his head down, collar turned up as if it were forty degrees outside rather than eighty.

SIXTEEN

E mmet was weary as he parked the car in the now-crowded driveway and made his way to the entrance of Ford's house. It had been a long day. He was deep in thought but made the decision not to dwell on the recent espionage drama he'd gotten into. His thoughts went to the man who died here. It might not be a pleasant discussion for the dinner table but he would have to bring it up. He knocked on the door and a woman answered.

Clara Ford had a pleasant, friendly face. She was not beautiful but something was inviting about the woman that made Emmet immediately like her. Her smile was demure but engaging, her dark eyes alive with kindness and warmth and embedded in a round face that looked as soft as pie dough.

"You must be Mr. MacWain," she said and curtsied as if she were greeting royalty. She held her hand out to Emmet, palm down, and he took her extended fingertips in his big, calloused hand.

Emmet bowed slightly but did not kiss her hand as she was married. "Yes, Mum," he said, "but call me Emmet."

"Aren't you a gentleman," she said. "But I still call my husband Mr. Ford while we're with company. We're what you'd call old-fashioned."

"How lovely," said Emmet. "I'm a bit old-fashioned myself. As you wish, Mrs. Ford."

Clara opened the door wide to allow Emmet in and welcomed him to their home with a sweep of her arm. "Make yourself at home, Mr. MacWain."

Emmet entered the house and noted the sounds of discussion in the nearby sitting room. Clara navigated him toward the room and offered to bring him an iced sweet tea. He accepted though he'd rather have had another scotch.

Ford noticed Emmet entering the room and glided over to him. He shook hands with him as if they had never met and said, quietly, "Thank you for coming, Mr. MacWain. Let me introduce you to my other guests, then we will have a little chat about the dead Jew at my mailbox."

Emmet did not care for Ford's demeaning way of dismissing the man and his tragic death. It seemed no more important to him than if someone had run over a cat in his driveway.

"Yes, we do need to talk about that, Mr. Ford. It's why I'm here," said Emmet, his voice as cold as a specter's.

"Well, of course, it is, Mr. MacWain. I'm just being hospitable. I may have been raised in a barn but I certainly don't live in one now. Point of fact, I invited the local sheriff here tonight, too. He has news to share which you may find interesting."

Emmet nodded gravely.

Ford placed his hand lightly on Emmet's arm and led him to the group, who turned their gaze upon them as they approached.

"Ladies and gentlemen, I'd like to introduce to you a special guest," said Ford, with much aplomb. "This is Mr. Emmet MacWain. An acquaintance of mine with the FBI recommended Mr. MacWain who used to work with Scotland Yard. He is going to look into the matter of the thief who died while pilfering through my mailbox."

Emmet watched the faces of the group, most of whom were men. Mrs. Ford and one other elderly lady were present. One man scowled at Emmet, and he deduced he was the sheriff and that he was not happy to see an interloper stepping into his territory. That man stood next to Harry Bennett and Emmet assumed the two of them had already had edgy conversations about him. There was another young man, handsome and well dressed, who held the face of his mother so much, Emmet knew he had to be a son of the Fords. Another man looked very corporate and a bit distressed and Emmet chanced a guess that he must be one of Ford's employees, probably in upper management.

"Please make him welcome. Now, I'll let you all chat before we sit down for supper," said Ford, then blended into the group and eventually made his way to the distressed businessman where they huddled in a corner of the room, whispering.

The young man approached him first and proffered his hand. "Hello, Mr. MacWain, I'm Edsel Ford. Call me Edsel, please. Should you need anything please let me know. I'm only going to be here a couple of days, but I'll make sure you have my phone number before I leave. I'm glad my father brought in a professional to investigate this matter."

"Thank you, Edsel," said Emmet. "A pleasure to meet you." They shook hands and Emmet thought: *how could a father and son be so different?* Then glanced at the man whom he believed to be the sheriff and who was now scowling at Emmet even more than previously.

Bennett came over, ever so reluctantly, like a student who has misbehaved and has been told by the teacher to say he's sorry. He had an amber-colored drink in his hand that he refreshed with a small sterling silver flask he withdrew from the inside pocket of his jacket. Though he had cleaned up and dressed in a rakish suit, the bruises he'd obtained from Emmet spread across his face like an infection.

"How about we start over Mr. MacWain? We might have to work together... if Mr. Ford decides to keep you around."

Emmet left his face expressionless and said, "No," then moved past him toward the scowling man.

"I'm Sheriff Carl Ross," the man said. His skin was pale pink, with light brown spots covering it. His hair was a dull red, styled in an odd bowl-cut one might expect on a street youngster whose family could not afford a barber's touch. His head was too small for his body and sat atop a long neck that had an Adam's apple the size of a golf ball, which rose and fell as he spoke.

"Hello, sir," said Emmet. "Good to meet you. I would like to talk to you about the man that died here when we can get a moment."

"Well, we can talk about it," said Ross, his yellow eyes narrowing, "but I'm wondering why Mr. Ford felt the need to bring you here in a professional capacity."

"Then you should ask him if it's a mystery to you," said Emmet. "Do you still have the package that came with the contents that, reportedly, killed the man?"

Ross shrugged and turned his mouth into an upside-down "U." "I believe Mr. Ford kept it. There was a bottle, or beaker, in it, too, but it was empty."

"Did you dust it to look at it for fingerprints?"

"C'mon, man," said Ross. We don't have a fancy lab around here. It was in the man's hand..."

"Which one?" queried Emmet. Right or left?"

Ross gripped his chin squeezing it like he was juicing a lemon and doing so would give him an answer. "I don't recall which hand but it's probably in my notes."

"Of course," said Emmet. "I'd like to see your notes, perhaps tomorrow?"

"Okay," said Ross, reluctantly, then added under his breath, "We've got the dead Jew in a refrigerator in the basement of the hospital if you want to see it."

"Him," Emmet corrected.

"What?" asked Ross.

"If I were you, I'd refer to anyone deceased as what they were before they died, such as a him, or a her, not an 'it.'"

"What?" Ross asked again, the point lost on him.

Emmet looked across the room and saw an elderly woman staring at him. When they made eye contact, she blinked her eyes as if embarrassed to be caught staring. Emmet left Ross with his mouth hanging open and approached the woman who'd been watching him.

"Good evening, Mum," said Emmet.

"Good evening, sir. I'm Mina Edison," she held out her hand and Emmet took it as he had with Clara. "I was married to Thomas Edison, you know, the inventor?"

"Of course," said Emmet. "America's genius."

Mina nodded, slightly, sadly, as if recalling the man she'd been married to for so long. "I'm telling you this to explain to you about the beakers, or tubes that my husband left for Henry, er, Mr. Ford."

Emmet frowned and cocked his head. "I know a beaker was sent here that, supposedly killed a man with one breath, but I was not aware that there were others that your husband left for Mr. Ford."

"Perhaps, you don't know the whole story then," said Mina. "Let me tell you." She looked out the nearest window as if it was a time-travel port and she could find memories there that she needed now. "As Mr. Edison was dying, our son, Charles, would try to capture his last breath." She looked back into Emmet's eyes to see if he was following her story so far. His intensity told her he was. She continued. "I'm not sure if my son wanted one for himself, too, but he intended to give what would be his father's final breath to Mr. Ford. It was sentimental and, some might say unusual, but no one was closer to Thomas than Mr. Ford. In all, there were forty-two beakers, or tubes, such as they use in laboratories. Because Charles never knew which breath would be Thomas's last, he kept and corked each one and sealed them with wax."

"I see," said Emmet. "So, are we assuming this was one of them that came in the mail, and, if so, why was it sent to Mr. Ford if he already had one?"

"Well, after Thomas died, we began to give away some things to friends and numerous museums who had contacted us. Some of Mr. Edison's smaller inventions, or copies of the patents he held for historical reference. But the box containing the beakers was lost. Then, one by one, every year, someone began sending the tubes to Mr. Ford. It's unknown who sends them but they come every year and are often from faraway places. Henry doesn't care who sends them but he gets...what's the word I want to use...*anxious*, perhaps, sad too, I think, if they don't show up."

Emmet wasn't sure what to say. What a bizarre tale, he thought. He was mesmerized by this kind lady's quiet and fascinating story, as unbelievable as it might sound. He looked over to Ford and saw him return his gaze. Emmet held up a finger as if to indicate to Ford he needed to talk to him for a moment.

Ford understood and made an apology to the stressed businessman with whom he was conversing, the only person Emmet had not talked to in the room.

Ford strolled over and put his arm around Mina. "I see you've met the lovely wife of my very best friend and mentor, Mr. Thomas Edison. She is a fine woman and dear friend of mine, as well, who still finds time to grace us with her presence."

Some people saying such a compliment would sound pretentious, but Emmet felt Ford was completely sincere. His eyes were wet and full of emotion as he spoke.

"Yes," said Emmet. "It's been my pleasure talking with you, Mrs. Edison."

"Thank you," said Mina, her face blushing slightly and a smile replacing the sadness in her own eyes. "There will never be another man like him."

"Too, true," said Ford. "So, Emmet, did you need something...?"

"Yes, sir," said Emmet, for the first time becoming excited to be a part of this investigation he was pressured into. "Please tell me you still have the beaker and the box in which it was mailed that killed the man at your postal box."

Ford nodded, "I do," he whispered. "I didn't want to give it to the local, and shall I say possibly inept, law enforcement people. I was also concerned that it might still be dangerous, so I capped it with the cork the thief had removed."

"I must see it right away," said Emmet with urgency.

Ford looked at his guests and hesitated. "Well, I believe dinner is ready and I shouldn't want to starve my guests..."

"Mr. Ford, you sent your man a long way to get me, and it was not without some trouble for both of us. Surely, if this matter meant enough for you to have sought me out so urgently, then we must get to the heart of the matter immediately. Wouldn't you agree?"

Ford locked eyes with Emmet for a moment and, as if it just occurred to him, he said, "Of course, you're right Mr. MacWain.

I placed the package and the test tube in Thomas's old laboratory across the street..."

"There's a laboratory here?" asked Emmet. "On these grounds?"

"Yes, of course," said Ford. "Thomas was an inventor after all."

"Is the lab still functional? That is, is it still equipped as Mr. Edison left it?"

"Of course, it's been some ten years since anyone worked in it but as far as I know, it's as functional as it was when Thomas was last here."

"Then, let's not waste any more time, sir."

SEVENTEEN

Ford led Emmet across the street walking with an urgency that surprised the former inspector.

"Mina gave the lab to the Department of Agriculture after Thomas died," Ford informed Emmet. "They have some personnel stop in occasionally and study the various plants that Thomas and I collected over the years. We were searching for the right trees from which to make rubber, a goal of mine that even with Thomas's diligent work, I failed. The cursed Brazilians still own the industry and demand exorbitant fees for the product, and we—myself—and other automotive producers, are forced to pay their outrageous fees. It should be criminal, and they should be taxed highly for their precious import. They make my profits bleed. I can tell you I have had many adversarial business negotiations with them."

"Enough for them to send you a package that might have killed you had you been the one to open it?"

Ford paused for a moment before acknowledging the possibility. "Yes."

They came to the laboratory and entered the building. The structure was quite large and filled with tables, cluttered with beakers, test tubes, Bunsen burners, and tubing linking many of the glass bottles and containers.

"We still have unrestricted access to the lab," said Ford. "Mina visits it occasionally; I believe to recall her fond memories of Thomas.

I seldom visit because it reminds me of failure which is something I loathe and, I'll admit, fear."

"We all fail from time to time," observed Emmet, his tone quiet.

"Yes," said Ford, though it seemed to pang him as he said it. "But it is a distasteful experience." He looked around, spied what he was looking for, and made for a side room off the main floor of the lab. He slipped his long fingers into his coat pocket and withdrew a small key then slipped it into the lock of a cabinet door and opened it. He was reaching for a long, rectangular box when Emmet stopped him.

"Mr. Ford, I'm going to ask you not to touch the package with your bare hands..."

"I handled it the other day when it came. No harm came to me."

"People handle guns all of the time and don't get hurt...until they do," said Emmet in a solemn tone. "Surely there are rubber gloves about. It is a lab after all."

Both men looked around for rubber gloves and, finding them, stretched them onto their hands.

"Emmet said, "May I?"

Ford nodded.

Emmet picked up the box carefully and slid one hand underneath it in case the packaging failed. "Let me have a look at it. You should stand back a few feet, Mr. Ford."

"I told you I handled it when..."

"Look, you said you wanted to hire me to investigate the origin of this package. My interest is piqued but I wouldn't be a very good inspector if the package still holds a threat, and I inadvertently killed my new employer. Wouldn't you agree?"

"Of course," said Ford. "You are the expert."

Emmet withdrew the package from the cabinet and carefully turned it over, slowly, in his gloved hands. All of his senses were heightened, his eyes tuned into the writing on the box—the block letters printed with a slight backward tilt, likely written by a left-handed person. The silence of the lab turned to a ringing in his ears as he concentrated, and his nostrils detected something familiar as he began to mentally thumb through some long, nearly forgotten memories.

The return address on the package was: Les Milandes, Castenaud-la-Chapelle, Nouvelle-Aquitaine, François.

"It's from France," Ford declared, straightening his posture, proudly, displaying his *eminence grise*.

"No, it's not," said Emmet.

"Look at the postage, man..." Ford began.

"Yes," said Emmet. "The postal stamps are French indeed. But it has not been stamped *Par Avion* as it would be if it were, indeed, mailed from France. There is no stamped date at all and, other than the end packaging being ripped open, the package does not appear to have changed hands the many times it would have had to if it were mailed from a foreign country."

"Why would anyone want me to think it was from France?" queried Ford.

"Perhaps to make anyone investigating the parcel believe it came from France," said Emmet. It might be a ruse or some contrivance to throw us off track of where it might have come from. Or someone decided to carry the package in their baggage rather than mail it and risk having the tube break. Besides, if someone was trying to kill you, do you believe they would be foolish enough to put their real return address on the package?"

Emmet continued concentrating on the packing. Satisfied the package had told him most of what it could, he tilted the box and gently shook the glass bottle into his hands. It appeared the sealing wax had been broken and the cork removed, then stuffed back in. It was a round bottle with a long neck but a relatively standard laboratory bottle, the round bottom still had a trace of soot from the tube having been heated.

"It's a Florence flask," said Emmet. "Is this the type of bottle that is sent to your house regularly?"

Ford shook his head. "No. It's typically a regular test tube that is sent. A larger one, perhaps twenty-five milliliters. Usually corked and waxed."

Emmet slowly tilted the bottle and looked closer, inside the bottom, where he could see a minuscule amount of powdered residue.

"Do you smell that?" Emmet asked Ford.

"No, I can't say that I do."

"When you retrieved it from the victim yesterday, do you recall smelling anything on the bottle, or perhaps on the man's body?"

Ford gazed at the ground as if trying to recall the scene. He began to say something, then stopped, then began again.

"I'm not sure," he said. "I thought I did smell a scent now that you mention it. I thought perhaps it was from some religious practice, or some oils, or unguents that maybe the Jews use in their rituals, or whatever they do."

Emmet reviled Ford's use of "rituals" as if the Jews were pagan worshipers, like ancient Druids, or cultists, but he didn't comment. He was keenly focused on his current observations.

"Tell me, man, what did it *smell* like?" Emmet demanded, glaring at Ford like a coiled snake.

"Well, I guess, it sort of like... something like flowers..."

"Yes...?"

"I couldn't tell you what kind, it was sort of sweet, subtle...like a perfume a woman might wear but not overpowering..."

"Was it lilac?"

Ford nodded slowly. "I suppose it could be."

"It does to me, even now," said Emmet, his nostrils flaring. "And it recalls another horrid time in our history in a world enamored with wars and killing. It was in France, during the big war. If I'm correct, you are very lucky to be alive, sir."

"What do you think it is?"

"Have you ever heard of White Cross? In terms of warfare, specifically?"

"No, I can't say I have."

"It's a gas, used exclusively as chemical warfare that's one of the deadliest contrivances ever made by man. It's a combination of several chemical compounds but most often bromoacetone or chloroacetone, bromo benzyl cyanide, bromomethyl ketone, and particularly, xylyl bromide, which was initially the main ingredient of what is commonly known as mustard gas."

Ford stood frowning, pondering Emmet's words. "I detest wars," he said, his voice sounding broken as if his throat were very dry.

Emmet surprised said, "Really?"

"Yes. Why are you surprised?"

Emmet paused before answering. He didn't want to give himself away and threaten his underlying mission, but he simply could not help himself. "I read Hitler's book, *Mein Kampf*, to try to understand how this depraved maniac could ever come into power. All I could discern was that Hitler's words appealed to the worst of his country's underlying hatred. He abhors anyone who is not of his made-up kingdom of an Aryan race and make no mistake, he will not stop if he defeats all of Europe. He will spread like a contagion across the sea until he has a foothold here in America. I've already seen some proof of that happening."

"What has that to do with me?"

Emmet stared at Ford. He was either an incredible liar, out of touch with reality, or had the best poker face in the world. But Emmet said none of that. "You're the only American he mentioned in his book, and it was with extreme admiration."

Ford smiled and shrugged. "It's no secret I have a manufacturing plant in Germany—have for years—so it is all business. Hitler told me personally he enjoyed my business acumen."

"How I read it was he enjoyed your stand against Jews. Now, here we are finding a deadly gas used exclusively by Germans and the murder of a Jew in your front yard. Is that a coincidence?"

"You suspect I may have had something to do with the Jew's death? Preposterous! I'm standing here with you, trying to help determine his cause of death. I even hired you to investigate the cause. I should fire you immediately."

"Sir, you can do whatever you like but I can promise you, whether I'm working for you or not, I will find this man's killer or killers. If you're one of them, don't believe for a second I'll let you escape justice."

"I won't let you stand there and bark at me like some junkyard dog," Ford yelled. "I...I..."

Suddenly, the door to the lab swung open as Ross entered the room, his pink skin now scarlet from running across the road. "Hello," he shouted, "Are you in here Mr. Ford?"

"Back here, Sheriff," said Ford, his eyes never leaving Emmet's face.

Ross dashed into the room out of breath, his face slick with sweat.

"What is it, man?" Ford demanded.

Ross looked from Ford to Emmet as he tried to regain his breath. "They..., they..." His huge Adam's apple bounced up and down as Ross tried to clear his throat of dried phlegm. Finally, it went down one more time and Ross was able to speak. "My deputy just called me. They found a body...some fishermen out...on the docks...hooked into something and when they tried to pull it up, a naked body came up. It's all bloated but they got it up onto the dock and they think... it's the postman."

Emmet glanced at Ford to see his reaction; he appeared dumbfounded, a quizzical frown on his face as if he had temporarily forgotten how to speak. Ford's lips moved but no words came forth. He reminded Emmet of an elderly man who could not recall who he was or where he was. It was almost painful for him to watch. Emmet recalled his own father wearing a similar confused look when he was not too much older than Emmet was now. The doctors said it was dementia. He pushed the dark memory from his mind. There were more pressing things to ponder now.

"What did they do with the man's body, Sheriff?" asked Emmet.

Ross turned to Emmet. "They're taking it to the hospital, to the basement where they took the dead rabbi fella."

Emmet did not hesitate as he addressed the Sheriff. "Take me to the hospital, sir, so I may look at both bodies and have your men close the dock where the postman was found. I'll need to see it, to look at everything. Why did you say 'rabbi,' Sheriff?"

"Well, he had those weird braids and the black suit...." said the perplexed sheriff.

"That doesn't necessarily mean he was a rabbi, but it sounds like he was of Hebrew heritage." Emmet paused, thinking of the man, picturing him going through Ford's mail. He had to know the package was coming and what it contained or was supposed to contain. Now, the postman was dead, too. He was also nude, which could mean someone had killed him and stolen his clothes. If that were the case, then whoever that was had to place that tube in the mailbox. Who would do that and why?

Turning back to Ford, Emmet added. "I'm afraid I'll have to forego dinner, Mr. Ford. You should stay here and keep some of your guests close by. This is not a mistake, nor a seemingly random, or accidental death. I believe whoever sent, or brought, the package to your home, knew your routine and fabricated its arrival by the postal service by killing the real postman and taking his place. Then he placed the package in the mailbox because he couldn't take the chance of the bottle of poisonous gas being broken while in transit." Emmet paused, frowning as he looked closer at the bottle.

"I need you to compose a list of all the people who might know of you receiving these packages from your friend Edison, a man who has been dead for some ten years, yes? We have few clues, other than the return address in France and now two dead men who can, perhaps, still tell me something. This is a conspiracy of murder, sir, and you, as well as others may be in grave danger."

EIGHTEEN

LES MILANDES, CASTENAUD-LA-CHAPELLE,

NOUVELLE-AQUITAINE, FRANCE

Jacques Abtey approached the gigantic oak doors at the entry of the Chateau with caution. It helped that the doors were obscured by domed arches that kept the entrance in darkness unless the sun was on high. Even this night, with a full, bright moon beaming down and illuminating the grounds, Abtey was shrouded in shadow. Still, he knocked quietly and hoped the occupants had received the note he'd sent with a local girl, named Pasquale, several days ago. The doors creaked open revealing a cautious eye, and Claude, Josephine's trusted servant, bade him to come in.

It was after midnight and though the house had electric power installed years earlier, Claude held a lantern, which meant they would be going to the cellar. Abtey entered the castle quickly to avoid being silhouetted in the doorway, a target for a possible assassin. Claude looked around as well, to see if anyone was following the captain of *Le Deuxiene Bureau*, a department of crypto-analytical agents who were being dissolved now that Germany had defeated France.

Satisfied there was no one following him, Claude joined Abtey, and they navigated a labyrinth of corridors that led to a small door that, if no one looked close enough, appeared to just be another part of the wall. Claude fingered the wall and found a stone that was slightly smoother than the others on the wall. He pushed it firmly and the small door, barely large enough for a child, opened. The men stooped to enter and descended the steps of the circular stone staircase that hugged the wall, the surface of which was cold and damp.

"*Bam...click....bam...click...bam,*" Abtey jumped when he heard the first shot ring out but Claude gripped his arm, leading the way, and assured him it was all right as they came to the bottom of the steps. Along a dark wall of stone that glistened with dampness was a line of candles, mounted on vertical posts, approximately twenty feet away and five feet apart.

A figure, most assuredly female, her outline visible through a gauzy nightgown and silhouetted in the glow of the candles, appeared.

Josephine Baker stood in a shooter's stance, her arms outstretched and holding a pistol.

"Hey fellas," she said without turning around. She aimed and fired the gun again. The shot snuffed out one of the candles. She pulled the hammer back on the gun again and fired without hesitation, hitting another lit candle wick and extinguishing it.

"Good evening, Josephine," said Abtey. "I see you haven't lost your aim. You know you don't always have to practice in the dark."

Without turning, Josephine quipped, "You taught me how to shoot a pistol down in the sewers in Paris, Jacques. This place seems like daylight and is certainly a better-smelling shooting gallery compared to that." She fired one more shot extinguishing the last candle and turned around, Claude's lantern illuminating the cave-like chambers and casting jerky shadows about the cellar. Wooden crates and barrels of wine lined the walls of the room except for the one that held the line of now-extinguished candles.

Josephine looked Jacques over in the orange glow of the lantern. He was tall, handsome—almost pretty, with features as fine as some women she'd known. He had dark, intense eyes with long black lashes, a thin, perfect nose, and full lips, made to look thicker with his pencil-thin mustache etched over his mouth as if by an artist's brushstrokes. His hair was slicked back with pomade and perfectly cut, and his ears were small and round, but from his neck down he was all man. Wide shoulders that tapered into a narrow waist and strong legs. He was wearing a black, wool turtleneck sweater under a fitted leather jacket and grey tweed pants that matched an Irish newsboy's tweed cap, that was tilted stylishly on his head.

Josephine glided over to him, hugged his chest, and fit her face into the cleave between his pectoral muscles smelling him as one animal might another. He smelled like the warmth of a wood-burning fire.

"You feel cold. How are doing Mr. Sanders?" asked Josephine. It was the name she came up with to keep his identity as the head of the *Maquis* secret.

"*Je vais bien,*" replied Abtey, beaming.

Josephine gave him a soft, little slap across his cheek. "No, no, no Mr. Jack Sanders," corrected Josephine. "Americans don't talk like that, even if they are my new 'artistic director.'"

Abtey corrected himself. "I'm doin' fine, ma'am," he said, like an American western cinema actor.

"They don't all talk like John Wayne either," she chuckled, "but I can live with that."

Abtey looked at the wildly popular, global entertainer, admiring her, not only for her pluck but for her exotic beauty. Her face was bright, beaming with a wide, salacious grin, and set with enormous, almond-shaped eyes. Her dancer's legs were lithe, muscular, and smooth, and her luscious skin was like cappuccino, light brown, and sweet.

"May I get you something, Mr. Sanders?" asked Claude, trying out his own English and Monsieur Abtey's new *nom de querre*.

Josephine interrupted before Abtey could answer. "Claude, if you'll lead the way up with your lamp, we can all sit in the parlor and sip some brandy. That should warm us up."

Claude nodded and led the way back up the winding stairs.

Once upstairs, Claude put together a silver tray with a fine crystal decanter with locally made fine brandy and a charcuterie plate.

From a distance, the group could hear bombs ripping apart yet another small town as they sat down, quietly, for refreshments.

After a taste of brandy, Abtey spoke. "I've come across some information that the Gestapo plans to do some 'home inspections," beginning with many of the chateaus. The true intent is to find fugitives from Germany."

"We've already heard this news," said Claude, sipping his brandy. "We know who is leading the campaign, but we haven't heard when."

Josephine gulped her brandy and reached for the bottle to refill. "We heard it might be Klaus Barbie," she said.

"Yes, that's right," said Abtey, his countenance suddenly hardened. "He's already started his campaign in the regions to the east. He's cleared chateaus up through Bourgogne and he'll be here within a matter of weeks. We need to be prepared. When he finds refugees, he kills them and the people who were hiding them, in the most unspeakable ways. He's said to have killed as many as ten thousand people already. If you are hiding anyone, you need to move them as fast as you can. If more come to you, your best bet is to move them to an outside haven. Don't be caught harboring them or you will be tortured before you are killed. Barbie is ruthless."

Josephine took another sip. "Let him come," she said. "He's a man and I am a woman. I've got the advantage over his weakness."

Abtey sat up and looked into her face, his tone hardened and serious. "His weakness, as you say, is to see people die. He enjoys the experience of watching people tortured. He is a butcher, Jo, and extremely dangerous."

Josephine playfully gargled a mouthful of brandy, inhaled sharply, and smirked, "So am I. Ask any of my ex-husbands."

Abtey stood up, upset by her nonchalance. "Do you desire to die, Josephine?"

Now, Josephine stood up, heat in her eyes, her fists clenched. "France made me what I am today. They gave me *everything*, especially their hearts. Yes, I am ready, Captain, to give my life to France!"

She paused to collect herself and took a deep breath. Her "style" was always supposed to be cool. "Now, who wants some more brandy?"

NINETEEN

E mmet and Sheriff Ross drove to the dock first. Emmet reminded Ross, "The dead men aren't going anywhere. We need to talk to the men who found the body before they wander off."

"My deputy is there," Ross tried to assure him.

"Is he competent, or at least bold?" Emmet asked.

Ross glanced at him quickly, said nothing but picked up the pace.

When they arrived at the waterfront, a fog had enveloped the dock so that one could not see the end of it. It was only November but there was an unseasonable chill in the air. It reminded Emmet of London and he felt somewhat at home, while Ross shivered as if it was snowing.

As they approached the end of the dock, Emmet could make out some figures silhouetted by lamps they held, evidently holding them over the water to see if there were any more bodies.

The deputy, a young, pudgy man with thinning, blonde hair approached them. He wore a khaki uniform, with a badge smaller than the Sheriff's.

"This is Jason Abram, my deputy," said Ross, to Emmet.

Emmet shook the young man's hand and introduced himself.

"These are the men that found the body, Sheriff Ross," said Abram. "They helped me take it to the hospital where we brought the rabbi the other day."

Ross nodded but said nothing, so Emmet jumped in. "I'd like to talk to the fishermen who first found the body and everyone else can go home. You won't find any more bodies here and the crime scene is getting trampled. If the deceased man is the postman, this was a planned murder to obtain his position and deliver the package to Ford's house. I'll talk with them and then I'd like to see the body, or bodies, if the rabbi is still there."

Abram politely thanked the men who were helping look around the dock and they began to filter off, glancing back at the man with the odd accent.

The fishermen told Emmet why they were there and when and how the body was found. Emmet took notes and names as they described the event. The one named Guillermo said he was fishing off the dock while his friend, Pietro, was casting a net for bait fish. Guillermo thought he had caught a fish, and believed it was surfacing. When he was able to see into the water, he saw he'd hooked a rope, and he bent down to untangle it from his line. As he pulled on the rope, the man's feet appeared, and he and Jose pulled the body out of the water and onto the dock. It was quite clear the man had not died from an accident.

"Did you hear anything or perhaps see anyone on the dock or leaving the area?" asked Emmet.

Guillermo glanced at Pietro. Pietro shrugged, then said, "There are often men down here. Some fish. Some just stand around and talk. Sometimes it is just two men, you know, together. How do you say...*maricons*?"

"You mean, homosexuals?" said Emmet.

"*Si*," said Pietro.

"Awe, c'mon MacWain, that's disgusting!" said Ross, indignant. "This ain't about queers. It's about a goddamn murder."

"Homosexual men kill each other, too, Sheriff."

Ross walked away, scowling, and said, "I'm going to talk to some of these other people."

"Why don't you do that," said Emmet relieved. Another small-town sheriff, Emmet thought. Experience told him it was not easy working with them, though there was one in Key West that, while ornery, helped him immensely...until he, too, joined the dead.

Turning back to the fishermen. "Por favor, mi amigos, continua tu historia."

"So, there is a place where these men meet," said Pietro. "It's called, The Dark Lantern Tavern. Men come from there and take walks on the pier. They don't bother us or cause problems. They come out here, maybe so they are not seen in the light."

Emmet nodded. "I understand. Did you talk to any of them or recall what any of them looked like?"

"No. Not tonight," said Guillermo, "but I was here the other night and I thought I saw the mailman, but he was with another man, over there in the shadows. I did not want to stare at them. It is none of my business, what they do."

"I see," said Emmet. "Can you describe the other man?"

"It was very dark, so I could not see him well. He was tall and had the uh, how do you say...*rubio*?"

"Blonde hair? Like the deputy?"

"Si, but no *gordo*. He was a much taller man, maybe your size?"

Emmet nodded. "Could you hear anything they were saying or doing?"

"No," said Guillermo. "What they say or do is not my business, so I look away. I'm just here to fish."

"*Bueno. Mucho gracias,*" said Emmet. "*Puedes irte ahora. Buenas noches.*"

Emmet looked around the dock and the area where the fishermen said they might have seen the postman and the tall blonde man. It was an alley area near the dock shrouded in darkness. As he stepped closer, two men appeared from behind some shipping crates, one adjusting his shirt, the other buttoning his pants. Emmet turned away, jotted a note, and ambled out to the end of the dock where the fishermen indicated they'd found the body.

The sheriff and his deputy were standing near a still-wet anchor and rope, chit-chatting until Emmet came over and they fell into silence.

"Is that rope the anchor line that was used to weigh down the postman's body?" he asked.

"Uh-huh," said Ross.

Emmet looked it over and noted the rope was secured to the anchor with a standard knot—an anchor bend—that most fishermen used to assure the knot would hold. But there were other knots in the rope that, while fishermen might use them, it was not common for them as much as, say, a climber would utilize. One, a barrel knot, stood out to Emmet. He'd learned a handful of knots while he was in the military, and some had stuck with him.

"You seen what you wanted to see, MacWain?" Ross asked, his embittered southern tone obvious.

"Yes," said Emmet. "Shall we go to the hospital now? I'd like to look at the victims."

Ross turned to Abram. "Mr. Ford has asked me to accommodate Mr. MacWain," he said, dryly, assuring his deputy, as well as Emmet, knew this was an imposition to him. "So why don't you canvas the neighborhood a bit more and see if anyone else knows anything or has seen anything."

"Yes, sir," said Abram. Then, to Emmet, "Good to meet you, sir."

Emmet shook hands with the young man and noted Ross's scowl directed at Abram. He made a note to himself to try to talk to Deputy Abram when Ross was not present.

TWENTY

At the hospital, Ross led Emmet to the basement where the bodies were stored in stainless steel drawers that were refrigerated to thwart decomposition, a mandatory concern in the heat of Florida. The dimly lit room reeked of chemicals: alcohol, formaldehyde, and menthol, the latter of which Emmet knew was used by people who could not stomach the smell of the dead, and rubbed it under their nostrils to mask the scent. Emmet knew that trick all too well having trudged through the alleys of London where dead people were as plentiful as stray cats.

There was a small man with an unkempt mass of hair the color and texture of steel wool. His spectacles were as thick as milk bottle glass as he fussed around a lab table that held various tubes, swabs, needles, bottles, and jars of various embalming fluids and blood, as well as some human organs.

"MacWain," said Ross, "this is the *Diener*, Walther Barndt. Walt this is Emmet MacWain. Used to be an inspector in London. He's working for Mr. Ford now and he needs to see the dead Jew and that body that was fished up from the bay tonight."

"You mean Butch Sevier, the postman?"

"Yup."

Emmet jotted down the name of the mailman but added the word "Diener," to his notes, too, along with a question mark. Most

Americans tended to call people who took care of the dead morticians. Perhaps "Diener" was from the German word *Leichendiener*, which meant, "corpse servant." It was an odd word for a small-town sheriff to use.

"And who was the Jewish man that died?" Emmet asked. "We seem to have skipped over his name."

Barndt and Ross looked at each other in a way that told Emmet they either did not know or did not care.

"Is there some reason you would know the postman's name and not the rabbi's?"

"Not at all," Barndt replied. "It's just that everyone knew Butch, the postman. The rabbi was not well known. In fact, if he was a rabbi, I don't know what synagogue he was affiliated with. Kind of a hermit is what I've learned. Nobody seems to have known him—at least no one has come to claim the body—but the sheriff found documents and photos of him in the tiny house he lived in on Larchmont. His name is Mordecai Hirsch."

"That's right," said Ross.

Emmet added this information to his notes with the question: *why didn't Ross tell me this previously?*

As Barndt looked through paperwork to locate which of the cold lockers held the body of the rabbi, Emmet felt the weariness of a long day come over him. His stomach growled and he fought back the fatigue that threatened to overwhelm him.

Barndt rolled out the freezer drawer that held Hirsch's body.

Emmet began to inspect the body of the rabbi. It had a thin white sheet covering him and a tag on the big toe of the right foot. His skin was the color of tallow. His hair was long and grayish blonde which, for reasons Emmet couldn't fathom at the time, seemed strange to him. He looked closer and found the payots—the sidelock hair many Jews wear as part of their belief—was not Hirsch's real hair. The sidelocks were *braided* into his own hair. Emmet wondered if that was normal practice but believed it was not. As the body had been drained of fluids, the eyes were sunken and shallow, flat rather than rounded. Emmet lifted the lids to examine them; they were blue eyes, one pupil larger than the other, suggesting brain injury which could've been from the chemical in the tube, or perhaps he hit his head on the ground and sustained a cerebral hemorrhage when he collapsed.

Hirsch was unusually tall, though his back was curved with osteoporosis so badly that his head was lifted off the gurney, and it made him appear as though he were attempting to rise off his deathbed. The rabbi had some tattoos, mostly letters, which appeared to be done by an amateur or perhaps by Hirsch, himself. This was unusual, Emmet thought. One tattoo appeared to be done by someone who knew the craft. It was clean-edged and larger in scale than the others. It looked like two bolts of lightning crossing each other.

Emmet thought he recalled that Jews were forbidden to have tattoos. Something in the Torah, he thought he remembered, that related to forbidden idolatry. His conclusion, which he did not discuss, was that Hirsch did not appear to be a man of the cloth. Other than the payot, or sidelocks, braided into his hair, Emmet doubted if he was Jewish at all. But if Hirsch wasn't a Jew, why did he try to appear to be?

"Have you a magnifying glass, Dr. Barndt?" asked Emmet. Barndt's eyes grew even bigger behind his thick-lensed glasses.

"I surely do," said Barndt, enthusiastically, grinning ear to ear.

"What's so amusing, Walther?" asked Ross.

"Oh, nothing, Carl. It's just been a long time since anyone called me doctor," said Barndt and handed the magnifier to Emmet.

Emmet peered closely at the tattoo. It was more like a backward "Z" laid sideways with another bold line crossing it. "I remember this," said Emmet to no one. "From somewhere." He was tired and tried to think of the name of what he was looking at, rubbing his closed eyes before finally saying. "It's a Wolfsangel."

"A what?" said Ross, frowning.

Emmet did not answer him but made additional entries in his notebook. The Wolfsangel was an old, heraldic symbol found on shields and flags in Germany for centuries, very odd for a Jew whose inherent religious laws forbade marking of the skin. Emmet also noted Hirsch's scalded nasal passages. He opened his mouth and saw the man's tortured throat, blistered and burned so severely that there were holes in the pharynx.

"The *Weisskrueuz*, or White Cross gas, that I believe was in the tube, killed this man rather quickly," said Emmet, "but it had to be extremely painful. Blatantly cruel. There are a number of ways to kill someone, but this was one meant to be particularly painful. Whoever planned this wanted this man, or Mr. Ford, to suffer."

"Dead is dead, one way or the other," Ross announced.

"Soldiers kill other soldiers to win wars," said Emmet, annoyed with Ross and his pathetic one-line and idiotic witticisms. "But there are some people who relish causing people great pain and suffering before they die. No one should do that." He paused, recalling things he'd seen in wars he'd rather forget, then said, "Let's have a look at the postman."

Barndt had not yet placed Siever's body into one of the cooler boxes. He was still on a gurney, covered with a damp sheet. Barndt pulled the sheet off revealing a man, of less than average height, with a thick, walrus-like mustache that covered his mouth like a broom. His eyes were open and slightly crossed.

Emmet glanced at him and immediately said, "Ligature marks on wrists and ankles that appear to be from the anchor rope we saw on the dock. Broken neck but it appears that was done with something else. Do you have his clothing, Dr. Barndt?"

"No sir, Mr. MacWain," said Barndt. "He came in naked as you see him." He paused, then held up a finger like a conductor's wand. "Wait, yes, of course, we do have his belt. It was around his neck." He waddled over to another box with a name scrawled on it: Siever, Bernard, "Butch."

"Yes, this it. It was around his neck. Most likely it's what broke it, too, if his assailant was strong enough and twisted it just so." He made an animated wrenching twist upward with his hands holding up the belt.

Emmet took the belt from Barndt and looked it over. It appeared to be a boy's belt as it was short in length for a man. He glanced at Siever and his wide, doughy waist. "This wasn't the postman's belt, so we have, essentially, the murder weapon right here. The rope and anchor were used just to hide the body. This belt belonged to a man with a much narrower waist. I think we can assume that this belt belonged to the killer. Let's see what else it can tell us."

Emmet turned the belt over in his hand. He held it next to his own long arm—helpful as a boxer—which he knew to be a thirty-four-inch sleeve length. From elbow point to the bony point of his wrist he knew was approximately twelve inches, an odd personal fact that allowed him to measure the approximate length, or width of a room's dimension, or a table, or window. The belt was at least a half-foot shorter than his arm, so he assumed the length was twenty-eight inches.

Emmet looked at Siever's neck. The belt-wide, purple indentation on his neck angled upward toward the back, so the killer was most likely taller unless the victim had been hanged from something, a possibility Emmet could not discard. He looked closer at the belt. "Huh," he said softly.

"Huh, what?" said Ross.

"Nothing much," said Emmet. He took out his pad again and scribbled a note.

"I'll remind you, that I am the sheriff. This man was a local and a friend to many people here who knew him well. If you're helping here, do you mind telling me what you're seeing?"

Emmet knew he was right. It was the man's job to pursue this murder. He was there to learn about the tube sent in the mail that had killed the other man, Hirsch, and why he was stealing the mail in the first place and then died from it. The circumstances of the postman's death—murder actually—were the sheriff's job.

"I just noted," said Emmet, "if this is the killer's belt, he was trim in the waist. The bruising on the neck angles up in the back, so the killer was tall and thin and behind the victim. I also noted the belt was made in Cologne, Germany. It's stamped into the leather underneath the buckle."

Ross started to say something when Henry Ford, accompanied by Harry Bennett, entered the room. They were accompanied by a tall, handsome, slender man.

"Gentlemen," said Ford. "I can see you are busy, but I have a special guest you need to meet."

"He doesn't need any introduction for me," said Ross, smiling as if he were a Christian and Jesus had walked into his church.

Ford glanced at Ross with a solemn, disdainful face, then began again. "Mr. MacWain, I'd like you to meet my dear friend, Mr. Charles Lindbergh."

TWENTY-ONE

T he group, minus Dr. Barndt, convened back at Ford's home, where servants were still cleaning up after dinner. It began to rain, and water splashed against the windows like waves against the portholes of a sinking ship.

"I'm sorry you men missed supper but if you still have an appetite, we can warm you up a dish," said Ford. "It's really quite wonderful."

"Thank you," said Emmet. "But it's late and I'm afraid I've lost my appetite for tonight."

"Sheriff?"

"I'll pass, too," said Ross. "I've got to be on my way. Good night." And with that, he put his wide-brimmed sheriff's hat on and left.

"Would anyone like some coffee or a drink?" asked Ford.

"I brought a bottle of Eiswein from my last trip to Europe," said the man in the suit, whom Emmet had not yet formally met. "It's a wonderfully sweet wine made from mature grapes that have gone through a frost. I had Clara put it in your icebox before dinner. It's perfect for dessert."

"I don't believe you've met my secretary, Mr. MacWain," said Ford, also standing now. "Ernest Liebold, please welcome Mr. MacWain."

Emmet stood per protocol to meet the man, but Liebold stayed seated.

"MacWain is the man I told you about. The one FBI Branch Director Serey suggested to us. I've retained him to investigate the man who was trying to steal my mail and, as misfortune would have it, died."

"Pleased to meet you, Mr. MacWain," said Liebold, with a slight nod. A handshake was not proffered.

Emmet gave a nod back, then said, "It wasn't misfortune, Mr. Ford. There's little doubt in my mind it was murder."

"Oh, you've come to that conclusion, have you?" asked Ford. He glanced at Liebold, "That's Mr. MacWain's former livelihood talking, Ernest. I think I shared with you that he was an inspector for Scotland Yard for some time."

Liebold stared at Emmet, his eyes steady as if he was staring through the scope of a rifle. "Yes, sir," he said. "You did. And I believe I shared my thoughts with you on that subject. I believe some industrial factory sent the package of some chemical that leaked and someone trying to steal your mail was unfortunate to open that package. I believe it's best to leave the matter with the local authorities."

Ford shrugged. "Ross is a decent man but let's face it, Ernest, he's no Sherlock Holmes, is he?"

"I don't think we need a professional sleuth. A filthy Jew tried to steal your mail and died. Not worth your time or resources, Henry. The sheriff can wrap it up and be done with it."

"I haven't actually been retained," said Emmet.

"You're right," Ford interrupted. "We should agree upon fee..."

"You gave me an automobile, sir," said Emmet, his eyes locked on Liebold's. "Let's agree that's my retainer..."

Liebold interrupted, "You're a bit long in the tooth to be doing this type of work, aren't you, MacWain? The local law enforcement will suffice..."

Emmet suddenly crossed the room so quickly, Liebold recoiled and pushed himself back into the plush chair he sat in. Emmet's eyes shown with heated anger for a moment, then he turned and extended his hand to Ford. "Deal?"

Ford grinned as he took Emmet's hand. "Deal, sir. You move rather quickly, MacWain. And even Bennett admitted you're handy with your fists." He glanced at Liebold. "I'm a little long in the tooth myself, Mr. MacWain, but I comfort myself knowing getting older usually means growing wiser. You should ponder that, Ernest."

A light sheen of sweat formed on Liebold's now scarlet face. His Adam's apple dipped in his throat, but he remained silent after Ford's admonishment.

Charles Lindbergh came into the room carrying a cup of coffee with Clara Ford at his side.

"Can you men stop discussing dark deeds and visit with our nation's most famous aviator and ambassador?" said Clara. "I've got some more cleaning up to do. Charles, it's so good to see you again, please give my regards to your lovely wife, Anne for me."

Lindbergh grinned, flashing an electric smile, "I'll surely do that Clara. Thank you for the use of your telephone and this wonderful coffee."

Clara dashed back into the kitchen and Lindbergh stood appraising the group of men in Ford's parlor.

"What did you find out Charles?" asked Ford.

"So, I'm sorry to say I cannot get out of my engagement with the America First Committee. They need me to spread my gospel, so to speak," said Lindbergh, his grin returning.

"And right you are to spread that word, Charles," said Ford. "It's not the Germans we need to worry about, it's the damned communists. They're against every man who yearns to make a dollar and then call us capitalists."

Lindbergh nodded and raised his coffee cup as if giving a toast. "Thank you, Henry. I do have an opportunity you might consider for your group. I can get you and your entourage to France on a cargo ship that left Tampa last night. They're stopped in Miami before heading to Brazil, then on to France. That might be a bit out of your way..."

"No, no, no," said Ford. "Not at all. That's perfect and it will allow me to travel incognito so to speak. I can kill two birds with one stone. I've been wanting to get back to Brazil to see what the savages have left of my city and the infrastructure I built there. They may have even been a part of this attempt on my life."

"I could book us on something more comfortable, Henry, or get us flights directly to France if that is where you wish to go..." Liebold began.

"Not at all Ernest," said Ford. "I'm tired of the press hounding me around and this will allow us to be more confidential in our investigation."

"Then I'll get the ball rolling...if I may use your phone again," said Lindbergh.

"Wonderful," said Ford. "What do you say, Mr. MacWain? Are you up for a transatlantic crossing with a stop along the way?"

Emmet had been absorbing the conversation and the odd, unaffected nature of this group of men who obviously did not care for the loss of one or two men's lives as long as they could keep to their schedules and continue their daily businesses.

Chewing on the inside of his cheek to keep from blurting out his thoughts, Emmet fought back the urge to tell them all to go to hell. But this is what Serey wanted from him, to ingratiate himself to their trust, infiltrate, and find out what their connection was to the Nazis. He did not want to go, nor spend another moment with these men, but he had nothing to hold on to and now, increasingly, more reason to look deeper into a case that was beginning to look like something more than the local murder of two men.

Emmet didn't want to appear too eager and played it that way. "I'll have to see if I can clear my schedule," he said. "How long do you think we'd be gone?"

Lindbergh addressed the question. "The ship is a quick cargo vessel, and they won't delay their shipment. They'll only stay in Brazil for two, maybe three days tops to load their coffee shipment and replenish fuel and supplies, then on to France. So, maybe ten days to two weeks at sea. I'm not sure how long Henry will need in France, but I'll be flying back to Germany in two weeks, and I'll bring a big enough plane to fly us all back. Would that work for you, Henry?"

"That would be splendid, Charles. Will you come with us Mr. MacWain, and help us unravel this intrigue?"

"I suppose it would be beneficial to go to France and see if we can find the address that was on the package," said Emmet, pondering the proposition. "I'll let you know in the morning. Let me think it over. It's been a long day," said Emmet, standing to go.

"As you wish, sir," said Lindbergh. "But if you want to hitch a ride, you better meet us here early, or at the airport by eight o'clock. The ship sails by noon. It's a quick flight to Miami but the captain won't wait for us if we're late."

"Understood," said Emmet. "I'll say good night and, one way or the other, I'll see you here in the morning around 7:00 AM."

"Splendid," said Ford. "I'm sure I can come up with some way to persuade you."

"Maybe another car?" Emmet said. As he took his leave, he heard Ford laugh and say, "Bravo!" in a foppish attempt at a Scottish accent. The group in the parlor chuckled it up. He glanced back before climbing into his new car and saw Liebold and Bennett standing close in conversation, watching him fade into the night.

TWENTY-TWO

Emmet was exhausted as he pulled up to the Royal Palm Hotel. There was a cool, brine-scented breeze blowing up from the bay that gave him some respite. He noted the bar was still open and hoped he could grab a nightcap and maybe a couple of those pickled eggs. At least the attractive, red-haired young lady was still laboring away. Upon entering the hotel, he drifted up to the empty counter. "Good evening, Miss Murphy," he said. "Are you still open for business?"

"I was about to close up for the evening, as it's slow tonight, but I'll keep the lights on if you need a splash," she said with a wink.

"That would be wonderful. Got any more of those pickled eggs?"

"Did you not have dinner, already?"

"No, I was called away and went without, I'm afraid."

"Well, you can't go to bed hungry, sir. I've got a chunk of corned beef and some rye bread in the kitchen. Would that suit you, sir?"

"Like a mother's hugs. A proper pint would be nice, too."

Bessie laughed. "Right away. Here's a couple of those eggs to hold you over while I warm up that sandwich for ya."

As he waited for his repast, he pondered the proposal to sail first to Brazil, then to France. *What had he gotten himself into?* Ford was a handful. Clever, ambitious, and tricky with a monumental ego. But he could deal with him. Bennett was like a wasp, he might be a challenge but if he became too much of a problem, could be easily swatted away. But Liebold was mysterious. His dark eyes buttoned into the expressionless face of a typical bureaucrat reminded Emmet of some of the killers he hunted in London a lifetime ago. Just from his demeanor, Emmet could tell he was hiding something, maybe many things, and he appeared hurt or wounded by Ford's words. Ford might have been dismissive of him, but he also listened and took counsel from him. *Why?* It was an odd relationship, to say the least. And what was Lindbergh doing there? Was it a coincidence that he would appear just as a man died—or was murdered—at Ford's house?

Emmet had read newspaper accounts of some of Lindbergh's speeches as the president of the American First Committee. They drew huge crowds who came to hear anti-communist speeches, but that rhetoric typically turned into pro-Nazi propaganda. And hadn't Hitler awarded Lindbergh the Iron Cross, the German's highest military honor? The Fuhrer had also written admiration for Henry Ford in his book, *Mein Kamph,* expressing he wanted to help "Heinrich to become the leading fascist in the United States." *They were all too cozy,* Emmet was thinking, *and now there was a dead postman, a rabbi who happened to have German tattoos? Unlikely at best.*

Bessie interrupted Emmet's thoughts when she placed a plate with the hot corned beef sandwich in front of him.

"That's on me, sir. Your tip earlier tonight was the biggest I've ever earned here."

"Oh, I couldn't possibly accept. You work hard for your money, Mum..."

"I won't hear it, Mr...."

"Emmet, please..."

Bessie nodded. "Emmet, please indulge a lady trying to do a kindness for a kindness."

"Done and done, then. Thank you, Bessie."

Emmet turned his attention to his late dinner, loading the sandwich with enough mustard and horseradish to water his eyes, clear his nose, and help wash his fatigue away. He watched Bessie put away the bottles of booze and finish washing dishes. Her skin was so pale, her arms were pink up to the elbows from being immersed in the hot water.

She disappeared into the kitchen but a mirror in the short hall that led to the back room showed her reflection. Emmet couldn't help but watch her and he saw her unbutton her shirt. He didn't mean to act like a Peeping Tom but was mesmerized by what she was doing. Believing no one was watching, she ran hot water over a dishtowel and washed her face, then her neck, and under her arms. She fanned herself off with another towel and replaced her shirt. She reemerged a moment later.

"Well, sir," she said, "I hate to leave a man to dine alone but I must get some rest. I've got to be back by 5:00 AM to help with the breakfast."

"Oh, I'm sorry," said Emmet. "I've kept you here late. Perhaps I'll see you for breakfast."

"That would be grand."

"Do you need a ride home, Bessie? I've got a car here."

"Ah, no thank you. I live right across the street, and I'll be fine."

"Well then, goodnight, and thank you again. You've filled my stomach and I'll sleep like a baby, I'm sure."

Bessie smiled and said, "My pleasure, Emmet. Have a good, restful night."

Emmet finished his pint and went to his room. It was spacious and elegant and contained the latest technology, including a telephone. He washed up and noted it was late but kept turning his gaze back to the phone. Was it too late? He knew Pauline would be awake and he wanted, needed, to talk to her. He dialed the operator and asked her to ring the number through.

Pauline answered, her voice small and listless.

"I'm sorry to call so late...," he began.

"S'okay," said Pauline. "I'm awake. How did your day go?"

"Eventful is probably the best way to say it. Busy and long."

"You should probably get some rest."

"I'm going to but I wanted to talk to you."

"About...?"

"A future."

"Emmet, we've talked about this, many times. It is what it is. We have what we have and I'm content. You should be, too."

"Living on my boat and seeing you only when I invite myself over?"

"That's not fair. You know I'm busy with the boys..."

"But it's accurate, yes?"

Pauline was silent, other than a deep breath Emmet could hear her exhale.

He didn't want to fight it anymore. "How are the boys, by the way?"

"They're gone for now. Ernest is taking them to Cuba for a couple of weeks before he goes back to France to cover the war for Collier magazine. He wants to take them with him to Europe..."

"That's a horrible idea."

"I think so, too, but he swears they will be safe."

"He can't guarantee that. The situation over there grows worse by the day. You need to talk him out of it."

"I've tried. Short of getting attorneys involved, which is very difficult in that he lives out of the country now, I can't do much to stop him."

Emmet pondered the matter, trying to think of what he could do to persuade Hemingway to leave his sons in Key West. "I can call him and try to reason..."

"Emmet, it's not your concern..."

"It *is* my concern. You know how fond of Gregory I am. What you mean is, it's none of my business."

Pauline went silent again and they both sat with the phones to their ears, listening to each other breathe.

"Pauline, I'm going to Europe myself. Agent Serey hooked me into this...situation, and I'm going to see it through. I'll try to reach out to Ernest whether you'd like me to or not. I'm not trying to butt into your family or life, but I cannot allow him to endanger those boys for a press opportunity."

"You should stay out of it. It's not your concern, nor your business."

Emmet felt a vein throb in his head and his face flush and a pang in his heart that was as palpable as a knife's blade. He heard all he needed to. His and Pauline's relationship had fizzled out like fireworks in a rainstorm. He had tried to relight the fuse but had grown as weary at the effort as Pauline had of him trying. He took a breath as if he were plunging underwater for an extended swim, then said the only thing he could.

"You take care of yourself, Mum. Good-bye."

Just before he placed the phone back on its hook, he heard her say something. But he didn't care. Not anymore.

Restless, Emmet went to the window to look out over the bay, seeking a balm for his bruised heart. Something below caught his eye. On the sidewalk near the alley that ran along the back of the hotel, he spied a woman tucking herself into the opening of the service doors. She had on a white shirt and her hair was flaming red. It was Bessie.

Was she going to sleep there? Emmet wondered. *Was she homeless?* He couldn't believe it. On the other hand, the country still wore the hangover of the decade-long depression and there were thousands of unfortunate people still suffering, without a home or shelter, many without food, and jobs were still difficult to find. He watched the street below as other homeless people, many of them intoxicated, sick—physically, or mentally—shuffled by, some with their hands out. Some moved on but there were a few who lingered, including two men who did not appear to be vagrants.

Emmet didn't bother to throw his shirt back on. He hurried from the room wearing an undershirt, hastily fastening his belt as he pushed the button to summon the elevator. He watched the floor indicator arrow slowly point from the first floor to the second, the third....He found himself holding his breath and uttering curses when the elevator car finally stopped and opened. He rushed inside and pounded the first-floor button repeatedly.

When he got to the ground floor, he ran from the car as if it were on fire and across the spacious lobby. Bursting through the front doors like a charging bull, he rounded the building and pushed toward the alley, his breath coming in gasps. As he entered the alley, his eyes had to adjust to the lack of lighting, but he could see the silhouettes of the two men and Bessie. One man held her arms, twisting them together with one of his hands, tearing at her blouse with the other hand, like a raptor pulling at the fur of a downed rabbit. The other man had circled around behind her and had one arm around her neck while he pulled up her skirt with his free hand.

Emmet never uttered a word as he charged into the shadows. He snatched the man behind Bessie by the greasy hair of his head and snapped back so hard he thought he broke his neck. The man uttered *"gack"* before the momentum of the assault threw him to the ground like a felled tree. His head hit the pavement like a coconut, with a resounding crack, but Emmet didn't bother to check on him. The second man barely had time to release Bessie before Emmet rushed forward with a wide, rounding right cross that found the man's face and smashed into it like a meteor. In the lightless alley, blood flew like black ink from the man's crushed nose. He staggered for a moment, then fell to one knee before collapsing into a crumbled pile.

Emmet swirled around to see if there were any more attackers before he turned back to Bessie. "Are you all right, Bessie? Did they hurt you?" he asked as he approached her and took her by her shoulders.

Bessie curled into his embrace, shivering and sobbing.

Emmet's eyes adjusted to the dark and he looked down into Bessie's tear-streaked face as she began to compose herself.

"My God, you're frightenin' aren't you?" she said with a voice husky with emotion.

"I...I'm sorry, Mum. Couldn't be any worse than these two brigands," said Emmet surveying the two men. He could see they were sailors from one of the ships. One of them—the one with long, dark, curled hair—wore an anchor tattoo on his forearm, with a ribbon wrapped around it that read, "crossed the Atlantic 1925," a time he noted when the world was not at war, at least not globally, so he could be a merchant marine. Navy sailors were forbidden to wear their hair long.

The other man was bald, his pate shining with blood as he lay there gasping. His shirt was torn open, and he had numerous tattoos of swallows. These tattoos were traditionally worn by sailors who had traveled at least five thousand nautical miles. Emmet counted six of them inked across the man's chest.

"No, Emmet. Don't be sorry. I...thank you," she said and wrapped her arms around him, squeezing him as if, when she let go, she'd fall off the earth.

"I was looking out my hotel window when I saw you down here. Why are you here? Do you not have a place to stay?"

Bessie shook her head between sobs. "I couldn't afford my flat anymore and I've been stayin' here the past couple weeks. It's been... okay, until tonight."

Emmet held her back so he could look into her face. He felt her trembling, her breath panting. "I don't want you to take this wrong— I'm not a brigand, Bessie—but I want you to come with me. I'll get you a room and you'll be safe."

"I couldn't..."

"Please, you must. You deserve better and I can afford it."

Bessie wiped away a tear that was routing her cheek like a streak of glycerin. She sniffled and gave an almost imperceptible nod. Then she gathered up a small bag of her belongings and they went back to the hotel. Emmet kept his arm around her shoulders as they walked. At the door to the lobby, Bessie stopped and looked up into Emmet's face.

"I don't want to be too forward, but would you do a lass a favor and let me stay with you? I don't want...to be alone tonight."

Emmet thought for a moment before saying, "Sure. And I'll do you one better than that. I'm working for a very wealthy man right now and he's provided my stay here at the hotel. I'm leaving tomorrow for a couple of weeks, maybe more. You can stay in my room until I return."

"Oh, my saints!" said Bessie, her tears welling up again.

"No more tears, lass. Now, let's get you some rest. We both have to be up in a few hours."

In the room, against Bessie's protestations, Emmet put a blanket and pillow on the couch while she took a proper bath. He laid down and began to drift off to sleep. Then, he felt a warm hand brush his face, soft, thick lips touched his, timidly at first, then with more fervor. A tongue teased his. A soft hand moved from his face to his chest, and further down.

"Come to bed with me, Emmet," whispered Bessie. "God sent you to me, kind sir, and I want to love you both."

Emmet chuckled. "If you insist, Mum, but can you ask him to look the other way?"

TWENTY-THREE

E mmet awoke at 6 AM. Though the window to his room faced the west and the sun peeked up in the east, the light reflected off the bay water and lit up the room like a spotlight. He sat up and stretched, feeling more relaxed than he had in years. Bessie was gone but left a note on the bedside table. It read:

Good morning, Emmet! Thank you very much for the hospitality. You are a gentleman and an animal! I look forward to round 2! Stop at the bar before you leave and I'll have a plate of biscuits and gravy ready for you and we can say so long, properly.

Your Bessie.

There was a kiss from her on the note accentuated by her deep red lipstick. The note brought a smile to Emmet, the first in a long time. A strand of red, curled hair lay across his pillow. He picked it up and smelled it—there was a hint of wildflowers such as grows in the grassy fields of Ireland, and he pictured the hair framing Bessie's pale, pretty face. He rolled out of bed with a spring in his step, showered, and put on fresh clothes. He hadn't unpacked his bag, so it was easy to pick up and go.

Emmet jaunted down the hall and into the elevator. A moment later, he stepped out and into the lobby and strolled over to the bar, his duffle bag slung over his shoulder like a sailor heading out to sea. The scents and sounds of eggs frying, bacon sizzling, and biscuits baking made his mouth water.

Bessie was serving breakfast to a couple of young, uniformed soldiers and spied Emmet. She winked at him and held up a finger indicating she'd be with him in a minute. He gave her a nod of understanding and helped himself to an urn of coffee at the end of the counter, watching her hips as she disappeared into the kitchen. She came back in a couple of minutes with a steaming plate of food in one hand and napkins and eating utensils in the other. With a wide, salacious smile on her face, she said, "Top o' the mornin' to ya!"

Emmet smiled and tipped the brim of his outback slouch hat, one side of the brim buttoned up, Aussie-style. He'd taken to wearing it as a young man while attached to one of the most famous cavalry units in history: Teddy Roosevelt's Rough Riders. They'd fought in Cuba and while Emmet detested war, he had to agree with Roosevelt's belief: "If you had to fight, it was better on the back of a horse, where you had some high ground than from the bottom of a trench." Amen.

Bessie set a plate on the bar for Emmet. It was loaded with biscuits and scrambled eggs covered in thick, steaming sausage gravy. "Let me know if you need more," she said with a wink.

"If I finish this plate, I might sink the ship," Emmet quipped.

"Eat up!" said Bessie. "It might be your last good meal for a while." Then, leaning forward, she whispered, "Are you sure you're okay with me staying in your room?"

"Of course. That way I know where to find you when I return," he said with a wink.

Bessie's face flushed, and then she seemed to recall something. "Did I mention to you I'll be working for the Ringling Brothers Circus next month when they come back to their hometown?"

"No," said Emmet, working on cleaning his plate. "Doing what?"

"I'll be returning as 'Bessie, The Empress of Flame!'"

"That sounds dangerous."

Bessie's eyes lit up. "It's fun! I get to ride a beautiful horse and jump through circles of fire."

"So, you're a bit crazy?"

"Aren't most of the best women?"

Emmet shrugged and finally nodded. "I can't argue with that..."

"Hey," said Bessie feigning anger, holding up a small fist.

"I used to ride horses, too," said Emmet. "Sometimes through fire. But I was in a cavalry then."

"I'd love to hear all about it...," said Bessie, her precious smile returning.

"And I would love to tell you, sweet lass, but I need to be going. Promise me you'll keep an eye open if you're out at night and enjoy the room here as long as you'd like."

"I certainly will. Thanks, again," said Bessie and ran around the end of the bar. "Give me a hug and you stay safe yourself."

Emmet hugged her tightly and for a moment considered staying. He didn't owe Ford, John Serey, Pauline, or anyone, anything. He wondered: *Would it be so bad for him to think of himself, to make himself happy just this once?*

Then, he thought about the two men already murdered and how many more there might be. His sense of responsibility for what he felt he owed his adopted country took over. He told himself he had no choice. He looked around, careful not to compromise Bessie in her workplace, and when he saw no one was looking at them, leaned down and gave her a kiss he hoped would last until he saw her again.

Bessie continued to squeeze him after the kiss, her head on his chest, then finally, let him go, her eyes wet with happiness. Looking up into his face, she said, "Luck o' the Irish be with ya, my grand man."

Emmet eyed Bessie up and down, admiring her youthful, springlike beauty, then grinned and said, "I've already got it." Then, he handed her a slip of folded paper and whispered into her ear, "If you need to contact me, there's a phone number on here for a man named John Serey. He always knows how to find me."

He tipped his hat to her and went out the hotel doors.

Bessie whispered aloud, "I think I could *love* this man," the "o" in love pronounced like "Oh," in her Irish brogue. She pushed the note discreetly under her shirt, into her brassiere, continuing to whisper. "I'll keep you close to my heart, Emmet MacWain."

TWENTY-FOUR

CHATEAU DES MILANDES

C laude heard hammering at the front door of the Chateau. He looked at his *Cartier* watch, a gift from his employer, Josephine Baker. It was 6:30 in the morning and his *patron dame* had only gone to bed about two hours earlier. He assumed the loud knocking was one of the local farmers to whom his patron had leased a field. Perhaps there had been an accident, or someone had left a gate open and some cows or sheep had run off. It was not uncommon but not appreciated either. Still, Claude answered the door with his usual aplomb.

When he opened the door, there were two officers in full military regalia. One was a high-ranking Vichy officer; the other was a Nazi whose rank Claude was not familiar with.

The obedient butler cleared his throat and swallowed. "Bonjour. What brings you here, gentlemen?" Then, unable to control himself, he added. "In these very early hours."

"I am Marshall Rene Pelletier from the Vichy gendarme, and this is *Oberleutnant* Hans Von Arent from the German Abwehr." Both men were armed with pistols.

Claude raised one of his considerable eyebrows. "*Oui*. I am Claude Durand, the master servant of this Chateau, of which Mademoiselle Baker is the owner. How may I be of service?"

"Don't you mean Madame Lion?" asked Pelletier, looking confused.

"No," said Claude. "Mademoiselle Baker is no longer married to Monsieur Lion. Again I ask, how may I help you?"

"We represent the interest of the German Reich. The Chateau des Milandes will be getting a visit from *Hauptsturnfurer* Barbie but we will speak to your master about this matter," said Von Arent. He approached Claude, looking at the tall butler as if from the vantage point of a defiant boy. While maintaining eye contact, he pushed open the entry door and brushed past Claude. Pellitier followed him and they spread out and began looking around.

Claude had to bite his tongue and breathe deeply to cool his anger. Before becoming a manservant, Claude had been a soldier. He'd killed dozens of Huns, the spiky-helmeted German soldiers that he fought with his fellow soldiers called *Tete de chou*—"cabbage heads"—or simply the Bosch. Claude was one of "The Hairy's," as the American Joes called them. He fought on the western front when his whole platoon was taken out with a deluge of bombs that left him deaf in his left ear, and more than "a little crazy in the head," as he would say when he was tipsy enough to tell the story. He fell in with the *Arditi*, the "Daring ones," the Italian assault units, when the Italians were on the good side of the Allies in the "Big War," before the world began to give wars numbers. Claude was then offered a place in an even crazier group of Italians—who called themselves, *Caimani del Piave*, or the "Alligators of the Piave," whose soldiers were so bold they did not use guns but swam the river with knives in their teeth and grenades in their pockets. Upon landing on the enemy's side of the river, they would throw the grenades into the cabbage heads' trenches, then dive into the trenches and reek carnage on them with their blades.

"I'll summon Mademoiselle Baker right away," said Claude, his jaw muscles flexing. He walked up the stairs slowly, an old anger brewing in his belly. Halfway up on the spiral staircase, there was a window that gave a birds-eye view of the long drive into the chateau. There was just one car in which their "guests" had arrived, and it was empty.

Claude went into Josephine's bedroom and found her sleeping face down, sprawled on the bed, nude, a sight so routine for him it did not embarrass him, nor would it bother her. She'd been near-naked in front of half the world in her bawdy sold-out shows. He placed his hand on her bare back and softly said, "We have *monstres* in our home."

Josephine awoke alert. She knew what the phrase meant. "Who is it this time?"

"One is a stinking kraut, and the other a Vichy lapdog. They want to look over the chateau and ensure it is up to par for Monsieur Barbie's upcoming visit. They are armed."

Josephine smiled, "Then let's dress accordingly." She opened the drawer next to her bed and withdrew a small, easily concealed Smith & Wesson .38. It was only a five-shot revolver but that was three more bullets than she needed. "What are you bringing to the party, *mi amour*?"

A cold grin stretched across his face. "You know I like the knife."

Josephine nodded approval and jumped out of bed. She pulled on a tiny, revealing robe with large pockets into which she slipped the small .38. Then she went into the bathroom to freshen up.

Claude removed, from its tattered scabbard, a French M-1916 Avenger Trench knife. It had been bathed in the blood of many adversaries who tried and failed to kill Claude Durand, most in the war, and a few afterward. Its edges were sharp enough to shave his face and it could be thrown as easily and accurately as a dart in an English pub.

Pelletier mounted the stairs and called out as he ascended, "Come down immediately or risk punishment."

"We will be down right away, sir," Claude shouted back, gritting his teeth.

"He's pretty demanding for a dead man," said Josephine as she emerged from the bathroom. "Let's not keep them waiting."

They began descending the stairs and Josephine smiled as if she were greeting one of her beloved fans. She almost laughed at Marshal Vichy's pencil-thin mustache amid a face that had a huge, alcohol-reddened nose and fat jowls created by too much cheese and croissants. Then she glanced at the German officer and while she feared no man, the Nazi had a face like a skull and the countenance of a corpse, without any expression but with pale blue eyes the color of ice.

She wondered how many people he had already killed or tortured and a fit of anger grew in her like a white-hot branding iron. Still, she managed to spread a smile across her face as she said, "Hey fellas, thanks for stopping by. How can I help you?"

"We will look around your castle and check that it is safe and clean enough for *mein Hauptsturmführer* Barbie's upcoming visit," said Von Arent.

"Oh, I can assure you it is clean, sir."

"Are there any *Untermensch* hiding here? Tell me now and things will be better for you."

"I'm sorry," said Josephine, "I don't speak Nazi."

Pelletier, his face redder now, interrupted, "It means sub-human."

"I'm sure you have a basement," said Von Arent. "You will show us now, *Schwarzer Teufel,* so we can see if you have a Jew hidden there."

At the mention of the name that Germans called her when she toured there, the "Black Devil," smiled and said, "Did you say *achoo*? Maybe I should get you a handkerchief if you've got a cold."

Von Arent unbuckled his holster. Pelletier followed suit, fumbling with his holster as if it were glued shut. Frustrated he said, "This is enough. We will check your cellar now."

"Of course, Marshall Marceau," said Josephine, alluding to the famous mime, who played "Bip," the clown and who was also a French Jew. Smiling, she added, "Let me lead the way," as she descended the steps and began the route to the cellar. Along the way, she continued her sarcasm, throwing verbal jabs that often went over their heads but made her chuckle aloud.

Her unwelcome company did not enjoy nor return the humor.

They made it to the locked door that led down to the cellar. She opened it and said, "Follow me but watch your step."

"Do you not have lights in here?" asked Pelletier.

"No, the wine likes it dark. Are you afraid of the dark, *Monsieur*?" Josephine quipped as she went down the steps she knew so well, she could navigate them with her eyes closed.

"*Nein!*" barked Von Arent.

Claude was behind the group and descended with them. "Keep one hand on the wall and it will help guide you down. There is a light at the bottom."

When Josephine got to the floor of the cellar, she turned, removed her .38, then looked up at the men silhouetted from the light at the entrance to the stairs as they continued to make their way down. "You okay, Claude?"

"I am," he said, withdrawing his knife, then added, "Now." Then he stepped up behind Von Arent grabbed the Nazi by the head and pulled it back, exposing his neck, and quickly stuck the trench knife into his windpipe so that he could drown in his own blood, cut off from life-giving air like the prisoners of war who were being stuffed into gas chambers. "That's from the *Caimani del Piave*, you stinking kraut."

Pelletier turned and tried again to free his pistol from the holster as fear came over him like a wave of lava. "Wha...?"

"I'm down here you Nazi *Leche-cul!*"

Pelletier turned, moving slowly as if he were caught in quicksand, gripped by an immobilizing fear. He opened his holster but still could not free the gun and, even if he could, it was too late. Josephine had her gun out and aimed. She pulled the trigger and even in the dim light leaking in from the hallway upstairs, she managed to find her target. The bullet drilled a hole in his forehead like a carpenter bee through soft wood.

Claude went back up the stairs and turned on the lights while laughing aloud. "Oh, *Mon Dieu!* Did you really call him a Nazi ass-licker?"

"I did. I hope it did not offend you," Josephine said, grinning like the character she performed on the stage.

"I'm glad you didn't shoot me. I was right behind him."

"I thought of that, but I already knew he had a hard head that was full of so much *merde,* it would stop the bullet."

Claude laughed then looking around, said, "*Sacre bleu*! We have a big mess to clean up!"

"Let's do that after dark. Get Peitro down at the vineyards. The Nazis killed his family when they first rolled in and I'm sure he would be glad to help. You could bury them in amongst the grapevines, but it might spoil the wine, and they could be found if the rodents got at them. Wrap the bodies in chains and cinder blocks and drop them into the river instead. Then pack for a trip. I think it might be good to get away for a while in case the goose steppers come looking for their dance partners."

"Good idea. But where are we going, Mademoiselle?"

"I've been offered a show in Brazil. I can perform on the ship going over and there's a huge nightclub that's been there forever where they still like to watch me shake my ass. The *Os Democraticos e Suas, Finalidades*. I get paid double and *Capitaine* Abtey has given me an assignment as well."

"A mission?"

"*Oui*, but the less you know about it, the better off you'll be. *D'accord*?

"*Oui*. But it would be nice to kill another Nazi. I'd forgotten how much I enjoyed it."

"Let's just say, you might get the chance. Brazil is crawling with them."

TWENTY-FIVE

mmet arrived at Ford's home at 6:30 AM. The sun was up bright, but not yet baking the Florida earth. There were several cars crowded into the driveway and Bennett was loading suitcases into them. Emmet spied Ford inside the house carrying on a discussion with Clara and Liebold. Edsel Ford was outside, standing off to the side of the house. He appeared pale, perhaps ill, as Emmet approached him.

"Good morning, Mr. Ford," said Emmet. "Are you all right?"

Sweat ran down the young Ford's face as if he were standing under a downspout. He leaned over and grasped his stomach, grimacing in pain. His legs were shaking and when he tried to answer, he simply groaned.

Emmet looked around—others had to notice the young man was suffering—but no one seemed alarmed. "Let me help you," said Emmet and bent down to get Edsel's arm around his shoulders. He was soaked with perspiration. The man was practically weightless to Emmet who all but carried him in like a child. He pushed through the front door with his foot and brought Edsel over to a couch.

Henry Ford glanced at his son but did not stop talking with Liebold. Clara noticed him and her face became pale.

"Oh, my, son," she said, rushing to him. "Are you sick?"

Edsel nodded but could not answer.

Liebold glanced over at the ailing young man. "I do hope it wasn't the coffee, Edsel. I tend to make it too strong at times."

"It's his stomach, Mum," said Emmet, while glaring at Liebold. "Do you have some bicarbonate, like baking powder, or soda water, or perhaps some peppermint?"

"Let me look," said Clara. She ran out of the room and was back in two minutes with all three.

"Very good," said Emmet. "Mrs. Ford, please mix a teaspoon of the baking soda with some water. Edsel, take a sip of this seltzer. It will make you burp and that might relieve the pain you're having."

Edsel sipped soda water and grimaced. Emmet noticed Mrs. Ford had returned with the mixture, her hands trembling.

"Edsel, take another sip of this," said Emmet. "It's more effective than just the seltzer and should neutralize any acid in your stomach, then swallow the peppermint. It'll help, too."

Edsel did as he was told and, slowly, his face began to relax as did the clinched hand he held to his stomach like a gut-shot soldier.

"We need to be going," said the elder Ford. "Charles is waiting for us at the airfield."

Emmet looked at Ford with astonishment and anger. "Your son should see a doctor. He needs treatment."

Ford looked at Emmet with disdain. "While I appreciate your intervention, Edsel has a tummy ache and he'll get over it. Right, son?"

Edsel nodded as he took a deep breath. "Thank you for your help, Mr. MacWain, but my father is right. This happens to me from time to time. I'll be fine, sir."

"He's under a lot of stress," said Clara.

Emmet noticed a handkerchief Edsel had been using. There were bright blots of blood on it. It reminded Emmet of his ailing wife as she died from consumption. "Does the pain come more frequently and has it grown worse over time?" asked Emmet.

"Yes, worse and more frequently, lately, but it will pass. Your concoction seemed to help quite a bit. Are you a physician?" Edsel queried.

"No, sir, but I've rendered medical aid in the field as a soldier. I'm glad it helped for now, but I could see you were in severe pain. I highly recommend you get further assessment by a doctor."

"That's good advice, Mr. MacWain but we really need to go," said Ford. "I'd hate to keep Charles waiting."

Emmet wanted to tell Ford to go on without him and was on the verge of telling him to go to hell, but he held off. He'd rather not go at all. Bessie was too young for him, but she was good company, beautiful, and seemed to enjoy his company as well. *Didn't he deserve to be happy or at least content?* Couldn't Serey and his G-men handle this investigation of Ford and his cronies on their own? Why did he have to get involved *again*?

A phone rang in the kitchen and Clara ran to get it. Within a minute she came back to the room, her face wrinkled with worry. "Mr. MacWain. You have a phone call. Is Edsel all right?"

Emmet was taken aback. "A call for me?"

"Yes, sir. I believe it is Mr. Serey."

Emmet wondered why Serey, who was trying to keep his presence unknown to Ford, would call him at the man's home. But, Serey had recommended Emmet to Ford, so perhaps they were not surprised or curious. Answering Clara's question, he said, "Your son seems better for now, but he should see a doctor."

Emmet quietly took Edsel's cup, then went to the kitchen, hid the cup under the sink, and picked up the phone. "Hello?"

"I'm going to speak quickly," said Serey. "So, if someone is near you, just answer yes or no, okay?"

"Okay. Currently, it's just us," Emmet whispered.

"Good, I've heard about your sudden trip. This is good. It appears Ford trusts you and that's what we want. I'm not sure what he's looking for in Brazil but there's over a million Germans living in the country now and a growing number of them have embraced the Nazi agenda."

Emmet wanted to ask some questions, but Serey was talking so quickly, he couldn't get a word in and, if he could, he wondered how he could make any inquiries in his present situation within earshot of Ford and his people.

Serey continued. "See what you can find out about the Teuto-Brazilians. They're a fascist group and share Hitler's dogma. If Ford meets with Getulio Vargas—he's the President of Brazil—let us know. Our information suggests that Vargas is bellying up to the Nazis, too. Has Ford indicated to you why he is going to Brazil?"

"Rubber," said Emmet, then wished he hadn't as he spied a faint shadow reflecting on the open door to the kitchen. It was a hulking shadow, too big for Bennett, too wide for Ford, Edsel was still seated, and the shadow certainly was not Clara's. It had to be made by the biggest man in the next room: Liebold.

"As I said," Emmet went on, "Rubbish…"

Serey was silent for a moment then whispered, "Is someone listening to you?"

"Yes."

"Damn. All right, I'll talk, and you just listen. Is that okay?"

"Yes."

"Okay," Serey continued. "See if you can see any evidence of an industry that might be utilized to make weapons, artillery, tanks, airplanes, armored vehicles, munitions, etcetera, you know, things made for war. Any items, including food, clothing, armament, or civilian needs that are being shipped to Germany, or any of their occupied territories. And names, I have an encyclopedia of names we are investigating and we're way behind on intelligence. Keep your ears and eyes open for someone referred to as 'Cheese' or 'The Cheese,' and another name, Gunther Hosp. Cheese is a mystery to us, we have no idea who he is but he's slippery, possibly Italian but that's only a guess. He's a true chameleon and can change identities as quickly as you can change your clothes. Hosp is an Austrian in the same mold as Hitler, a natural-born killer who was a seaman until he was recruited to become an assassin for the Abwehr. They're part of a group of 'sub-agents.' People so deep undercover that they make Gestapo agents seem like well-known celebrities. Also, one last thing. You can't trust any of your present crowd, including the local sheriff there, but you can trust his deputy, the young guy, named Abram. He has some information he needs to share with you. And, keep in mind, that women can be spies, too. I'm not trying to tell you how to run your life, but I know you're a big-hearted guy and tend to trust people more than I would, but we're already tracking a group we're calling The Duquesne Ring. Duquesne is the ringleader, but he's got several broads working with him, one named Lily who is basically a good-looking nymphomaniac who meets targeted guys in nightclubs, sleeps with them, and sucks information out of them like a vampire bat."

Serey paused for a moment then added, "Sorry about that description but you just need to know, right? Look, I know this is not what you signed up for, Emmet, but this is an opportunity we cannot pass up. You understand?"

Emmet had been watching the shadow near the kitchen. It hadn't moved and he knew whoever it was, was trying to eavesdrop on him. "Yes. I understand. You are going to owe me," said Emmet, then whispered, "Look under the sink here in the kitchen, there's a coffee cup under the drainpipe. Have your lab people check it for prints and poison."

Serey nodded, "Understood."

Emmet quietly hung up the phone and tip-toed over to the kitchen door, where the shadow still loomed. He could hear the listener breathing heavily. He listened for another moment and heard Clara doting over Edsel, then he stepped into the parlor quickly, nearly bumping into Liebold.

"Er, uh, excuse me," said Liebold. "Just going to refresh my coffee before we leave..."

"Of course, you are," said Emmet. "Be careful though. The cream might be bad. I believe young Edsel had some in his coffee," he added, then smirked and pushed past Liebold whose face took on a sheen of shame as his rubbery jowls went scarlet.

TWENTY-SIX

As Ford, Bennett, Liebold, and Emmet loaded their bags into their cars, the sheriff's car glided into the drive behind them. But it was not Sheriff Ross who stepped from the car. It was his young deputy, Jason Abram.

Ford stepped forward; his raptor-like countenance exaggerated when he was perturbed. "Can I help you, son? We're just leaving to catch a plane."

"I'm sorry, sir. I just needed to talk to Mr. MacWain for a moment," said the young deputy, his voice high from his nervousness.

"You'll have to wait a few weeks. We're leaving, immediately and..."

"It's okay. Mr. Ford," said Emmet. "Why don't you go ahead, and I'll meet you there?"

Ford shook his head. "You'd better be quick, Mr. MacWain. We won't wait," said Ford, indignant.

"As you wish and at your own peril, sir," Emmet replied. "I won't be long."

"Fifteen minutes, MacWain, then your usefulness may be determined to be not worth the time," said Ford, then got into his car, with Liebold climbing into the backseat and Bennett behind the driver's wheel. They pulled from the driveway, the sun glinting off the car's shined finish while Bennett gunned the motor and sprayed gravel as they sped away.

"I'm sorry, Mr. MacWain," said Abram. "But I need to tell someone what I know just in case something happens to me and I don't know who else to turn to."

"Does it involve the murder of the postman?"

"In a manner of speaking but it involves Rabbi Hirsch, more specifically."

"Why can't you discuss it with Sheriff Ross? It's his responsibility."

Abram looked at the ground, took a deep breath, and exhaled. "I just can't, sir. But I need someone to know the truth and I think you're that person. I think you're here to learn more than what killed a Jew in a small town like this."

Emmet wondered what the young man did know and was eager to find out. It was the death of the "mail thief" that began this task and initiated Emmet into his present role as a spy.

"What do you mean?" asked Emmet.

"You know what I mean. Let me take you to Hirsh's home. We'll talk more along the way."

"It'll have to be quick. I don't want to miss that plane."

Abram stepped closer and whispered to Emmet, "You're not going to. There will be a slight delay there, so you'll have plenty of time. Now, let's go. Bring your car and follow me."

Emmet did as Abram requested and followed the young deputy down the Royal Palm tree-lined street, a breeze rustling the umbrellas of huge palm fronds. They arrived within minutes at a small house nearly invisible from the street and covered with purple-flowered, Queen's Wreath vines outlining an arched front door that seemed too small for an ordinary-sized man to enter.

They parked the cars and Abram hurried to the door, dug into a nearby flowerpot to retrieve a key, opened the tiny, front door, and quickly entered the diminutive house.

Emmet followed cautiously, stooping over so he could go inside. He was allowing his eyes to adjust to the interior darkness when Abram came into focus. He appeared nervous or at least hurried.

"FBI Director Serey said we should talk," said Abram. "Save your questions for now. I know you must leave soon, so I'm going to be fast. Sheriff Ross has regular weekly meetings for anti-communist supporters, which is a clever way of saying fascists—Nazi supporters—right here in little old Ft. Myers. Most of them are just dumb rednecks but a bunch of them are members of the Silver Legion, like the KKK, they just don't wear their sheets at the meetings. You know about them, right?"

"Of course," said Emmet, eager to ask questions but knowing it wasn't the time.

"Mordecai Hirsch wasn't a rabbi, but he might have been a Jew, I saw him in the synagogue where I used to worship before I went into law enforcement. So, yeah, in case you're wondering, I'm a Jew, too. I came to know Serey when I applied for a position with the FBI a few months ago. I filled him in on what's going on around here and he said I'm in with the bureau, but it would be advantageous to stay in my role as deputy right now, so I'm undercover. I had to quit going to the Chabad and try to act like I was raised as a gentile."

Abram paused for a moment as if wondering if he was saying too much.

Emmet said, "Go on."

"Look, I didn't plan it this way, but I'm kind of doing an apprenticeship right now," Abram continued. "I attend the fascist meetings and hoot and holler just like all the idiots there, so they'll buy my act. But these murders have got me on edge and convinced me that not only does this town have some real problems, but our whole nation does. Serey says there are not only American Nazi sympathizers in our communities but spies in big businesses and even government jobs who are agents for the Fuhrer. We're looking into a group called the Duquesne Ring but there are many, many more. They're all spies, Mr. MacWain, deeply ingrained in our society and there are hundreds, if not thousands of them."

"Where is Serey now?"

"He had to go back to Miami last night, so he asked me to talk with you. I know it's a lot of information but we're doing this thing on the fly, so to speak."

Emmet wasn't sure if he should trust the young deputy but felt he had no choice. He needed to hear what the man had to say and then get to the airport if he was going to continue to infiltrate Ford's inner circle. He knew what Abram was saying was true. He'd noticed the deputy was nervous and seemed as if he wanted to talk the night before on the dock. With what he told him about Sheriff Ross, he could comprehend that now.

Emmet nodded finally and said, "Okay. I understand and appreciate your willingness to share what you know. Serey and I talked this morning, but I couldn't speak openly when he called. You've told me some things I suspected and more. I appreciate that but I must warn you, too, you should be very careful. I've dealt with some of these people before. They are cunning and cruel beyond your imagination."

"Oh, I got that, sir," said Abram, trying to swallow with a dry throat. "On Passover, Jews used to mark their front doors with lamb's blood. But, on Passover here, some of our members at the Chabad had their doors covered with pig's blood and guts."

"Do you think Hirsch was murdered, or that someone was trying to murder Ford?"

Abram glanced out one of the windows as if he could find an answer there, then shook his head. "I don't know. I've been back and forth with that same question since this happened. The dead postman raises even more questions."

Emmet wanted to hear more but time was running out. He wanted to share what he suspected already but the less anyone knew of what he was thinking or doing, the better. "Is there anything else? I need to catch a plane."

"Yes," said Abram. "I wanted to tell you that I think Hirsch was from Germany. I know a lot of Jews have fled from there, but he was more Aryan than Jew if you know what I mean."

"I'm not sure I follow..."

"Take a look at this," said Abrams, drawing something from a drawer in a huge desk that nearly filled the tiny room. "It had to be written by Hirsch but it's in German."

Emmet took the letter from Abrams and read it: *Ich bin absolut unschuldig an Verbrechen, für die ich angeklagt werde.* It was signed *BH.* Emmet thought of the *wolfsangel* tattoo on Hirsch.

"I am absolutely innocent of crimes for which I will be charged,'" said Abrams, then went on. "I think he'd been a soldier, and soldiers, especially German soldiers, do what they're told to do. Maybe he was disgruntled, maybe he'd been discharged, or he deserted. I don't know. I do know he was mentally unstable. We talked a few times, and he was friendly enough to me but seemed, I don't know...like there was something wrong with him. It was like he was here for a reason. And look at this," said Abram, opening a drawer in a desk that nearly took up the whole space of the small living room. "How many people do you know that have one of these?" Abram held up a Luger pistol, the standard sidearm of German soldiers.

Emmet recalled the tattoo on Hirsch's body and the fake *payots*. As he looked over the pistol, he asked Abram, "Can you confirm something for me, sir? Am I mistaken that Jews are not allowed to have tattoos?"

"You're not mistaken. We cannot have tattoos. It's in the Torah. It says: 'You shall not make gashes in your flesh or incise any marks on yourselves: I am the Lord.' That's in Leviticus 19:28. Why do you ask?"

"Hirsch had a tattoo," said Emmet. "It was an image of a Wolfsangel. It's a common military symbol in Germany."

"So, he *was* a German soldier at one time?" whispered Abram, like a child sharing a secret.

"It's not inconceivable. It's possible he still was. Did he seem physically ill to you?"

Abram thought for a moment. "Now that you mention it, he did have a persistent cough. I asked him about it one time and said it was from a childhood illness."

"See if you can find out from Dr. Barndt if Hirsch was sick, maybe terminal. That could be very important to us. Maybe he was willing to be a martyr, though a regretful one. Another thing, Jason, if you don't mind. I noticed you do not wear the sidelocks, the *payots*, I believe they're called. Aren't Jewish men supposed to wear them?"

Abram tilted his head. "It's traditional but it's not a requirement at the Chabad I attend and, as I said, I'm trying not to be a Jew right now."

"I examined Hirsch at the hospital," said Emmet. The payots he wore were weaved into his hair, not grown naturally, and you said Hirsch attended your Chabad, too. So, why would he wear them if they were not required?"

Abram shrugged but kept increasingly intense eye contact with Emmet. Then, his eyes went wide in surprise. "It's not disallowed but it's not uncommon in my Chabad... maybe...Hirsch was trying to make people believe he was a Jew?"

Emmet allowed a smile and nodded to the young deputy. "Good job, Deputy Abram. I think you're a good copper. You'll do well at the Bureau."

Abram's face flushed and he looked down modestly. "Thank you, sir. That's a compliment coming from you. Director Serey told me you used to be with Scotland Yard."

Emmet nodded. "I was. I could tell you some stories, young man, but that will have to be another time. For now, thank you," he said and extended his hand.

Abram shook his hand and said, "Are we going to be okay, sir?"

Emmet pondered the question for a moment. "We must be. For everyone's sake."

They were almost out the door when Emmet thought of something else. He turned back to the young deputy. "Could you do me a favor, son?"

"Yes, sir," said Abram, without hesitation.

"I have a room under Ford's name at The Royal Palm Hotel. There is a woman who tends the bar there, named Bessie Murphy."

"The pretty red-headed lady?"

"That's the one. Could you check in on her, now and then? We've ...become friends. She was attacked by some local brigands last night and I ...helped her out. I'm letting her use my room while I'm away. If you could keep an eye on her, I'd consider it a gesture for which I'd be most grateful."

Without hesitation, the young deputy said, "You can count on me, sir."

TWENTY-SEVEN

E mmet made the plane with time to spare. It seems someone had disconnected a fuel line to the plane's engine. It was obvious to Lindbergh, and he fixed it easily, but it put him on high alert, and he insisted on going over the plane thoroughly. After his close inspection, they still had to refuel, and Ford and his crew were noticeably upset. Though it was November, it was still warm in Florida and the group all insisted on wearing their nicely tailored wool suits, which were ringed with semi-circular arcs of sweat under the arms.

Emmet was cool in his short-sleeved linen shirt, canvas belt, and cotton cargo pants. His shoes were doughboy-style, high-top boots. He didn't see the practicality of wearing fancy clothes on a cargo ship or while possibly slogging through the hot Brazilian jungle. France, already in the grip of Nazis, would not be maintaining a civil dress code either. It would behoove all of them to travel in journeymen's clothing rather than stand out with their tweed and tailored suits. But that wasn't Emmet's problem.

Lindbergh completed the plane's refueling and cranked the engines. Before leaving, Lindbergh gave an informative lesson on the plane, filled with admiration for its German origins. The plane was a Messerschmitt/Caudron, an eight-passenger plane powered by Argus AS 411 inline engines, a workhorse built in Nazi-occupied

France. It could fly some twelve hundred miles with a cruising speed of almost two-hundred-forty miles per hour. This particular aircraft was the first of its kind and was yet another *gift* from the Fuhrer to Lindbergh, who asked him to "put it through its paces and report if it was worthy of mass production."

Once again, Emmet was chagrined at the chummy relationship between the successful American pilot/hero and a madman seeking to rule the world.

Lindbergh throttled it up and maneuvered the aircraft through the sky like a magic carpet. Emmet noticed that while Ford appeared comfortable and admired the plane's performance, Bennett was suffering from motion sickness. Liebold seemed comfortable enough with the flight, but Emmet would catch the secretary watching him with furtive glances and wondered if he had heard much of his phone conversation with Serey at Ford's house.

As the experimental aircraft ripped through the sky, Emmet peered out the window and imagined faces in the clouds. One appeared to have the face of a woman and though it lacked facial details, he couldn't help but think of his departed wife, Solana, and wondered what life would have been like had she lived. Would there have been children? What would their names have been?

From one lost love to another, Emmet's imagination soared with the plane. His thoughts turned to Pauline Hemingway and their all-but-over romance. Her hatred for her divorced husband lingered in her like a disease, one that grew worse every year. Emmet had finally realized he could not cure it. He would not try anymore.

The drone of the plane's engines began to lure him to slumber. He was almost asleep when the its wheels bounced onto the landing strip.

They arrived in Miami in just over an hour. Ford had called ahead and had a car waiting for the group. Lindbergh left the plane's engine running and bid farewell to all, then turned the plane on the tarmac and taxied out to take off. He waved out the window with a gloved hand as he circled before departure, just as he had when he'd set out to cross the Atlantic in his *"Spirit of St Louis,"* in a time when there might have been a shred of innocence left in his soul.

The balance of the group filed into the waiting car; Bennett was obviously more comfortable on land than in the air. Ford allowed him to sit in the front seat to drive and avoid more motion sickness, while he, Liebold, and Emmet filled the backseat.

The automotive magnate poked fun at Bennett, asking him, "If you can't take the air, how will you do at sea, man?"

"I was in the Navy, remember?" Bennett barked.

Liebold chimed in. "What was your position? The anchor?" He and Ford laughed it up like hyenas while Bennett scowled like a child being picked on by bigger kids. They drove this way to the Miami port and found the *SS Brazilian* at the dock, fueling up for the crossing to Brazil, some thirty-two hundred nautical miles away.

Ford paid the driver of the car, and the group went to the dockmaster's office with bags in hand to clear customs and received passage on the cargo ship. Liebold had called ahead and made all arrangements, and the process went quickly.

With paperwork in hand, they boarded the ship and met with the captain, a Brazilian himself with a serious and professional demeanor. Emmet initially tried speaking some Spanish with Captain Alves but recalled they speak Portuguese in Brazil, and the languages were more varied than he originally thought. In the end, Alves said it was easier to just use English, so it was in this language the captain called for his first mate to show the American group their quarters.

Ford and Captain Alves spoke briefly about travel time, the weather and the seas, and the brief stop—only two days—in Brazil. Between the route there, then on to France, Alves said it would be at least three weeks, depending on the weight of the load they picked up in Brazil. They could travel up to twenty-five knots with an empty vessel but would slow to twenty knots, perhaps even fifteen knots if the ship's cargo was filled to capacity. So, the trip to Brazil was going to be much quicker than the trip to France.

Emmet watched Ford hand the captain a thick envelope which quickly disappeared into his peacoat.

Captain Alves added, "The cargo crates stacked about the ship are empty but strapped down. We will trade most of them for full crates in Brazil. They typically move less when they are full but with nothing in them, they can become loose. We caution all aboard to keep your eyes on items shifting, not only in your quarters but particularly on deck."

Emmet heard someone approaching up the stairs leading into the bridge and turned to see a tall man with a neck as thick as a fire hydrant that rooted down into mountainous shoulders and arms as swollen as those of the cartoon sailor, "Popeye." On one of those arms was a tattoo. It was a swallow, similar to one on the arm of one of the two sailors Emmet has thrashed as they tried to assault Bessie, the night before.

"Ah, here he is," said Captain Alves. "Gentlemen, this is my first mate and he'll show you to your cabins. We're not a passenger luxury liner but we're honored to have Mr. Ford aboard with us and we'll make you as comfortable as possible. So, if you need anything, just call for Mr. Hosp and he'll be glad to help."

The former Scotland Yard inspector had to bite his lip to keep from saying anything. Hosp was one of the names Serey had given him to watch out for. He wondered: *Would the as-yet unidentified spy nicknamed "Cheese," also be on board?* As the ship pulled in its dock lines and slowly moved out to sea, Emmet wondered what kind of serpent's nest he'd stepped into.

TWENTY-EIGHT

PORT OF BAYONNE, FRANCE

On a luxury passenger liner, named the *SS Pearl*—one that was part of the luxurious White Star Lines collection—nestled in the port of Bayonne, Josephine, also known as "The Black Pearl," and Claude Durand orchestrated the loading of her show's props and personnel onto the ship for an updated version of her *"La Revue Negre"* and her wildly popular, *"Danse Sauvage."* She had learned from her first manager and part-time lover, Count Pepito Avatino, how to put together all the pieces and the business of promoting her show. Now, she could do it herself and make more money.

Josephine summoned up most of the orchestra, technicians, and roadies who were still trying to shake off a decade of economic depression as well as the loss of their beloved country to Nazi aggression. With most of them, she didn't get past, *"Bonjour,"* before they asked, "When do we go?" Still, there were many new faces joining them as well. In fact, the cruise ship was at full capacity.

As the crews finished loading and moving into their quarters, Josephine strolled to the bow of the ship and gazed out over the turquoise sea that turned sapphire as it deepened to the west. A light fog hung on the horizon like a mysterious veil hiding what might come her way. She breathed in the saline scent of the ocean and hugged herself as the cool air enveloped her.

Claude strolled up to her carrying two brandy snifter the short stems lost in the fingers of his huge hand, while the other hand held a bottle of cognac.

"No champagne, good sir?" quipped Josephine.

Claude handed her the glasses to hold as he poured some of the amber liquid into them. "I thought the cognac would warm you."

"You spoil me."

"It is my job."

The glasses clinked as they tapped the snifters and toasted and Claude added, "*Je leve mon verre a la liberte*," a popular toast typically said on Bastille Day.

"*Oui*," said Josephine. "I raise my glass to freedom."

Claude raised his glass to her toast and held a bit of the amber liquid in his mouth, pulling in some air through his teeth to better taste the heat and flavor of the cognac. After swallowing, he said, "I couldn't help but notice many of our entourage are new..."

"Indeed," said Josephine, non-committal.

"And many of them presented visas and documents from Portugal. All with the same signature."

Josephine's eyes locked with Claude's.

"Are you trying to ask me something, Claude?"

He smiled. "No. Well, not really. I suppose I want to say something in the interest of safety but I believe the pussy has my tongue."

Josephine almost choked on her cognac before howling with laughter. "The phrase is 'the cat has got your tongue."

Claude, looking embarrassed, corrected himself. "As it were. So, I will take the cat off my tongue and ask you. If I could notice that their travel documents were all signed by Monsieur Sousa Mendes, the Portuguese consul general in Bordeaux, then perhaps others might see it as, how do you say, obvious?"

"Ah, I did not wish to worry you, *mon ami*, but yes, it is so. Monsieur Mendes is a fan and a friend of mine. He also hates the Nazis as much as we do."

"*Je comprends*, Mademoiselle. I am just watching out for you. It is my job, *oui*?"

Josephine placed her palm against Claude's cheek. She felt as warm as fresh baguettes against his skin. The scent of perfume on her wrist wafted into his nostrils.

"It is your job and you do it so well. I don't know what I'd do without you." She reached up on tiptoes and gave him a quick kiss. "Thank you for being so vigilant and for being so good to me."

Claude's eyes became wet, perhaps because of the cool sea air, or because of a heart filled with love. He retrieved a handkerchief from his jacket pocket to dab at them.

They finished their cognac leaning against the rail that enclosed the bow of the ship and watched as the Pyrenees Mountain range turned into a blue, reclining hulk that served as a natural border between France and Spain and caught the light of the setting sun.

As the night enveloped them, floodlights lit up the boat and took away the charm of the evening onset.

"I'm going to my cabin," said Josephine. "See if I can still slip into my banana skirt. Been a long time since these hips had a banana around..." Then she did her crossed-eyes, kissy-lips face that made her popular around the world and always drew a laugh, as it did then with Claude. He had to force himself to stop laughing and regain his proper butler role.

"*Bonn nuit, Mademoiselle*," he said, still chuckling.

Josephine turned, shook her famous hips, and did a slow, music-less dance back to her quarters, her arms in the air, her fingers snapping to a beat only she could hear.

TWENTY-NINE

H osp led Emmet and the Ford team to their rooms. Captain Alves gave up his quarters to Ford, perhaps the envelope, thick with cash, helped. It was a rather nicely appointed room with a real bed, a table with chairs, and a desk, all affixed to the floor to prevent sliding. Liebold and Bennett were given a common guestroom with a bunk on either side, each with its own nightstand and closets for their luggage. Emmet couldn't help but grin, thinking of these two men whose obvious contempt for each other grew out of their one-up-manship feud to be Ford's Number One guy.

The first mate and the captain exchanged shifts running the helm of the ship, so the two offered to share the mate's cabin.

"My dear friend, Thomas Edison took a nap every day," said Ford, to his group. "Not all day, but short interludes of respite that he swore kept him sharp. He would often nap right at his desk in the lab, holding ball bearings in his hand. When his sleep got too deep, his hands would relax, release the bearings, fall to the ground, and wake him up," Ford chuckled. "I'm not going to go through all that trouble, but I will follow Thomas's advice and take a well-needed snooze. I'll catch up with you men later for dinner."

Liebold and Bennett nodded and awkwardly went to their own, shared quarters.

Emmet was assigned to the boatswain's cabin next to the engineer's quarters on the deck below. The boatswain had quit the job a few weeks earlier and had not yet been replaced. Emmet was pleased he had some distance between himself and his traveling companions. He was not enamored by any of their company and it would give him time to sort through things and go for walks around the ship at his leisure.

The rooms were all slathered thick with fresh paint, in the usual battleship grey, and each had its own porthole, lavatory, and toilet. It was not as nice as the Royal Palm Hotel, but Emmet had slept in worse places. The towels and bed linens were all off-white and starched stiff, but the room was spick and span clean.

Thinking of the hotel, Emmet wondered how Bessie was doing as he made himself comfortable in his temporary quarters. He wondered if she was working her shift yet and hoped she would still be there when he returned, though he held no false beliefs that she would. She was so young and working toward a goal of entertaining in a show that never stopped traveling. Once she got on with the Ringling Brother's Circus, it was likely she would be gone to him, possibly forever, though he did so hope to see her again.

The scent of her hair and her freshly showered skin stuck in his nostrils as if she was still laying there next to him and he felt a fleeting loss that he told himself was naïve and foolish. He thought of Pauline, as well, and wondered how she was doing. Maybe he should have called her again, but their last conversation underscored how resistant she was to change. Though divorced from Hemingway she would always be his wife, in her mind if not his. That meant she would never be Emmet's and that realization had finally dawned on him. His short time with Bessie helped lighten his heart and he hoped he would see her again but was wizened enough to know their age difference could be a barrier if they ever did cross paths. Their lovemaking was her way of thanking him, that was all. Emmet tried to push her and Pauline from his mind as he put his things away in the cabin.

The captain had advised Ford's group that three meals a day were served in the mess hall and coffee was always available. Convenient for Emmet, as it was just down the hall from his room. He went to check it out and found a friendly Brazilian cook who was more than happy to make him a cup of tea with lemon and honey. They chatted amiably, Emmet standing while they did so, as he knew this was the best way to get his legs acclimated to the slow roll of the ocean.

He was a bit sleepy after his tea and decided to go back to his bunk for a nap, too. He'd had a late night with the enthusiastic Bessie, then an early start, and the idea of catching forty winks was too strong to ignore. He opened the porthole to his room and laid down on his bunk. A cool breeze wafted into the room, scented by the sea, and combined with the rhythmic roll of the Atlantic, Emmet was soon dozing.

Dreams filled with seemingly unrelated images filled his sleeping mind. The haunting memory of his wife on her death bed; a perennial memory that had not faded after more than twenty-plus years. Another brought in Pauline Hemingway, flashes of their initial meeting when she came to hire him to clear her husband of a murder, a tear falling on her sheer dress, making it temporarily see-through and exposing a lacey bra strap. Another had Bessie atop him, her flame-colored hair splayed over her pale breasts as she moved slowly, then with more urgency as if riding a horse, trotting at first, then going into a full gallop before shivering to a stop and collapsing on his chest.

Emmet awoke, slowly, smiling, and not wanting that last image to fade so soon. He sat up in bed and shook off the slumber and felt good as he stretched and stood.

He decided he would go for a stroll, perhaps get himself acquainted with the layout of the boat. It was advantageous to know where you were on a ship, how to get out of the boat—night or day—if it was taking on water, and where the lifeboats and safety equipment were kept. He stuffed a pipe with some tobacco and put a couple of Diamond Blue-Tip strike-anywhere matches in his pocket.

Emmet ambled down the narrow hall, ascended a small ladder, and emerged from the lower, darker deck into a sunlit but cool deck. The breeze off the ocean hinted at the cooler, deeper sea ahead and it was already late afternoon. It would get cooler as the sun went down.

Emmet walked the circumference of the boat, locating the lifeboats, flares, and flotation vests.

Henry Ford emerged from his cabin, appearing to be shaking off his own bit of slumber. The man was always dressed in a high-collared, rounded-lapel shirt and Windsor-knotted tie. He spied Emmet, nodded, and turned his way, coming toward him for what Emmet hoped would be an unusually pleasant conversation. They were both in the deck-wide shadow of the cargo boxes that stood three stories high secured to the deck.

The ocean wind was blowing, and Emmet sidled up next to the tall stack of cargo boxes to block the breeze and light his pipe. He bent forward, stopping to scratch the blue tip match on the rough deck surface. It burst into flame, and he stuffed it into his pipe, welcoming the cherry scent of the tobacco. Something caught his eye along the outline of the shadow on the deck. It, too, was a shadow, almost simian in appearance, with long arms and legs and a long, thin torso, as it scurried along the top of the empty but heavy cargo boxes.

As Emmet stepped back, craning his neck to see what was up there, he heard a snap and initially thought it was his aging, often-injured knee protesting, but then a giant rectangular shadow blotted out the sun, like the hand of God making geometric shadow puppets, and Emmet saw a crate the size of a railcar toppling over from above. He had only a second to lurch forward and grab Ford by the waist, tackling, then rolling with him across the deck, toward the wall of cargo bins, before the massive wooden crate crashed down and exploded into slivers as if it were loaded with grenades.

THIRTY

E mmet awoke in a cabin that appeared to be lit by the sun, or several suns. Vague silhouettes loomed above him moving about like dark specters, their heads haloed by the bright lights above.

"Dim the lights," said one of the specters. "We're blinding the man."

Someone obeyed the order, and the lights were dimmed enough to allow faces to be seen. One face was unfamiliar to Emmet, and it was the one talking.

"Hello, Mr. MacWain," said the man. "I'm the Chief Medical Officer on board. Name is Hal Hallonquist, but you can call me 'Doc Hal,' as most people do."

"Aack," said Emmet, attempting to clear his parched throat.

"Help me sit him up and let's get the man some water," said Doc Hal.

The rest of the surrounding crowd was Captain Alves, First Mate Hosp, Bennett, and Henry Ford, who was grinning at Emmet as if he were his first-born son. There was an abrasion on his head.

"You are a hero," said Ford. "Just like Serey said." He stopped beaming to help Emmet sit up as Doc Hal put a glass to Emmet's lips.

"Serey has a vivid imagination," croaked Emmet.

"You're a lucky man, Mr. MacWain," said Doc Hal. "You and Mr. Ford should've been another stain on our deck. As it is, you've got a busted arm, technically a fracture of the Radius and Ulna bones in your forearm, hence the cast. It was angled a bit but I reduced it with a little pull and it seemed to pop together well. Still got a pulse and good blood flow to your fingers."

Emmet lifted his arm and saw it was covered in a cast made of gauze and plaster of Paris. The fingers were purple and throbbed. "At least I can still play the piano," Emmet said, after gulping the water.

Ford laughed and for once, Emmet saw Bennett smile, when he said, "You trying to take my job, ya crazy mick?"

"I'm a Scot, you lunk," said Emmet.

"You saved my life," said Ford, again. "I don't know how I can ever repay you. If you wouldn't have acted so quickly...well, you moved like a...like a tiger, sir. Grabbing me and rolling toward the pile of crates. Most people would've tried to roll away. Had you done so, we'd both be dead. *That* is thinking sir. Just incredibly brave thinking."

Emmet stared at him and thought to himself, *could someone be trying to kill Ford after all?* First, the White Cross poison in the tube, and now the mysterious falling crate. Then, another thought. *Or was it me they were after? Am I getting too close to the truth?*

"Why...how did the crate fall?" Emmet asked. "I thought I saw someone up there just before..."

Captain Alves interrupted him, a look of deep concern on his face. "My sincere apologies, Mr. MacWain. The crates are secured with canvas straps that are buckled down. Sometimes the straps get old and fragile. The crates are empty but still weigh over a half-ton and with the sea rocking them, pulling on the straps, they can fail. We don't see it happen often, thank God, but sometimes it does. To make amends, I've brought you a bottle of the finest rum, from Nicaragua. It's my favorite and I hope it will be yours, too."

Emmet nodded. "Done and done. We're good, captain, but may I have a look at that strap? Just to ease my mind."

"Of course, Mr. MacWain," said Alves, then turned to his First Mate. "Mr. Hosp, please secure the strap that held that crate..."

"I believe the broken crate and the strap were picked up from the deck. Probably disposed of by now..."

"Mr. Hosp, just do as I requested," said Alves, bluntly. "Unless you threw it into the sea, it should still be on board."

Hosp nodded, his face grim, then turned, his back straight, arms stiff, and exited the room.

Doc Hal interrupted the awkward moment. "Mr. MacWain, I want you to keep me informed of how you're feeling. You seem to be fine, but you did lose consciousness due to striking your head. There's a hematoma on the back of it, probably from when you hit the deck. You have some bruises on your chest, abdomen, and some various contusions here and there. I've palpated your ribs, and they seem to be fine, no fractures. Lung sounds are clear. I did have to remove some rather large splinters of wood, mostly embedded in one leg, hence the stitched areas. Let me know if you require a cane and I'll find one for you. I'll check on you daily until we reach port. I'll leave you something for pain. Use it when you need it."

The Medical Officer handed Emmet a small bottle labeled: *Laudenum.*

"Ah, you can keep that, sir."

"Are you sure? It's quite effective for pain."

"And quite addictive, too. I saw lots of people in the devil's vice in the dirge of opium dens we had in London when I was a copper. Thanks, but no thanks, sir. I'll take some aspirin. If you have some horse liniment, that's good for the aches and pain, too."

"Old school, eh? Well, your call. If you need anything else, just call me on the ship's comms and I'll come to you. Okay?"

"Yes, sir. And thank you, Doctor Hallonquist."

"You bet. Get some rest and stay away from falling objects."

"Count on that."

Doc Hal grinned, then took his leave.

Emmet sat up, wincing with a groan.

"You should take it easy, man," said Ford.

"Well," said Emmet, "that's not my way. Could we speak alone for a moment?"

Ford looked to the others and nodded to Bennett. Bennett glanced at Emmet but nodded and left as requested.

"I need to get back to the bridge, gentlemen," said Captain Alves. "Please let me know if you need anything." Then he was gone, and it was just Ford and Emmet in the room which now seemed as quiet as a vacuum.

"I'm not sure if someone was trying to kill me, or you, sir," said Emmet.

"You don't believe it was an accident?"

"I know it was not. Just before the crate fell, I saw the shadow of someone on top of the shipping crates. I looked up but the sun was in my eyes. I couldn't make out who it was, but it seemed like a tall, thin man."

Ford guffawed. "Heh, that could be any one of the sailors on board..."

"Or it could be the man who killed the postman."

Ford gripped his chin, closed his eyes, and seemed to go into a meditative mode. "That's a leap of logic, don't you think?"

"No, or I wouldn't have said it. I didn't tell you but last night at my hotel, two men were assaulting a lady who works the bar there. I stopped it but I saw some tattoos on them that suggested they were sailors. Mr. Hosp has some of those same tattoos and I'd bet you my bottom dollar that those men came from this ship."

"Well then, man, we should tell Captain Alves. Why didn't you say something?"

"Because, sir, I'm the kind of player who doesn't like to show his cards until I know what game I'm playing."

"You think this is some sort of game, Mr. MacWain? What are you talking about?"

"Yes, it is a game. A deadly one, but I believe this whole case is a deception. From the man found dead at your house, a man I now know was not a rabbi, perhaps not even a Jew, but he, or someone else, obviously wanted others to think he was. The tubes of Edison's breath you've been receiving for years until one shows up filled with White Cross, an obscure poison gas used by Germans. Why would the Germans want to kill you? You are obviously admired by their Fuhrer. And who sends those tubes to you? With your resources, surely, you could have found the answer to that by now. I'm beginning to feel as though you're gaslighting me. I'm going to need to hear the truth if you want me to continue working with you."

Ford smiled, his lips stretching across his face in a malevolent smirk. "Mr. MacWain, we were both almost killed. Had you not reacted so quickly, we two would be getting mopped off the deck even now. Admittedly, there have been some rather odd circumstances lately. It's why I called Agent Serey in the first place. My question is why did he send you?"

A question answered with a question...often a formula for deception, Emmet thought and suddenly realized he should not have revealed his curiosity. By doing so he had just risked giving away his chance to observe and report his findings—whatever they might be—to Serey and the FBI. He needed to cool off, continue to observe, and report when he could, but he needed to proceed with extreme caution.

"Serey sent me because the FBI does not get involved in singular murders, especially when it appears the death of a person might have been an accident. They don't pursue murder cases unless they are multiple and cross state lines. Serey trusted me and my...abilities...to investigate this incident at your home. But the murder of the postman and now an attempt on our lives has...confused me."

"I'm sorry to hear that, Mr. MacWain. If you need to resign from this appointment, I'd be disappointed but understand. I can arrange for you to be flown back to the States when we get to Brazil if you so choose."

Emmet had to think fast. The friendly offer of *discharge* from Ford was another clever ruse. Emmet's growing rage over nearly being killed had sparked his old and constant companion, *anger*, and he was now on the brink of losing Ford's trust. If that happened, he would never find out the truth, and the FBI's investigation into a spy ring in which Ford might be an accomplice could hit a dead end.

"I don't like to give up," said Emmet, swinging his legs off the gurney he was on. "I suppose I'll continue on with you, but I expect you to be completely open with me if you truly want to know what is occuring with these inexplicable deaths and accidents that seem to surround you."

Ford clapped his hands together. "Splendid, sir. Let's continue the hunt together, then! Now, I must admit that tumble and near miss have fatigued me. I believe I'll return to my quarters and lie back down with an ice pack on my head. I suspect you could use some additional rest yourself. Do you need any assistance to return to your room?"

"No, sir. I'll be fine."

Ford opened the door to the ship's infirmary and began to step out when he turned around. "I do have a question, MacWain. What does the word, 'gaslighting' mean?"

"It essentially means someone who denies, diverts, or manipulates the truth in order to obtain their own goals."

The skull-like grin returned to Ford's face. "That's a good word. I'll have to remember that. I could use such a word in my company's board meetings." As he stepped out the doorway he added, "You're educating me every day, Mr. MacWain. See you at dinner."

THIRTY-ONE

Night fell over the cargo ship and the moonless sky rendered it as black as a pirate ship's sails.

Hosp met with the two sailors who had accosted the Irish woman behind the Royal Palm Hotel the night before. He was not pleased.

"You were supposed to take *him* out. The woman was supposed to be the bait. You two were supposed to be the fishermen, right?"

The sailors, Budzinski, a Pole, and Krum, from Bulgaria, listened to their reprimand. Krum ran his fingers through his hair, nervously twisting the shiny black curls, while Budzinski, repeatedly wiped his near-bald head because it felt like hardened sand. The personal grooming gestures just served to anger Hosp more.

"*Nie wywiuj wilka z lasu,*" said Hosp, speaking Polish. "Isn't that one of your sayings in Poland, Budzinski? 'You don't call a wolf out of the woods, especially if you don't bring a gun to kill it!"

The Pole quit stroking his head and cast his eyes downward.

"We thought we had it handled," said Krum. "But, for an old man, he moved so fast."

"I can vouch for that," said a voice from the shadows. Edvard Heinz emerged from the shadows cast by the bulkhead that housed the entrance to the engine and storage area at the rear of the ship. "He managed to dodge a falling crate."

"The 'Cheese,' won't care to listen to more of your failings," barked Hosp. "This plan is set in motion, and we need to fulfill our part of it. If we can't, then the whole thing could fall apart and if that happens, the Fuhrer himself would mete out his discontent for your failing."

"I will take care of it," said Heinz. "Maybe he is another converted Jew..."

"*Nein!*" hissed Hosp. "You are supposed to keep a low profile. Stay in your quarters, and limit conversations. Your connection to the SS could be disclosed and that is the last thing the Cheese would want." He turned back to Krum and Budzinski. "You two will finish what you did not before. The Scot must go. He is a...restless man."

He paused and cranked his head on his shoulders until it made a popping sound in his neck that seemed to give him some relief. "We will be at sea for at least another week. You will have opportunities. Look for him when he is alone, perhaps taking a stroll, or having a smoke. He is injured, maybe unstable walking. Perhaps he slips and falls overboard."

Heinz began to say something again, but Hosp held up a hand, like a traffic guard at a school crossing, indicating Heinz should stop. "That is all. You will not get involved for reasons I've already stated. Now, go and stay out of view."

Heinz's face turned scarlet, his eyes fixed with a cold menace, his jaw muscles flexing.

Krum giggled, just a little, but it was enough.

With his hand still extended in the halt gesture, Hosp turned with unexpected agility and quickness for a man his size and backhanded Krum across the face. Through his teeth, he warned, "You and your useless partner will stay out of sight, too. Do your job on board but avoid the Scot. He will recognize you from last night. He might want to question you two idiots. Certainly he would not believe your presence onboard would be a coincidence. If that happens, you might as well be dead."

"I will be manning the bridge at night," said Hosp. "That is the only time you can come out and do what you must do. I will arrange your schedules for the night shift, and I'll find a way to draw out the Scot. Then you will finish your task. *Guten Nacht*," he said, and watched them disburse, then strode to the bridge, his heavy footsteps pounding on the steel deck like a hammer on an anvil.

Hosp was pleased with one thing that these buffoons did right this night; before they met with him for their harsh review, they threw the smashed crate into the sea.

What he didn't know was that as soon as Emmet was left alone to rest and heal, he had hobbled down to the lower decks where the ship's refuse was held for disposal. He found the splintered cargo crate and, most importantly, the strap that held it, which had clearly been cut with a knife.

***

In New York's Madison Square Garden, Charles Lindbergh gave a speech to the America First group for which he had become its traveling ambassador. Over the chanting of hundreds of an all-white crowd and wearing the Service Cross of the German Eagle that was presented to him by *Reichsmarschall des Grossdeutschen Reiches*, or "The Marshal of The Empire," Hermann Goering, Lindbergh reemphasized his beliefs.

"Europe, and the entire world, is fortunate that Nazi Germany lies at present, between Communistic Russia and a demoralized France." He went on over the din of an adoring audience to add, "The British, Jews and the Roosevelt administration are war agitators who have used misinformation and propaganda to mislead and frighten the American public." Then shared his belief that "modern aviation is a uniquely Western innovation and one of those priceless possessions which permit the White race to live at all in a pressing sea of skin color: Yellow, Black, and Brown, all of which are inferior to the White race, even more so to the Aryan race!"

THIRTY-TWO

For the first few days after his near demise, Emmet committed himself to his quarters. He felt as if he'd been squeezed through a giant set of teeth-wielding gears. The first night after the "accident," he'd had enough adrenaline flowing through his veins to fuel his curiosity and explore the ship's lower decks and locate the refuse of the pulverized cargo box. He'd also found the strap that held the crate to the other shipping containers. He'd removed the length of the strap—with some difficulty as it had been twisted into the wreckage of the splintered wood—and took it back to his room for scrutiny. The strap was obviously cut with a sharp blade such as many of the seamen wore on their belts. But which one of them had cut the strap?

As Emmet reclined in his berth, he thought of the rail-thin shadow that he'd seen atop the cargo boxes, like that of a long, thin alley cat creeping atop the load. He had glanced up to see the figure but was momentarily blinded by the sun, then had to make the instant decision to jump, grab, and roll, and ultimately save Ford's life. He could've run out of the danger zone as quickly as he'd rolled across it but, if he had, the world's leading car manufacturer would be dead. *Then, how would the FBI learn the depth of what Ford was doing for the Germans? Would someone else pick up the work of looking into those questionable deals?*

Emmet thought of Edsel, Ford's son, whom he believed was nothing like his father. *Would money motivate him to embrace the Nazi agenda?* Emmet didn't believe it would. Emmet saw something in the young man's eyes that did not reflect in those of his father's, which were akin to those of an animal that enjoyed toying with its prey before it devoured them. *So why did I save him?* Emmet wondered. *An old soldier, turned copper's instincts? Or, am I trying to find the truth as much, or more, than FBI Director Serey?*

There was a knock on his cabin door like the clapper in a huge, heavy bell. Emmet pulled himself up with a groan, ambled to the door, and opened it. It was Liebold.

"Good afternoon, Mr. MacWain," said Liebold. His cheeks and neck were flushed as if he were embarrassed to be there. His neck seemed garroted by the diamond-patterned tie he wore, and his gray, wool suit struggled against his girth. It was not raining but a heavy mist had descended upon the ship so that beads of moisture spread across Liebold's shoulders like heavy dew. He wore a charcoal-colored fedora that the damp air had caused to droop into his face and made it appear as if he were hiding under it. His round eyeglasses were fogged-up and he took them off and wiped the lenses with a handkerchief.

Emmet thought of Edsel Ford again, recalling this man at his door might have poisoned the young Ford. If that were true, Emmet wondered, what motivation might he have had to do such a thing? He'd noticed Liebold craved Ford's attention, and it seemed to bother him greatly when he was not the subject of his employer's admiration. Also, he did not get along well with Bennett either, perhaps because he'd become Ford's "main man," almost always present when Ford was out and about...except the day the cargo crate fell, something else to ponder. Liebold was also absent that day.

Liebold smelled strongly of cologne. Emmet had noticed this before, but it was particularly overpowering this day. He had persistent halitosis, with breath that smelled worse than an open manhole in the street, perhaps the reason for the cologne. Emmet tried not to inhale through his nose as he addressed Liebold.

"Good day, Mr. Liebold. What can I do for you?" Emmet noticed Liebold looking over his shoulder into his room. *For what?* He wondered.

"I was, uh...Mr. Ford charged me with asking you to be his, uh, *our* guest at dinner tonight. We've arranged a private supper in the mess hall before the ship's seamen are to dine." He looked Emmet over and added, "About six o'clock," he added, looking at his watch. "That is if you're up to it."

"I think I can manage," said Emmet. "Tell Mr. Ford I'll be there."

Liebold's eyes, which had continued darting around Emmet trying to see behind him, returned to Emmet's face. "Very well, then," he said, glancing at his wristwatch. "At six, then."

"Tell him, I'll bring the rum."

"Oh, Mr. Ford does not drink spirits," said Liebold.

"Huh," said Emmet, "no wonder I don't trust him."

Liebold's face went solemn.

"Just a joke," said Emmet grinning.

Liebold nodded, appearing confused, then sauntered off, his sewer-scented breath still hanging in the air.

Emmet watched him waddle away, an odd man, to be sure.

It was nearly five o'clock and the thick atmosphere had almost pushed the day away. It was already darker than it should've been at that hour. Emmet bathed and shaved and put on a light wool, taupe-colored suit that had managed to avoid becoming wrinkled. He was barely able to get the suit sleeve over the arm with the cast. The suit would keep out the damp weather—the last thing he needed was a case of the sniffles—and he added a chestnut brown vest and matching bow tie. Not exactly Saville Row but not too shabby either. He trimmed his graying beard and slicked back his thinning hair.

He thought of the last time he wore the suit, an evening out to dinner with Pauline Hemingway when she had been in a good mood, and the evening had been light and the possibility of love was still lingering. Emmet's heart murmured her name again, a pang he needed to exorcise if he wanted to truly get past her.

Then he recalled his only night with Bessie, the fiery lass with flame-colored hair and that memory eased the painful throb in his heart. He breathed deeply and shook off a chill that had crept into his quarters. Glancing at the watch he kept in his vest pocket, he noticed it was close to the arranged dinner time, so he stepped out of his room and into a cool evening that descended too quickly.

Still limping from his near-miss with a crushing end, he made his way through an atmosphere that turned gray with fog, toward the part of the ship that held the dining quarters. He thought he heard a step thudding behind him on the iron deck and turned quickly just in time to see one of the sailors disappear behind a bulkhead. He waited a moment to see if the sailor would reappear but heard the steps fading away.

Emmet turned back and nearly ran into Bennett.

The little man with the tough sneer raised his chin in recognition. "You doing okay, MacWain?"

"I'm healing like Jesus," Emmet replied.

Bennett hesitated, mulling over the comment, then let out a laugh that doubled him over. "Tha..that's funny." His laughter subsided, finally, and he actually wiped tears from his eyes. Then he straightened and said, "Let me be straight for a sec' here. Do you think that cargo box fell by accident or maybe had some help?"

There was no reason to lie. "It was not an accident," said Emmet.

"So, if it wasn't an accident, was someone trying to kill you, or Mr. Ford?"

"I should reserve this conversation for Mr. Ford, don't you think?"

"I respect that but, you know, I'm supposed to be his bodyguard as well."

"Where were you when the crate fell?"

Bennett appeared angry at first, but his face melted into a shameful look and he kept his eyes cast downward as he admitted, "I was in the head, seasick, puking my guts out."

"You're over that now?"

"More or less. It's better. Captain Alves had the cook make me some ginger tea and he gave me some salty crackers and soda water. Told me to keep the porthole open and get fresh air. Seemed to work. Maybe you just get used to the boat rocking. I don't know. Mr. Ford moved Liebold to another room, which was helpful, too. Geez, just the smell of that guy breathing can make ya puke."

Emmet thought about that for a moment. It told him something, not a lot, but an insight he hadn't picked up before. Ford made Liebold move rooms, not Bennett. So, maybe Ford held Bennett in a higher light than Liebold? Emmet believed that might be important but put the thought away for now.

Just then, Emmet noticed the silhouettes of two men in conversation. They were near the bow of the ship and were obscured by the increasingly dense fog. One of the men appeared to be Liebold. Emmet could not make out who the other man was, but he was tall. Very tall and thin, one could say *elongated* with a waist as small as a woman's.

"Well, perhaps this is a conversation we can have when we're not going to dinner," said Emmet, turning back to the conversation with Bennett.

"You got that right," said Bennett. "Speaking of that, we oughta get going."

"One moment," Emmet requested. "Who is that man that Liebold is talking to?"

Bennett turned and looked, squinted, and shrugged, then said, "I have no idea. Looks like another one of the seamen. Must not have a sense of smell, right?" Bennett laughed at his own joke.

Emmet smiled perfunctorily.

Dinner was a scrumptious meal that was not the usual sailor's fare. The captain had ordered extra provisions for his special guests and joined them for the meal, along with Medical Officer Hallonquist and First Mate Hosp.

The crews often fished off the side of the ship between duty shifts and brought up the sea's fresh fish bounty. There were slabs of grilled wahoo and kingfish, seabass, and a spicy chowder made with fresh snapper, ripe tomatoes, onions, potatoes, and okra. There were fresh baguettes and croissants and *Touteau Fromager*, made with fresh strawberries, goat cheese, and *crème fraiche*. The chef, a Frenchman named Jean, was a huge, round man with a whiskered, ruddy face to which a permanent smile was affixed. He bowed with every compliment that came his way and even the wooden Henry Ford was exuberant and grateful.

Once again, Ford took the time to do what he enjoyed most and became the center of attention. He stood up and tapped his glass with the handle of his fork. Murmuring came to a stop and all gazed at their benefactor. The abrasion on his forehead was gone, leaving behind a small, healing spot of pink skin.

"First, I want to express my gratitude to our wonderful host for this delicious dinner. Thank you, Captain Alves." Glasses were raised and cheers of, "Here, here," resounded. Ford continued, "And a special toast to our very talented, Chez Jean," which he pronounced correctly as "*Che* Jean." The group applauded again, and Chez Jean made a slight bow as Bennett yelled, "*Bravo!*"

"Last but not least," Ford continued, "I must thank one more person, without whom, I would not be here, enjoying this fine meal and the company of such wonderful hosts and friends..." He paused for effect as the room grew mostly silent. "Here's to Mr. Emmet MacWain, investigator extraordinaire, the man who moved with cat-like reflexes and saved me from becoming the world's largest pancake!"

A round of exuberant applause and Emmet saw Alves, Hallonquist, and even Bennett heartily raising their glasses to the toast. Liebold nodded slightly, but when Emmet glanced at Hosp, he noted only a cool stare.

Then Ford went on. "He is also a former soldier and rode with Teddy Roosevelt's Rough Riders, fought in The Big War, then spent a life of public service as a Scotland Yard Inspector..."

Emmet grew uncomfortable as the speech went on. He felt his face begin to flush from embarrassment. He'd much rather not have his personal information thrown out among people he knew, much less those he did not. After all, it could compromise him, or lead to something even more nefarious altogether. He nodded to Ford and held up his hand as if to say, *Okay, you can stop,* now but Ford continued with information that he had not heard from Emmet.

"Mr. MacWain, as an investigator for hire, also cleared our country's over spoken, and may I say, very *liberal,* American novelist,

Ernest Hemingway, of a murder. The victim was a pillar of the community, too, a prostitute with whom Hemingway was having a dalliance as he does with every other woman he meets, only this one was gutted, properly I might add, after she helped smuggle into our blessed country dozens, if not hundreds, of illegal immigrants, many of them, who were filthy Jews."

The small crowd grew so silent, they could hear only the drone of the ship's engines, the soft sizzle of cooking grease from the kitchen, and the breathing of the person next to them.

Ford continued. "So, here's to you, Mr. MacWain, the righteous defender of useless causes..." He raised his glass grinning like a skull, but only one person raised his glass slightly to share the toast and that was Liebold.

Everyone else in the room fell silent, their faces flushed from embarrassment, except Emmet's. His face was that of a man who seethed with anger and a strong desire to kill Henry Ford with his bare hands.

Emmet stood and approached Ford, who seemed to suddenly shrink in size as Emmet approached him with his glass of wine. "Here's to you, Henry," said Emmet, then added, "and to your friend, the Fuhrer." After that, he threw his wine into Ford's face, turned, and strode out of the room, trying not to limp.

THIRTY-THREE

Emmet stepped out and into the night which had grown unusually cold. He hobbled across the deck moving toward the stern of the ship, thinking perhaps a bowl of good tobacco would calm him down. *Why did Ford suddenly feel the urge to try to belittle him in front of his own people?* After all, as far as Ford knew, Emmet was there to help him with his situation. Unless, Ford had learned that Serey was not his friendly acquaintance, not just the amicable director of the FBI 's Miami offices he'd met on occasions, but a government agent, a cop, who had every intention of taking him down by using Emmet, a civilian, as his spy. *But how would he know that? Did Serey share the information about "Papa" Hemingway's "problem" with Ford in order to gain his trust?*

Emmet pondered this conundrum. Ford seemed to enjoy this game, like the cat who ate the canary. But if Emmet was supposed to be the canary, he would not be so easily eaten.

He drifted to the back of the ship, puffing on his pipe, and occasionally looking up at the wall of empty cargo crates as he heard the wood groan when the ship rocked gently on the ocean. Drifting to the starboard side of the ship, Emmet wanted to look over the side and see the ocean lit only by a partial moon.

He tapped the ashes of his pipe against the rail but just as he did so, it was if *Kali*, the multi-armed Hindu goddess of destruction grasped him. Two arms wrapped around his elbows immobilizing his own arms. As he grappled against his assailant, two other hands grabbed his legs and pulled them out from under him. His head banged against the hard, metal deck and a fist found his nose, producing a crunching sound.

"That's payback for busting my nose, Scotty!" a voice growled.

Another fist grazed Emmet's forehead and he saw a flash of light like a grenade exploding inside his head. A sticky, sanguine taste filled his mouth as his eyes blurred from the impact. He blinked and tried to make out who had grabbed him. As Emmet bucked against his attackers, he saw the tattooed images of an anchor on an arm.

The other man who had been holding onto Emmet's legs stood up now, his greasy black, curled hair shined, lit by a deck light. Suddenly, he pulled a long, curved knife from his belt and slashed down at Emmet who tried to roll out of the way. He felt the knife tug at his side and knew he had to get out from under these two men whom he now recognized. They were the sailors who had attacked Bessie in the alley.

With his legs free, he kicked up wildly and felt his foot drive into a soft spot—a belly or a groin—and heard a "Gwooof," come from the curly-haired man. Then, through a rain of fists pummeling his head, Emmet reached up quickly and grabbed blindly, hoping beyond reason to find something to clinch his hands on, and found the slick, bald head of the man who had just broken his nose. He felt the man's face and aimed his thumbs where he thought the eyes would be. One thumb, surrounded by the cast on his hand, slipped off the face altogether, but the other thumb managed to find a socket and gouged into it. The bald man screamed and let go.

Emmet rolled to his side and managed to get to his feet just as the sound of gunfire roared across the deck. Emmet and his attackers came to a standstill and peered around.

"Hold it right there, you guys," a familiar voice said, "Or the next slug goes into some flesh."

Wiping blood that had flowed from his nose into his eyes, Emmet looked up and saw Bennett standing, with his pistol still pointed at the sky having just fired a warning shot. Behind him, a throng of men were running to catch up to Bennett as he lowered his firearm but kept it pointed at Emmet's assailants.

Ford, Liebold, and the ship's crew that had been at dinner with them moments earlier came to an abrupt stop, some with their mouths hanging open.

Captain Alves came forward, squinting in the dim light to see who it was. "Budzinski?" queried Alves. "Is that Krum with you? What in the hell are you doing?" Krum had fallen to the ground and got to his knees, just as Emmet heard Bennett shout, "What are you...?"

There was another gun blast and blood splattered Emmet as Budzinski went down. Another blast followed quickly and a chunk of something flew across the deck as Krum fell down face-first.

Even in the dim light, Emmet could see both men had been shot in the head, Budzinski's wound clearly in the middle of his forehead. Krum's headshot had removed the left side of his skull.

"Why the hell did you do that?" yelled Bennett, his voice higher than usual.

Emmet looked up to the crowd now that stood where Bennett had fired his initial warning shot.

"I had them sighted in," yelled Bennett. "The fight was over, ya dumb fat ass."

Emmet saw who had the gun now. It was Liebold, his arm still outstretched, the gun still on point, a curl of inky smoke wafting up from the barrel.

"I...thought I saw one of them reaching for a weapon," said Liebold, as if in a trance.

Captain Alves rushed over and quickly disarmed Liebold.

"That's my gun," shouted Bennett.

"It's mine until we reach our destination," said Alves. "I'm the captain of this ship as well as the judge and jury of crimes at sea. Obviously, there will not be a trial, but there will be an investigation." He turned to Emmet, walked over, and stuck out his hand to help

Emmet. "What happened Mr. MacWain? Two of my seamen are dead and here you are, wounded it appears."

Emmet found a handkerchief in his coat pocket and wiped his face. He wiped the blood from his eyes and then his nose. When he found it was broken, he gripped the bridge of his nose between thumb and forefinger and gave it a twist to straighten it. There was a pop and blood trickled down his upper lip. *Easier now than later*, Emmet thought.

"These two men attacked me," said Emmet, his nose stuffed with blood, making him sound as if he had a bad cold. "They are the same men who were attacking a woman outside my hotel the night before we departed on this never-ending fun cruise."

Alves looked down upon the dead seamen and said rather matter-of-factly, "I wondered why they looked beaten up when they showed up the day we shoved off. I thought they were just in a barroom brawl."

Emmet felt something warm run down his abdomen and into his trousers. He looked down and saw his vest was torn where Krum had slashed him with the knife. He opened the vest and saw the blade had gone through the garment and tore his shirt as well. "Bloody hell," he said.

Hallonquist, who had come over and kneeled to look at the dead seamen, glanced up and saw the slice in the shirt. "Better let me look at that," he said standing. "Someone bring me a light, please." He went to Emmet and told him to remove his jacket and vest. First mate, Hosp, appeared quickly with a lantern.

"Hold it up," ordered Hallonquist, then he stuck his fingers in Emmet's shirt where the tear was and ripped it open. "This might smart," he warned Emmet, probing with his fingers.

"It would be the only thing that has been this evening," Emmet quipped.

"It's not deep but it could use a stitch or two. You seem bent on keeping me busy, sir. We should get you to the infirmary and take a look for any other wounds. Can you make it on your own?"

"Sure," said Emmet. "I've had worse."

"I'll be along in a few minutes, Hal," said Alves. "I'll need to...do something with these two ne'er do wells. Mr. Hosp, fetch a few men to help put these two brigands in boxes until we can do something with their bodies. Look at their employment records and see if there is any next of kin. Either way, we'll most likely do a burial at sea. And get this mess cleaned up," he said, waving his hand toward the pools of blood on the deck.

"Am...will I be in trouble?" asked Liebold, glancing back and forth between the ship's captain and Hosp.

Ford slid from behind his entourage, seemingly to take charge now. "I don't believe there's going to be any..."

"That's quite enough from you, Mr. Ford," said Alves. "While I have appreciated your...largesse, shall we say, your grandiose presence on my ship has become an irritant, and now your secretary has killed two men. They may have well deserved it after attacking Mr. MacWain, but I need to find out what motivated them to do such a thing and I don't need your opinion on the matter."

Ford stood with his mouth hanging open in surprise. As Emmet limped toward the infirmary with Hallonquist helping him along, he couldn't help but chuckle and wonder, *when last had anyone told Henry Ford to shut up?*

Alves turned to Liebold and said, "In answer to your question, sir, I'll have to do a report for the authorities. There's a knife here and it's obvious these men were assaulting Mr. MacWain, perhaps attempting to murder him. So, no, you won't be in trouble inasmuch as I'm concerned, but I will have to talk with you tomorrow and get a statement. Port authorities are not very understanding when you arrive with dead people aboard." He turned and scanned the crowd. "Now, I suggest everyone turn in or just stay out of my way. I have much to do. Mr. Hosp, please join me on the bridge when you've taken care of this...mess."

THIRTY-FOUR

Several days into their trip and halfway across the Atlantic, Josephine Baker just finished her onboard performance to a grateful, yet reserved, crowd. She did her usual acts for the audience and didn't hold back. She did the Zouzou performance from the giant birdcage they—her new and inexperienced stagehands—assembled on stage. The bird perch she was seated on while she sang fell apart but she shrugged it off with a joke and kept going. She followed up with the usual swan songs and wrapped up with her banana dance, and then her frenetic Charleston. Her top "titty containers" as she called her fanciful brassiere, fell off sometime during the show and though she didn't notice, most of the crowd did and, while some of them might have been offended by her risqué show, no one complained.

After the show, Josephine went to her impromptu dressing room. Claude was there arranging some comforts for her, a small table of cheese, snacks, and champagne. She came in sweat-slicked skin, stripped, and slid into the small shipboard shower provided to her, completely uninhibited. Claude was used to it. He held a towel for her, while looking away, when she came out.

As she dried off, she asked, "So, how did it go?"

Claude was honest. "Of course, you're always wonderful."

"Be honest, Claude."

"Very well. I was worried when the swing slipped off the cable."

"It's okay, *mon ami*. Did I sing well?"

"Beautiful as always," said Claude.

Claude looked away. He was her servant and though she treated him as a friend and confidant, he was always aware of his position. "And 'Jack Sanders'? Where is he? Doesn't he typically act as your manager, your... what is the American word, *cover*?"

"Captain Abtey has his hands full right now, in France," said Josephine. She stood up and came over to him. "Claude, I know you worry about me. You know, you are not *just* my servant, you are my friend, too. I could not do what I am doing now without your help. If you are becoming too uncomfortable with what we are doing, I understand. It is dangerous and I don't want to place you in peril. If you do not want to stay with me, you can go back to the chateau when we reach Brazil. I need you there and I would miss you terribly but I have to do what I have to do."

Claude appeared deflated. He stared at the floor for a long time. "I will always be by your side. I just want you to be safe."

"And I will be as long as you are by my side, *mon ami*," she said, then hugged him, tight.

***

"Heil Hitler," said Klaus Barbie, calling a subordinate on the phone.

"Heil Hitler, *Hauptsturmfuhrer* Barbie," said SS Colonel Major Kurt Lieber. "What a privilege to hear from you. For what do I owe this honor?"

Barbie's chest swelled with pride. He loved the title, which when translated into English was, "Head Storm Leader." The title made him feel like Thor, the God of Thunder, from Viking mythology. The Vikings were another conquering group, mostly Danes and Nords, but close enough to the Saxon brutality of early Germanic tribes. They were extremely barbaric, a quality Barbie thought was essential for a country that was planning to conquer the world, and he believed that is where his family name came from, the word, *barbaric*.

Barbie also enjoyed the ring-kissing his position demanded, even from other German military leaders. Groveling was a spectator sport to him, and he enjoyed it immensely.

"I'm calling to let you know," said Barbie, "I've been informed by the Fuhrer himself that I will be transferred to France soon, as early as the new year, perhaps," said Barbie. "How do you like it down there?"

"Ah, what good news," Lieber lied, enthusiastically. "It is...good here." If Klaus Barbie was coming to France, that would mean *he* was not going to continue to be the lead Gestapo anymore. Lieber tried to be humorous. "I hope that does not mean the Fuhrer is dissatisfied with my job performance...ha, ha," he ended with a weak laugh.

"*Nein*," said Barbie. "Your performance is...adequate."

Lieber's heart sank, then he swallowed dryly as Barbie continued.

"I've heard the country is nice and there are many *frauleins* who will lift their skirts for anyone, and they use their mouths for sex as if it were nothing."

"*Ja!*" said Lieber, feeling relieved, even chummy with Barbie. "The *frauleins* are uninhibited and you can do anything you want to them..."

"My father was assigned to France during the war in 1914 and was shot in the neck. He never fully recovered, and he hated the French for the rest of his life. It made him an alcoholic and a very abusive man."

"I...I'm sorry to hear that, sir...," said Lieber, becoming most uncomfortable with the conversation.

"I've also heard you might have lost an *Oberlieutenant*...?"

Now Lieber was even more uncomfortable, sweat popped from his pate like dew and he felt it trickle down his neck. "Uh...it is true... *Oberlieutenent* Hans Arent and Marshall Rene Pelletier of the Vichy police went *scouting*, if you will. That is, they do frequent inspections of various homes, farms, and chateaus in the countryside just to make their presence known and, of course, to see if they can spot any signs of Jews or other illegal refugees."

"And so, they went on this scouting mission and failed to return, and you did not send a police officer, or soldiers to find them?" asked Barbie, his voice was as iced as the fields along the eastern fronts.

154 - EDISON'S LAST BREATH

"Well, sir, they are not under my direct supervision...My offices are in Paris..."

"You are the Colonel of the Security Police, in charge of policing this fallen country, as well as a former SS and Gestapo officer. You should be more aware of what is happening in your assigned region."

"I was only told this news a couple of days ago and I have made a note to check back on this matter. I assure you I will do so as soon as our conversation is ended..."

"See that you do, Colonel. I will be 'scouting' down there, too, in a few weeks. Getting a feel, as it were, of the country of my new assignment. I expect you will have this mystery solved or an answer to it, one way or the other. Perhaps I can show you some of my interrogation techniques. Lately, I've found sticking the offender's head into a simple bucket of ammonia is quite simple and effective. It's so easy but if that fails, we stick thin glass rods into the male's penis or a champagne glass into the female's vagina. They typically will tell you anything you want to know after that. For a brief moment, it's exhilarating to watch the relief they have when they believe we will remove the glass, and the look it turns into when we break the glass anyway is...priceless. I'll demonstrate the techniques when I arrive, eh? It's always fun to learn new things, *ja* Colonel?"

There was silence for a moment, then Barbie added, "Am I clear, Colonel Lieber?"

"Absolutely, sir. I will make it my priority to locate the missing gendarmes. Is there...?" He heard a click, then a dial tone, and realized *Hauptsturmfuhrer* Barbie had hung up on him. He was soaked with sweat and his heart was beating so fast, he thought it might explode. He loosened his collar, reached for a bottle of Scotch he kept in his desk drawer, poured a shot glass full, and downed it. He suddenly had to urinate, but the thought of the glass rods Barbie spoke of disturbed him so greatly that he put it out of his mind. Instead, he began making urgent phone calls.

THIRTY-FIVE

THE PORT OF RIO DE JANEIRO, BRAZIL

T he *SS Brazilian* slowly entered the port, a tugboat guide leading them into their berth in Guanabara Bay. Emmet watched from the deck as they eased in, passing conical-shaped mountains pushing out of the sea like gigantic, fat fingers. He was quite pleased to see land again and looked forward to getting his feet on firm ground.

As they drifted by other vessels of all sizes originating from numerous international ports, Emmet spied several huge billboards advertising the *"Espectaculo Especial, con Josephine Baker,"* who was playing for the week at the *Os Democraticos e Suas, Finalidades!* Pictures of the unusual-looking entertainer, with curls of her short hair pasted to her forehead, her eyes crossed playfully, and wearing a skirt made up of bananas, made Emmet wonder how an act like hers got to be so popular. Other pictures of the uniquely beautiful "Creole Goddess" in various costumes and levels of undress splayed across the advertisements for the show with a sexuality that would not be allowed in the U.S. Nudity in Brazil was not a crime, Emmet noted, as the ship cruised slowly by the heavily populate beaches.

The deck of the *SS Brazilian* was bathed in a bright-orange, morning light as they idled into the bay. The turquoise sea lapped at beaches filled with tanned, topless women, wearing bathing suits that were about the size and shape of an eyepatch, showing no inhibitions about their lack of modesty. It was not unlike the beaches in Europe, though the Brazilians seemed even less inhibited than the Italian, Spanish, and French female sunbathers Emmet had seen.

With his hand over his brow shading his face, Emmet smiled for the first time since they'd gone to sea. The approaching land was a welcome view and the sights of an exciting civilization he knew too little about lifted his spirits.

He'd been keeping a low profile staying in his cabin, allowing his wounds to heal. The swelling in the broken forearm was beginning to ease as was the pain, the cast on his arm was loose now, and the numerous puncture wounds inflicted by the splintered shipping container had mostly gone away. But the knife wound on his abdomen pinched him with every move he made. Despite Doc Hallonquist cleaning and stitching the cut—a half-crescent slice that looked like a small smile—it appeared infected and felt warm.

Ford and Emmet had not spoken much since the dinner that ended with the car magnate dabbing red wine from his face. The following attack by the seamen had aggravated Emmet's previous wounds and gave him the smiling scar on his stomach, but it also had underscored the danger in which he had immersed himself. Hallonquist seemed trustworthy, and some of the deckhands seemed friendly enough, but Emmet was rattled by the two near-misses on his life. He no longer took casual strolls with his pipe late at night and alone.

In his cabin, he pondered the elements of the case and the key information FBI Director Serey had shared with him. He came to believe it was Liebold who might be the man referred to as "Cheese," for two reasons. One: Why did he shoot the sailors that had attacked him? They had already stopped their assault after Bennett fired a warning shot. Did they know something or were they connected to Liebold in some fashion? Two: Liebold smelled bad, literally, and figuratively. Emmet came to believe it was because he loved to eat cheese, particularly the odiferous Limburger cheese. Whether he was the elusive spy Serey was interested in, Emmet was not sure, but he was certain that he was hiding, and possibly planning, something covert. He was always too nervous around Emmet.

Captain Alves sought Emmet out and checked on his recovery regularly. He was a strange man, too, but seemed trustworthy. Once while passing each other on the deck, Alves had asked how he was doing. When Emmet answered he was on the mend, the captain said, "Good. I am glad, sir." Then added, under his breath, "I enjoyed Mr. Ford's expression when you threw your wine into his face! I am being paid well to assure he gets to his destination but he is not a likeable man."

"That's putting it nicely," said Emmet, and the two men shook hands in what Emmet felt was an unspoken bond between them.

Alves turned to get back to the ship's bridge, stopped, and returned to Emmet. "Maybe you should consider a different mode of transportation for the rest of your journey after our stop in Brazil," he whispered. Then he whirled around and quickly strode away, leaving Emmet questioning why he would say that. He left another question in Emmet's mind: Alves' accent sounded more Italian that day than Portuguese. Italians tend to speak with a sing-song cadence, while the Portuguese are a little less so. It was a little thing but, like many things that Emmet entered into his mind's journal, it was another piece of a puzzle that would irritate him like an annoying mental mosquito bite.

The *SS Brazilian* slowly bumped its way into the dock like a cumbersome circus elephant being loaded onto a train, finally settling in, its line moored and the anchor dropped.

Ford's entourage began to assemble near the exit ramp. Emmet had his bags packed for the next leg of this misadventure and met them there. As he approached the group, Liebold spoke up.

"There's no need to bring all of your luggage, MacWain," said Liebold. "I've arranged a car to pick us up and a charter flight to whisk us to Fordlandia. We only have the 2 days, so we'll be back by tomorrow evening."

At that, Bennett's face turned visibly gray. "Maybe I'll stay here, you know, until you get back..."

Liebold shrugged, then continued, "We might stay there one night and fly back here to continue our journey to France. An overnight bag should suffice."

Emmet nodded. "I like to keep my belongings together, Mr. Liebold. You can never tell when plans might change." At this point, Emmet wished they would.

"Very well," said Liebold.

As they prepared to depart the ship, Ford approached Emmet. "I suppose we should engage in conversation again, Mr. MacWain. I'm still relying on your investigative experience as I'm sure Director Serey is."

"Okay," said Emmet. "Let's begin with why you want to go back to Fordlandia?"

"As we discussed, I had enemies there, people who thwarted my every move and caused my creation to fail. Besides, I think the gas in that tube meant to kill me may have originated from there. There were so many witch doctors there, you could swing a cat and hit a dozen of them nearby."

Emmet wanted to say, "You caused Fordlandia to fail with your oversized ego and greed," but he addressed the origin of the gas instead. "You know as well as I do that concoction did not originate here."

"Oh, I'm not sure we concluded that...or anything, really."

"I've concluded a few things, Mr. Ford. The White Cross gas is a German construct..."

"Anyone could have made it," Ford interrupted. "That's why we're going to France, too, which is where the package was mailed from...".

"Let me finish now that we're having this chat. I also have serious doubts that the so-called rabbi who died opening your mail was a Jew. The package was *not* mailed from France and I am beginning to believe this whole odyssey you're conducting is a subterfuge for some other plan that's been set in motion."

Ford looked away as if completely disinterested. "Hmmn," he said, finally. "Anything else?"

"Yes," said Emmet. "You are, without doubt, the biggest arse of a man I've ever met."

Ford stood stoically for a moment, letting the morning Brazilian sun warm his face, his eyes closed.

When he opened them, Emmet thought they were the color of a ghost's eyes—Emmet had many specters with eyes like that who haunted him—so light blue as to almost be white, with a pinpoint pupil that seemed reptilian. Then Ford burst into laughter. "Oh, Mr. MacWain, you are so entertaining." With that, he began to descend the staired plank to the dock.

Emmet was about to debark, too, when Captain Alves came up behind him, an intense look on his face, as if he had just heard bad news, or had some to share. His bushy eyebrows curled into a frown like two furry caterpillars facing off with each other. "Mr. MacWain, may I have a moment before you leave?"

Emmet turned to him. "Of course."

Alves leaned forward and whispered to Emmet. "You must keep this secret in order to save your own life. When you return...if you return, you must not board my ship."

Emmet was confused. "Oh?"

"Hear me, sir. This ship is not just picking up coffee. I found a bill of lading that I was not supposed to find. My first mate, Mr. Hosp, is a spy for the Germans and he has brought aboard another man whom I believe is the same man you were seeking for the murder of the postman. That man is Edvard Heinz and I also believe he is the one who tried to drop the cargo box on you as the intended target, not Ford." He paused for a moment as if searching for the right words to express his sincerity. Then, emotionless, he said, "This ship will be loading munitions for the Germans, sir. I will assure Medical Officer Hallonquist and the few good men that are still aboard are reassigned to another ship."

"What? If you knew that, why didn't you tell me? It's my purpose for being here in the first place."

"Let me finish, sir. It became clear to me, early on, that this ship was filled with spies. It was less clear to me who they were and what their purpose was. It was my purpose to find out why. You and I have a mutual friend...." Alves paused to look around, then came back, his voice harsh with the urgency of his message. "Mr. Serey..."

"You know Serey?" said Emmet, shocked as if he had just been inflicted by one of Edison's electrified inventions in the making.

Alves held up his hand. "I do. I am the 'Cheese' he told you to look out for. It is a silly codename, but we are working on a common objective, just as you are. To stop these Nazis from taking over the world. It is a monumental undertaking and we are far behind, trying to play catch up. The codename was given to me by the Brits, because *cheese* is what you use to catch rats. I am what is commonly called a 'double agent' in the espionage world. Ostensibly, I am working for the Germans under the name Roberto and they believe me to be loyal to them. They would be astounded—and I would be dead—if they knew I was an Italian Jew. I am telling you this now because Serey told me to. He said you can be trusted and I have learned he is a man of his word. As you take your brief trip through this country, look around. It has become a manufacturing hub and a haven for Germany. It is also filled with Nazis, so you must be very careful, especially with the group you are traveling with. They are either Nazis themselves or sympathizers, perhaps financiers, for the Nazi cause. Now, go, quickly, so your traveling companions do not become suspicious."

Alves, or "Cheese," extended his open hand. Emmet took it slowly, his mouth hanging open in surprise. He cleared his throat. "Thank you, er, uh...Captain. For everything..."

"Everything you believe, all the horror you suspect, is true," said Alves. "Trust no one. Goodbye, and good luck, sir." With that, he turned on one heel and walked away, briskly.

THIRTY-SIX

Josephine's skin glistened with sweat as she wrapped up the evening show doing her Banana Dance, topless, which was not only allowed but encouraged in Brazil, though it was still banned in most English-speaking countries. She would dance naked if they let her, though she did like to have a little something on while she sang. It kept the audience's imagination going and imagination helped sell tickets. Give the crowd a tempting little piece, but don't give them the whole pie.

The crowd was sold out and the applause was deafening. Josephine loved the adoration; it was an electric vibe that jolted her performance. The more they cheered, the more she gave them. She came to the forestage making her overreaching bows, extending her rubber arms as if to embrace the whole audience. The crowd showed their appreciation by throwing roses onto the stage. She picked one flower up, tore two pedals off, and placed them over her nipples. The audience roared past the point where Josephine could even hear hearing them anymore.

In the front row seats, as close as anyone could get to the apron of the stage, a squat white man with a bald, shining head sat throughout the show holding a bouquet of roses that appeared to be red, white, and blue. He stood up wearing a grin on his onion-looking head and walked up to the stage as Josephine picked up parts of her costume she had doffed during her last act.

The man handed her the flowers wrapped with white crepe paper. Josephine squatted down, to accept the flowers, her breasts practically in his face.

"That was a wonderful show," said the man and added, "Yes...sir-ry."

That was the agreed-upon password, "sir-ry" was a play on "Serey."

Josephine winked at him, then took her sequined brassiere, put it on her forefinger, and swirled it around like an airplane propeller before she planted a red-lip-sticked kiss on it and handed it to the man. "I hope you'll come back!" she said.

Serey nodded, stuffed the bra into his suitcoat, kissed his palm, and blew a kiss back to her.

Josephine stood up, shook her rubbery legs as if she were having an orgasm, then bowed deeply to the audience as they stamped their feet. The light dimmed leaving only a single spot in the performer's lovely face. She exaggerated a wink they could see even from the balcony seats.

The spotlight came back on, and Josephine glided backstage carrying her bouquet in the darkened backstage hall, then into her dressing room. There, Claude was waiting for her, the lights on but dimmed. Before she sat down, she unwrapped the paper, turned up her make-up mirror light, and looked at it. Inside the flower's wrapping was a message that read: *Keep an eye out for a Scotsman, named MacWain. He's the most trusted man I know. You'll love him and he needs it. S*

"Eeewwweee," said Josephine. "I love me some Scotty's." Then, she tore the note into pieces and flushed it down the toilet.

Back in his hotel room, Serey locked the door, practically ran to the desk, and flipped on a lamp. He pulled the brassier out of his jacket and began looking through it. Inside the sweat-dampened cups, he could see writing, though sweat had smeared some of the ink.

"Nazi's advancing to front, some reports say as many as 20,000 troops with heavy artillery. Vichy offer no help and they are aiding the Nazis. Resistance took out some leadership. We expect backlash. They are going door to door and robbing and killing residents inside the unoccupied zone. Need help. Expedite. JS"

Serey, read the letter, his anger increasing with every word. "JS" was the initials for the code name for John Sanders/Jacques Abtey. He was a good man whom Serey would call a friend; one of the few they had in Europe. Still, without a declaration of war on Germany, the U.S. could only help through covert operations.

"So, okay," muttered Serey to himself. "I'll send you the best I can for now." Now, he just needed to find Emmet MacWain.

THIRTY-SEVEN

Ford allowed Bennett to stay behind, at his request. He wasn't sure if he was up to another nausea inducing plane ride. Ford knew many of the locals he used to employ in his failed factory might hold animus toward him, but he also knew they would not act on it. He was like a god to them and while not every god is loved, they are revered, and in this primitive jungle world, he was. So, he would not need Bennett as bodyguard for this quick trip.

Ford's group: himself, Liebold, and Emmet flew low over the mountainous countryside and the lush, emerald foliage of the jungle. Occasionally, the dense jungle gave way to clearings around small villages, and a few potholed dirt roads that would suddenly appear like serpentine scars. The plane that Ford's group flew this time was not as nice as Lindbergh's, nor was the pilot as skilled in flying as was the historic aviator of the old *Spirit of St Louis*. There were sudden, stomach-dropping dips and turns. The pilot, who spoke very little English said he was "Eduardo," but otherwise spoke very little.

After a few hours, the plane bounced down along a dirt landing strip outside the city of *Brasilia*, refueled, and slowly lifted off again, its wings tipping back and forth like a seesaw. The engine was noisy and belched out dark, oily-scented smoke. The plane's cabin was warm, and all passengers were soaked with sweat, though

Emmet had wisely slipped into some khaki shorts and a light shirt and brought a canteen. Ford and Liebold maintained their habit of wearing wool suits, with collars and ties cinched up to their Adam's apples, appearing as if their heads might pop off from the pressure.

When they landed a few hours later, the perspiring group practically leaped out the moment the plane rolled to a stop. Eduardo, suddenly finding a few more words in English, as well as some provisions he had not shared along the way, said he would sleep in the plane, and they would leave at sunup.

An old man not much taller than a boy stood on the makeshift runway near Ford's former factory. The little man looked like a weathered old coin purse; his skin leathered from working in the sun for eight decades. His bright, blue eyes were startling in the shadow of a huge straw hat. He gripped a walking stick that was taller than him and held one hand up, palm open as if halting the roll of the taxiing plane with the gesture.

"That's Carlos," said Ford, staring at the little man for a moment, then adding, "He's the only employee who stayed loyal to me."

Liebold rolled out of the plane as soon as it stopped, holding his crotch, and ran over to the edge of the landing strip to relieve himself. Ford stepped out, followed by Emmet, who gazed at the surrounding jungle then decided to scare Liebold.

"Watch out for the Jaguar, Liebold!" Emmet yelled, suddenly.

Liebold jerked about, urinating down his pant leg as his fear-filled eyes darted all around.

Emmet laughed so hard, he had to bend over to catch his breath.

Even Ford managed a grin when he said, "God almighty, Ernest. You fell for that?" Then, he introduced Emmet to Carlos, who said, "Good to meet you, sir," with perfect English and a smile.

"Nice to meet you, too, sir," said Emmet. Jokingly, he asked, "Will you be introducing us to the witch doctors?"

"Do you need one, sir?" Asked the little man, without hesitation. "We have a very good *Curanderos*, who lives nearby. She can cure almost anything," then added, "And see the future."

Emmet glanced at Ford who turned to Carlos and said, "That won't be necessary, Carlos. But please show us around. I have not been here for years, and I want to see what's left of my once promising vision."

"Of course," said Carlos.

Liebold rejoined the group, giving Emmet a dour look as Carlos led the way through the thickening foliage.

"There is also a bad *Kalku*," Carlos went on. "What you call a witch doctor, who came from Chile. One of the villager's sons drowned in the *Tapajos* River near here. The *Kalku* works with the *Anchimayen*, a spirit creature who brings dead children back to life. There was a ceremony, and the boy did come back to life, but he is what we call a *zumbi* now. He roams through the village, and he is neither alive nor dead. I tell you this because you might see him walking around here. Do not look at his eyes or you may never sleep again."

Emmet pondered that information, and a chill ran up his spine. Local beliefs and customs were always strange to outsiders but the lore they spoke of often had some truth to it.

The group traveled on. It was farther than Emmet thought it would be, but he was up to the task. Liebold was not. He wheezed and panted along, still sweating profusely. Carlos produced a bottle of water and gave it to Liebold. Then he gave him a small green leaf and told him to chew on it and it would give him energy. Liebold complied. Within a short while, Emmet noticed Liebold had a little pep in his step and wondered if the leaf was from the coca plant. Soon, Liebold was jabbering like a child who just learned he could talk.

As they approached Ford's former rubber factory, Emmet saw some cattle roaming about in the nearby fields and noticed they bore a brand. He couldn't make it out at first but some of the cows began walking toward the group and the ranch's brand on the cattle's haunches came into clear view. It was a swastika.

Emmet was squinting his eyes to see the brand better when he felt he, too, was being observed. Between the slick green leaves of foliage, he spied a boy peering at him with large, black eyes, his small, thin arms held down the bushes through which he peered. A white scar was branded onto his shoulder. It, too, was a swastika.

Emmet's blood boiled but he kept it to himself, recalling Serey telling him to watch out for any signs that indicated Nazi presence but cautioning him to "keep it under his hat." Making a stir while in the company of his traveling partners might make him a target. Emmet was sure he already was a target after the two near-fatal incidents on the ship. Now, in the jungle's ruthless heart of darkness, where cows and children wandered through its damp, green underbelly, bearing symbols of the Third Reich, it was an ominous sign that the Nazis' dark reach was already very long and growing longer.

THIRTY-EIGHT

To Emmet's surprise, much of what had been Fordlandia was still there. Jungles grow quickly with heat and moisture and this area in the Amazon rainforest had plenty of both. But, as if wary of its stern owner, the jungles had reached for, but not yet grasped, the factory where Ford's dream became his nightmare.

Windows had been smashed out in a worker's revolt, cobwebs hugged the ceilings as big as fishermen's nets, and rust had crusted the sides of the metal buildings like scabs on abrasions. A water tower still stood tall, like a sentinel overlooking the grounds which contained small, American-styled homes that looked as out of place as the tailored suits that Ford consistently and stubbornly wore, even here. It was apparent Ford's lack of recognition for the mores and values of the native people had been his downfall, along with his resistance to learning from those same people how to harvest rubber from the trees that were part of their natural habitat had led to his failure.

Now, he stood staring at the factory as a nemesis, his face clouded, brows furrowed, arms crossed upon his chest. Ford still resisting the fact that he failed like a gambler refusing to acknowledge his losses in a game he never knew. As he stepped toward the doors to the empty facility, Liebold began to follow him in, but Ford held up his hand and waved him away.

"I'd like to go in alone for a few minutes, Ernest," said Ford, in a tone that made Emmet feel a tad sorry for him.

Emmet had known loss as well—in life, if not business—though he lacked the stunning hubris with which Ford cloaked himself. Loss, by its very nature Emmet believed, is supposed to be something from which we grow. From the way one deals with the loss of a loved one, to one who loses that which they strove to accomplish with an idea, a dream, or greed. Loss is a vacuum that most people cannot fill.

The undisputed giant of automobile production walked board straight, one hesitant step in front of another, like a man walking toward the gallows as he disappeared into the emptiness that only severe loss, or failure, can produce.

Emmet glanced around the former would-be manufacturing town and noted some of the surrounding locals who had either stayed there or had filtered in from the surrounding villages. Some of them were elusive, shy, or scared of outsiders. Others stood erect, frowning, and glared at the white-skinned outsiders as if wanting to challenge them. Overall, the place held a menacing feel, like a town that had been bombed, the surrounding jungle creeping in to regain its geography.

"MacWain!" cried a shrill voice with a pitch between anger and fear. It was Ford inside the cavernous building he'd entered.

Despite Emmet loathing the man, it was his nature to run toward trouble rather than away from it, and he did so now while Liebold stood still, his eyes wide with fright. Emmet bounded past him and Carlos, up the steps and into the building. It was dark inside and his eyes had to adjust for a moment before he spied Ford across the room standing near a dusty, cobwebbed table, trembling in terror.

Emmet crossed the room and approached Ford, who turned to face him, his eyes wide, urgent.

"Take a look," said Ford, pointing with a finger that shook with fright. "I told you there are shamans here! Godless practitioners of voodoo and evil! See here."

Emmet looked at the tabletop in the dim light. There were two wooden dolls laid next to each other, dotted with blood. Both were clothed much like Ford was that day, with little business suits sewn onto them. One doll had gray hair painted on it and an uncanny resemblance to Ford, with his signature, high-collared shirt, and wrinkles carved into the face. The other doll had dark hair and resembled Ford's son, Edsel. The gray-haired doll had a needle shoved into its head, while the dark-haired doll had a needle stuck in its stomach.

A dead chicken lay next to the dolls, its head wrenched off, flies crawling over its corpse like a dark, living blanket. A *Ford* emblem from one of his cars held the head of the chicken, like a platter.

Ford stood and stared at the dolls, rubbing the side of his head as if it ached. A vein stood out along his temple, throbbing. "I think I'm going to be sick," he said, before turning away and retching. After a moment, he stood and pulled out a handkerchief to dab at his mouth, his hands shaking, his face pale and sweating.

"You...see why I abandoned this primitive hell hole," said Ford.

You left because you failed, Emmet thought, but said, "Did you touch the dolls?"

"No...," said Ford, his voice hesitant.

Emmet opened his knapsack, took out some leather gloves, and slipped them on. He looked at the dolls closely, trying to see if there was any powder that could be inhaled or something that might suddenly stick out of the doll and prick the finger. He was wary of ancient, primitive practices, and booby traps that could be utilized, possibly poisoning whoever picked them up. But nothing happened. Despite their resemblance to the Fords, the figures were harmless dolls. Still, Emmet found some rags in the shop and wrapped the dolls in them before placing them in his backpack.

"Is something wrong?" asked Liebold, slowly stepping forward, as if he expected the floor to have a trapdoor in it.

"Just some creepy dolls," said Emmet, then added for Ford, "They can only hurt you as much as you let them. That's the strength of voodoo. Its believers give it power."

"Well, you know damn good and well I don't believe in that malarkey," said Ford.

Emmet looked at him, his face a mask of concern. "I hope not, because it can only hurt you if you give it credibility. That said, it's obvious that someone has it out for you and your son." Emmet paused, contemplating. "What about Edsel? Do you think he might believe in this type of witchcraft? Did he ever come here with you?"

"He did, several times. I think he's an earnest young man and we brought him up to believe in the only God there is, a Christian one. But he was also cursed with an artsy, 'open mind' and has had some fantastical ideas from time to time. Many of those cost the company a great deal of money."

"Forget the corporate woes, man. I noticed he has stomach issues..."

"And?" barked Ford, impatient with the line of questioning.

"The doll that resembled him had the needle stuck in its stomach."

Ford said nothing for a moment, contemplating what Emmet said. "And mine had a needle in its head and there is nothing wrong with my head."

"It will be what kills, you, Senor Ford," said Carlos, appearing suddenly from behind Emmet. "Maybe not right away, but once the curse is made...," he paused, then added, "It is the curse of the *Kalku.*"

"Enough of this supernatural dribble," Ford growled. "I only brought your attention to this matter because I wanted to prove that someone is out to threaten me, or worse, and I believe this ill will has come aborning right from here. *Your* people, Carlos, always despised me, no matter that I was trying to help them."

"What about the French mailing address that was on the package?" asked Emmet, a sarcastic lilt in his tone. "Do you think these people put that on the package to throw you off the scent?"

"Of course not!" barked Ford, his face flushing. "These people wouldn't know which side of the stamp to lick to post the package. That's why we're getting back on the ship and continuing to France."

Emmet glanced at Carlos, who was staring at Ford, his pupils enlarged, his breaths coming faster. Emmet wondered if that was from the coca leaves or anger. He suspected the latter.

"I have made the accommodations you requested for tonight, sir," said Carlos. "You will be the guests of the woman who lives in one of the abandoned workhouses. Her name is Rocio. She will have food and sleeping quarters ready for you." He started to lead the way to their lodging when Carlos turned back to Ford and added, "Be kind to her, Senor Ford. Rocio is the *Curanderos* that I told you about and she is well-liked here. The villagers—many of your former workers—would not be pleased if you were...disrespectful to her. Maybe she can help you lift this curse."

Carlos stepped out of the delipidated factory and out of voice range when Ford spat more venom. "Damned, lazy vagabonds, squatting on my property and demanding respect. Hogwash. I should have a demolition crew come in here and blow this place to hell."

Emmet grabbed Ford by the arm and squeezed so tight that Ford winced and his eyes watered. Outside, the wind picked up and the temperature seemed to plummet as the scent of rain filled their nostrils.

"Listen to me," said Emmet. "This isn't Fair Lane, old chap. You can't disparage these people and expect they will look the other way out of civility. This is a jungle and a dangerous place to be as you've already seen. I'm not your bodyguard so I don't care if they slide a poison adder into your bedding or send in a quiet killer who will take your head."

Emmet paused to let the words sink into Ford's thick skull, then continued with a warning. "Have you heard of the *Shuar*? They're a head-hunting tribe who shrink their trophies after sewing their mouths shut so their victim's soul cannot escape and seek revenge. Then they blacken the skin and eyes with charcoal so the victim's spirit can't see them. So, when I say to you, mind your manners and keep your head, so to speak, I mean it."

Ford turned pale and goosebumps ran down his neck.

Emmet turned and left the room, looking about for Carlos to lead the way, then chuckled to himself. "Keep your head," he said to himself under his breath. "That's rather funny."

THIRTY-NINE

KEY WEST

Pauline Hemingway was cleaning her house, again, bored. The boys, Patrick and Gregory were with "the X," as she referred to Ernest, in Cuba, fishing, hanging out with "Papa" and his newest wife, Martha Gellhorn. It was Ernest's court-given time to spend with his sons and though he did not always fulfill that obligation, this time he insisted. Pauline had filled the vacuum by doing the rounds with all her friends in town, doing some volunteer work for the church, planting some flowers in the garden, and tidying up the house, again and again.

It was approaching the holidays, and the weather was a little cooler than usual, which in Key West meant it was a nice 78 degrees rather than 98 degrees. Pauline had just decided to go for a swim in the pool when the phone rang. Another minute and she would have missed it, but this was one of those moments that fortune or providence, as the religiously devoted Pauline would refer to it, would change the lives of so many people.

She didn't want to seem as if she were doing nothing, though she was, so she let the phone ring three times before she grabbed it and tried not to sound so desperately lonely.

"Hello?"

"Hello, Pauline, how are you today?" said a boisterous, gruff, and slightly drunken voice—though it was only noon—of "the X," Ernest Hemingway.

Oh, Lord, thought Pauline. *What now?* Then her heart missed a beat. "Are the boys all right, Ernest?"

"Wha...why of course, they're all right. They're with me, aren't they?"

Exactly why the question came to mind, she thought, then let out a pent-up breath. "Very...good. Then why are you calling?"

"Well, I'm getting ready to take a trip. I've got the boys for a few more weeks and thought I'd take them with me to Europe."

"Europe?" asked Pauline, her heart beating faster again. "What part of Europe were you thinking? You know there's a war going on there," she added, her voice laced with sarcasm she was using to hide a slow, creeping fear.

"Yes, of course, I know that. That's why I'm taking them. I'll be staying in the free zone, in the Dordogne area. They'll be safe as houses, and they'll get to see how other people live while I take a few days to report on the occupied front for Collier. It's a good education for them."

Now, the creeping fear turned into complete terror as Pauline recognized her helplessness. She knew Ernest made impetuous decisions but this one she could not abide. She also knew he would not listen to her try to reason with him. But she had to try. "Have you seen what the Nazis are doing? Ernest...puh, please don't do this. I would die if anything happened to them.... please!"

"Sorry, Pauline, the plane is waiting, and I owe Collier's a story. The boys will be safe with me."

"Then at least let me know where you'll be...please," she pleaded.

"All right, I'll send you a cable," he chuckled a bit, then in a honey-oozing voice said, "Hey, uh, I'm considering taking the boys to Le Grau-du Roi. Show them where I took their mother for our honeymoon. Marty's covering a story in London, maybe you and I can rekindle things in our honeymoon spot..."

"Not a chance in hell, you *bastard*," said Pauline genuflecting as she said it. "You just make sure I get the address of where the boys are, or so help me God, I'll find you and cut your little penis off!"

Hemingway roared with laughter. "I sure miss that spunk! I'll let you know where we end up. Maybe you'll change your mind about a romp when you get there!" With that he hung up, laughing.

Pauline's head hurt and she rubbed the vein in her temple like a genie's lamp, trying to soothe the aching throb there. Her heart and mind raced in a full-blown panic. Then, an idea popped into her head.

She dug through the kitchen drawers and found the phone number she was looking for. Sweat formed across her forehead and upper lip as she dialed the number. She heard the phone pick up.

"FBI, Miami Bureau, this is Robert Holly." The voice was that of a young man, with a touch of the South in it. There was a glass cover on the desk where he sat. He could see a mirror image of himself, his hair slicked back and parted in the middle, just like Howard Hughes, a man he admired despite his defiance of federal laws. How could he not like him? Hughes was a fellow Texan.

"What? I'm sorry," said Pauline. "Did I call the wrong number? I was looking for Director John Serey."

"No Ma'am. You've got the right number. Director Serey is out of town currently. I'm the Assistant Director filling in while he's gone. May I help you?"

"I...I don't know. This is Pauline Hemingway. My ex-husband, Ernest Hemingway, you know the author? Well, he has done something...wrong."

"Yes, Ma'am. I do know who Mr. Hemingway is. I've been following some of his publications from the war in Europe. He's quite a writer. I've also been briefed on Director Serey's ...um...cases, uh... recent past and current. I'm aware he worked on a case a year or so ago with your husband. Is your hus...excuse me, ex-husband, in some sort of danger?"

Pauline sighed. "He's always in some sort of danger. But this time he has done something stupid that threatens the life of my sons."

Holly sat forward in his chair, authentically concerned. The son of an abusive father, he had a particular interest in cases of domestic violence. He also knew, from what Serey had told him, that Ernest "Papa" Hemingway was a "certified loose cannon and the subject of an ongoing FBI file that was already quite thick." "What has he done, now, ma'am?"

"He's taking my boys to France while he covers the frontlines for a story on the war," Pauline had started to cry, her voice cracked and came in spurts between sobs. "I need...I...need...to know...there's a man, who helped Director Serey when he was in here, in Key West. His name is Emmet MacWain. Do you know who he is?"

Now, Holly was quiet. He had to think. He *did* know who Emmet MacWain was. He also knew MacWain was working on something with Serey that was top secret, and secrets are supposed to be just that, *secret*. It involved MacWain, some murders in Ft. Myers for which Henry Ford might be responsible, and quite possibly, some Nazi spies. It was not something he could discuss with a hysterical woman who called looking for her wayward ex-husband."

"I'm sorry," said Holly. "I can't talk to you about ...um... some things...."

"Do you know how I can reach Mr. Serey?"

Now, Holly felt a dollop of sweat creep from his scalp and run down the side of his face. The first time stepping up to fill in for his boss, he was being asked to compromise the trust that put him there.

"Ma'am, the best that I can do is try to get hold of Director Serey, but he is out of the country and might not be so easy to contact... .I'm sorry...but if this is an emergency...you should call your local police department."

Pauline thought that her head might explode. She was torn between uncontrollable anger and gripping fear. She spoke slowly, deliberately. "My...ex-husband... may... be... putting... my... *children*.... in... harm's way. If anything happened to them...," she decided to try a different tactic. "Listen, I...need Emmet MacWain. He can help...he *will* help me with this. If you talk to Director Serey, would you tell him that? Please?"

She began to sob, and Holly felt his face grow hot listening to her.

"I'll do my best, ma'am. I can't make any promises," he began, but he heard a click, then silence, and knew she had hung up the phone.

He chided himself as he had failed to get the troubled woman's phone number. Even an overworked beat cop would have done that.

Holly sat at Serey's desk, in his chair, a place he wanted to end up one day. He wondered if Serey would be upset with him if he called to say a woman phoned to report her kids were taken by their famous father and were heading toward the worst place they could go: France, where the war was spreading like typhoid fever.

Holly sat in Serey's chair for a long time, contemplating, trying to think like the man who had been mentoring him—a man he much admired—pondering what he would do. If he called Serey, he might be upset. But if he didn't call him, something worse might happen.

Finally, he reached for the phone on his boss's desk. He dialed "o" and Gladys, the Miami bureau's switchboard operator answered.

"Hello, Mr. Holly, how can I help you?"

"Gladys, can you call the hotel where Director Serey is? I need to get hold of him."

"That's in Brazil, sir. They are about two hours ahead of us, I believe."

Holly looked at his watch. "I know, so it's evening there. Maybe he's out for dinner but if you get him, patch it through to me. If you don't, leave a message at the front desk of his hotel. Tell them just to have him call me, please."

"Yes, sir," said Gladys. "Will we be working late tonight?"

Holly thought for a moment. "Yeah, we just might be."

FORTY

BRAZIL

W hen they arrived at the house where they would stay the night, the tenant, a lovely Brazilian, in her mid-thirties, Emmet guessed, greeted them. Her name was Rocio though Ford referred to her as the "Squatter." She was a beautiful, slender woman, with long, brown hair, streaked with blonde from the sun. Her supple skin was the color of cinnamon. She wore no makeup, and while she was one of the tallest women Emmet had ever seen, she walked with the balance and grace of a yogi.

Rocio showed the men their rooms, in which she had made up small but clean beds for each of them. She had prepared a wonderful meal of smoked wild pig and squash and beans. As the men sat down to dinner, Carlos told them he would return in the morning and bade them all, "*Buenas noches.*" Emmet thought Carlos should have stayed for dinner as the food was spiced in a way that Emmet had never encountered. It was delicious and Carlos was missing out.

Rocio was a quiet woman until spoken to and, much to Emmet's remorse, knew English well. This was established when Ford spoke salaciously of her—the man who cloaked himself in Christianity—smacked her bottom and mused on how the locals must enjoy "riding" her. Rocio was cutting up some fruit on the counter by the sink when Ford uttered the crude remark. She turned abruptly and stepped forward. She was taller than Ford by several inches and said, "If you mock me again, I will break your fingers." Then she glided out of the room as elegant as a silver screen actress.

Emmet liked her.

Ford looked like a dirty, little schoolboy caught looking up the teacher's dress. "I suppose I should be turning in now," said Ford, sheepishly, his face pale but his cheeks a bright scarlet, as if he'd been slapped.

Liebold, ever Ford's shadow, lifted himself from the kitchen table with great effort. He'd eaten too much, and the tiring journey had worn him down to the point he could no longer keep his eyes open. It was as if he'd been drugged. He mumbled a groggy good night and sauntered off to his appointed room in the small house.

Several boys, very young, came to Rocio's house as she was cleaning up after dinner. "*Hola Niño's*," said Rocio. "*Hola*," said the boys, looking up at her with giant eyes that shone with love and respect for her. The kids sat at the table, and she served them all food. They went at it hungrily, without speaking anymore. Emmet noticed that many of them had elaborate tattoos on their arms, usually creatures: snakes, birds, or fish. He thought it was unusual for children to have tattoos but chalked it up to the different cultures.

Rocio made some coffee and poured herself and Emmet a cup, then they went outside and sat on the small porch on the back of the house as the children finished their meal, then without prompting, washed the dishes. The rain had cooled the evening then died out to a light drizzle that tapped the huge leaves in the jungle with a gentle, soothing sound that made Emmet's eyelids grow heavy.

"Who are your little friends?" asked Emmet, drowsy.

Rocio peered into his eyes suspiciously, as if trying to assess why he asked the question.

"Why are you here, Senor MacWain?" Rocio inquired. "You are not like Senor Ford or his *gordo amigo*."

Emmet chuckled at the description of Ford's "fat friend," and then his smile faded. "There was a murder at Ford's house in Florida. I'm looking into it."

If Rocio was surprised, she did not show it. "You are a policeman?"

"I was, many years ago. Somehow, I never seem to get away from it though."

Rocio considered this for a moment, then asked, "You like this work?"

Emmet thought for a moment. "Not particularly."

"Then why do you continue to do it?"

"Because I like answers."

Rocio pondered this then, finally, said. "The boys are orphans. Our village takes care of them." She paused, then added, "They escaped the camps."

"Camps?"

Rocio hesitated again. "I believe I can trust you..."

"You've been a kind hostess to myself and my traveling companions, despite some of their vulgar displays. I owe you, and you can trust me."

Rocio nodded slightly, took a deep breath, leaned forward, and whispered, "The boys were held as prisoners, slaves, to the *teuto-brasileiros*, in the camps nearby. Many of them are descendants of German immigrants and they sympathize with the Nazis."

Emmet sat up, his interest keen. "I think I saw one of them in the jungle as we came here."

"Yes, they keep them on farms where they are forced to work to raise beef and produce to send to the German military. I've helped some of them escape. I put spells on the Nazis so they can't see me, or the boys and I bring them back here."

Emmet questioned the "spells" but also knew the world is full of strange customs and beliefs and did not question her claim. One could believe in magic just as easily as in miracles. He wondered if Ford knew about these "camps," prisons more like it, and if that was another reason they were there. "Are these camps nearby?" he asked.

"The camps are about fifteen kilometers from here, but it is through the jungle, and it is a perilous trip filled with danger. It takes me all day to get there, and it is even slower coming back with the Niño's. I have to bring as much water and food as I can carry. That's why I cannot take many each time I go. Carlos helps me sometimes, but he is old, and it is hard on him."

"Why do the children have tattoos?"

Rocio smiled. "I did that. I wanted to cover the numbers the Nazis tattooed on them. That way, if the Nazis come looking for them, they might not recognize the children as their former slaves. And...the children like the animals I tattoo on them. They believe they have the power of the animal in the tattoos."

Emmet pondered this. He recalled seeing the cows and the one child with Nazi brands as they approached Fordlandia. Serey would want to know about this as well. He made a mental note to direct Eduardo, their pilot, to fly south and low. Perhaps he could see the camps when they returned and report the location to Serey.

"I have something I'd like to show you, Rocio," said Emmet. "To get your opinion. Would you mind?"

"Of course, not."

"I'll be right back," said Emmet. He stood and went inside and grabbed an item among his belongings. He came back and pulled his chair closer to Rocio and put on his gloves. He reached into a burlap bag that held the items he wanted to discuss with her. He took out the "voodoo dolls" that were made in the image of Ford and his son, Edsel. "I'm not sure you should touch these, in case they have poison on them, or something."

Rocio smiled. "Thank you for caring about me to be concerned, but they are safe to hold. I could smell them if they had *veneno* on them." She took them into her hands.

"You can smell poison?"

"Si, it is part of my *mágica*."

"You're a brave and good woman, Rocio," said Emmet.

Rocio looked the dolls over. "This one is Mr. Ford, I can see." Does he get bad headaches?"

Emmet hesitated, trying to recall. "I think so. He's a busy man, running a giant business, among other things. I've seen him rubbing his temples frequently."

"He will die one day from a *Golpe*, what you call a stroke, I believe. But it will not be because of this doll that has the needle in its head. Not directly anyway."

"Really?"

"*Si*. But the doll might make him believe that could happen. Such is its power."

"And the other doll? That one is supposed to be his son, Edsel. I've met him and he does have stomach problems."

"Someone else must know that, too, and that's why the needles were put into his stomach."

Emmet shook his head in disbelief. "I just wonder who would have made these dolls and what was their purpose."

"The children who live in the camps of the *teuto-brasiliro*. They tell the kids to make these dolls to scare their enemies. The dolls have no power, other than what the person who sees himself in them, gives them. But that can be powerful, too.

Emmet shook his head in wonder. "I know the son, Edsel, too. He has very bad stomach problems and he has never seen the dolls."

"Someone else must know that, too, and maybe they told the *teuto-brasiliro* people, many of them work with the Nazis and dislike Americans, especially one like Senor Ford, who treated them badly when he was here. Someone that knows Senor Ford well, I believe, that would know his son is sick in the stomach."

Emmet sat quietly, pondering this new knowledge.

Rocio noted Emmet wore a gold wedding band on the ring finger of his left hand. "Does your wife mind that you are in this dangerous business?"

Emmet sighed, wearily. "*Mi esposa esta muerta.*"

Rocio leaned forward, noticing his sadness. "Oh, *lo siento mucho*," she said, then reached her hand out and gently touched Emmet's hand.

"*Gracias*," said Emmet, then feeling the need to clear his throat. "She's been gone for many years."

Rocio stared at Emmet. "They say a broken heart is never cured."

Emmet nodded, slowly, his eyes wet. "They're right about that."

She was silent for a moment, then stood, bent over, and kissed Emmet, lightly, on his mouth. Her breath was warm and smelled like coffee. "Do you wish for me to share your bed with you?"

Emmet reached up and gently placed his hand on her face. She was beautiful, her olive eyes shining in the dim light. "That would be so nice, dear lady, but I can't do that. Your hospitality has been so wonderful, I wouldn't want to take advantage of your kindness. And I don't think my wife would approve."

"You said she was dead."

"She is."

Rocio looked a bit forlorn, her eyes looking down as if in self-observance, then she looked back into Emmet's eyes. "You're a good man, Mr. MacWain." She kissed his forehead. "I'll say goodnight then. I pray you sleep well."

Emmet sat on the porch for a while longer, listening to the rhythmic tapping of the rain, growing drowsy. He thought about Pauline, curious how she was doing, then his thoughts turned to the ginger-haired bartender, Bessie Murphy, and their brief encounter— an anomaly—for him, and her yearning to be a circus star. Bessie and Pauline both held a place in his heart now, but he wondered if anyone would ever hold all of it. Rocio was beautiful but Emmet had never been a man who was just filling up a scorecard of romances, and you don't repay kindness with lechery.

He stood, took his coffee cup to the kitchen, and rinsed it out, then found his room with help from a moon that shone through the windows of the small house. He fell into bed and was asleep in minutes, dreaming of the women he'd loved and lost.

FORTY-TWO

Robert Holly called the Hotel Gloria where Serey was staying and was put on hold. The hotel was a luxurious architectural beauty built in the 1920s. With a wonderful view of Guanabara Bay, it quickly became a go-to landmark in Rio de Janeiro. It was the hottest spot for royalty and dignitaries from all over the world. It was no accident that Serey chose the hotel. The grand palace was also a den of spies.

"This is John Serey."

"Good evening, Boss. It's Robert Holly."

"Hello, Robert. Everything okay?"

"Everything is swell, sir, but I thought I should call to tell you about an unusual circumstance that may coincide with your current endeavor."

"I've had a few unusual circumstances down here myself. Tell me about yours."

"Okay. In short, Pauline Hemingway called me to tell me her ex-husband, Ernest, was taking their kids—against her wishes—to France, so he could cover the war there. Naturally, she was quite upset but, beyond that, I recalled our conversation about you possibly going to France as well and I just thought...well, is this coincidence, or is it something going on with what you're doing, or am I just thinking about it too much?"

Serey considered the situation for a moment, biting his lower lip, trying to decipher the possibility that it might be a coincidence, or could it be some trickery, some spy bullshit? *Hemingway*, he thought. *What a pain in the ass.*

"You're not thinking too much about it, Robert. That's for sure. Our business has little to do with coincidence, and when we start thinking that way is...well, that's when one of us gets killed. The term, 'cloak and daggers,' comes from somewhere, you know? It's good you called to tell me. Let me think about this, uh...situation and I'll get back to you if needed. But while we are on the phone, see if Gladys can patch me through to the Director. I've got some critical information I need to discuss with him."

"Anything I need to know or can lend some assistance to, sir?"

"Thanks, Robert, but no. I'll keep this under my hat for now. The less people that know things these days, the better. I'll handle the Hemingway issue on my end. *Capiche?*"

"Understood, sir. Wait a second while I get Gladys to help with that connection. I wish you well and look forward to your return, sir."

"Thank you, Robert. I look forward to returning myself. Great job letting me know about Hemingway. Keep up the good work."

Holly said, "So long," before he transferred the connection to Gladys.

"Gladys?" said Serey.

"Yes, sir. How are you?" she inquired, with her nasal voice. "Enjoying the beaches in Brazil?"

"Not so much, but thanks for asking. I have an urgent request. Can you patch me through to the Director from your office?"

"The Director? Do you mean, *The* Director?"

"Yes, Gladys. That one."

"Oh, my. You must be onto something *very* important. This is so exciting. Just give me a moment sir, I don't do this every day."

Serey heard her shuffling around, probably looking up how to make that kind of patch, then she said, "Here it is. I'm going to pass you through, but I want to say, please stay safe, sir. We miss you here."

Serey was able to say, "Thank you," before there was a click, a humming noise, more clicks, and then J. Edgar Hoover answered the phone.

"Hoover," he said.

"It's Miami Director Serey."

"I know, and...?"

Serey was always taken aback by Hoover's bluntness. "We need to talk, sir."

"I know that, too, Mr. Serey. Are you calling to tell me the Nazis are in our country?"

"Yes, sir, they are," he paused. "In fact, sir, they're everywhere."

***

BERLIN

Deputy Fuhrer Rudolph Hess sat at his desk in Berlin contemplating his future, while pondering his past. His upbringing in Egypt spawned his distrust of dark-skinned people—always poor and reaching out to him like lepers to a priest—and his now begrudging admiration of the English, who ruled the stygian-skinned savages with a riding crop.

He was greatly relieved when his family moved to Germany where he felt comfortable within its clean streets and modern buildings. He'd learned the trade business from his father but spent most of his life in the military fighting for his adopted country in the Big War and earning an Iron Cross, but also earning scars from bomb shrapnel and bullets. After that fiasco, he'd studied geopolitics, and befriended Adolf Hitler, who pushed him to marry Ilse Pröhl, then became godfather to their child whom he named "Wolf," which is what Adolph's closest friends called him.

He'd also spent time with Hitler in Landsberg prison after their failed *coup d'etat* and helped edit the book, *Mein Kamph*, which would help cement the Nazi Party as a political dynamo and turn the Nazi Party into the world's most feared army since Napoleon Bonaparte's. He'd also been injured while shielding Hitler from a bomb that was planted by Marxists.

But his relationship with the Fuhrer had become frayed. Perhaps it was because he protested too much about their overly zealous expansion, but that was because he was a geopolitical statistician who was absolutely sure they could not fight and win on two active fronts. Yes, they could defeat almost any enemy army they fought, and they were on a very successful run of conquering one country after the other in Europe, but Hess was deeply concerned. *How many countries could they conquer and hold?* How soon would Germany's perfectly trained and weaponized soldiers become so thinned out that they would become ineffective and vulnerable? Where was the funding going to come from to continue this unprecedented gobbling up of the world while still defending their own? If they were to follow the global appetites of Caesar, Napoleon, and Genghis Khan, would they not follow the pattern of their losses as well?

Hitler did not like that kind of speculation verbalized and he saw Hess's growing concerns as weakness. The Fuhrer was listening more to the counsel of Martin Bormann these days and less to his longtime friend who had been by his side, even in prison. Hess was beginning to believe he was being shut out of the inner circle, and his old friend was turning more toward men who seemed to favor the taste of blood and the smell of more, and bigger, battles rather than diplomacy. Men, like Klaus Barbie, whom Hitler had recently announced would be going to Lyon, France to lead the Gestapo.

Barbie was considered a monster, even by the darkest of Nazi officers such as Goring and Himmler, who admired his rapacious appetite for torturing and killing prisoners.

Hess was beginning to believe he had to do *something*. As he thought of Barbie and his French assignment, he began to think more about France. Hess knew of the two officers that had seemingly vanished during a "scouting" mission, supposedly one in which they had visited the famous entertainer, Josephine Baker's home, an American negress whom some rumors suggested was a spy.

Slowly, but with inspiring clarity, a plan began to form for Hess. He decided to call Klaus Barbie.

Barbie answered his phone on the first ring.

"Chief Barbie, this is Deputy Fuhrer Hess."

"Yes, sir," said Barbie. "What can I do for you?"

"I was calling to congratulate you on your new assignment, as Chief of our Gestapo in Lyon."

"*Danke, Kommandant,*" said Barbie, wondering about the unexpected call.

"I also understand you are putting together a team to investigate the disappearance of one of our officers and a missing Vichy gendarme."

"That's correct," said Barbie, suddenly defensive. "*Oberleutnant* Hans Arent and Marshall Rene Peletier."

"Yes," said Hess. "I am curious about this case as well. That's why I was calling today. I am going to change your orders regarding this investigation as I am going to look into it myself. I will utilize SS Colonel Major Kurt Lieber and his men to assist, as it should have been his responsibility in the first place."

"Oh?" said Barbie, concerned why Hess would take the responsibility away from him. "Why would someone of your rank and prestige take on such a task? I'm sure you have more important matters that require your attention."

"Of course," said Hess. "But I knew Hans Arent's family, and I told them I would look into this personally."

"I...see," said Barbie. "But it is *my* new assignment in my region and I'm sure you are already so busy..."

"I *said* I will look into it, Herr Barbie," Hess said, abruptly. "I am not asking you for your permission. I am telling you this is what is happening. Do you understand?"

"Yes...sir," said Barbie.

"Very, good then. "Consider the matter done. And good luck with your new position. *Auf Wiedersehen,*" said Hess, then hung up the phone. But he was uncomfortable. He was a higher-ranking officer than Barbie, but he had heard of the man's relentless dedication, as well as his sadistic, one might say demented, character. He would have to be careful.

Klaus Barbie sat down and considered the conversation with Hess. It was unusual, particularly with a man who, until recently, was the Fuhrer's closest high-ranking officer and confidant. But some rumors were floating around, too. Some said Hitler and Hess were not so close now. Disagreements in battle strategies, was it? Talk of a different position for Hess? Barbie could not recall the specifics, but he would see if he could find out more. In any case, he would still "unofficially" be going to *Chateau Des Milandes,* whether Hess approved, or not.

Intelligence had reported "unusual" activity at Josephine Baker's residence. Barbie wondered what the *Schwarzer Teufel* would do if he took her to his inquisition room. He found himself becoming aroused as he thought of seeing what it took to break her. The broken glass shoved into an orifice? No, something special for the special songstress. Maybe if he cut out her vocal cords...

FORTY-TWO

Emmet awoke, dressed, and washed his face in a bowl with a pitcher of water left there for this purpose. He dabbed his face and noted he needed a shave but that could wait. What he needed most was to get back to someplace where he could use a phone and hope that he could connect with Serey.

He ambled out to the kitchen, scratching his prickly face, and found Carlos, their guide, sitting at the table with Rocio having coffee and chatting like two old friends. Perhaps they were.

Rocio greeted Emmet and asked him to sit down, then went to the stove and poured him some coffee. She brought it to him and said, "*Buenos dias*. Did you sleep well, Emmet?"

Emmet took the coffee from her. "Thank you," he said, "Yes, I did. Very much so."

It was then he noticed his cast was gone as was the persistent ache in his side where he'd been slashed with a knife when he fought with the two sailors trying to kill him. His bruised, discolored skin was now back to normal. He felt refreshed, no, *renewed*. No aches or pains anywhere. It was uncanny and, in a way, somewhat scary. Emmet felt the hair rise on the back of his neck as if a ghost had blown cold breath on him.

Rocio looked at him, thoughtfully, the morning sun finding her face, even more beautiful than the night before, especially when she smiled. Her tongue parted her lips and slid from side to side leaving her mouth wet and shining. "I blessed you at night, as you slept. I hope I didn't wake you."

Emmet shook his head, confused. "I never knew you were there."

"I didn't want you to," she said as the smile returned, though it had a slightly risqué look to it as if there was a twilight mystery that Emmet had missed. "I wanted you to believe me when I say I can cast spells."

He tried to recall if she had slid into the bed with him—surely, he would recall that—but he didn't. He did remember his erotic dreams *but those were just visions of former lovers, weren't they?* he asked himself. Emmet was not sure and felt slightly embarrassed about it.

"You've been a wonderful hostess, Rocio," said Emmet. "Thank you."

Rocio held out her hand. In it, was a single mushroom. "Look," she whispered, and suddenly her voice seemed far away to Emmet. For a moment, he felt dizzy, and darkness enveloped him as he stared at the mushroom and watched it grow until it towered over him, and he thought he felt the earth shake. Then a bright light came from the center of the giant mushroom and, suddenly, Emmet was back in the kitchen, Rocio leaning over him, her face close to his.

"Are you all right, Emmet?" she asked. "Sometimes my treatments have, what do you call them? Hangovers? Breathe deeply and remember, from something small, great power can be produced."

Emmet's head cleared as if the vision he'd just had never occurred, like the wounds he had that were not there now. He felt an energy within him as if he was a younger, stronger version of himself. He felt something in the palm of his hand and when he looked the mushroom was there.

Rocio smiled again and gave him a quick wink just as Ford and Liebold came in. Her smile faded quickly.

Both men had bags under their eyes and looked road weary. It was uncommon to see either of these automobile magnates unshaven or disheveled but here they were looking like men who could use some spare change.

"There is coffee and there are some *catibias* there on the counter," said Rocio, amicably but without the warmth with which she addressed Emmet. "Some are filled with guava and cheese and some with beef. You might know them as empanadas."

Ford, rudely, ignored her. "Carlos, Ernest, and I are packed and ready to go back to the plane. I've found what I needed to find here and wish to leave this god-forsaken place as soon as possible. Make sure you fill some canteens with water. We have a long flight back." Then, he turned and walked out of the house.

Liebold shrugged his shoulders and grabbed a couple of the *catibias,* stuffing some in his pants pockets and one in his mouth. He addressed Rocio with a nod and hurried out of the house.

"I'm sorry for my traveling companions lack of gratitude," said Emmet. He took some money from his billfold, stood, and placed it on the counter. "I hope this serves as my gratitude for your wonderful hospitality."

Rocio nodded. *"Gracias, mi amor.* Take some food, the lighter ones have the fruit and the darker ones, the beef. The pastry is made from yucca. It's like your potato."

Emmet picked out two *catibias* and drank a cup of coffee then filled his canteen with water. Thank you very much," he said, then smiled and added, "for everything."

Rocio and Carlos stood up at the same time.

Carlos nodded and went to the door. "I am pleased you are leaving after two nights here. It isn't safe for Senor Ford."

"What?" said Emmet. "We...were only here overnight."

"No, sir, it was two nights," Carlos affirmed.

Emmet looked at Rocio who smiled slightly, knowingly, looking like a Latina Mona Lisa, a woman with secrets to keep.

"You needed the rest," she said. "See how your wounds have healed." She glided over to Emmet, slid her slender arms under his, and hugged him. "I will see you again, good sir," she said.

Emmet smiling said, "You sound so sure."

"I am," she said. "You will feel better today than you have in a long time, then better tomorrow, and best when we meet again."

Emmet laughed, still thinking the locals must be playing a joke on him. "Until then." He leaned forward and kissed Rocio's forehead. She was almost as tall as he was. "Again, *mucho gracias.*" He waited until she stopped hugging him, then slowly turned and with a final wave, said "So long," as he stepped outside the small house. He wondered if he should tell Ford they'd lost a day.

Grabbing his knapsack, and accompanied by Carlos, they caught up with Ford and Liebold, just as the two of them stood at a crossroad of two trails wondering which way to go. Emmet considered telling the two of them about their extended stay as they did not seem any more aware of it than he did. But he didn't have to. Coming from the left side trail of the crossroad was Eduardo, the pilot of the plane that brought them here.

"I heard you were finally awake," he said. I did not know Americanos liked to sleep so much."

Ford and Liebold looked at each other, frowning dumbly. Finally, Ford said, "I hope you haven't had too much fermented guava juice or whatever the hell you people get drunk on. We need you to fly us back."

Eduardo grinned. "I've been waiting until you were well enough for the trip..."

"What the hell are you talking about, man?"

Eduardo opened his mouth to say something but noticed Emmet, standing behind Ford, shaking his head, side to side, and holding a finger against his lips.

Eduardo shrugged his shoulders and held his palms up in a gesture of surrender. "The plane is ready, so let's be on our way."

FORTY-THREE

FORT MYERS, FLORIDA

D eputy Abram pondered the invitation from his boss, Sheriff Ross. They'd been working together for over a year and the Sheriff had never been particularly sociable with him, though they'd seen each other at some of the Christian "rallies." But just after lunch that day, he'd invited him to come to his Methodist church to share a night of fellowship that evening and listen to the radio show called "The Radio Priest." Ross added, "The priest, Father Coughlin, is a Catholic, but we don't hold that against him," said Ross, with a chuckle while giving Abram a little nudge with his elbow. "He broadcasts out of Detroit. That's where Mr. Ford's car factory is, I believe."

Abram was hesitant, but how could he say no to his boss? The offer was a bit more enticing with the reference to Ford. Maybe he could find out a bit more about the recently elusive automobile magnate.

"Well..." Abram began. He'd been to some of the Sheriff's "social gatherings," and was always wary about the company. His name "Abram" was a name suggesting his Jewish heritage, a subject he managed to avoid, particularly in the company of his boss and his associates. They were open about their praise of Hitler's ideals. Thankfully, many of them were not well educated.

"C'mon, son," said Ross. "The church ladies—and there are a few pretty, single gals there—will make a batch of fried chicken with sides of cucumber salad, mashed taters, green beans with bacon, cookies... Gosh, I'm making myself hungry all over again. What do you say?"

"Well, all right. That sounds mighty nice, sir."

"Very good," Ross exclaimed. "And when it's just you and I talking, you don't have to be so formal. Call me Carl."

Abram chuckled and said, "That might be awkward sir, uh, *Carl*, but I'll give it a try."

"Great," said Ross. "Be there at six o'clock. You know the church, right? It's just three blocks south of the station."

"Yes, sir."

"All right then."

The two law officers parted ways, each heading home to get ready for the evening.

At his tiny but immaculate cottage, Deputy Jason Abram removed his khaki uniform, hung up his pants and shirt, and took a moment to shine his Deputy Sheriff badge. It was smaller than the sheriff's but the FBI badge he kept hidden in the nightstand drawer was bigger and he'd be carrying that one soon.

After showing Director Serey he could do undercover work—keeping an eye on the sheriff and his cronies, covertly filing reports, and assessing their next move, he'd be done with this little town. He'd be in Miami, the bright lights and big city, where the big gangsters operated. Arresting mob guys like Lansky and Capone. He couldn't wait to take down some of those big money hoods. Show them that a Jewish kid, who grew up overweight and picked on by neighborhood bullies, still became a man, a law enforcement officer, someone to reckon with.

He bathed and put on his best plaid and pressed shirt and tucked it into pants he'd laundered and ironed himself. They were a little tight in the waist, but looking in the mirror, his thin blonde hair combed, belt and shoes shined, he thought, *Okay. Some ladies like a guy with a little heft. Skinny guys can't wrestle mouthy, belligerent drunks to the ground, or settle squabbles among citizens and tourists who came to see if they could get a glimpse of the Ford and Edison homes, but he could.* He took a deep breath and returned a nod of approval to himself in the mirror.

Abram left his house with confident strides, his face aglow with the tangerine light of a setting sun coloring his freshly shaven cheeks.

When he arrived at the church, he could hear voices from inside and the loud, tinny sound of a radio show with an overly angered announcer on a full tirade. He went inside trying not to be the center of attention and inched his way around a giant table set up with about two dozen chairs, mostly full of men already seated. Women in proper long dresses rushed around the table bringing steaming dishes of hot food out of a kitchen in the back of the church.

Abram spied the sheriff, "Carl," who saw him, too, and motioned to come over and sit next to him. Abram complied, glancing around the table, noting familiar faces, some he'd known from around town: the milkman who delivered his eggs and milk, the butcher from the meat market, the baker he bought his bread from, some bar owners and fishermen from the docks. Most of them made eye contact with him and gave him a slight nod. A few shook his hand.

Ross stood and pulled out a chair for him, talking into his ear, so that Abram could hear him over the loud announcer whose voice came from the giant radio, the size of a gun cabinet that was placed, oddly, near the steps leading up to the church's altar.

As he sat next to the sheriff, he glanced and noticed all eyes were on him. Heads nodded in an unspoken greeting, a welcome. Abram nodded back.

Women, the wives of the men at the table and some single ladies, Abram assumed, floated around the table quietly, their shoes oddly soundless as if they were hovering like angels. A couple of the younger ladies glanced at him, then looked away like proper young women do. But one of them smiled demurely at him. Her hair was dark, short, and wavy over a round, kind face. She was a full-bodied girl, as they say, and was wearing a modest, blue and white plaid dress.

She walked the length of the table carrying a tray of glasses on a platter as if she did it every day. When she got to the young deputy's chair, she asked, "Sweet or unsweet?" Her voice sounded as if she were from Mississippi or Alabama.

"Sweet, Ma'am, please."

She leaned over the deputy, placing the tea in front of him, and whispered, "I'm Lily."

Abram said, "I'm Jason. Pleased to meet you."

Lily gave a slight nod and before continuing her rounds, said, "I like plaid, too."

Sheriff Ross stood and said grace, and Abram was glad he came to the dinner. The din of the crowd around the table had drowned out the sound of the radio briefly, but as they settled into eating someone turned up the old, waist-high, Zenith Upright so that the diners could hear better as forks and knives clattered against plates.

Father Charles Coughlin spewed his radio sermon with urgency, with fire and brimstone warnings against complacency, announcing that, "sloth was one of the seven deadly sins..."

Abram listened to "The Radio Priest" and slowly began to concentrate on the reverend's message.

"We must remain vigilant to the increasing number of Jews who have crept into our society, bringing in their conniving, under-handed, and duplicitous practices! Every Jew I've ever met was a communist and every communist I've ever met was a Jew. They will say hello to you and ask about your family while shaking your right hand, while their left-hand slips into your pants pocket and steals your wallet."

Abram's mouth was suddenly dry, his appetite gone. He placed his eating utensils on his plate, having barely made a dent in his food. He felt his face flush and began looking at his fellow diners as the radio show continued.

"And mark my word, our president, Franklin Roosevelt, is one of them. We must not allow him to push us into a war that he tries to convince us is necessary. Germany's Chancellor Adolf Hitler is right in his bid to exterminate these vermin and if we are to do anything with this European conflict, it should be to side with the German Reich..."

Abram looked around at his table guests who, while still eating, began to glance at him. He felt his scalp turn hot and a dollop of sweat ran down the side of his face. He dabbed at the perspiration and tried to stay calm. He gulped some iced tea trying to push down the food that clogged in his tightening throat.

"Are you all right, Jason?" asked Ross. "You look a tad pale, son. Get a chicken bone stuck in your throat?"

Abram cleared his throat. "No, I mean, yes...I'm ok. Just took too big a bite of my chicken, sir."

Ross nodded. "I understand, that is some mighty nice fried bird there," he said, going back to eating, his pronounced Adam's apple undulating as he swallowed another bite, like a barn snake sliding a mouse down its throat. He sipped some tea himself and said, "When we finish up, let's you, and me and the guys go out back and smoke some cigars. Maybe sip a little brandy," he said in a conspiratorial whisper, "... while the ladies pick up the dishes and serve up some dessert."

Abram picked at his food, trying to regain his composure and stay on task. The sweat ring around his neck and under his arms chilled and he smelled a scent like vinegar wafting up from his body. He nodded to Ross and tried to swallow again; his throat so dry it made the attempt impossible. He gripped the glass of iced tea and brought it to his lips, his hands shaking from both anger and fear.

Most of the men had already devoured their dinners and were beginning to get up from the table to saunter out back. None of them showed the good etiquette of offering to help clean up.

Abram found the strength to rise, his legs quivering, his bowels churning now, he fell into the line of men that were exiting the church's back door. He looked back at Lily and saw her watching him. He lifted his chin, smiled nervously, then mouthed the words, "Thank you."

"You're welcome," Lily mouthed back to him.

Deputy Abram just reached the bottom step of a set of wooden stairs and was approaching a group of men who had already lit up their cigars and were watching him like turkey vultures on a branch. He sauntered toward them, trying to act casual, his hands in his pockets, and was about to say, "Hello, gentlemen," but never got past "Hell..." when the butt of a gun slammed down on the base of his skull. He felt the earth fall out from under his feet, and everything went black, but before his senses were entirely gone, he heard the hiss of one word: "*Jew.*"

***

When Abram woke up, he couldn't feel the right side of his body, which was a good thing he thought, because he was nailed to a cross.

He assessed himself. The blow to the head must've done something to kill half his body. Hurt his spine or something. He'd known people in the small farming town he'd grown up in, who had fallen off a tractor, or old folks who fell downstairs and could no longer walk. He must've been laying on his face for a while because one of his eyes was filled with blood that probably came from the initial assault on his head.

He was stripped naked, and his hands were outstretched in the crucifix position, with what looked like railroad spikes driven through them. His feet looked mauled, as if his attackers *tried* to nail him to the cross, couldn't figure out how to get a spike through both feet, so just bound them tightly with a sisal rope. Abram thought it looked very much like the rope found on the postman they'd pulled out of the water around the fishing dock.

Surrounding him, were thirteen men, all dressed in silver shirts with a red "L" sewn over the left breast pockets. Abram thought they looked like overgrown Boy Scouts. They were carrying torches and wearing pointed hoods that covered their faces. At first, Abram believed they were wearing witches' hats, but he determined that they were more like those hoods the Ku Klux Klan wore. This crowd must have been an offshoot of that crazed horde, the white-robed costumes of the hateful, murdering group who openly hated Jews and Negroes and just about everyone else, save for the goosestepping Nazis who were advancing across Europe like a disease, but he had not seen the silver shirts and dark hoods before.

As if in answer to the questions in his head, one of the hooded men leaned down and growled said with an overly dramatic voice, "We are the Silver Shirts. We are here to save good people, Christians, from the likes of you and other substandard heathens. You're a conniving Jew. Jews don't believe Jesus was our savior, so we will show you what he felt as he died. Maybe then you'll know he is real."

"Sheriff?" croaked Abram. "Carl?

When the man didn't answer, Abram, with blood dripping from his swollen lips added, "Shirts look kinda blue to me...baby blue..." He smiled at his own joke, as much as his mouth would allow.

The man stood up and moved away from him as if bitten by a snake. He looked to the group lined up behind him and said, "Do it."

They moved forward and each grabbed a handhold on the cross on which Abram was nailed. There was a deep hole dug next to the cross that held him. They hefted the cross up, then dropped the foot of it into the hole.

The weight of his body pulled down and Abram could feel pain on the left side of his body, particularly in the one hand that could still feel pain. Fresh blood seeped from the spikes in both hands. His left shoulder seemed to bear the weight of his whole body and developed a throbbing ache immediately as it bore his weight. He felt the joint in the shoulder begin to separate. It was hard for him to breathe. His heart raced. He lifted his head to peer around, trying to see where they were.

In the moonlit night, he could see the area was filled with trees and the smell of pine and muck. There were no sounds of cars or lights of businesses or homes. Must have been somewhere in the swampy woods, east of Ft. Myers, where no one could hear them.

After they secured the cross into the ground, the silver-clad figures began to pile branches and logs around the base of the structure on which Abrams hung, like a side of beef, butchered and ready to cook. They poured kerosene around the base, then the tall one Abram already identified as Sheriff Carl Ross, lit the fire.

Dark clouds hidden by the night rolled across the sky like silent Panzer tanks, their insides beginning to glow and flicker as energy grew within them, like a vengeance.

"Beg for mercy, Jew pig," said the fire starter.

"Nope," Abram said.

"I wonder if he'll squeal?" said one of the cloaked men. Another said, "His God is called Yahweh! Let's see if he screams Yow-wee!" This was followed by insane laughter.

Rain began to fall, slow at first, then building into bullet sized drops that threatened to drown the fire. The ebony clouds growled.

The Yahweh jab provoked laughter but as the flame licked at Abram's mauled feet, blistered its way up his legs, and his abdomen, which heaved in and out like a billows as he tried to contain a scream. The crowd's laughter subsided into silence.

The young deputy's pain was such that he welcomed it to assure an end that would surely come soon. It would be excruciating but brief and he thanked Yahweh for giving him the strength to bear it. He thanked him, too, for the foresight to write a letter to Emmet MacWain, telling him where he was going that night, what he was doing, and with whom, that he'd left in the drawer of the nightstand with his new, well-earned FBI badge. He thanked Yahweh for his brief but good life.

Then his God reached down with an explosive lightning bolt, stopped his heart and his pain, and sent his tormentors running into the forest like the cowards they were.

The next day, Sheriff Ross was walking down the street, having left his office to lunch at a local diner he frequented when he passed a young lady who had been at the church dinner the night before.

"Hello Sheriff," said Lily.

"How do you do?" said Ross, tipping the brim of his hat.

"I'm very fine, today, thank you," she said. "

"Say, what happened to the nice young man that was wearing the plaid shirt last night? I think his name is Jason. Someone told me he was your deputy?"

"Uh, that's right," said Ross, his enormous Adam's apple sliding up and down as he swallowed. "He, um, he said, eh, he was feeling a tad bit queasy and left early."

"I'm sorry to hear that. He did seem as if something was bothering him. Will he be at the station today? Maybe I'll stop by and bring him some of the leftover desserts we had in abundance."

"Eh, well, no," said Ross. "In fact, he quit the job. Said he was going back to his home state. I think he had a job offer up there."

202 - EDISON'S LAST BREATH

Lily frowned at the Sheriff. "Hmmn. That's odd. One of the ladies told me he was from around here. Seems like he would've given notice, perhaps a few weeks ahead of time."

Ross shook his head, "Well, I don't know. He, uh, just seemed like he was bound to leave. Now, I'm ready to eat lunch, so, if you'll excuse me ma'am..." he said, then tipped his hat and quickened his pace toward the diner.

Lily Fields felt that something had happened. Maybe the young man, "former" Deputy Sheriff Jason Abrams had been fired. Why would he suddenly quit? Maybe he had not left town yet. Lily wasn't sure why she wanted to know more about him, or why he would want to leave so quickly. He seemed friendly, even interested in her, and she felt the same way about him if she was to be honest with herself. She also knew where he lived.

"I'll go see for myself," she said under her breath, then proceeded to walk the few blocks to his modest house. It was a small, yellow, plastered house that was partially covered with Queen's Wreath vines, whose brilliant violet color on top of the yellow walls made her think of Easter, a day of rebirth.

Lily knocked on the front door, but the house sounded empty. "Deputy Abrams?" She tried. "Jason...are you here?" she twisted the doorknob of the entry door. It was open. Lily went inside and repeated, "Jason? It's Lily. We met last night at the church social?"

The house was nothing more than a hotplate kitchenette extended into the same room sharing a small living space. One door was a combination of a bath and closet, which still held clothes. Next to that was another door that led into a room only long enough to hold the length of a single bed with a nightstand next to it, no bigger than the size of a bible with legs on it. And a drawer.

Lily was drawn to it like it was talking to her. She approached cautiously and opened that singular nightstand drawer. Inside, there were a few pennies, a comb, a shaving cup, and brush, still damp from using it the night before. There was a gleaming silver badge with block letters on its shield that read FBI, attached to an agent identification card, with Jason's name on it. Underneath it was a letter, which Lily drew out from under it. The envelope read: *For Inspector Emmet MacWain.*

FORTY-THREE

RIO DE JANEIRO

It was only five o'clock in the morning, the sky a pale grey-blue as the sun began to rise, but Serey was already up—had been up most of the night. Busy. With too many things to list. To worry about. To do. To lose sleep over. To begin. To end. One of those was now. He gazed toward the harbor where the *SS Brazilian* had pulled out, away from the dock and from other boats and the few fishermen and workers already at work.

Serey looked at his watch and found himself holding his breath, then exhaling and taking a deeper breath, then returning his gaze toward the ship, getting smaller as it pulled out to sea. Serey suffered from Hyperhidrosis—excessive sweating—even when he was cool-headed and calm, even though he showered several times a day, even when he was a sniper in the Big War, when he had to bury himself in snow as a troop of German soldiers marched over him and he sweated profusely and froze his flesh. To this day, it still peeled off his bald pate like onion skin.

The explosion in the harbor was so intense it rocked the Hotel Gloria, sending shock waves and shattering windows on the upper floors. Serey covered his face at the last second and ducked under the windowsill. He had not expected the blast to be so...catastrophic. Disoriented, he looked around the room, the floors sparkling with shards of broken glass. Looking out the now-open window, Serey saw a pillar of black smoke rise and expand in the sky like a fire-filled tornado from hell. Waves washed over the docks in seconds. Small boats rocked and pulled against their anchors and tugged at their moors.

Serey pulled himself up and used a newspaper to dust off splinters of glass, then found some binoculars in his baggage and went back to the window. He could see the ship, shorn in two, the stern where the weight of the engines and most of its deadly cargo lay, already gone under. The bow still pointed up, like the arm of a desperate drowning man, flames billowing on its deck like the torch that Lady Liberty held. Serey wondered if she'd be proud of the work he was doing to protect her these days.

He looked at his watch again and wondered when Emmet MacWain would be back from his journey to Fordlandia. He should've been back yesterday at the latest.

Serey recalled there was a bank of phones in the lobby downstairs. He needed to make some calls and it occurred to him that he should do that before every tenant in the hotel was rushing down there to call loved ones to assure them, they were ok, or reporters called to share the news that a freighter had just exploded and sank into the Porto Do Rio Janeiro.

None of them, other than Serey, and some terribly upset German leaders, would ever know the ship's cache of weapons for the Nazi Army was now strewn across the ocean floor, along with whatever was left of a dangerous group of spies. He hoped he got most, if not all, of them.

Captain Alves aka "the cheese," the code name the Germans had dubbed him, had worked with Serey to obtain, and then plant the charges in strategic areas of the ship to limit the outward explosion of the blast. Explosives were placed in the hull under the Nazis' smuggled armament to assure it would be destroyed and the ship foundered.

The beleaguered FBI branch director sweated out the explosion, as it was to be ignited by a timer that was set to go off once the ship was out to sea, but delays in the now all-German crew in departing the dock caused the explosion to occur closer to the port than he had hoped. Still, the job was finished and, in terms of the loss to the Nazis, it was catastrophic. The U.S. from all outward appearances might not be "engaged" in the European conflict but they were certainly dipping their toes into the pool, so to speak. While many politicos argued over the reasons not to engage in what would be another global conflict, some Americans knew the conflict was taking place, and the United States was already threatened by spies and saboteurs within the country's borders. If they didn't get into the fight, Serey knew it would only be a matter of time before Hitler had citizens goose-stepping down Main Street in every city in the country.

Some Americans already were. Some like the silver-shirts legion.

Serey called his Miami office where Gladys patched him through a protected line straight to the Director in DC. No names were used, nor were greetings utilized. Serey simply said, "Add one to Davy Jones's locker."

***

The plane carrying Emmet and Ford's entourage circled over Rio De Janeiro, in the late afternoon. A strong tailwind pushed them along like a cutter through calm seas. From their vantage point, the plane's occupants could see something was amiss. Police lined the streets. Traffic was bottle-necked on every street. Crowds squashed against each other as they tried, in vain, to move one way or the other, seeking shelter or escape.

Emmet was pleased to get back, though he could see something catastrophic had occurred. Other than meeting the exotically beautiful and mysterious Rocio, his trip into Fordlandia had been claustrophobic and dark. What he learned, if anything, was what he expected: Ford usurped the area, and hired natives whom he disrespected. Most of them eventually revolted and turned on him, or simply left. But their hatred of him was still there.

Emmet had to ask himself: Could one of them pursue a vendetta against him? Sure. But how many of them could find the means to travel to Florida, or concoct a poisonous gas that utilized chemicals more common to established countries with histories of seeking war, unlike the simple—if mysterious—people of the jungle? And what of the French address used on the package?

Emmet was ready to move on, get to France, and see where this case—as it were—led him. He had already come to some conclusions, but this denouement was not satisfactory to him. Even if he had proof of murder and a suspect, or suspects, the rich defy laws that commoners live under. He wanted to ensure that would not happen now.

As the plane taxied down the runway Emmet could see something was amiss. Soldiers, many from the Brazilian Expeditionary Force, also known as the *Cobras Fumantes*, or Smoking Snakes, lined egresses to the airport. Local police and other soldiers were present in the streets and were particularly heavy at the harbor.

Ford's entourage deplaned and was quickly escorted to customs agents where passports, and the little luggage the group had, were thoroughly checked in full view of the many armed soldiers. They were cleared and the car Ford had waiting for them took them into the city to their hotel. Along the way, they saw windows blown out and general disarray with pedestrians running about hurriedly, obviously panicked, and soldiers in the streets with rifles held at the low ready position.

The driver of the car informed them a ship had exploded in the harbor. When they learned the ship was the SS Brazilian, Ford turned toward Emmet, his face grave. "So, Mr. MacWain, do you think that was an accident?"

Emmet did not answer but he was sure of one thing, it certainly *was not* an accident. It was the reason Captain Alves, or "Cheese" had told him not to return to the ship. He hoped the innocent people, like "Doc" Hallonquist, and others on that Nazi-loaded ship were safe. He had no regrets for the rest of them. As he pondered his thoughts, one thing became quite clear to him. The European war that had started less than two years ago was spreading globally like a deadly plague. It had to be stopped at any measure, at any cost.

Winding through the streets to their hotel, the English-speaking refuge from Luxembourg, and constantly chatting driver of Ford's hired car, remarked on the ship's sinking. "You should have seen the explosion," he said. "It was bigger than anything I've ever seen, and I fought in the big war when I was a young man. The cloud that it produced rose into the sky as much as a kilometer I believe, then curled back at the top. It looked just like a giant mushroom," he exclaimed.

As soon as the word had escaped his mouth, Emmet's memory of Rocio staring into his eyes as he cleared his head that morning, the mushroom he envisioned, then found in the palm of his hand. A cold dampness ringed his neck and he recalled Carlos, Ford's former employee at Fordlandia, speaking of the *"Curanderos*, who lives nearby. She can cure almost anything," then added, "And see the future..."

Emmet was sure Rocio was that *Curanderos*. She had "cured him," and now he genuinely believed she could see the future. But he also wondered if this was the last deadly "mushroom," he would hear of. Or would there be more? He loathed himself for not being more open to things she might have shared with him.

Remembering the inexplicable crimes he investigated as a Scotland Yard Inspector, he had learned this lesson: You can never underestimate the mysteries of the human race, nor neglect to realize some things are beyond explanation. Such as the case of "Jack the Ripper."

Emmet had been given some "busy work" to investigate the unsolved murders that had been attributed to the mysterious and elusive, "Jack the Ripper." It was an inside challenge and a sort of rite of passage that many young investigators were assigned. Most of the time, the inexperienced inspectors came back with similar inconclusive endings.

The six victims that were attributed to The Ripper were: Mary Ann Nichols, Annie Chapman, Elizabeth Strides, Catherine Eddowes, Frances Coles, and Mary Kelly.

Among the list of some thirty-three suspects were: Montague Druitt, Aaron Kosmiski, Walther Sickert, David Cohen, and Thomas Cutbush, among others, with Kosminski being the favorite suspect. But it made no sense to Emmet. Most of these men had alibis: some were out of town when the murders occurred, or known to have been at a function, or with someone who could corroborate their whereabouts.

Emmet looked elsewhere and found there was a royal coach often seen the night of each murder. The coach was not the color of a royal coach, indeed there were few like it. It was painted a scarlet color, so dark it was almost black. It was an unusual sight in the downtrodden areas where the murders occurred. He found and interviewed witnesses who not only remembered the coach but could describe it. As he was allowed access to archives that included the Royal Family, he poured through the history of every relative and their places of residence, not all of which were palaces, though many were large estates. Emmet looked into the estate owner's possessions, particularly their livery stables, and their hired personnel. He found the number and style of coaches for each estate and their perspective drivers. The only distant relative to the Royal family was a Viscount, named Harold Jonathan Tydwell who went by the name of Jonathan, or John. John is often substituted for "Jack" as a manner of casual speaking. Tydwell owned a dark red coach. He was also irrational and troublesome and was finally put into an asylum for mentally ill patients.

Within a few weeks, Emmet had cleared all the suspects— timelines for when and where the suspects were on the nights of the murders. They simply did not tie in with any of the timelines and places of when and where the women were killed—and Emmet found several more possible victims to be added to the lists of murdered women. Then he connected all, or most, of the killings to the Viscount. He thought it was all too simple and wondered why there was such a mystery about the case in the first place. Moreover, why wasn't there an arrest? He brought his conclusions to his supervising officer.

Emmet's "busy work" was immediately terminated, and he was put into the field to investigate current murders full-time. Emmet always wondered if he solved the case, or if it was just an exercise to determine if, as one elder cop told him, "New inspectors couldn't find their own arses, with their own hands." When he followed up with his superiors, they told him it was just that, an *exercise*, the case was too old and there was no more interest from the public or private parties, with a final command to "just work on the many current cases."

After completing an entire career in law enforcement and investigations, first with the City of London Police, then with Scotland Yard, Emmet didn't miss the work.

FORTY-FIVE

W hen Ford's car arrived at their hotel, they witnessed the damage from the *SS Brazilian* blast. Chunks of plaster were missing as were all the windows. They had lost power and running water and the steps leading up to the hotel were filled with guests, sitting around with their luggage, disoriented, and trying to find new accommodations, many sprinkled with dust from the hotel's crumbling walls. A few wore makeshift bandages. There was a smell of ozone and sulfur in the air.

Bennett was nearby, sitting at an open-air bar, and saw them arrive. He ran over to tell them the news which was all too apparent.

"Hey, Mr. Ford," said Bennett. "I guess you heard what happened."

"We did not until we landed at the airport," Ford replied. "There were no radio broadcasts in that God-forsaken, primitive jungle town. I can't wait to sell the damn place and get rid of it and its unpleasant memories."

"Yeah, so our ship got blown up and the hotel is damaged and they're trying to find places for their guests in other hotels. They got us rooms at a place across town called the Hotel Gloria because I told them who you are. Supposed to be nice. I went by there earlier and they got some windows knocked out but not too bad and it's a swanky joint. They wouldn't let me into your rooms here to get your baggage but now that you're here, maybe they will."

They went inside and talked to the manager, who was shuffling through paperwork, trying to find guests other accommodations, with a phone stuck between his face and neck, talking loud and fast.

Ford stood in line to conclude business at the front desk while Liebold and Emmet went to their rooms to fetch theirs, and Ford's, bags.

Emmet did not have much to retrieve but assured himself he had all he had brought with him when he arrived. The floor was covered with broken glass like the rest of the hotel, some lamps were knocked over, but the bed was still made, covered with broken plaster and other refuse from the blast of the exploded ship. He realized he had never slept there before they ran off into the jungle.

As he stepped out of the room and was about to close the door, he saw a man approaching Liebold's room. There was something familiar about him, his stature, the stride of his walk—*something*.

He was squatty in stature but took long strides. His hair was black and slicked back. *A wig, perhaps?* Emmet wondered. He wore round, green-tinted glasses over a thick, black mustache the shape and size of a man's pocket comb and a devilish, pointed goatee on his chin. There was a cardboard tube under one arm, such as would hold a rolled-up painting or perhaps a map, or *blueprints*. Emmet recalled when Liebold had shown some blueprints to a newspaper reporter previously for a bomber Ford's company had designed. Was that stupidity? Or vanity to show off a project he was supposed to be overseeing? What did this man in the dapper suit have to share with him? And why now, as the hotel was being vacated?

The man's suit was a double-breasted wool, brown with light-yellow pinstripes, such as a gangster might wear, and certainly too hot for Brazil. Nice yellow tie to match the suit's stripes and highly polished wingtip shoes. As he drew close to Liebold's room, he stopped and looked around, thoroughly, to see if anyone had followed him or was watching him, then pulled out a handkerchief and dabbed his neck and brow.

Emmet had stepped behind his door already and peered through the opening of the hinged side. He worried about leaving the door ajar, but in all the disarray, who would notice? Some of the cleaning people might have already been in rooms doing their jobs, so okay, maybe?

The well-dressed man stared at Emmet's door intently and he wondered if the man could see him peering through the hinged crack. Emmet held his breath and watched as the dapper but overdressed man eventually turned and knocked gently on the door to Liebold's room.

Liebold opened the door and the two men chatted for a moment. Even from a distance, the dapper man's voice sounded familiar, though slightly different, from one Emmet thought he knew. *Perhaps it was an attempt at an accent?* The man slipped inside Liebold's room.

Emmet moved quickly but quietly across the lushly carpeted aisles to Liebold's room, thanking God that they were not polished wooden floors that would make footsteps sound like cannon shots. He gently placed his ear to the door.

"I'm pleased you came today," said Liebold. "Mr. Ford and I are changing hotels due to the ship explosion and subsequent damage. Were you here for that? Mr. Ford and I were in the god-forsaken jungle, ruminating over his former rubber plant at the ill-fated Fordlandia. Surely one of the worst ideas he has ever had."

"As a man of business, I'm aware of this miscalculation," said the stranger, his voice an odd mix, thought Emmet. Eastern European, maybe?

"And yes, I was here waiting for you and Mr. Ford to return. It was a calamity, buildings shaken, windows blown out of anything close to the harbor, some docks destroyed, and small boats sunk. Some people were injured, dozens, perhaps hundreds, but I have not heard of any deaths, thank God." He paused, then inquired, "Do you have the money we agreed upon?"

Was that a Romanian or Polish accent? Emmet wondered.

"Of course," said Liebold. "Did you bring what you said you have?"

"I did," said the stranger.

Emmet heard papers shuffling around and spreading open on what he supposed was a table or countertop.

"Do you know what you're looking at, Mr. Liebold?" asked the stranger.

There was silence for what seemed like a long time to Emmet. Then, in a voice that seemed to verge on anger, Liebold replied, "I...am...overseeing the building of the best bomber planes ever engineered, patrol boats that can locate submarines, armor-plated tanks, personnel trucks, amphibious vehicles that can float then hit the beaches driving like a jeep, and numerous other bombs, such as this incredible weapon of war. I *know* what I'm looking at," he said, drawing a breath. "Now, I must ask how you came upon these plans for this...instrument?"

There was silence for a moment, then the stranger said," Have you heard of a man named Oppenheimer?"

"The physicist?" Liebold inquired.

"The same," said the stranger.

"Of course."

"I've worked with him on some projects. This is a thing that he has labored on, a theory, for some years now. But it is no longer a theory. It is a realm of science never fully understood before now. It will be an unparalleled source of immense power. Theoretically, it will be able to deliver electricity to millions of people, much more efficiently than coal or oil. But it can also be the source of a military weapon, the likes of which no one has ever seen. It is beyond imagination. We know the Germans are working on such things, but they are way behind. My consortium of like-minded people, true Americans, such as you and I, would like to help the Germans succeed in their endeavors and they will do so if they have these blueprints. Also, they would pay handsomely for this information. You must know this, too, or you would never have been open to this singular, momentous, offer I am bringing to you today. I would have offered it to the Germans myself, but I do not have the relationship with them that you and Mr. Ford do."

There was more silence, then the rustling around of papers again.

"Mr. Ford and I do have an extraordinarily strong relationship with the Fuhrer and his staff. We have for years due to our automotive plant in Cologne."

"So, who will you sell these to, Mr. Liebold?" asked the stranger. "Himmler? Goering?"

Liebold said, "No, we will not go the route of the usual military food chain. They cannot be directly connected to this transaction, or their internal arguments could delay this project for years," said Liebold, with more than a note of braggadocio. "No, it will be someone more at my level. A man the Fuhrer can trust, as Mr. Ford trusts me. His personal secretary controls all information that comes or goes with Hitler. The man referred to as the Deputy Fuhrer."

"Rudolf Hess?" asked the stranger.

Liebold paused, smiled, then said, "That's all I'll say, other than thank you. I believe our business is completed."

"Well, then," said the stranger. "I'll be on my way, but I would like something more than a handshake to take back to my colleagues. Perhaps a letter with an agreement signed by yourself?"

Liebold hesitated. "Isn't the money enough?"

"My colleagues will want to know that the plans went into the right hands, someone who can assure they will be placed into the hands of the Fuhrer...."

For several moments, there was silence. Then, "I can only write something of an obscure nature," said Liebold. "A letter of gratitude on Mr. Ford's stationery will have to do."

"Very well," said the stranger.

There was a rustle of paper and a scratching of an ink pen.

"My colleagues will be pleased," said the man. "Now, I must be on my way. It was good to meet you, sir. Our regards to Mr. Ford. Heil Hitler."

Upon hearing this, Emmet looked around, he could never make it back to his room without being seen. He didn't want Liebold to know that he'd been overheard while he brokered his traitorous deal. With most of the rooms now vacant after the harbor explosion, perhaps he could find a door that had been left unlocked. His heart pounded as he looked around, finally making the call to go to the nearest guest room, hoping beyond hope it might be open. If it wasn't he'd be standing there, obvious to all, he'd been listening through the door.

Running would be too loud even on the carpeted floors. He was ten steps away from the nearest room but with his long legs, Emmet made it five big, quiet steps.

He grabbed the doorknob and turned. It opened and he ducked inside, closing the door as quietly as he could. He hadn't had the time to think through it all, but now as he took some deep breaths trying to calm himself, he couldn't get past the question he kept asking himself.

Why would FBI Branch Director John Serey disguise himself and bring plans for some sort of bomb, or war weapon, or whatever it was, to Liebold, Ford's right-hand man, and a person of questionable motives at best?

FORTY-SIX

When Emmet came down to the lobby, Ford was at the clerk's desk completing some paperwork. Liebold was next to him whispering in his ear. He was not holding the cardboard tube that Emmet had seen the stranger bring to him. Emmet assumed Liebold had probably taken the blueprints from the tube and folded them into his suitcase. He would not have had time to hand them off to someone else.

Ford finished his business with the hotel desk clerk and turned his attention to Liebold. He held his pointer finger to his lips indicating that he did not want Liebold to say anything more in the crowded lobby.

Liebold looked around as if to see if anyone was listening to him. His eyes scanned the lobby, then rose to the staircase where Emmet was descending. Their eyes locked.

Emmet paused, then realized he must act as if everything was normal, they were just getting their things from the hotel and moving to the next one. He continued down the stairs into the lobby. He spied Bennett standing amongst a pile of luggage, chewing gum, and twirling a wristwatch by its leather strap like it was a miniature airplane propeller.

Emmet strolled over, his small bag slung over his shoulder, and approached Bennett. "Are you preparing to fly away with that watch?" Emmet joked.

Bennett looked down and chuckled. "Ha. Didn't know I was even doing that." He paused, then leaned toward Emmet. "Isn't it kinda, you know, suspicious, that the boat we came here in got blown up?"

"Yes," said Emmet. "What are your thoughts on that untimely event?"

Bennett paused before answering, then looked into Emmet's eyes, leaned forward, and whispered. "I think someone is trying to kill Mr. Ford." He paused as if waiting for a reaction from Emmet and added, "Again. Like with the poison in the glass tube that guy put in the mailbox. What do you think, Mr. Scotland Yard, detective?"

Emmet shrugged. "I wonder what was on the ship?" said Emmet and added, "Besides a crew that turned out to be mostly German sailors who, perhaps, might be devoted to their Fuhrer."

Bennett stood straight, his face blank, eyes blinking rapidly as if the suggestion hit him in the face like a baseball. "You think?" said Bennett, surprised. "Why would they do that? I mean, Mr. Ford and Hitler are friends, kind of."

"Do you believe that Nazi madman has friends?" asked Emmet.

Bennett looked around the room, then back to Ford who waved him over.

"Let's go," said Bennett to Emmet. "The boss is ready to leave."

The two men went to Ford, Bennett grabbed Ford's luggage, and then they left the bustling lobby of the hotel.

Outside the sounds of sirens, cars honking horns, and policemen blowing whistles, the din sounded like an orchestrated cacophony. The sun was high in the sky, beaming brilliantly as if nothing had happened, the sky still blue and clear and promising. The scents of restaurants returning to their business produced smells that made Emmet's mouth water and his stomach growl.

"I heard that, Mr. MacWain," said Ford. "I know a starving stomach when I hear it. Shall we stop for lunch on the way to the new hotel? I, too, am famished."

"Sure," said Emmet. "The sooner, the better."

"I could eat the south side of a northbound horse, right now," Bennett added. "How about you, Ernie?"

Liebold looked at Bennett and replied, "You know I hate that. If you must refer to me, please call me by my given name, Ernest. But to answer your question, I am not starving but could, perhaps, have a libation and nibble on something."

"Maybe you've got a nervous stomach or something," Bennett continued.

"And why would that be?"

"Geez, I dunno. Maybe all the projects you're working on."

Liebold scowled at Bennett and was about to say something when Ford interrupted.

"Why are you two bickering again? Please have a little decorum and act like *men*, if not gentlemen."

As they looked about for a café that was not too crowded, Emmet pondered the situation. Liebold obviously told Ford about the plans he'd just taken into his possession. Did Bennett know as well? If so, what did that mean? Was he an accomplice in this transaction and in agreement with what it could mean, not only to the United States but to the world? Or did he see it as one more thing that Liebold was doing to win Ford's favor and push Bennett out of the picture?

Only time could tell, and time was a commodity of which Emmet had precious little.

The incongruous group continued on and found a café near the Hotel Gloria. They parked and Liebold, a man who did not like to miss a meal, immediately vacated the car, and darted into the restaurant.

"Geez," said Bennett. "That chowhound broke his leash to be the first to grab some grub."

Ford turned his head to address Bennett. "Are you and Ernest at odds again, Harry?"

"We always will be, sir."

"And why is that?"

"You know why."

"Remind me, because I don't like to have to bear discontent among my closest associates."

Bennett looked out the window, pondering his next words, watching the horde of unsettled masses darting about, still confused by the after-effect of the bomb exploding a ship in the harbor. A ship that had brought them here. Without turning back to Ford, Bennett said, "Because he can't be trusted."

Ford continued to stare at Bennett until he turned his face back toward him. "We'll speak of this matter later, Harry."

Emmet continued to look as if he had no interest in the conversation of bickering co-workers, but he most certainly did. He made a mental note of the discontent between Ford's closest personal employees. He might be able to utilize this mistrust at another time. Perhaps to gain information that could answer some of the questions that were increasing every day.

In the café, they found Liebold already seated at a table with a cup of coffee and a basket of *Pao Frances* in front of him from which he had already consumed several of the tasty rolls.

The rest of the group sat down and ordered their choices, then ate in silence. It was uncomfortable for Emmet, but what did he have to talk about among this entourage of men who all seemed flawed, distrustful, and got along as well as a pack of wolves would with a pride of lions.

The local food included *Bauru*, a hard-crusted sandwich with the inside soft bread scooped out and replaced with cheese, tomatoes, pickles, and roasted beef. *Moqueca capixaba*, fish, lime juice, and coriander, with vegetables such as onions, tomatoes, and garlic, all nicely colored with *annatto*, a spice similar to paprika. Emmet enjoyed the Bauru and had just finished it when he happened to glance out the window and spied the man whom he had seen dart into Liebold's room to arrange their deal.

Emmet excused himself to the restroom but acted as if he wasn't sure where it was, a subterfuge that allowed him to walk to the front of the café and watch the hotel across the street where, surprisingly, he clearly saw FBI Branch Director Serey, now without the theatrical wig and facial hair but in the same striped brown suit as the man that had met with Liebold. He trotted up the steps with an energized pace, going to the same place where Emmet was staying, The Hotel Gloria.

Emmet's beliefs now confirmed, he wondered why Serey would be foolish enough to wear that same distinguishable suit.

***

Inside the hotel, Serey went straight to the hotel elevator. He knew where he was going, had been there before. He also knew the woman he was going to see would be in her room, perhaps still sleeping off last night's exhaustive show.

"May I help you, sir?" the front desk clerk inquired.

"No, thanks," said Serey, walking briskly, carrying a thin attaché. "I'm a guest here."

Then he turned and walked across the hotel's lush, grand lobby and into the elevator, where the doors closed like vertical lips keeping their secrets.

FORTY-SEVEN

COMPIEGNE, FRANCE

Hemingway, with his sons, Patrick and Gregory, hunkered behind a building that had been bombed out by the Germans nearly six months earlier. The loss of Compiègne initiated the end of the formal war in France and the taking of most of the country by the Nazi regime. An Armistice was reached in the same city where one had been signed in 1918 when Germany had lost the first war. Now, in an historical irony that Hitler had arranged, France had officially surrendered to the Germans, part of which would be under the watchful eye of the German-friendly Vichy in the south.

As the war progressed throughout Europe, Compiègne was under the control of the Nazis and a reluctant peace was initiated. But it was a fragile peace as the civilian resistance, called by many names: freedom fighters, *maquis*, partisans, French underground, and other more derogatory names by the Germans, were in full battle mode.

Hemingway had traveled to Compiègne to do a story for Collier's magazine about the French resistance. Now, for want of ego-centric prestige and a couple thousand dollars for an article he needed to stay alive to write, he and his sons were in harm's way.

Gunshots rang out as resistance fighters boldly performed impromptu attacks on the occupied city, occasionally taking out

German soldiers assigned to hold the city. The Nazis often responded with a hail of bullets, bombs, and finally, tanks they pulled in from the guarded perimeter of the city. The French onslaught was typically quelled quickly after that, only to be repeated another time in another place. France's guerilla soldiers' goal was to weaken the Germans even if they could not defeat them. Many of them paid for these assaults with their lives.

One of the Panzer tanks had just fired a round into a building where resistance fighters had taken higher ground and continued a fight that seemed as ludicrous as David with his sling against the giant Goliath. The parapet walls above the roof of this once-residential building tumbled down and missed Hemingway, Patrick, and Gregory by inches. Hemingway snapped some pictures and told his sons to follow him. Closely. He was trembling with fear but tried to hide it as he had already seen Gregory, whom he insisted on calling Gigi, with streaks of tears running through the battle dust on his face. He realized bringing his sons into a war zone to *write a story* may have been the stupidest thing he'd ever done, and he'd done plenty.

"Look, Papa!" said Patrick, trying not to point and give a target to the Nazis.

Hemingway whirled around and saw a group of resistance fighters, hiding in the shadows and rubble of an apartment building whose upper floors were demolished, providing the fighters with a sniper's nest and good cover. One of them was waving them over, though doing so might give away their position. Hemingway's heart was pounding, sweat dripping from his chin.

He'd made an inexcusable mistake but now he needed to find a way to get his sons to safety. While he wore a press card clipped to his shirt pocket, he learned that the Nazis did not conform to typical Western values that prohibited reporters from being targeted. Wearing a helmet and a soldier's uniform didn't help. From a distance, he looked like any infantryman, which meant he was a target for some young, sharpshooting Nazi sniper. But he had to make a decision and soon. He saw the young resistance fighter waving him over again while trying to stay under protected cover himself.

"All right, boys," said Hemingway. "We're getting out of here. You guys run toward that foxhole where that soldier who waved us over. I want you to run zig-zag, you know, back and forth but not too far apart. I'll run behind you and give you cover. Don't look back. If I get hit, you keep going. If Frenchie has communications, you try to get through to a correspondence officer by the name of Alan Moorehead. He's with a group of reporters in Paris, south of here. He's a friend of mine and knows the ropes. He'll get you home. Understand?"

Patrick nodded; his eyes now filled with tears. Gregory stood, hugging himself, shivering.

"Listen, boys, I know I messed up bringing you along," said Hemingway. "I didn't think we'd get into the thick of it. Thought we were just following the troops as they moved forward and cleared areas. But we're going to get out of here, so help me God. That tank has moved on to another block with most of the Nazis. We've got some distance between us. This is our best chance."

The boys stood, ready to go. Hemingway gave a thumbs-up to the resistance fighters. Two of them raised their rifles and began shooting at the building from where the Germans had last fired shots.

"Go," said Hemingway and the boys shot off, running like rabbits, zig-zagging as their father had told them to. Hemingway ran behind them, trying to make himself as big as he could to shelter the boys. He heard the crack of a rifle behind him that kicked up some dust about three feet to his right, but the shooter must have been firing off a pot shot while he kept himself barricaded from the resistance fighter's hail of bullets.

The boys dove into the dark cave of rubble, then Hemingway squeezed in behind them. As he crawled in behind their saviors. He quipped, "*Bonne journée mes amis!*"

One of the French snipers replied, "*Imbécile!*"

Hemingway shrugged, then turned to his sons. "You young men, okay?"

Patrick nodded but Gregory just sat, his arms around himself, trembling.

"You guys did great!" Hemingway exalted. Then he turned to the resistance fighters and stuck out his hand to the soldier who had not called him an imbecile. "Ernest Hemingway," he said.

"*Le célèbre auteur*?" asked the soldier who gripped his hand and smiled widely. "I have read your books! *L'adieu aux armes!*"

"*Oui? Merci*," Hemingway said. "When I wrote it, I thought it might stop wars. *Comment t'appelles-tu?*

"I am Pierre Rocuet," said the young Frenchman.

"I'm very grateful to you, sir. *Merci*," said Hemingway, flashing his smile again. "Now, how do we get outta here?"

Pierre pointed to the back of their makeshift foxhole and with much enthusiasm, said, "*Les tunnels!*"

"Merci, mon amie," said Hemingway. "Bonne chance."

Hemingway looked through the darkness as his eyes adjusted from the sun to the dark and he saw a hole carved into the ground. A tunnel that, hopefully, led to salvation. He unclipped an Army flashlight from his utility belt and crawled toward the hole. He turned back to his sons and said, "Let's go boys, while the gettin' is good."

"Where are we going, Papa?" Patrick asked.

Hemingway looked back to his sons. He wasn't quite sure where they could go that might be safe. Then he thought of something. "We're going to head south. It's under the control of the Vichy but it's better than sticking around all these damn Nazis. I have an acquaintance down there in the wine country. Nice chateau, you know, like a castle. She can put us up until we can book a safe fare back to the U.S. You'll get a kick out of it," Hemingway concluded, trying to keep his toothy grin and give the boys some comfort. But as he led the way down through the tunnel, flashlight in hand, he knew they were not in a good place. They would be lucky to get out of northern France without being caught, or worse.

FORTY-EIGHT

THE HOTEL GLORIA, BRAZIL

Josephine Baker was inventorying her bags and needed supplies for their trip. Claude, her butler, was assisting.

Josephine: "Costumes?"

Claude: "*Verifier,* or shall I say 'check'?"

Josephine: "Well, you are working on your English."

Claude: "Check."

Josephine: "Makeup?"

Claude, grinning: "Check."

Josephine: "Food?"

Claude: "Check."

Josephine: "Booze?"

Claude: "Of course."

Josephine: "Okay, that's all for me," she chuckled. "Now, let's get to everyone else's needs."

"Including the refugees, we smuggled out of France?" Claude asked.

"No, Claude. I am sure they do not want to go back to the place they just escaped."

"Good point."

"Many of them have already found places to go, some hoping to get into the U.S.—good luck on that—and some here, in Brazil. Others are making their way to Ecuador and Bolivia."

"Hmm, I've heard the U.S. is not as welcoming as it used to be. They've established a quota. Particularly with the Jews. Once the annual quota is met, they turn refugees away. A ship, the *M.S. St. Louis* was denied entry into first Cuba, then the U.S, then Canada."

"You're right, Claude. The U.S. is very welcoming to many of us who were born there, but if your skin is black, or you are a Jew, or if you're Asian, or Hispanic, or Native American, the same indigenous people that welcomed them in when *they* were refugees, they don't want you there, even if you were born there. They don't like anyone unless you are white-bread, churchgoing, middle-to-high-class, nine-to-fivers, who do not want change for their pale existence...." She was standing up now, waving her long, lithe arms around, as if she were doing one of her banana dances.

"Oh my. I think I did what you call, touched a nerve?"

Josephine strolled over to Claude and placed her hand on his cheek. "No, Claude. It's just that, I was born there and grew up there. I know how I was treated as an underclass citizen. But I also know that if you believe in yourself, you can rise above it all. The only limits people have are those they place on themselves. If I could become what I am, then anyone can."

Claude smiled with admiration. "I don't concur, my dear. You are special. One of a kind, as they say."

"Oh, Claude," said Josephine. "You are so sweet. Why haven't I married you yet?"

"I'm flattered, Mademoiselle, but I'd like to stay in your company and my experience is that your husbands do not."

Josephine laughed so hard, she had to hold her stomach and try to get her breath back. "You are too funny, Claude."

Just then, there was a light knock at their hotel room door. They were not expecting company, so they followed their usual routine. They quietly and quickly found their weapons, Claude going for his combat knife and Josephine her pistol.

Josephine discreetly hid one gun under a sofa cushion and another in a robe with large pockets. Claude hid his knife up his sleeve where a special sheath loaded with a spring release held the deadly dagger, ready to be ejected for a quick throw. They were now ready to greet their unexpected guest.

Josephine perched herself on a divan, colorfully embroidered with mystical-looking peacocks, while she attempted to cover her see-through negligee with her red silk robe.

Claude opened the door.

"Hello, Claude," said the guest.

"Oh, hello, *officier de police*," Claude replied.

"*C'est le directeur du FBI, monsieur*," said Serey, utilizing his familiarity with the language. Having darted into his own room at the Hotel Gloria, Serey was no longer wearing his "disguise," but he did have a document rolled up, held under his arm.

Josephine stood up and floated across the room with her usual grace. "*Bonjour, directeur Serey.*"

"*Bonjour, Mademoiselle Baker,*" Serey replied. "I hope you're doing well."

"Always, John. What's new?"

"I need to ask another favor."

"Why did I know that?" said Josephine. "What is it this time, John? You want me to write more secrets on my underwear instead of my brassier?"

Serey gave a crooked half-smile. "No, but thanks for the thought. This one is a little bigger request, I'm afraid."

Josephine sauntered around the room, slowly making her way to the window where she looked out over the unsettled harbor as if she needed the time to make up her mind.

Serey walked up behind her. A breeze blew into the room through the open window and pushed the fragrance of her expensive perfume into his nostrils. Goose bumps ran across his skin, and he shivered, though it must've been a balmy, seventy-five degrees in her luxuriant room.

"Does this have anything to do with that ship blowing up in the harbor?" asked Josephine.

Serey was silent for just a moment then, knowing she could tell if he was lying—as she always did—he decided on the truth. "Yup," he answered. Then he got to the punchline. "We're going to need your boat to get to France."

"Who is "we?" she said, turning toward him, stepping closer, into his space where she utilized the power of proximity to a gorgeous woman, for which most men had no defense. Her face was so close to Serey's, he could feel the warmth of her breath and smell her lush perfume. The formula was intoxicating, and he felt weak. Never a nervous man, now he felt his throat parch, his tongue tie, and a stir in his loins that made him extremely uncomfortable.

"*We*' is Henry Ford, and his personal entourage of Ernest Liebold, secretary, and his, shall we say, *enforcer*, Harry Bennett."

"That's all?" said Josephine, her eyes narrowing like a cat's.

"There's another man, Emmet MacWain. He's a former Scotland Yard Inspector who is, uh, sort of working with me on a case."

"Sort of? That's a weak word selection, John. Sounds kinda half-ass, if you know what I mean. Is this a *case* that will be ongoing while on my ship?"

"No," Serey said, taking a step back. "But, uh...we need to talk about something."

"I thought we were," said Josephine. Then turning to Claude, said, "I think we are going to need a drink. What will you have, John?"

"Well, I am working, so I shouldn't..."

"Settle down, John. I need more information and I can see that you're uncomfortable," she said, placing the warm palm of her hand on his face. "Claude, would you be so kind as to make our guest and me some Negronis?"

"I'd be honored," said Claude, with a crooked smile that assured his comment was in jest. He made the drinks: One shot of gin, one shot of sweet vermouth, and one shot of Campari, a curl of orange rind as a twist, and he quickly returned to the living room.

Josephine was sitting with Serey on the couch. He looked very nervous, and she was her usual model of cool. "Wow, that was quick, Claude. Agent Serey hasn't even started to tell me why he is so uncomfortable," she quipped.

Claude placed the drinks on a small table, along with a bowl of olives and a plate of sliced cheeses.

Serey quickly grabbed his Negroni and took a gulp.

"Wow, John," said Josephine. "We didn't even clink glasses."

"Oh, excuse me," said Serey. "To um...freedom."

"Good one," said Josephine and tapped her glass against his.

Serey took another gulp, then went into it. "So, I should say, I not only need your ship but your chateau as well."

Josephine grinned and leaned forward, a salacious grin on her face. "Is that all you need, honey?"

Sweat beaded on Serey's forehead and he gulped more Negroni. He leaned forward, looking directly into his hostesses' eyes. "Here is what it is. Henry Ford and Thomas Edison were friends, Edison was a mentor, personally and professionally, to Ford and used to employ him before Ford became what he is today."

"An asshole?" said Josephine.

"Well, I won't argue with you on that. But I mean the most successful automobile manufacturer in the world. And, admittedly, he's also become a target due to his, uh, antisemitic views."

"I am well aware of that, John. He and that other bastard, Liebold, that you want me to take on my vessel, published that wonderful 'newspaper.' *The Dearborn Independent,* that spewed hatred for anyone who wasn't white, male, and Christian, throughout America. Do you wonder why I live in France? And now those fuckers are pals with Hitler? Do you know what that bastard has done to my beautiful, adopted country? Do you want to see it?" Josephine was sitting up now, her face flushed with anger.

Serey held up his hand in a gesture to stop, like a cop directing traffic. "Listen. Please just sit down and listen. You've been a wonderful asset to our country and especially to the European allies. We wouldn't have any of the extremely important information we have now, if not for you. But we need more so that we can try to turn the tide of this war."

"*Your* country is not even in it, yet, John," said Josephine, her voice quivering with anger.

"*I* am," said Serey, his patience slipping.

For a moment, neither of them spoke. Claude came in and brought fresh Negroni's. To break the silence he quipped, "Did this turn into a mime show?"

Josephine was the first to crack up and let out a guffaw of laughter.

Serey was slow to return the humor but eventually chuckled a bit and smiled. Then, he went back to business. "Josephine, I have to tell you something, if you will let me continue."

"Go ahead. I'm not stopping you."

"As I said, there was a package sent to Ford's winter home in Ft. Myers, Florida, several weeks ago. A man, supposedly a rabbi, stole the package from Ford's mailbox. It held a sealed, glass tube. The man opened the tube and removed the wax and cork that sealed it. He inhaled whatever was in the otherwise empty tube and died immediately."

Josephine was silent for a moment, then said, "Why would he do that?"

"It's an odd, and long story, but I'll try to condense it. Henry Ford admired Edison so much, that as Edison was dying, Ford asked his son, Charles, to try to capture Edison's last breath before he died. Edison never knew when his last breath would come, so forty-two vials were filled until he died. Then, they went missing. But each year, someone sends a tube to Ford. Ford opens the tubes and inhales the breath of his long, lost friend. He believes it gives him wisdom and strength."

Josephine's face was a mixed mask, morphing from disgust and unbelievability to an almost comical frown.

"That's the weirdest damn thing I've ever heard," she said, finally. "So, someone is trying to kill the wannabee Nazi car magnate? Why should I give a damn? I say bravo."

Serey took a breath, his eyes blinking rapidly, and now a dollop of sweat trickled from his bald scalp, down the side of his face. He swallowed, then placed his hand on top of hers and said, "Because, my dear diva, the return address on the package that held the tube, that killed that man, was *your* chateau's address in France."

FORTY-NINE

After Emmet and the rest of Ford's group checked into the Hotel Gloria, he decided to try to send a telegraph to The Royal Palm Hotel in Ft. Myers, to see if he might be able to leave a message for Bessie. The hotel clerk assured him he could and led him to the communications room near the front desk.

Emmet wrote: Dear Bessie. How are you doing? Did you begin your job with the circus yet? I am in Brazil now, but we will be leaving for France soon when we find passage. This old man thinks of you often. If you get this message, please telegraph me at The Hotel Gloria in Rio de Janeiro. Affectionately, Emmet.

Emmet found his face was a bit flushed. He was embarrassed by his feelings for such a young lady. But she had seemed as interested in him as he in her, and he hoped she would still be there, in Ft. Myers, when he returned. He went back to his room to lie down for a short nap. He was worn out from a number of things that taxed him.

Emmet laid down and thought about the drive to Ft. Myers and the Donnybrooks with the unlikeable Harry Bennett. Meeting Ford and his distrustful minions, the most dangerous of which Emmet knew now, was Liebold. The long ocean trip to Brazil with the perils onboard that almost killed him twice, and then Liebold shooting the two sailors who attacked him. *Why?* Did he really care what happened to him? Emmet thought not. Perhaps they knew something that Liebold did not want to be revealed?

Emmet tried to let it all go and just enjoy the nap, but the memories kept coming, like a jigsaw puzzle that begged to be finished so one could see its final image. He recalled the bumpy flight into Fordlandia, now just a decaying part of an unforgiving jungle. The roaming cattle branded with Nazi symbols. The beautiful but strange local woman, the *bruja*, Rocio, who helped make him well—overnight, was it? The mystery of that entire odyssey—for surely that's what it was—had been interesting but quite challenging. A brief respite found in a short nap would be greatly appreciated, if he could let it all just go, for a moment...

Emmet was just dozing off, that wonderful feeling of floating just before he would drift off to sweet dreams of either the wonderful women who had been a part of his adventurous life, or the nightmares of the many murder cases that he'd investigated that would flash through his mind like horror movies in a dark theater.

There was an urgent knock at the door to Emmet's room. "Jesus," he groaned, wearily. What now? He reached into the nightstand next to his bed and took out his Smith & Wesson .38 special, a trusty sidekick from his years as an inspector who had been to a score of places that required its use. It fitted his hand like a wedding ring.

He went to his door and, without thinking about it, stood against the wall to one side of the door as if waiting for a bullet to bore its way in. "Who is it?" he asked.

A voice, barely above a whisper answered. "It's Serey."

Emmet unlocked the door and opened it, still standing behind it, his gun at the ready, held hip high.

Serey was looking the other way and Emmet shut the door abruptly. Serey whirled, saw the gun, and locked eyes with Emmet.

"Would you like to explain why you went to Liebold's room?"

"What are you talking about?" Serey huffed.

"C'mon, John," said Emmet, exasperated. "That ridiculous costume you wore might have fooled someone else but not me." He cocked the gun.

Serey squinted at him, his jaw working as if he were chewing on leather. "I can't say, but you must trust me."

"I don't trust anyone anymore, John," said Emmet.

"You're getting jaded."

"I'm getting tired and pissed off. You've forced me into this global run around and now I see you dressed up like some dandy. As I was hired as an inspector, I took the liberty of listening in on your conversation. Either Liebold is the stupidest man I've ever known not to see through your attempt at a disguise, or he doesn't care..."

"He and I have never met so he does not know who I am."

"Okay. But Ford does. What would you have done had he seen you?"

"I suspect he wouldn't recognize me. People like him are so infatuated with themselves that they seldom take a good look at anything else."

"That doesn't make any difference to me. What does, is that you went to his room for a prearranged meeting. You brought him some blueprints, evidently of some sort of bomb or weapon. You know these men are dealing with the Nazis, that Ford is friends with this madman, Hitler. Tell me why I shouldn't shoot you right now as a traitor to your country?"

"I'm sorry, Emmet, I can't tell you. If you feel you must shoot me, go ahead. But know this, if you do, you might mess up a chance for us to do something bold. Something that could allow us to strike a blow at the Nazis, our nation's biggest threat ever."

By now, Serey's delivery had reached the fervor of one of President Roosevelt's heart-wrenching, motivational speeches. Emmet put his thumb on the hammer of the gun and let it down carefully releasing the taught trigger.

"Why did you bring me into this thing anyway, John? Tell me the truth because you know, I will know if you're lying. I might not kill you, but I will damn sure walk away from this debacle."

"Because you are smart and can be trusted. And now, I need you to trust me a little longer. I, *we*, do have a plan and I need you to be a part of it. I brought you in, initially to look into the man who was murdered at Ford's house. I think you know more about that than I do, and we will conclude that case, but that event has led, shall I say to an international issue. An *opportunity*, actually. But I must ask you to be patient. Work with me. You and I worked together on the Hemingway issue, standing side by side as we were attacked by a mob. We fought together, were wounded together, and made it through together. And we located a Nazi spy working in America. I'm pleading with you to remember that and work with me one more time."

Emmet shook his head, exasperated. "I don't like this cloak-and-dagger shite."

"I don't either, but we are playing a role that will change the future. America is going to be pulled into this war, sooner than later. All it will take is one ... *thing*. I don't know what it will be, but it will be provocative. We need to be prepared for that and the best way we can do that is to try to get ahead of the enemies we have in-state, in our own country. I must tell you something first, Emmet..."

"I'm still listening."

Serey took a deep breath and went to the window as if he needed to look outside to find the fortitude to continue. He inhaled deeply, then turned back to Emmet. "Deputy Abram is dead."

Emmet started toward Serey. He was not sure why, but he felt a violence rising in himself that was like a dark and deadly specter come a calling. One that he knew too well and did not like. Its name was *anger* and it rose through Emmet's body like a fire. He felt its heat, pushing his body's blood into his head like a thermometer.

Serey began, "I know you took him under your wing...he told me you and he had figured out some things about the death of the so-called rabbi and he'd told you he was working with us undercover..."

"Who killed him?" Emmet interrupted through clenched teeth. "And how?"

Serey's lips quivered, and his eyes watered. The muscles in his jaws worked as if he were chewing something and it tasted like bile. "We believe it was a group of the Silver Legion, also known as the Silver Shirts because of the outfits they wear. They are antisemitic and encourage and participate in violence against Jews. A knock-off group of Klansmen who call themselves Christians but are anything but. There is a group of them in Ft. Myers."

"You answered what, not who, or how."

Serey looked at his feet as if noticing them for the first time. It allowed him to look away from Emmet, whose rage was something he'd seen before, and it was frightening. He was uneasy and his voice broke as he said, "They crucified him on a cross in the woods. Some campers found him. They say it appeared he was struck by lightning in a thunderstorm that went through as he was being tortured. My deputy director from the Miami office, Robert Holly, is in Ft. Myers now, leading the investigation. We will find..."

Emmet cut him off, "Who did it?"

Serey was hesitant, then said, "Holly has been canvasing neighborhoods. A woman named Lily Fields approached Holly and said she had talked to Abram briefly the night he went missing. They were at a church function if you can believe that. She took a liking to him and when she went looking for him the next day, she couldn't find him. She ran into Sheriff Ross and she said he acted strangely. He told her that Abram had just up and quit and moved back home."

Emmet had been walking back and forth, chin in hand, his pace increasing as Serey told his story. Now, Emmet stopped and found he was standing in front of a mirror. He looked at himself, feeling impotent and hollow, angered about the horrible story, about the loss of a young man who was only trying to do right, and finally, angry at himself.

He should have told Abram to be careful, to watch his back, to be especially careful because monsters do exist, and to not ask too many questions without either him, or Serey, there to back him up. Anger gripped him until he could stand it no longer. He suddenly drove his fist into the mirror, smashing it into a thousand smaller mirrors that fell to the carpet of the hotel room and looked like a thousand eyes peering up at Emmet and seeing a monster aborning. His fist dripped blood as if he had just murdered someone.

Then, someone knocked at the door.

***

Liebold slid into a phone booth and made the call to the number he had been given. It was a German phone number, more specifically, a Nazi phone number.

"*Hallo*," said a voice, cool and calculated. "This is Barbie."

"Hello, *Hauptsturnfurer* Barbie," said Liebold. "We met when the Fuhrer held a gala for my employer, Mr. Henry Ford, in Cologne?"

Barbie sat for a moment, trying to remember who he met at the event. He did recall meeting Herr Ford, who was a close friend to the Fuhrer. He was with another man, who stuck close by his side, though Barbie could not recall his face or name.

"Yes," said Barbie, lying and wondering why one of Ford's people would be calling him. "I think I recall meeting you."

"Very good, sir," said Liebold. "I have come across something that I would like to share with you and, of course the Fuhrer."

Barbie thought perhaps the man was going to send a case of wine, or something to endear him to the Fuhrer, so he could meet with him. He knew that Ford, the car manufacturer, was friends with Hitler and that Ford had signed an agreement with the German military to supply trucks for their Wehrmacht. So, he would hear him out.

"What is it you would like to share, Herr Liebold?" asked Barbie, looking at his fingernails, checking to see if they had any residual blood after his morning torturing prisoners.

"I have a design for a bomb so powerful, one of them would ensure the victory for Germany."

Now, Barbie sat up, his heartbeat accelerated, his interest piqued. "This is very interesting Herr Liebold. Tell me more..."

FIFTY

Emmet wrapped his bleeding hand with a towel. The blood quickly soaked through. "Are you expecting someone, John?" he said, his tone gruff.

Serey quietly said, "Yes."

Emmet went to the door and opened it. In the hallway was a beautiful black woman, her curled hair pasted to her forehead. Her shapely figure was lithe, barely hidden by a shimmering dress that extended to just below her pelvis. Her huge eyes were as deep and dark as oil wells but sparkled with mischief, set into a beautiful face, its skin the color of coffee with sweet cream. Her fragrance was like that of fresh-cut flowers. She pursed her thick lips while her eyes assessed Emmet from head to foot. They locked on the bloody towel around Emmet's fist.

"I see you're a southpaw," she said, as her mouth formed into a salacious grin.

Behind her was a giant man in full butler attire, pressed black suit, white shirt with wing-tipped collar, though no white gloves. Shoes polished so glossy one could see one's image in them. Around his neck was a silver and red-striped ribbon that held a bronze medal that Emmet recognized as the *"Croix du Combatant"* or, Combatant's Cross, which was only awarded to soldiers who battled on the frontline, those that witnessed and dealt with the fiercest of military combat. Emmet immediately respected him.

Emmet locked eyes with the big man, assessing him as the Frenchman assessed him in return. A common trait among former soldiers who had seen many enemies and were always ready to encounter another should the need arise. They each gave the other a slight nod that acknowledged their unspoken personal evaluations of each other.

Josephine Baker noticed and stuck out her hand to Emmet, who took it, his hand under hers, accompanied by a light bow.

"I'm Josephine Baker, sir," she said, her words dripping with her natural sexuality. She wasn't pretentious. It was just the way she was. She noticed his nostrils flare, as he smelled her scent that held traces of patchouli, carnations, and vanilla. "You like my perfume, huh?" It wasn't a question. "It's *Tabu*, my favorite thing," she said, then licked her lips. "Sometimes it's all I wear."

"Emmet MacWain, Madam," he said, blushing, his neck suddenly cool with sweat. "I know who you are. I've seen the billboards and advertisements." I'm sorry, my business here has not allowed me time to see your show."

Josephine smiled, "Maybe we can change that. I love your accent. Not a Brit, you're not stiff, upper-lipped enough for that. I'm guessing...a Scot?"

"Yes, mum," he said. He had never seen anyone quite like her. He'd never met anyone so comfortable with who they were, and he was immediately fond of her. She was beautiful, flirtatious, quick-witted, and humorous. He noted she was not wearing a brassiere and her dress was practically see-through. He tried not to stare.

"Mmm-mm," she said, with a carnivorous grin.

"May I ask what I can do for you?" said Emmet.

"Well, I guess, Mr. Serey did not tell you he had invited me to stop by..."

Emmet turned back to Serey, who was already red-faced and sweating more than usual.

"Eh...," Serey began, but Emmet cut him off.

"Well, Mr. Serey is not well practiced as a gentleman but, whatever your business is, please come in."

"Well, thank you, sir," said Josephine. "And this big guy behind me is my valet, Claude Durand."

Emmet extended his right hand—the one without blood dripping from it—to Durand. "Honored to meet you, sir," he said, his eyes acknowledging the medal.

"And you, sir," he replied, then, "Where did you serve?"

"I managed to go through several wars. The first when I was not much more than a boy, was the Battle of San Juan in Cuba."

"Oh, the cavalry with no horses?"

Emmet smiled, "Yes, the battle started before the horses arrived from the U.S."

"I heard of the battle. Roosevelt's Rough Riders. Remarkable. And you said that was your *first* war?"

"Yes, the other one was in the big war, in Cambrai, as well as other unpleasant places," said Emmet.

"Oh, my, what fun that was. No horses there either. All trench fighting." Claude paused, contemplating. "Were you one of the seventy-four by any chance?" He asked, referring to the seventy-four Scottish soldiers awarded the Victorian Cross.

"As a matter of fact, yes," Emmet replied.

"I was with the *Caimani del Piave*. Maybe you heard of us?"

Emmet shivered, recalling the stories of these men who swam the cold rivers in the night, with daggers held in their teeth, and attacked the enemy as quietly as Comanches. "Yes, I recall, the Americans referred to your team as 'The Alligators.' You fought along with the Italians?"

Claude nodded with pride.

Emmet nodded as well, the two men acknowledging each other's now historic military backgrounds.

Claude, looking at Emmet's hand wrapped in a bloody towel, said, "I did some first aid in the war." He turned to Josephine and inquired, "Madame, would you mind if I returned to our room to fetch my medical bag.? This soldier could use some first aid."

"Not at all, Claude," said Josephine, her eyes never leaving Emmet. "Please do."

Serey broke the moment. "Excuse me but I have to tell you both something of utmost importance and secrecy."

Emmet frowned, then looked at Josephine, puzzled.

"You must be a spy, too?" she said casually.

"Not at all," said Emmet. "I'm a former Scotland Yard Inspector and now, a victim of circumstance."

She laughed. "Yes, Mr. Serey here seems to attract that type." She looked back at Serey. "Go ahead, John."

Serey rubbed his face with one hand as if the gesture would help him say what he needed to say. "I need you both to return to France, as soon as possible."

"But we just met," said Josephine, grinning.

Emmet had to smile, as well.

"We have an opportunity to... get ahead of something. We need you, Josephine, specifically, to meet with some Nazis that are going to come to your chateau."

"Why would they come to my house, John?"

Serey stared at her for a moment, then glanced at Emmet.

He was about to answer when Claude came back. "Let's get that hand cleaned up, Mr. MacWain," he said.

"There's a sink over here," said Emmet, gesturing with his head toward the lavatory across the room. He unraveled his fist and wrist, holding his arm over the sink, while Claude pulled gauze and tape from his med kit. When Emmet finished washing the wound, he dabbed it off with the clean end of the bloody towel and held the hand over the sink. It dripped blood slowly from several lacerations across his knuckles.

"Not too bad, for a soldier," said Claude, with a grin. "Now, keep it over the sink while I apply some iodine. It will smart a bit."

Emmet nodded as Claude poured the red liquid over the wounds. Emmet's jaws flexed but he didn't make a sound as Claude gently cleaned and then dressed the wound, wrapping it with a roll of gauze and securing it with tape.

"There you are, sir," said Claude. "That should keep any infection out."

"Thank you, good sir," said Emmet. "I'm much obliged."

"You're most welcome," said Claude. Then, he turned toward Serey. "You were saying, sir?"

"I was just telling Miss Baker, that you need to return to France, as soon as possible. That some Nazi officers are coming to the chateau. I think you know why."

"No," said Claude. "I have no idea, but it is not uncommon for these German officers to stop in and check on us. They are, as you Americans say...nosey."

"They're about ready to get nosier. It seems there were two such officers who stopped by several weeks ago. They haven't been seen since."

Claude looked toward Josephine, raising his eyebrows in an unspoken question. She responded by stepping up to Serey as if to challenge him. Standing there, face to face, defiantly, she said, "That's because we killed them, John."

FIFTY-ONE

FORT MYERS, FLORIDA

Lily Fields stood in the shade of the Arcade Theater, waiting. She was nervous but driven. She only met Jason Abram one time, one evening at a church social, and then he disappeared. The odd thing was, she knew something had happened to him. But that one time, she had seen kindness in him she did not see in the local men who lived in her hometown of Ft. Myers, Florida. The ones that called her "chubby," or that she heard saying "oink, oink, oink," as they passed her on the street.

When she could not find him the next day, she became worried. When she found out he had been murdered the same night they met at the church dinner, she was appalled and angry. When Lily Fields got angry, she was a woman not to be trifled with.

It was her talk with Sheriff Carl Ross, the morning after the church gathering and she'd asked about the polite Deputy Sheriff, Jason Abram. Sheriff Ross said that Jason had suddenly quit and gone back home. Lily just knew that was not true. *Dang it, it was just an outright fib!* She believed in love at first sight, and she knew in her heart that something sparked between her and Jacob Abram. When she heard that he'd been found crucified and buried on a cross in the nearby woods, she could hear the voice of the Lord tell her, don't let those *bastards* get away with this. *Okay, maybe he didn't say, bastards*, thought Lily, but she knew *He* wanted her to help find the truth about what happened to that nice young man. She called the FBI's office in Miami the next day.

Now, she was waiting for the Deputy Director of the FBI's Miami bureau to come speak to her personally. Robert Holly told her he was very interested in what she had to tell him and after their conversation was over, he said he would be down the next day and he would be driving a government-issued car, a black, unmarked Ford Model-18, standard issue for most law enforcement officers. She knew which car that was and waited patiently, having arrived at the designated meeting place a half-hour early so she wouldn't miss Agent Holly.

When the clean-as-a-whistle car pulled up in front of her, a man, a gentleman she could tell, stepped out and said, "Good morning, Miss Field?"

"Good morning, Mr.... or should I say, *Agent* Holly?"

"Robert is fine, Miss Field," said the handsome young man.

"Then, please call me Lily," she said, thinking, *Wow, what a nice, mannered man.*

"Okay, Lily. Is there a place where we can talk...privately?"

"Of course. I volunteer here in the theater. I work the ticket window for them," said Lily, digging into her purse and retrieving a ring filled with keys that Holly estimated weighed about five pounds. "We can go inside. There's a little office in there where we can talk."

Lily opened the theater door and went inside as if she lived there. Like most theaters, it was cool and dark, and Holly wondered why that was. Perhaps because most people didn't visit theaters unless they were watching a show. Then the building came alive with the lights and sounds of live theater, and even scents—sweating thespians and perfumed ladies, floors cleaned with Lestoil, and, always, the lingering scent of fancy libations for the audience. Past the box office, there was a small meeting room. Lily opened it with the help of her giant ring of keys.

"This is our meeting room. Would you like a cup of joe, Agent Holly?" Lily offered.

"That sounds swell, thank you," said Holly. "It was a long ride over from Miami this morning."

"Okay," said Lily. "I'll have it ready in a jiff. Have a seat and I'll tell you what I know and what I believe if that's okay."

"Sure," said Holly. "Of course. Our organization often has to work off speculation, though from what you said on the phone and the fact that Jason Abram was murdered, this doesn't sound like speculation."

"Oh?" said Lily. "Frankly, I was surprised your department had any interest. I mean, Deputy Abram was just a local lawman..."

"Well, I must be honest with you, Lily...'"

"Of course, sir," she said eagerly. "Please do."

"I also must ask you to keep our conversation in the strictest confidence..."

"Yes, sir. I understand."

"Jason Abram was one our men. Working undercover to root out some Nazi sympathizers over here."

Lily turned and placed a cup of coffee in front of Holly. "Cream? Sugar?"

"No, thanks, ma'am. Hot and black is good for me," said Holly.

"I suspected as much when I found his FBI badge in his home," Lilly sniffled. "I hope you get the people who did this awful thing to him."

"After today, I expect you won't have to worry about Sheriff Ross or any of his cronies."

"Really? How can you be so sure?"

"Well, from what you told me on the phone, we know Sheriff Ross was lying. But, just to confirm, you said he told you that Deputy Abram had just up and quit his job and said he was going home, correct?"

"Yes, sir. That's what he told me when I asked him where, Jason, Mr. Abram, was the next day. As I believe I told you, Mr. Abram was at the church social—I believe Sheriff Ross asked him there. After dinner, they both went outside to smoke some cigars, as all the men do after dinner, and the next thing I know, they were both gone as well as some of the local men who are friends or associates of the sheriff."

"I see. And that was the last time you saw Deputy Abram?"

"Yes, sir."

"From what I've learned, that was the last time anyone saw Jason, alive."

"That's right. I didn't know who else to call, so I called your office. It's...it's horrible what happened to him."

"Yes, it is," said Holly, and Lily thought she saw his eyes shine with tears forming. He continued. "I'm glad you called, Miss Fields. We've had some questionable things that have happened here. My boss was here several weeks ago working on another investigation. I have a feeling it's connected somehow."

"Oh, my," said Lily. "Sometimes I wonder if the world is ending, what with the war in Europe and these...terrible things right here in our little town."

"Well, ma'am... Lily. We can only do what the Lord put us on his earth to do," said Holly, and he meant it. "So, I've got some work to do myself before I go back to Miami. I can't thank you enough for sharing what you know. Jason was a good man."

"You mean you knew him, personally?" asked Lily.

"I shouldn't say, Lily, but I can't see the harm now. Yes, I knew him. He was a lawman just like me. He was a law-abiding man, and he didn't deserve what he got. But I know you are a woman of the Bible, so I'm telling you this. Our God is a vengeful one. I'm sure whoever was responsible for Jason's ending, will pay for it."

"Yes, sir," said Lily, tears in her eyes. She stood up to say goodbye but couldn't without bursting into tears.

Holly took her into his arms and held her while she sobbed, her body trembling as if she'd lost a child.

"Now, now, Ms. Lily," said Holly. "We're going to make it right. Jason was a good man and I'm going to make it right. I promise. Now, can you remember some of the other men who were at the church that night?"

Lily gave Holly some of the names of the men, who also slipped out of the church dinner when Jason disappeared. Then she recalled something she almost forgot.

"Oh, she said, "There was one other thing." She turned away from Holly and pulled a letter out of her brassiere. "Excuse me for being so coarse but I didn't want anyone to see me with this. The next day after the church gathering, I went to Jason's house to check on him. He wasn't there but the door was open, so I looked around. I wasn't trying to be nosey, but I just had a feeling Jason was gone and might not return. That's when I found his FBI identification and that's why I called your office—but I also found this."

She handed an envelope to Holly, who looked at it. It was addressed to Emmet MacWain. "I thought it might be of interest to you," said Lily, then excused herself and said, "Good-bye, sir. Let me know if I can be of any help."

FBI Agent Holly walked into Sheriff Ross's office with a little bomb ticking in his head. It was probably his blood pressure. A doctor had told him it was high. He said stress made it higher. Robert Holly was stressed. Yesterday he was on the phone with Jason Abram's parents, trying to explain their son, who was right out of federal officer training, was undercover acting as a Deputy keeping tabs on a crooked Sheriff who probably killed him because he was a Jew. Today he listened to a nice lady whose heart was breaking after meeting their son one time. Holly had met Abram more than once. Holly had been his field training officer.

Sheriff Carl Ross was at his desk fumbling through some paperwork. His hat was pushed back on his head, red tufts of hair sticking out from under it, making him look clownish. He'd been chewing on a wad of tobacco and when he looked up at Holly, he kept his eyes on Holly's eyes as he leaned over and spit the tobacco into a wastebasket. He swallowed and the Adam's apple in his overly long neck slid up and down like a snake that just swallowed a rat.

"Can I he'p you?" he said.

Holly noted Ross had hung his holstered gun and belt on the coat rack next to his desk.

"Yes," said Holly. "I'm new in town and I thought it would be good to come in and meet the local gendarme."

"The what?" said Ross, his teeth stained with tobacco juice, some of which dribbled from the corner of his mouth.

"The Sheriff of this town."

"That's me. The only one here."

"You don't have any other officers?"

"Nope. Had a deputy but he got kilt."

"Oh, I'm sorry to hear that," said Holly. He walked around the side of the desk. He looked up and down, then at the curtained window as if he were a building inspector.

"What're you lookin' for?"

Holly looked at him barely able to withhold his anger. He felt his face get hot, maybe beginning to turn red. Damn blood pressure. "Oh, excuse me. I'm just nosey. Is that your gun?"

"Yeah, who else's would it be?"

Holly took the gun from the holster. "Geez, that's nice," he said. "Nice heft. That's an old Colt revolver.45 caliber, yes?"

"Yeah," said Ross, but he was getting antsy. *What was with this guy?* He thought to himself. It was the last thought that would go through his mind.

Holly swirled quickly, crouching himself to approximately the level of Ross's head, the Colt revolver's hammer already pulled back, the gun at the end of his extended arm, next to Ross's ear, and pulled the trigger. The bullet exited the side of his head as if it weren't there—because most of it wasn't anymore—then drilled into the office wall like a wood-boring beetle.

Holly ignored the ringing in his ears, quickly pulled a handkerchief out of his pocket, and wiped the handle and trigger of the revolver. Holding the gun by its still-hot barrel, careful to keep the handkerchief between his hand and the gun, he placed it in Ross's right hand, with which he'd seen him using it to write something.

He looked himself over to see if he had any blood on himself and was pleased to see there was none. The impact at such close range blasted everything out the opposite side of Ross's head.

"That's for Jason, and that's how the Feds do it, you cud-chewing, murdering hick," growled Holly. He wiped the handle of the sheriff's gun, then placed it into his placed it into Ross's hand. Then he put his hat back on, took a deep breath, and composed himself. He looked out the window to see if anyone was walking by on the sidewalk, saw it was clear, and left the dead sheriff's office.

FIFTY-TWO

RIO DE JANEIRO

"I didn't want to hear that," said Serey, his face reddening.

"So, now you have," said Josephine, her eyes flashing heat. "You know how it works, John. You can get involved from a safe distance, but I can't. These Nazis, these... *monsters* are in my country, in my home! Do you think I can just sit there and let them do what they're doing? The French people took me in and by God, I'm going to fight for them."

Serey walked around the hotel room, his head down, his hands locked behind him as if they were in manacles. "So now, we use it to our advantage."

"How so?" said Claude, stepping forward, his voice raised, protective of his employer.

Serey stopped pacing and turned to look up at Claude. "I need *all* of you to return to France immediately." He looked at Emmet. "I need you to go, too."

"Why, me?" Emmet asked.

"Because I need *you* to monitor the situation, report back to me, perhaps *control* the situation. I cannot go."

"And why not?

Serey hesitated before answering the question. "I am a United States citizen and a deputized federal law enforcement officer. If my identity were to be discovered, it would be suspected I was part of a plot to undermine the Germans. That might bring the U.S. into the war and we're not ready for that. It would be an international debacle."

Emmet frowned. "I'm a U.S. citizen, as well..."

"I'm sorry, Emmet, currently, you're not," said Serey.

"You told me that before, but later said you were bluffing to push me into the murder investigation at Ford's home in Ft. Myers."

"I'm not bluffing now," said Serey. "For our needs, it's best you're *not* a U.S. citizen."

Emmet's jaw muscles flexed as he stepped toward Serey, his fists balled.

Josephine stepped between the two men. "Now, now, boys. Let's play nice." She turned toward Emmet, placing her hand on his chest. "Mr. MacWain, let me tell you something," she said, her face so close to his chest, that he could feel her warm breath on his neck. "I'm being used, too."

Her hand slid up to his face, her touch like a soothing balm. "But I've been used all my life. I learned to live with it, honey, and I learned how to make it work in my favor. *We* can do this. If it allows us to get a leg up, so to speak, on the Nazis...," she said, hesitant, her smile mischievous and sensual at the same time, "Then I'm all in."

Emmet softened. "Ma'am..."

"Call me, Jo," she said.

"It's just... that I *am* a citizen of the United States. I earned that right, by fighting in wars for them, more than once. This man and I circumvented a Nazi spy in Key West last year." He looked at Serey with menace. "I don't like being forced into anything."

Josephine moved closer to Emmet, her hand sliding around the back of Emmet's neck as if she were pulling his face down to hers for a kiss. "I've been forced to do a lot of things I didn't want to do, either baby. But I learned to use that, to make myself better, find some...*power*, that most women do not possess, and even less 'Negro' women have. Now, why don't you come along with me? I can see you're a fighter. I am, too." She paused, then addressed Serey, while keeping her eyes locked on Emmet's. "John. Why don't you tell us what the plan is? I'll make adjustments as necessary."

Serey pondered what he should say. His mission was supposed to be Top Secret, Eyes Only, to designated agents from several U.S. departments: The Department of State, The U.S. Armed Services Department, the Office of Strategic Services, and the FBI. All of the departments were angling to be in charge of intelligence gathering and management, so it was easy to make a misstep. Every department had leaders with huge egos and agents with eyes on moving up in the quickly growing federal government. Serey just wanted to keep his job. Pressure on him was heavy but he still had to go with his instincts and his instincts were telling him that, despite their differences, Emmet MacWain was a good man. A trusted man, and he was taking advantage of him. Still, it was his job.

Josephine Baker was already working with the collective departments, with Serey acting as her liaison. He was using her, too, but she was already a French citizen, so if she were caught, it wouldn't reflect on him or, more importantly, his country. Emmet's citizenship had to be buried and he did that so that he could use him.

"Okay," said Serey. "Here is what is going to happen and why. Please have a seat, except for you, Monsieur Durand. I'm afraid I must ask you to leave for now."

"No sir," said Josephine. "That's not going to happen."

"Miss Baker," said Serey, "This is a matter of utmost top-secret intelligence. The fewer people that know what our intentions are, the better."

"Does this concern those Nazis that went missing after they visited my home?"

Serey didn't know how to answer. His mouth tried to move, as he looked from Josephine to Emmet, to Claude.

"Claude knows all about that," said Josephine. "We work together if you know what I mean."

Serey thought for a moment, then began to nod his head slowly. "Okay, then," he said, "I know what you've been doing for our country as well as for France. You're a brave woman and we appreciate your help. Let's move on with it, then. Time is critical and we don't have much of it."

"Some Nazi officers are coming to Miss Baker's home, soon. They are very high-ranking officers, and they are investigating the disappearance of two other officers, one German officer, and one the head of the Vichy police who visited Miss Baker's chateau, the same two she just admitted she and Claude killed."

"Our intelligence has informed us that at least one of these Nazi officers wants to defect to the U.S. We're not sure which one..."

Josephine interrupted. "Who is your informant?"

Serey hesitated, sweated some more, and shook his head. He didn't try to resist. He knew too well how much Josephine had helped with intelligence for the French underground, as well as the British and their allies.

"It's your friend, uh, Jack Sanders," Serey replied.

Josephine smiled and turned to Emmet. "That's the code name for my friend Jacques Abtey. He's a captain in the French underground unit called the Maquis, whom I do some...favors for. He's a good man. May I call you Emmet, Mr. MacWain? I feel we've known each other forever."

Emmet's face reddened but he said, "Yes, of course"

Serey, obviously irritated, pleaded, "May we continue?"

Josephine turned back to him and winked, "Go ahead, baby."

Flummoxed, Serey continued.

"We need you to entertain these German officers and try to discern which one wants to defect, and those that are there to look into their missing fellow officers, you need to try to throw them off."

"And how do we do that?" asked Emmet.

"We think Liebold will."

"What?" said Emmet frowning. "You know you can't trust that man. And now, you've sold him some blueprints for a weapon..." Then the truth came to Emmet and he stopped talking. He held his hand up, as if to stop the conversation and lowered his gaze to the floor, thinking...*thinking*...putting the puzzle together. "Liebold has done this before, yes?"

Serey nodded.

Emmet continued. "The time he showed a reporter the blueprints of a bomber Ford was making for the government. Liebold...likes to show off, make himself seem more important, like someone who craves to be...liked, or admired...." He stopped to think for a moment, pacing back and forth, his hand on his chin. "You're giving him blueprints for a bomb that is fake."

Serey allowed himself a slight smile. "Our hope is that it will throw the Germans' technology off, at least long enough for us to do what we must."

Emmet smiled for the first time in many weeks. "You're not quite the arse I thought you were!" Then he quietly muttered, "Bravo. I'm glad you finally let me in on that." Then he strode over to Serey and extended his right hand, the one that was not bandaged. "I understand now, why you went through the trouble to take away my citizenship. It's a sneaky bastard thing to do, but I can comprehend your motivation now."

Serey took Emmet's hand sheepishly and smiled, sort of.

Emmet said, "I'm in."

"And that pleases me," said Josephine, then turned to Durand. "How does this sit with you, Claude?"

Claude nodded slightly. "Anything that grieves the Germans, and pleases you, madame, pleases me, as well."

"Outstanding," said Serey, smiling for the first time in many weeks. "I've got a plane here that will fly you all back to France. The sooner everyone gets packed, the better."

"What about my Miss Baker's ship?" asked Claude.

"Good point," said Serey. "I suppose your crew could head back, or they could wait for you here. I'm sure we can fly you back here. The choice is yours if you could handle that...?"

"Have them return, Claude. My remaining shows here have been postponed due to the unfortunate ship explosion," said Josephine, while giving Serey an icy, narrowed-eyed glance. "Have them dock in Portugal where we have some neutrality still. I'd rather we have some escape choices if this all goes to hell, and we have to get out of France quickly. You can stay with the captain and crew to oversee the ship's return."

Claude looked as if he'd been slapped in the face. "I would prefer to be with you, ma'am, you know, in case there is... trouble with the... visitors."

"I appreciate that, Claude, but you know how important it is we get the ship back. We have other...friends who may need safe passage out of Europe."

Claude nodded, a mixture of discontent and sadness on his face. "I'll see to the ship's safe return, then," he said, passionless. He sauntered over to Emmet and said, "May I speak to you for a moment?"

"Of course," Emmet replied. They moved away from the others. Claude whispered but with a direct tone that was unmistakable. "You *must* keep Miss Baker, safe, *oui*. She is brave, perhaps too much so. If something happened to her..." he paused as tears began to well in his eyes.

Emmet put his unbandaged hand on Claude's shoulder and gave it a reassuring squeeze. "As one old soldier to another, you have my word. I will keep her safe, my friend."

Claude nodded and whispered, "*Merci.*" Then he turned toward the door and without looking back said, "I will see to your baggage, then, Mademoiselle." As he left the room, he muttered, "*Que Dieu soit avec vous.*"

Emmet watched as the Frenchman moped out of the room. While they had just met, they'd become instant comrades, each knowing they had a bond of trust. "God be with you too, Claude," said Emmet.

FIFTY-THREE

Ford, Liebold, and Bennett were in the lobby waiting impatiently when Emmet came down with his luggage. Claude Durand brought some of Josephine's luggage down and said his farewell, his eyes still moist and red, practically mourning having to leave her to travel on her own even if it was back to her home in France. It was obvious to all that he was incredibly loyal to his "boss" and his concern was evident on his face. Emmet reassured him, once again, he would look after her, then met with Ford, waving him aside to introduce him to Josephine, whom he had escorted down the stairs.

"Miss Baker, I'd like you to meet Mr. Henry Ford," said Emmet.

"How do you do, Miss Baker," said Ford, his delivery as stiff as over-starched laundry. He did not stick out his hand but managed to make a slight bow. His face could not hide his curiosity about why they were meeting.

"Very, well, sir," said Josephine, her sexuality oozing from every pore of her dark skin.

"Miss Baker must get back to France, urgently," said Emmet, who had descended the stairs with her, helping Claude carry their baggage to the lobby. "I told her the ship that sank in the harbor was our mode of transportation, that we needed to get to France as well, and she graciously offered to give us a lift, so to speak."

"Well... that's very kind of you," said Ford. "But we wouldn't want to intrude on your privacy."

Josephine laughed. "I don't know if you've ever seen one of my shows, Mr. Ford, but I can assure you, privacy is not one of my virtues."

Ford's face turned as red as a fire hydrant.

"Come now, Ford," said Emmet. "Even with the ship intact, it would've taken a couple of weeks to get to France. Now, we can be there in a couple of days. Then we can get on with our...odyssey. I'm telling you now, if I am to continue on this mission with you, I'm taking Miss Baker's offer of a plane."

"Sounds good to me," said Bennett, stepping up to meet Josephine. Sticking his hand out like a hungry politician, he added, "I'm Harry Bennett. Mr. Ford's associate. And that guy over there, is another associate of ours, Ernest Liebold. He's, um, not quite the charmer I am but we keep him around to make sure no one is overcharging us for our meals and rooms." He laughed at his own joke, though Ford and Liebold did not.

"It's a pleasure to meet you, sir," said Josephine. She stuck out her hand and Bennett took it gingerly. Liebold did not move toward her but simply gave her a nod.

"Shall we resume our journey, then?" said Emmet. "Miss Baker's man will take care of her bags and we can follow in our rented car."

"What happened to your hand," Mr. MacWain," asked Liebold, awkwardly.

Emmet shrugged. "I, uh... shaving accident." This drew uncomfortable glances within Ford's group, but no one questioned him further. There was a noticeable discomfort among them, except Josephine, a woman who had learned to roll with the punches, follow fate's uncanny lead, and see what happens. She often managed to make the most of a situation, even if it was dangerous.

The incongruous group was about to depart when the desk clerk in the hotel lobby spoke up.

"Um, Mr. MacWain," he said. "I received a telegraph for you."

Emmet excused himself and rushed over to the clerk, accepting the telegraph with the excitement of a boy on Christmas morning. It had to be from Bessie and he was anxious to see what she had to say. He felt his heartbeat quicken and found himself smiling as he read the message.

It read: "Dear Emmet. I hope you are doing well! I am doing wonderful. I met with the circus people and performed my horse routine. They loved it so much they offered to make me one of their star acts! The Ringmaster took me to dinner and told me the news. He is such a sweet man, his name is Tommy Mandet, and we're spending a lot of time together as he trains me. He gave me the name, "The Princess of Fire!" I will be doing riding stunts including jumping through a ring of fire! It's scary but audiences love it! I received your telegram just as I was leaving the hotel and I am so glad I did. I hope you stay safe. The circus headquarters is in Sarasota and you can find where we will be traveling and doing shows if you ever want to meet up again. Wishing you the best, Bessie."

Emmet had been smiling as he read the message but by the time he finished it, he was not smiling anymore. A wave of nausea seemed to overcome him as he read the message again and the part where Bessie said she'd gone to dinner with the Ringmaster "Tommy" seemed to poke his heart with a sharp stick.

"Mr. MacWain," said Liebold, his tone irritable. "Will you be joining us anytime soon?"

Emmet turned around and stared at Liebold, his face reddened with emotion, his eyes hardened like black glass. "Shut up," he said. Then he eyed the other travelers: Ford frowned, Bennett stood, mouth agape, but Josephine looked at him with compassion as if she had read the note herself. She glided over to him and wrapped her arm around his. Looking up at his face, she said, "Would you be a gentleman and escort me to our car, good sir?"

Emmet nodded, wordlessly, and swallowed, his throat so dry, he could not talk right away. There was no breeze outside and the humid day made it difficult to breathe. A street vendor had set up a stand outside the hotel and was selling iced refreshments. Emmet spied a bottle of Brahma beer poking out of the ice and bought one. He paid the vendor who opened the beer for him, then upended the bottle and drank half of the beer quickly.

"Can I have a sip?" Josephine asked. "Sure," Emmet said and handed her the bottle, noticing tiny beads of sweat on Josephine's temples, too. She sipped demurely and handed him back the bottle. "Mmmm. I like that."

Ford and the others watched on, a look of disgust on their faces, making it obvious they were appalled by him sharing a beer with a colored woman. Emmet finished the beer and bought two more. He did not offer to buy one for them.

***

Serey had commandeered an aging but beautifully-crafted Pan American Boeing Clipper to carry Emmet, Josephine, and Ford's entourage. The plane came with an ex-pat, Aussie pilot named Jerome at the controls. He welcomed the group aboard with a "G'day mates, 'ave a seat,"

then went forward and began throttling up. A flight servant was wearing a tuxedo, an elegant man with long, thin fingers who told the passengers to buckle up until they were in the air, and then he would come around and take orders for snacks and libations.

Soon the plane was aloft. Emmet stared out the window and saw the pool of rainbow-colored fuel spread out on the water indicating where the ship had gone down. Some boats with deep-sea divers encircled the site, some already donning their copper helmets attached to hose lines that supplied air to the divers.

Emmet, always concerned about being aware of where he was and how to get out of it in a hurry if needed, looked about the plane. It was, essentially, a boat with wings. Its interior was filled with lush mahogany paneling and chrome-edged tables and cabinets, plush carpet, and velvet seats. It launched from the continuously active harbor in Rio De Janeiro, as the smell of burned petroleum still bubbled up from the depths where the bombed-out ship, its hull filled with weapons of war, lay at the bottom, and smoke lingered in the otherwise sunny air like wispy phantoms looking for a place to stay.

Within a quarter-hour, the hum of the plane's engines had already lulled some of the passengers to sleep. Ford seemed to be catching forty winks and Bennett's head bobbled as he fought to stay awake. Liebold sat board straight, eyes wide open, writing something on a pad.

Josephine was sleepy, too, and curled up against Emmet's shoulder as comfortable as a cat on a lap. The scent of her skin was the fragrance of flowers and Emmet's anger over Bessie Murphy's telegram began to subside. *What right did he have to be upset anyway?* he asked himself. They'd only spent one night together and while it was special, it did not give him the right to question what she did, nor how she lived her life. Her dream of joining a circus and seeing the world was not unlike many young people who did not have the money to attend university. Besides, as he'd told her, he was practically old enough to be her father.

Emmet began to grow sleepy, too, but as soon as he laid his head back the man in the tuxedo asked if he could bring him something, as he placed glasses of water on the dining table in front of his and Josephine's seats.

"Not right now," said Emmet. "Perhaps after the lady has had a bit of a nap."

The tuxedoed man bowed his head slightly, understanding, and whispered, "I'll check back then."

Emmet stood and stretched, and noticed Ford was now awake and looking at him. He waved Emmet over and he scooted around the table and went to him.

"I have to ask you something, Mr. MacWain," said Ford.

"Go ahead," said Emmet, holding one of the grips attached to the aircraft's ceiling so passengers could steady themselves if they had to get around the cabin.

"Did you know, the return address on the package that contained the poison that killed the mail was the same as Miss Baker's?"

"Yes," said Emmet.

"And that does not seem suspicious to you?"

"It might if I hadn't come to know her. But I've found Miss Baker has our country's security clearance as well as that of France and England."

"So, why would her address be on the package, addressed to me, which ultimately, killed a man?"

"Well, that's the mystery, isn't it? But, moreover, why did a man, with German soldier tattoos, dressed like a rabbi, know about the delivery of the package, wait for it, then run to your house, open said package, and inhale its contents? And, worse, why was the young deputy sheriff, Jason Abrams, nailed to a cross and brutally murdered?"

Ford paused to consider the question. "I...I can't answer that."

Emmet grinned, "Currently, I can't either but I'm working on it. There's a mystery of all of this and we must follow all leads. That is what you hired me for and that is what I intend to do and when I have my answers, I swear this to you, I will see those responsible for these crimes will pay, dearly."

Ford nodded, then turned his gaze to the window.

"Now, I'm going to return to my seat, have a bite to eat, then try to take a nap," said Emmet. "We'll stop in Sierra Leone by this evening to refuel, then continue into the night to France, which should decrease our chances of getting shot down by Nazi ships. Rest well, sir," said Emmet, then added, "If you can."

FIFTY-FOUR

CROSSING THE ATLANTIC

It was night, clouds blanketing the stars, but with favorable winds, as the plane carrying Emmet, Josephine, and Ford's companions, landed in the port of Sierra Leone off the western tip of Africa. The country was still a British colony and, as early as 1938, the Brits had begun to militarize the area, setting up refueling docks and maintaining a presence. While fighting had not begun there, Freetown had been prepared for the support of troops, and allied forces who had already established a presence there.

Emmet felt at ease as the plane docked into a fueling station and its passengers stepped out to stretch their legs. Of course, when Josephine stepped out, some of the locals, as well as the servicemen stationed there immediately recognized her, and within a few minutes, the dock was loaded with locals whistling and asking her to sing a song, which she did. It was a sweet, quiet love song, not one that she typically used in her act. The crowd roared with excitement and applause as she finished the song and items—pieces of torn newspapers, service caps, even a belt—were pushed toward her for an autograph. She did as many as she could, until the boat-plane was fueled, and she passed them back to the servicemen like offerings at a church.

The pilots switched places before the plane skimmed along the choppy surface of the port, then pushed into the air like a giant albatross, continuing its path to France. Ford's group was mostly silent, with Bennett—paper bag in hand—still uncomfortable flying, more so as they flew over a sea as black and shiny as asphalt and seemingly endless. Ford and Liebold barely said a word to each other, or anyone else, and Bennett was back and forth to the plane's bathroom time and again.

After several hours, the food and beverage servant came into the cabin and informed the small group of passengers that as they drew closer to France, they would turn off the lights on the plane for safety reasons, primarily so that they would not be targeted by German vessels at sea. Bennett appeared even more ill at ease, but the rest of the passengers took the news quietly. Emmet, the only one with military experience, approved. The plane was not one of the new, experimental aircraft with pressured cabins, so they had to fly under 20,000 feet, which could make them vulnerable to ground fire, or other enemy planes patrolling the coast.

Emmet occasionally fell off to sleep, with Josephine cuddled up next to him like a housecat. He had embarrassed himself with his anger over Bessie Murphy's telegram to him, but he was over it now. He had just been foolish—not the first time, probably not the last— over her admitting she was starstruck with the circus announcer, who was undoubtedly closer to her age than Emmet. He told himself to enjoy the memory of the evening they spent together and to get over his adolescent jealousy.

He needed to concentrate on what he was doing now; following the strings of a mystery that had begun with the death of a fake rabbi, whom Emmet suspected was a Nazi, at the home of the world's most successful automotive manufacturer, from a gas that was used by the Germans in the Big War, that came in a package with the return address of one of the world's most popular entertainers to throw blame toward her. A complicated scheme but one that might have worked had he and Serey not got involved.

Now, here he was, with the car maker and the songstress on the way to her chateau in France to oversee a meeting with the Nazi officers who were also en route to her home to investigate one of their missing officers as well as the missing Vichy officer. To complicate that meeting they were trying to "bait" the Nazi officers, and either Ford, Bennett, or Liebold with swapping blueprints for a weapon that hadn't been created yet, but if it were to be, would jeopardize the entire world.

Emmet shook his head in disbelief at his present circumstances. He was a retired criminal inspector, not an international spy, without knowledge and experience in espionage and subterfuge. This whole plan, invented by Serey, an FBI director—and a man whom he was unsure he could trust anymore—was preposterous, and Emmet's likelihood of being caught and executed appeared a lot more plausible than his managing to pull off the whole operation.

"God, help me," Emmet muttered under his breath. Liebold had bought the weapon's plans from Serey, who was poorly disguised as a scientist who had supposedly helped create the bomb in the blueprints. But would Liebold be the one who offered them to the Germans? Or would he hand them off to Ford to reveal them? Certainly, Bennett wouldn't be the agent of exchange. He was simply an enforcer, not someone who could handle the finesse of brokering a deal with high-ranking SS officers. And what would Emmet's role be after the exchange other than staying alive and informing Serey that the insane plan had either worked, or it didn't, in which case, he would be dead?

Of course, he *had* to let it happen for two reasons. One: it would give the Nazis plans that could lead them down a rabbit hole to nowhere. Two: it would reveal if Ford, or one, or both of his two closest advisors were traitors.

Emmet would have to be constantly vigilant to witness the exchange if, indeed, it even happened at all. For all Emmet knew, the SS officers might arrive at Josephine's chateau and just have them all killed. And what would the Germans think of him? Who was he supposed to be and why was he there?

Josephine stirred out of her slumber as if she had heard what Emmet was thinking about. The moonlit night shone through the window next to their seats and she could certainly see he was concentrating on something important, his brow in a deep frown, arms crossed, staring out of a tiny window into the blackness of a sea that could provide no answers. "A penny for your thoughts, sir," she said.

Emmet looked back to the others to see if they might be listening. They were all asleep now—even Bennett—and the drone of the plane's engines would certainly prevent them from hearing what he and Josephine were talking about. Still, he brought his head down to her and whispered. "I'm trying to figure out how, when, and why Liebold, or possibly Ford, might offer up the blueprints to the Nazis. What occasion would bring us all into the room to be privy to that exchange—if it happens at all?"

Josephine placed the soft palm of her hand on Emmet's face and leaned toward him.

At first, he thought she might kiss him, so intimate was her gesture.

Josephine whispered, "Don't worry," she said, moving her hand up to his brow, her fingers lightly touching the frown as if trying to rub it away. "I've got something in mind. This is my arena, Emmet. I've been shuckin' and jivin' these krauts for some time now. Just follow my lead, baby, and play your role."

"And what is my role?" Emmet whispered with some urgency. "Why would a displaced Scottish American man be at your home?"

Josephine leaned in close, her face next to his, her eyes locked onto his. "Because you're my new lover." Then she tilted her head and kissed his mouth, lightly at first, then as he responded, her tongue played over his lips with more urgency, then slid into his mouth. She looked back over Emmet's shoulders to assure the others were asleep, opened his pants, and pulled him out. Then, with a movement as quick and nimble as the dancer she was, pulled up her dress, slipped off her panties, and mounted him.

Emmet whispered, "You're crazy," but nevertheless, did not stave off her lusty advance. The dim starlight that peeked through their window shone on her skin and it was a delicious pearlescent black, her gardenia scent like that of a heady flower opening. Emmet's hands, weathered with time and work but still as strong as a vise, ran over her soft skin and pulled her into him. Their mouths locked onto each other's, separating only long enough to gulp some air quietly. It ended quietly, other than a tiny yelp Josephine emitted along with a sustained shudder, then she slumped into Emmet's arms and breathed warm air into his ear as she continued to kiss his neck and face.

Emmet whispered, "For a moment I thought I was back in the cavalry riding my horse."

This drew a giggle from the beautiful woman who sat, straddling his lap, the dim light peeking through the window like a voyeur, and highlighting her beauty.

FIFTY-FIVE

FRANCE

The plane flew in through the southern tip of France, where the German occupation was less than in other areas, and into the so-called free zone where the biggest threat was the Nazi-friendly, Vichy puppet police. It was near noon when the plane set down in the Dordogne River and anchored near Josephine's Chateau des Milandes. Claude had arranged for some of the caretaking staff to pick up her and her guests, while Serey had arranged for the plane to be refueled with a nearby fueling service. Emmet made a point of thanking the pilots, shaking their hands, and wishing them luck returning to Brazil.

The caretakers were led by a short, red-haired, bearded man in overalls, named Henri, who embraced Josephine, obviously overjoyed to see her return. They spoke in French before she introduced Emmet to him, then they were loaded into a car. Ford, Bennett and Liebold were loaded into another car along with their bags.

Approaching Josephine's home, Emmet was amazed. "Oh, my," he said, quietly, gazing at the ancient building's grandeur.

"You like?" asked Josephine. "It was built in 1489. We've done a little remodeling and updates but have tried to keep it as close to the original as possible. It's had many owners over the years, from royalty to squatters but one of the owners, Charles Claverie hired an architect and redid the towers, stained-glass windows, and the surrounding structures, and hired a landscape designer for the gardens. Most of what you see was done in the early 1900s, I just had it...refreshed." She paused briefly, then added, "I...love it here. It is a place I find solace."

"It's just beautiful," said Emmet, looking at Josephine and noticing her eyes were wet with tears, he added, "Just like you."

With that, Josephine leaned over and kissed him. "I...like you, Emmet. A lot."

Emmet trying to lighten things up for her quipped, "I won't hold that against you."

Once at the Chateau, Henri took the guests and their bags to their rooms. Josephine wanted Emmet to stay in her room but he thought it might be best for both of them if he did not.

"Why?" asked Josephine, with a salacious grin. "Didn't you enjoy our plane ride?"

"Very much so," said Emmet. "But I don't want your other guests to have ammunition for gossip, especially Liebold who has trouble keeping secrets. Besides, at my age, your enthusiasm might kill me."

"But what a way to go, *oui*?" Josephine blew him a kiss, then added, "Make sure to come visit my room when these fascist bastards are sleeping, okay?"

Henri returned before Emmet could answer. "This way, sir."

Emmet gave Josephine a wink, and silently mouthed the word, "later" then followed Henri to a room that had a view of the chateau's wonderful vista. He thanked Henri, then took a bath, dressed, and laid down for what he thought would be a moment of respite. The windows were open and a cool, flower-scented breeze pushed into the room from the French countryside, where goldfinches in a multitude of colors tweeted about, some landing on the window sill to Emmet's room, looking for handouts that the proprietor of the house typically fed them. Emmet felt at peace for the first time in what seemed a long time, dozed off, and slept for hours.

***

Deputy Fuhrer Rudolph Hess waited in a hotel in Paris for the rest of his investigative team to arrive. Investigating missing persons was not something that would be normally assigned to him at his rank, no, *position*, as it were, which was now that of custodian. But he had his reasons for volunteering for the "investigation" and he'd declared to his former friend, Adolf, he would take care of it.

He had saved Hitler's life by diving on him, as a bomb planted by Marxists, exploded in the Hofbräuhaus in München. His leg was injured but his friend, Adolf, was safe. When they both were imprisoned in Landsberg, he helped edit his friend's manuscript, *Mein Kamph*. The two of them were as close as friends could be, then Hitler appointed him to the Council of Ministers for the Defense of the Reich, which turned out to be a pencil-pushing desk job. Worse, Hitler had inexplicably replaced his position as personal secretary to the Fuhrer, with Martin Borman. Hess's importance to Hitler was lessened and his grave concerns about invading Britain and fighting on two fronts were ignored. He believed Hitler had come to think of him as *schwach*, but Hess would show his old friend he was not weak.

Now, he might get the chance he'd been waiting for, something so secret he had not discussed it with anyone else, including his wife. If he had, he would already be dead. He felt he must stop the confrontation with England, at any cost. Of course, no one could know this, not even his wife. Hess had told the psychic that he'd been seeing about his dreams and the psychic told him that it was not a dream but a mission that God was telling him to do.

There was an added pleasure to the assignment, too: he got the opportunity to tell Klaus Barbie that *he* would be in charge of the investigation, and that would be very satisfying. He'd never cared for Barbie; he was an arrogant monster who wasn't focused on winning a war, as much as he was on torturing and killing people in the most brutal ways.

A sharp rap on the door to his room startled him. He took a deep breath and stood up. "Enter," he said.

The door opened and two men entered: SS Colonel Major Lieber, and *Oberleutnant* Edvard Heinz.

"Good afternoon, gentlemen. It is good to see you again," said Hess. He stepped from behind the desk where he'd been pondering the Britain situation, along with the reports of the missing men, of one of their own soldiers, *Oberleutnant* Hans Arent, and the Vichy Marshall Rene Pelletier in the Dordogne area. "I am surprised to see you again," said Hess to Heinz. "I was told you were on a ship that exploded in the harbor of Rio De Janeiro."

"Sir, it is good to see you, again," said Heinz. "I was on the ship, but fate had other things in mind for me. As you are aware I was on a special mission in the United States. In addition to working with some Americans who are part of the Silver Shirts movement there, I was assigned to observe a man who is a close associate of our Fuhrer, Mr. Henry Ford, and create an international situation that would implicate the horrendous Jews and justify Mr. Ford's alliance with the Fuhrer.

"Ford was on the same ship as me that came from Florida, along with his closest colleagues. He was returning to Brazil to his failed factory, called Fordlandia. He was not aware, but our secret mission was to pick up a load of armament there which, unfortunately, went down with the ship. I was not on the ship as I was surveilling Mr. Ford and his companions."

"How fortunate for you, *Oberleutant*," said Hess. "And what are your responsibilities in this matter, Colonel Major Lieber?"

Lieber was slow to answer, twisting his mouth thoughtfully, and gazing briefly out the window mulling his answer. "My position is the same as yours, to investigate the disappearance of one of our soldiers and the Vichy Marshal, both who were last known to be visiting a chateau in the Dordogne, owned by the "Black Devil," the former American entertainer and whore, Josephine Baker."

"I'm confused," said Hess, his caterpillar-like eyebrows squirming on his forehead.

"If you don't mind, sir," said Heinz. "There has been some suspicion that Baker might be assisting the French underground. Her home has been visited previously, several times. There was no evidence found and she is welcome and open to inspections. Still, given the chance she is not what she appears to be, I put her address on the package that was placed in Mr. Ford's mailbox. One that held a deadly poison."

"I am confused," said Hess, arching one of his furry eyebrows.

Colonel Major Lieber explained. "Our Fuhrer is...fond of Mr. Ford. He has a portrait of Mr. Ford in his office and considers him a friend and professional ally. They have signed contracts for Mr. Ford to manufacture vehicles for our *Wehrmacht* and he has factories in both Cologne and Berlin, but by doing so, Ford has drawn detractors in his own country. His American sales are down. Our Fuhrer wanted to help him, so several of us put together a plan. If it appeared that a filthy Jew was trying to kill Mr. Ford, the public might be...how shall I say, more favorable to Mr. Ford and his company. So, we— *Oberleutant* Heinz—with the help of the Silver Shirts in the United States, devised a plan to change Mr. Ford's image to his buyers." Lieber paused for a moment. "*Oberleutant* Heinz, would you care to tell Deputy Fuhrer Hess the rest?"

"Of course," said Heinz. "One of our soldiers, volunteered to be a part of our plan. He lived in the city of Ft. Myers where Mr. Ford has a winter home. Our volunteer was valuable as a spy for us by assuming the role of a Jew, a rabbi, in fact. He played that role for several months and when we were ready to make our move, he willingly gave up his life by going to Ford's house and removing a package, a piece of mail that had a tube of deadly gas in it. It appeared to have been sent by the popular singer, Josephine Baker, and intended for Mr. Ford and that our man, pretending to be a stinking, low-life Jew, stole it and inhaled, only to die."

Hess was still confused and growing impatient. "But why would anyone want to breathe in a tube of poisonous gas?"

"This is why, and it is very interesting," said Heinz. "Mr. Ford receives one of the tubes of every year. Of course, it is not poison gas...it is a tube of his best friend's breath!"

"What?" asked Hess.

"Yes," said Heinz. "Ford's best friend was none other than Thomas Edison, the inventor. They were very close. And, as Edison was dying, he breathed into a glass tube, time and again, thinking each time it would be his last breath, and he wanted his friend, Henry Ford, to have it. Rumor has it, that when he receives these packages yearly, Ford immediately breathes them in."

"Can that be true?" asked Hess.

"It is!" Heinz assured. "And enough people know about this, ritual, if you will, that we decided if we could do this, and put someone's name on the return address, they would be blamed for trying to kill Mr. Ford. Someone who might be an enemy of our Fuhrer." Heinz was clearly excited, even proud, to tell this story.

Hess frowned again but his brow softened, then a slight smile came to his face. He shook his head, in disbelief. When it all made sense to him, he said, "Oberleutant Heinz, that is quite clever."

"Perhaps," said Lieber, "we should bring at least a small *Armeezug* with us to deal with any resistance we might incur from the *negersmach and her staff.*

Hess considered this. He didn't want his superiors to question why he was taking a platoon of soldiers into the part of France with whom they had signed an armistice previously, he had already been repositioned, losing his Deputy Fuhrer position to Borman. But there were some missing men who were last seen at Baker's chateau. He would have to tread lightly but assuredly with this investigation. If it went right, he might regain his close relationship with the Fuhrer. But if the mission failed, then he could lose not only the standing he had now but his life as well.

FIFTY-SIX

CHATEAU DE MILANDES

When Emmet awoke, he heard voices downstairs. He could not understand what was being said, but one of the voices was melodic—had to be Josephine—and the other was a dry, irritable voice, most likely Ford's. Emmet had wondered when Ford would approach Josephine about her address being on the package sent to his house and he didn't want to miss the exchange, so he splashed some cool water on his face, toweled off, and went downstairs as quickly as possible.

"How the hell would I know, Henry?" said Josephine, just as Emmet came off the last step of the stairs and into the living room downstairs. Ford was seated—never an advantageous position from which to argue a point—while Josephine was standing, facing him with one hand on her hip, the other pointing a finger at his face.

"If I would have sent a package with poison in it, wouldn't it be pretty stupid if I did put my home as the return address, just in case it got lost and the mail service would send me back a package full of poison?"

"Maybe it was a clever trick you did to confuse everyone..."

Emmet interrupted the conversation. "Excuse me, if I may say something..."

"I wish you would, Emmet. I let this unpleasant cracker, Nazi-ass-kisser into my home and he tries to insult me."

"I don't have to take that..." Ford began but Josephine stopped him.

"Yeah," she said, "You kinda do. You have got some of your goose-stepping pals coming here, soon. I don't like it, but I know how to play the game. I've done it before. They come here often to stick their noses in my business. I get it, they have taken over part of France, so I must play that game because I want to keep working. But I don't have to like it. And so far, they take a look around and they go. So, let us all keep it civil, and you mind your manners in my home, or we can send you back with your Kraut pals and see if Adolf will put you up for a few days."

And with that, the premier entertainer of the world turned and strode out of the room.

Emmet shrugged his shoulders. "I was going to try to help you out, Ford, but hell hath no fury like a woman's scorn and you walked right into that one."

"I merely was asking a question...," Ford tried.

"I don't care. You're in her house. Besides, you should know she isn't your biggest problem."

"So, what is my...biggest problem?" Ford said, his snarky attitude on full display.

"Your biggest problem is you need to know who *did* send you that package and if my hunch is right, it will be the Nazis, or one of their agents, coming here to meet you. You have a chummy relationship with the maniac Fuhrer who has perpetuated this war on Europeans in general, and Jews specifically, but you must know deep down inside, that the man is as crazy as a shithouse rat. Perhaps some of his own men, maybe one very close to him, might be undermining him for their own glory. It wouldn't take too much deep thinking, or speculation, to believe he might have a coup boiling up underneath his rather fractured view, even as we speak."

Ford sat silently on the couch for a moment, looking down, contemplating, his face slightly reddened. Then, he stood and looked at Emmet. He said nothing but nodded his head, then turned and walked toward the door. He opened it and looked back at Emmet. "I think I'll stroll the gardens. They are...quite beautiful."

***

Claude Durand felt like a useless fool. He'd promised that he would assure the ship and crew would get back to France under his guidance. What he had not known when he made the promise was that their luxury yacht had been heavily damaged, when the *SS Brazilian*—carrying German armament—was blown up in the harbor.

Claude did what he could. He managed to find their captain and crew quarters in which to stay until their ship was repaired. He had found a local shipbuilder who took on the repairs their ship needed, though he was behind with all his work, and it would take weeks for their yacht to be completed. So, what was he to do? He was intensely loyal to his employer, and she had tasked him with returning their boat and he was working on that directive. But he was also intensely worried about her.

Josephine Baker might be the biggest entertainer in the world, but she had also made many enemies. Not the least of which was Hitler's Nazis who were spreading across Europe like the black plague, killing tens of thousands as well as destroying the precious infrastructure of countries with all the impunity of Genghis Khan.

Claude was worried about *his* Josephine Baker, not just because she was his employer but, like most men who met her, he loved her. He was concerned that the Nazis would pay her another visit as they did from time to time. She always managed to either schmooze them and if that failed, dispose of them but what would happen now? Claude and Emmet had bonded based on their military experiences, but they were traveling with Henry Ford, too, and he was a bit too Nazi-friendly for Claude's taste.

He knew what he had to do. Claude told the boat captain he would return in a few weeks, and to keep the crew out of trouble or heads would roll. Then he found a flight going to Barcelona, Spain, leaving in the morning. He would have to find a way back into France, but he could lease a car, or steal one for that matter. The southern part of France was still free from enemy occupation other than the Vichy lackeys, but Claude knew he would not have problems with them. They traveled in small groups and were scattered and few in numbers. If he kept to the backroads, he should be okay. At least that is what he told himself, then softly muttered, "*C'est quoi ça!*"

FIFTY-SEVEN

CHATEAU DES MILANDES

Three days passed. Josephine went on with her life as usual, discussing upcoming shows with her staff, talking to venue owners, preparing variations in her act, and practicing some new songs.

Ford had found Josephine's library and displayed patience, at least in appearance, occasionally making phone calls to various businesses and reading book after book. Liebold and Bennett went to a nearby train station that had a telegraph service and sent telegraphs on behalf of Ford. At the end of their day, Liebold and Bennett would return and have hushed conversations with Ford, then fall silent when Emmet came into the room.

Liebold was also making calls and went out of his way to keep them private, occasionally attempting to speak broken German. Emmet suspected he was talking to one of the higher-ranking officers in Hitler's upper-ranking echelon. Emmet heard him stumble over words that he didn't know in German, like "blueprints."

There was a nearby farmhouse and vineyard and Josephine knew the owner, Gerard Choffard, who raised and sold fine horses. She introduced Emmet to him, and they became fast friends as they shared stories of the Big War in which Choffard was in the cavalry.

He offered Emmet various horses to ride, and Emmet took him up on the offer, riding every day, to pass the time as they waited for the proposed Nazi visit. He enjoyed the beautiful countryside, with its nearby river, and bucolic rolling hills and forests.

Each day, Choffard allowed Emmet to pick a different horse, and he did—one day a majestic and spirited French trotter, another a beautiful white Camargue, one of the oldest breeds in France— but Emmet's favorite was the Auvergne, a rather large horse with somewhat shorter legs that made them less likely to break while in battle, hence their use for cavalry horses in the Big War. The horse— its name was "*Rouillé*," or "Rusty," in English, from its coloring— followed him around when he would stop for a rest and then would come running when Emmet whistled for him. The sugar cubes Emmet kept in his pocket assured the alliance.

Emmet rode him back to Chateau Des Milandes to show him to Josephine. He got off the horse, letting it graze on the estate's manicured grass as he went in to find Josephine. He noticed tire marks on the lawn, going around to the back of the property, and wondered if one of the groundsmen had tipped a few too many Cabernets and driven off the paved walkway in their work truck.

When he entered the chateau, he found Josephine entertaining a group of Nazi soldiers in the parlor. His blood stopped in his veins and hair stood up on the nape of his neck. His heart seemed to move up and into his throat and he tried to swallow. There were three officers, seated, and three soldiers standing behind them, blonde and blue-eyed as if they were all manufactured in the same Nazi incubator.

Emmet had no way of knowing how many others might be there. He took a deep breath to slow down his heart, which beat with the ferocity of a drum before a battle charge.

Bennett stood near the soldiers and locked eyes with Emmet. He appeared taught and uncomfortable but gave Emmet a slight nod.

Ford was sitting next to one of the officers—the one that had the most medals on his jacket, as if they were old friends. Certainly, they knew each other. Emmet recognized the officer from the newspaper as Rudolph Hess, Deputy Fuhrer. His ice-blue eyes were cold and lifeless, shaded by eyebrows that grew together to form a long, black, serpentine shroud. His face was expressionless. Emmet suspected he was insane, as was Hitler, and wondered, with much trepidation, if all the Nazis were.

"Ah," said Josephine, walking toward him, "Darling, you're finally home. Gentlemen, let me introduce my husband from the Emerald Isle, Mr. James O'Connor." Then she went to Emmet and gave him a kiss.

Emmet realized what she was doing. Ireland was still a neutral country that was not engaged in the war on Europe. As an Irish citizen, he would be of little interest to the Germans. But that did not mean they would not kill him anyway.

Liebold was sitting on the other side of Hess, all of them looking comfortable and chummy with each other. Hess wore the three-branch insignia of the SS on his collar, as did another officer, Emmet deduced was a colonel, or something close to that rank. The other man seated was of a lesser rank, that Emmet recognized as a lieutenant. He also thought he might have seen him somewhere, a narrow-waisted man, who also bore the same lifeless eyes. The officers were all seated, but the lower-ranking soldiers stood, all still wearing helmets, their rifles at their sides.

Ford stood up and for a moment, Emmet thought he might tell his Nazi friends who Emmet really was. Then, with a slight smile, Ford said, "Mr. O'Connor, let me introduce, Deputy Fuhrer Hess, Colonel Major Kurt Lieber, and *Oberleutnant* Edvard Heinz."

Emmet stepped forward and shook hands with Hess, first, adding, "What a pleasure to meet you, Deputy Fuhrer." Then, he shook hands with Colonel Major Lieber, but when he came to Heinz, he took his hand and held it tightly, remembering who he was. Emmet noted the man's small, boy-like waist and recalled catching glimpses of the same man on the ship that brought them to Brazil. The same man, who had killed the postman, strangling him with his small-sized belt, so that they could replace the mail carrier and plant the tube with the poison gas in Ford's mailbox. The poison was inhaled by a fake rabbi with artificial payots in his hair, and Nazi Wolfangels tattooed on his arms.

When Emmet shook hands with Heinz, he gripped it tightly, consciously holding it too long and too tight. The two men stared at each other.

Jaw muscles flexed in Heinz's face and his lips quivered before he finally pulled his hand away. "My, Mr. O'Connor, you have a strong grip. What type of work do you do?"

Emmet tried to overcome his anger and think straight. "I...uh..."

Josephine slid up next to him. "James was a professional boxer before he parlayed his winnings into manufacturing saddles and equestrian products."

"Yes," said Ford, suddenly, standing. "That's one reason I came here, to persuade, Mr. O'Connor to take on a contract for doing the upholstery for the seats in my cars."

Emmet was surprised by Ford's quick intervention, especially considering his fondness for the Germans. Perhaps he was smart enough to know when Nazis showed up where you were staying, it wasn't because they were just being neighborly.

"Yes," said Emmet, his mind racing. "Mr. Ford and I share ideas on manufacturing quality, as well as other ideas, some of which could, possibly, change the world."

"And what might those ideas entail?" asked Hess.

Now, Emmet wasn't sure which way to go. He could not mention the plans for a nuclear bomb after just meeting anyone, let alone the world's would-be conquerors. He glanced at Josephine, hoping she might come up with something. She did, once again reminding Emmet how special she was.

"Gentlemen, can we forestall the subject of business, right now?" she said, with all the natural charm she had. "I have not had a visit from my Deutsch friends in some time. Let me rally my staff and get some refreshments served. I can show you around my home and then you men can chat about mutual interests. *Jawohl, Commandant*?"

Hess smiled, as did the foot soldiers, though Lieber and Heinz did not. "I thought we were here to discuss some of our missing colleagues, sir," said Lieber.

"Let's not be rude, Colonel," said Hess, frowning at Lieber. "We are not in a hurry. I would enjoy some refreshments with Mademoiselle Baker. Then she can show us around her beautiful home."

Emmet took advantage of the situation. If he could get away for a moment, he could make his way up to his room and get his pistol. The officers were all armed with Lugers and the soldiers had rifles, but if he could surprise them, they might have a chance. And there was a possibility the momentary pause could push Liebold into his pastime of sharing things with people he should not be sharing them with.

"Perhaps Mr. Ford and Mr. Liebold can entertain you for a few moments while I put my horse up?" said Emmet.

Liebold suddenly lit up. "Yes, we have much to talk about since we last met, Deputy Fuhrer Hess." Then, as if it were an afterthought, "I think I have something that would interest the Fuhrer."

"Oh?" said Hess. "Are you planning on another factory in our Fatherland?"

Liebold laughed for the first time that Emmet had ever witnessed. It was creepy, sounding forced, but it was a perfect distraction for him to step out and do some reconnaissance. But before he left the room, he stopped in the kitchen to eavesdrop on the conversation.

"Possibly," said Liebold, "but I think this is something of dynamic importance, Deputy Fuhrer Hess. Something so big, it might end this war that has been so devastating—I think you will agree—to both sides. I am sure that Adolph will want to see it. In fact, I must insist. Let me fetch the plans."

Emmet was surprised that Liebold was so forthright, to call Hitler by his first name. It was obvious he, and of course, Ford, had met the Fuhrer previously. Then, too, Hitler did not mind being called "Adolf," as the name came from old Germanic and it meant, "Noble Wolf."

Ford said nothing and his frown was not an indicator of how he felt because he wore it all the time.

Emmet wondered what Ford and his pals would do if it came to a firefight. *Whose side would he be loyal to?*

Liebold was back in a moment to show Hess the plans.

Hess angled his head, looking at the blueprints, like a curious dog. "Are these what I think they are?" he asked.

"Yes, sir," said Liebold. "Your Fuhrer will be most pleased, I'm sure."

There, the bait was offered and taken, thought Emmet. *Serey's crazy plan might just work.* But Emmet was not going to depend on that as a plan to survive. Hess and his soldiers were there to investigate where their missing comrades were and, as mesmerizing as Josephine was, Hess might not buy her story—if she had one at all—and they might all be lined up for a firing squad right after they finished their tea.

Hess sat back down to look at the plans for a moment. "I'll take these to our Fuhrer," said Hess. "Perhaps, you and Mr. Ford will accompany me, and we can present them to him together. I have not seen him much since I was placed on the Council of Ministers."

"That would be wonderful," said Ford. "It's been a while since I've seen him, as well."

"If you'll excuse me," said Emmet, feeling some bile in the back of his throat. It was hard for him to stomach, Ford and Liebold's willingness to see Hitler as just another business associate. Though he knew the bomb's plans were fake, they did not. But he had to hide his displeasure with them and act as if he knew nothing about their intent to deliver what they believed was a real atomic bomb.

"I need to tend to our neighbor's horse," said Emmet. He fetched *Rouillé* and took the horse around the back of the chateau to temporarily put him in Josephine's barn until he could return him to his owner, *Monsieur* Choffard. Emmet suspected if he tried to just ride away to return "Rusty," the Nazis would just shoot him. He noted there were three more soldiers standing near a truck behind the house, so nine Nazis in all. He wondered if things went to hell in a handbag, what Ford, Liebold, or Bennett would do.

Emmet took the horse to the barn behind the Chateau, filled a bucket with water for the horse, and was going to fetch some hay when he heard, "*Pssst*." For a moment he thought the horse had sneezed. Then he heard it again and began to look around. A pile of hay stirred. Emmet spied a machete hanging on a nail in the barn. He took it in hand and moved toward the hay, which moved, as if it was coming to life.

Suddenly a head popped up, its hair filled with straw like a living scarecrow. It said, "Emmet, *mon ami*, it is I, Claude Durand."

Emmet grinned and dropped the machete. "What in God's name? Where did you...I thought you stayed in Rio to bring the boat back."

"*Qu'ai-je à perdre?*" whispered Claude.

When Emmet looked quizzically at him, Claude translated. "What Have I to lose?" Then explained. "The boat had damage from the ship that exploded in the harbor. It will take weeks to repair. While I trust you, I could not leave my sweet employer and friend to fend for herself while living amid these barbaric Huns! I left the repairs in the capable hands of the captain and found a flight to northern Spain, stole a car, and here I am."

Emmet gave Claude a hand and pulled him up, then helped brush him off as he explained the situation.

"Well, you may have gone from out of the frying pan into the fire coming here," said Emmet.

"What does that mean, Emmet?"

"That you were safe but now you have landed in a pit of vipers. In addition to three *Boches* just outside, there are six more in the house, where Josephine is trying to charm them, and Ford's man, Liebold, is trying to give the Nazis plans for a bomb."

Claude thought for a moment, a worried look on his face. "Then we must kill them all." He pulled his always-present throwing knife from a sheath under his shirt sleeve. "

"Damn right," said Emmet, picking up the machete, which he carefully slid down the leg of his trousers. "You stay back, then sneak up from behind after I have a few words with them. I'll give you this signal: I'll raise my pipe and laugh."

Claude acknowledged the plan and Emmet walked casually over to the soldiers, digging a pipe from his pocket.

The soldiers were all smoking cigarettes. They looked like they were barely out of school, and Emmet regretted what he had to do. He was saddened these young soldiers, most of whom were drugged up with meth or cocaine to fight harder, faster, slaves to a false, crazed, and evil prophet, who made them believe they were descendants of an archaeological superior race, the Aryans, who were never real, but a made-up myth originally based on Persians, not Germans. A lie that was perpetuated into a belief in a superior race that was doomed as surely as the Romans.

Out of the corner of his eye, Emmet saw Claude sneaking forward. He held up his pipe, looking for a light and asked, *"Hast du ein Licht?*

The soldiers looked grumpy but one dipped into his pocket and came out with some matches.

"Vielen Dank," said Emmet, thanking the soldier. Then, "How foolish of me," he said. *"Ich habe keinen Tabak mehr!"* he laughed, then raised his pipe, indicating he had no tobacco.

Emmet had barely put the pipe back into his pocket when there was a slapping sound like a butcher's blade cutting into bone and meat. Claude's knife came through the soldier's neck. The man instantly grabbed at his throat, trying to stem the gushing blood, to no avail as it sprayed out of the punctured vessels as if from a torn hose. Emmet immediately pulled the machete from his waistband, swung it in an arc and hacked into one of the two soldiers still standing, striking so hard, the soldier was almost decapitated.

The last soldier fiddled with his rifle, trying to get the strap off of his shoulder, trying to pull the bolt back, trying to live...before Claude came up and retrieved his knife from the soldier he killed, then quickly used it to stab the young man a dozen times before he could do anything of consequence.

Wordlessly, Emmet and Claude moved the bodies behind the soldier's truck. They found some rags and water in the truck and wiped the blood off their arms and faces.

"Take their pistols and any magazines you find," said Emmet. "It would be obvious and clumsy if we walked in with rifles... and you are supposed to be in Brazil, so stay back a step or two. They will not expect you and the surprise will help us. The soldiers inside all have rifles, except the officers. We should be able to beat the soldiers to the draw. We have eight rounds in each magazine, so grab a couple extra just in case. I want to get as close to these goose-stepping bastards as we can, assure Josephine is safe, then take them out as quickly as possible. You stay in the kitchen until you hear the first shot. Then run in raining hell down on them."

They tucked the Luger P08s into the back of their waistbands. "Ready, *mon ami*?" asked Claude.

Emmet nodded, "Yes, let's go save the lady, shall we?"

They strode up to the back of the chateau and went in through the kitchen. Claude stayed back as instructed as Emmet entered the room. He heard chatter in the living room and as he entered the room, words escaped him. Absent were Ford, Liebold, and Bennett. Present was Josephine, her eyes huge and wet, her face, usually the mask of cool, was now filled with terror. She was sitting sandwiched by Deputy Fuhrer Hess on one side, whose expressionless eyes looked like blue ice under his single eyebrow, his jaw muscles flexing.

On the other side was a man Emmet knew too well and for whom he had mixed feelings. "Well, hello, Emmet MacWain," said Ernest Hemingway. "What in the hell are you doing here?"

FIFTY-EIGHT

Before Emmet could shoot any of the officers, Hess placed a small pistol against Josephine's head.

"Drop your gun, Mr. O'Conner, or MacWain, or whoever you are, or I will shoot *Fräulein* Baker in her beautiful head," said the Deputy Fuhrer.

Emmet's stomach knotted, his mind raced trying to figure out the next step and constantly asking the same question: *why the hell was Hemingway there—the idiot—and how can I save Josephine?*

"Raise your shirt and let me see if you have any weapons," said Hess. "Then I think we should all go for a tour of this house, don't you, *Fräulein* Baker?"

As Emmet followed Hess's directive, he turned very slowly. As he did so, he looked for Claude and spotted him in the kitchen. The whole confrontation had taken less than thirty seconds and he knew that Claude had not come into the room, guns blazing, because he feared for Josephine's safety. Emmet was relieved for that, because if Claude had launched an assault, they all would probably have perished, starting with Josephine.

Claude was staring at him, his eyebrows raised as if asking, "What now?"

Emmet locked eyes with Claude for a moment and signaled downward, indicating that Claude should go to the cellar, hoping beyond hope that Claude would understand him. If he did, they might have a chance at overcoming Hess and his depleted minions. No one knew Claude was there, not even Josephine, so maybe they could still pull off this coup.

One of the soldiers found the Luger in his waistband and pulled it out roughly. Emmet turned back slowly, glancing at Josephine, who was trying to keep her usual cool. But Emmet saw a tear roll down her cheek. That tear made him lose any fear, any caution and stirred a hatred, a rage that began to bubble up in him like lava in a volcano. Blood pumped into his head, and he felt like it might explode. He turned his gaze toward Hess, and it was filled with rage.

"I don't like this imposter's insolence," said *Oberleutnant* Heinz, standing. "I believe he was the investigator who found out the dead rabbi was one of our own men who gave his life for the Fatherland. I will kill him, Deputy Fuhrer Hess," he said, unholstering his gun.

"*Nein*," said Hess, "Go find Herr Ford and his companions. I want to know what they know about this man. Take Colonel Liebert with you in case they are up to something."

"But what about you, Deputy Fuhrer?" Heinz asked. "What if there are others in league with these *Verräters*?"

"Then I will kill them all, starting with *Fräulein* Baker. Now go and do as I say and search the rest of the house, too. Be thorough and take these soldiers with you."

Heinz locked eyes with Hess for a moment, his jaws flexing with indignance. Then he and Colonel Lieber left the room, both glaring at their leader.

Hess stood up and put his back toward a wall. "Get up, Herr Hemingway," he ordered.

Hemingway did as he was told. "Now, keep in mind, I'm a reporter, not a soldier..."

"I know who you are," said Hess, his voice like sharp ice. "And what you are. Go stand next to O'Conner, or MacWain, or whomever this spy is. You, too, *Fräulein* Baker."

Emmet wanted to know where Hemingway's sons were but did not want to bring the subject up, just in case Hemmingway was smart enough to have secured them in a safe place, or if he was smart enough to get them out of this war-torn country and back home.

Hemingway did as he was told.

After Heinz and Lieber left the room, Hess did something unexpected. He holstered his gun, then looked down the hall to see if his fellow officers were around. When he was satisfied they were not, he approached his captives.

"I have to tell you something, quickly," said Hess, as if they were meeting in a coffee shop to discuss the latest news. "My friend, a former professor, Karl Haushofer, the philosopher who pushed the idea of *Lebensraum* that became Germany's goal to expand our space, has discussed something with me."

Emmet, Josephine, and Hemingway all looked at each other, confused.

Hess paused for a moment and looked around again for his officers. "Haushofer is a genius but as we've moved forward with our country's dream of German Expansionism, Haushofer contacted me and has convinced me of something." Hess paused again as if considering what he was doing. His face was pale and for a moment, his hand went to his stomach as if he was going to vomit. "He, we... have discovered that *Lebensraum* will not work because it requires too many soldiers to hold the fronts. Hitler, my former friend, has grown...unreliable. When I spoke to him about my concerns, he moved me to the Council of Ministers for the Defense of the Reich and does not listen to me anymore. He is planning on expanding the war to another front. It's a battle we can't win against Russia. We are, if I am to be honest, quite overwhelmed trying to maintain a war on too many fronts now."

Emmet thought Hess looked maniacal as if he had not slept for days, and wondered if he was taking the same stimulant drugs the soldiers were issued.

Hess's eyes darted to each of his captives' faces as if looking for answers, before he continued, talking so fast, he was almost unintelligible. "Haushofer told me that King George of Britain is opposed to the way Churchill is running the war. He believes the King wants to replace Churchill and take a different direction. Haushofer has written to the Duke of Hamilton to see if we can meet and make a...compromise. Haushofer believes they will meet with me and discuss some other alternatives that might end this war and the countless loss of lives. My hope is that we can do something to keep Germany from falling because of our voracious appetite to conquer. I believe our reach has exceeded our grasp, as you say."

Hess paused and while Emmet wasn't sure if Hess could be trusted, he took the opportunity to ask some questions, if for nothing else but to buy time. "So, what is your intent, sir? If it is something that may lead to peace, how can we help?"

Hess looked at Emmet, then Josephine, and finally at Hemingway, and to all said, "First I must have Herr Hemingway's promise he will not write about this meeting and what I am telling you. Obviously, it would mean my instant death by firing squad."

Everyone looked at Hemingway. "Well, sir, I am a reporter as well as a writer..." he began.

"Shut up," said Emmet. "This man is trying to broker a possible peace treaty. You *won't* write about this," said Emmet directly. "What do you say, Josephine?"

"I say we should listen to what Herr Hess says. I mean, he's still the only one of us who has a gun."

Hess lowered the gun. "I have to trust you," said Hess. "More importantly, *you* have to trust me. If you do, we can save thousands of lives."

Emmet looked at Hemingway who gave him a nod, then to Josephine. Another nod.

"All right," said Emmet. "A truce, for now. How can we help?"

Hess continued. "Lieber and Heinz are underlings to Klaus Barbie. He was supposed to come here, but I outranked him and told him I wanted to see what was going on here myself." Here he paused first, stepped toward the hall, and assured himself that no one was listening to him.

"The truth is, my intent is to fly to Britain, myself, and negotiate a peace with them. I need some papers made up with a new identity, so they don't kill me right away. If I tried to have them made in Germany, I would be discovered and killed along with my family and my plan for peace would never be heard."

"I can help you with that," said Josephine, stepping forward. But before she could discuss the details with him, they heard steps coming and stepped back. Hess heard them, too, and took his gun from his holster to act like he was still keeping guard on Josephine and her guests.

Heinz and Lieber entered the room. With them were Ford, Liebold, and Bennett.

"My God," said Ford. "What is going on here?"

"Your friend killed our soldiers," said Heinz. "And he would have killed us all if Deputy Fuhrer Hess, had not put a gun to the black devil's head."

"What were you thinking, MacWain?" said Ford, his face flushed. Then he turned to Hemingway whom he recognized. "And what are you doing here, Mr. Hemingway?"

"Just thought I'd stop in and see an old friend but wasn't expecting she'd have such a mix of company," said Hemingway, with a smirk. "You really ought to rethink your guest list next time, Miss Baker."

Colonel Liebert butted in. "I have taken the liberty of calling in another *Schwarm* that are some thirty kilometers from here. They were working with the undermanned and spineless Vichy Police. It seems there has been a scourge of French resistance fighters in the area that they had to help control. Do you know anything about this, *Fraulein* Baker?"

"No, I don't," said Josephine, indignant. "I'm just a performer, not a resistance leader."

Hess stepped in. "Enough of this, Colonel. Have you and Heinz completed your search of the premises?"

"Yes, we have," said Heinz. "All but a hidden cellar that we just learned about from one of the servants. I believe Henri was his name," he said, smirking. "I think that's what he said before he died."

Josephine stepped forward; her face morphed into a mask of hatred. "You killed Henri? You cowardly, fucking bastard," she said, then spit in Heinz's face.

Heinz wiped the spittle from his face. "We will kill you, too, black whore, perhaps let some of the men have their way with you before we leave."

"That's enough," said Hess. "I will say who we will kill and who we will not. For now, I think a check of the cellar is in order. If it is clear, we will take Mr. MacWain in our custody and leave the rest of her guests here. Is that understood, *Oberleutnaut?*"

"Yes, sir, Deputy Fuhrer Hess," said Heinz, his face flushed with anger.

"Herr Ford," said Hess, "You and your men can stay up here. My soldiers will stay with you and notify me if there are any more surprises. Please prepare yourselves for a trip to meet with the Fuhrer so that we can share your plans with him. I'm sure he will be pleased. Mr. MacWain, come with us so we can keep an eye on you. For killing our soldiers, you will be held as our prisoner. Do you understand?"

"I do," said Emmet.

"Then lead on," said Hess to Heinz and Liebert.

"I'll come with you," said Josephine. "I have a torch and you will need me to open the locked door and show you around."

"What about me?" asked Hemingway.

Hess stared at Hemingway for a long time before answering him. "What for, *Papa?*"

"So you can write more inflammatory rhetoric about us *Jerry's?*"

"No," said Hemingway. "Nothing like that. I mean as far as *Heine's* go, you don't seem like a bad guy." He said then gesturing toward Henry Ford, added. "I just don't want to keep company with this Kraut lover."

Ford said nothing but Bennett stepped forward. "Watch your mouth...*writer*," he said as if that was the worst thing he could think of calling Hemingway.

Emmet grimaced, noting Hess's face turn red, a vein throbbing on his temple.

Hess smiled as if the words meant nothing to him, then said, "Yes, come along. If we find anything in the cellar that indicates *Fraulein* Baker had something to do with our missing officer, then we can shoot you all in one place."

The group—Emmet, Josephine, Hemingway, and Hess—along with the three Nazi soldiers came to a place in the basement of the chateau where Josephine had to point out the door to the cellar.

They would not have found it otherwise. Josephine removed a stone and there was a handle inside the hole where the stone had been. She grasped the handle and turned it. There was a sound like gears grinding on gears and the door slowly opened. Cool air blew up through the dark hole that was the entrance to the cellar and the group began to descend.

Josephine held a torch but stopped along the winding stairway to light candles that produced flickering shadows to the descent. It was cool and dank, perfect to keep wine, but some of the steps were slippery. The songstress was at the lead with Heinz and Liebert behind her, then Emmet, Hemingway, then Hess, and the three soldiers, as they descended into the stygian darkness. They were about halfway down to the bottom of the cellar when Hess heard the soldiers bickering with someone.

It was Liebold.

"What are you doing, Herr Liebold?" asked Hess.

"Uh, Mr. Ford asked me to go with you..." said Liebold.

Hess stared at him for a moment, then said, "All right. We will have a look at this lair, then you and I must talk more about those plans. I'm sure there is some financial agreement you wish to discuss."

Then the group continued descending into the cellar, some slipping along the way in the flickering light, their shadows, elongated like boney stickmen.

Emmet was sure not all of them would be ascending. He was making a plan that would guaranty that.

FIFTY-NINE

THE CELLAR

Hess was going through the motions of an investigation, but it was just for show for Heinz and Liebert, who would undoubtedly go back to Klaus Barbie, or even the Fuhrer with their reports. That fact alone angered Hess, who until recently was second in the chain of power. Still, as the group made their way to the floor of the cellar, he could easily believe, this dark hole was where Jews and other "undesirables," escaping Europe—running from Hitler's onslaught—sought refuge.

Now, Liebert and Heinz—cronies of Barbie—were in the mix and they would only complicate things with their overzealous "inspections." Both searching every inch of the cellar with their *Taschenlampe*, the hand-wound pocket lights.

Emmet watched as Josephine tried to use her charm to distract Heinz and Liebert, but it was pearls before the swine, so to speak, as neither they nor the stormtroopers that accompanied them were impressed with her sensual talents. Emmet looked back toward the three *Wehrmachts* to see if they had found anything incriminating and noticed something no one else had: now, there were only two soldiers. *What happened to the other one?* He wondered, though he thought he knew the answer.

Claude Durand was in the cellar, too. Emmet looked into the shadows and the small rooms that held various casks of wine. He thought he saw an outline of a man squeezed against a door but did not want to look closer and draw attention. But as he glanced at the shadow again, there was a flash of metal catching the light of a candle and Emmet knew what it was. Claude was signaling him with the blade of his throwing knife. Without looking back in his direction, Emmet nodded his head slightly. He wondered if Claude still had the Luger, they took off one of the soldiers they killed outside.

A hand gripped Emmet's shoulder. It was Hemingway and his lips were close to Emmet's ear as he whispered, "The boys are down here..."

Emmet stopped, briefly and looked back into Hemingway's shadowed face. He wanted to tell him what a fool he was bringing his sons to a war zone and now, placing them in even greater danger. If the bullets began to fly...an interruption below refocused Emmet's attention.

Heinz was looking at something on the floor with his flashlight. He ordered one of the soldiers to come to him with another light.

Emmet made a plan and a quick decision. He slowly inched toward Heinz. It was now or never.

"Is that a blood stain?" Heinz asked. As the soldier knelt next to Heinz to look at the floor, Emmet approached the two squatting men as if to see better himself. He set his legs, balling up the fist of his right hand, then twisted at the waist and pivoted using the momentum to launch a hard right cross toward Heinz.

Heinz turned his head just before the punch landed and Emmet felt his knuckles smash against the back of his head. Heinz went down and dropped his flashlight, but he was not out of the fight. The soldier who had crouched down with him tried to stand up and shoulder his rifle but there was a *thwap* and a dagger appeared, as if by magic, in his back. The soldier reached back to pull at the weapon, his breathing already labored, when Emmet threw a left hook that caught the soldier in the Adam's apple of his neck. He went down choking as the room exploded into gunshots and flashlight beams were directed around the room in feared haste.

Emmet grabbed the soldier's rifle but had no time, nor room to shoulder and shoot. He swung the butt of the rifle and caught the remaining soldier in his head. He was not sure if he'd knocked him out or killed him as someone else, probably Josephine, or Claude—who both knew the cellar well—was dousing the candles. Emmet heard footsteps on the stairs and more candles went out. Shots rang out and Emmet pushed his back against a wall so no one could come up from behind him. Then he closed his eyes for a moment to adjust them to the darkness.

When he opened them, he saw a flashlight someone had dropped in a corner, then a quick movement to his left and the silhouette of a man just before it threw a belt over his head and around his neck and began to squeeze.

"Let's see how strong you are now, Scotsman," Heinz hissed. Emmet tried to shift his body weight to lessen the tight grip around his throat. He reached back but Heinz was fast and ducked Emmet's grasp. Black dots were already floating in front of his eyes as his fingers grabbed impotently at the belt that cinched tighter, the blood pushing into his head like an oil rig before it blew.

There was a meaty smack and a sound like a coconut falling on concrete and the belt loosened.

Emmet slumped onto his knees, the floor coming back into focus, and began to breathe again. He looked up to see Hemingway grinning like a cartoon character. "How are you doing, Scotty," said Hemingway. "Aren't you glad I tagged along?"

"Whe...where...are ...the boys?" Emmet croaked.

Josephine suddenly appeared and squatted in front of Emmet. "The boys are safe in my room," she said. "There is a secret door in the back of the cellar I told the boys about. It goes up to a closet in my room. "Are you okay, baby?"

Emmet nodded and a trickle of blood came from his nostrils. He used the wall to pull himself up with Hemingway on one side and Josephine on the other. "Thank you both," said Emmet. "Where's Claude?"

Josephine looked at Hemingway, who shrugged, then back to Emmet. "I didn't know he was here," she said.

"He was," said Emmet, pointing to the dim corner where Claude had been hiding. "He was over there. He took out two of the soldiers before it all went to hell."

Josephine found her flashlight and rushed over to where Emmet had pointed. Then she screamed. Hemingway ran over to her, Emmet got to his feet and stumbled over, his throat feeling as if he had swallowed a razor blade.

Claude was on his back, his breathing labored, his skin pale and sweating profusely. He was also bleeding from a bullet that had bore through his upper chest and out his back. Tears ran down Josephine's cheeks as she alternated between hugging Claude and trying to get him to sit up. "C'mon, my French baby," she said. "I need you, sweet man."

"Who got you, my friend?" asked Emmet. "Could you see?"

Claude nodded, slightly. "*Oui*. It was...Li..." He stopped and coughed, then tried to continue as blood came from the corner of his mouth. "Lieb..." he tried, then stopped and lost consciousness.

Emmet shook Claude by his shoulders. "Liebert, the Colonel?" Emmet asked. "Or Liebold, Ford's lackey?" Still no answer. Emmet searched Claude's belt, then rolled him over to see if he still had the Luger. He found it behind him where it must have fallen when Claude went down.

"Leave him on his side, Jo, so he doesn't choke on his blood," said Emmet. "Keep this pistol with you. I saw a medical kit in the Germans' truck. I'll go fetch it and see where everyone else is. Ernest, you should go check on your boys. Grab one of the soldier's rifles. Keep them safe if they're still in the room. I'll be back here as soon as I can. Did anyone see Hess?"

"I saw him going up the stairs when I was helping get Heinz off your back," said Hemingway. "I think he was going after Liebert, or Liebold, one or both of those bastards. But he was limping Emmet. Looked like he took one in the leg."

Emmet nodded. "Okay," he said. "I'll try to find him, too. Colonel Liebert said he had called in another platoon of soldiers. Maybe Hess can stop them if I can find him."

"Or order in more," said Hemingway.

"Let's hope not," said Emmet, as he looked around for, and found, another pistol on one of the dead soldiers. "Jo, you are going to be okay, here. Ernest, let's go. I'll cover for you until you get up the stairs. He gathered the dead soldiers' rifles and handed one to Hemingway. Keep the boys in Josephine's room. Let me know if you find Hess. I'll fetch the med kit in the truck out back and come back here for Jo and Claude."

"Roger that," said Hemingway. Then both men ran up the blood-soaked stairs, trying not to slip in the red ooze that dripped off of the steps like a creek running out of water.

***

Emmet and Hemingway stopped at the top of the stairs and looked down the dark corridor that led back to the main house. With their backs against the wall, Emmet looked forward as Hemingway looked back to assure that they were not being followed, or ambushed, from behind. They made their way back to the main living room. A trail of blood dappled the floor, boot prints smeared through it.

"You go upstairs and fetch the boys," Emmet whispered. "When you find them, you get the hell out of here."

"No can do, my man," said Hemingway. "I'm not leaving you here to face off with a *Schwarm* of these goosestepping bastards alone."

"Okay, just make sure the boys are all right," said Emmet. "I'll follow the blood and see who it leads to."

Hemingway nodded. "Be careful, pal. We know Liebert is a skunk. Liebold is questionable at best, and we're not sure about Hess. He seems...unstable. If I were you, I'd shoot first and ask questions later." Then he took off running in a crouch, headed for the stairs.

Emmet wondered where Ford and Bennett were. He also wondered where their loyalties stood. He was sure Liebold could not be counted on. He'd been eager to share with Hess what he believed were blueprints to a world-changing bomb, so it was reasonable to believe he would do anything to save himself. And what about Ford and Bennett? Bennett seemed like a thug, but Emmett couldn't see him being favorable to the Nazis. But Ford was a personal friend of the worst madman in history. Whose side would he be on if it came down to choosing?

A thought came to Emmet. He had to get the medical bag from the German's truck out back. Maybe he could do that and come back into the house from a different direction? One that no one would be monitoring.

He crouched and ran through the kitchen and out the back door, his eyes darting back and forth for a head to pop up, aiming a gun, or the glint of light reflecting off the barrel of a rifle. Once outside he bolted for the truck, retrieved the med bag, and was sprinting back to the house when there was a hard slap on his upper arm, followed by the sound of a gun firing. He instinctively glanced at his arm and saw he had been shot, then hit the ground and rolled back under the truck. Suddenly, the truck was bouncing from repeated shots, pinging off the fenders, exploding the windows, some rounds tearing through the canvas canopy on the back of the truck. One shot blew the mirror off the truck's door.

Whenever Emmet tried to peek toward the house, the shooter barraged the ground around him. If he tried to get up and run on the opposite side of the truck toward the barn, he would still be a target in the field before he could make it.

He felt his wound throb as if his heart had relocated there. He probed the wound and his fingers fell into a hole where some flesh used to be. He tore the rest of the sleeve away and pulled it off his arm, then made a tourniquet from it and put it above the wound. As he was doing that, the sun kept glinting into his eyes. He looked for the source of the light and saw the truck's rearview mirror lying under the truck near him. An idea formed in his head. He took a chance and grabbed the mirror and the ground exploded up again from a rain of bullets.

Now Emmet rolled toward the other, safer side of the truck and positioned himself with his head toward the house, then used the mirror to site the shooter without having to stick his head up to see him. He spied an open window and fixed the mirror on it. He could see the shooter reluctantly filling the window space, and from time to time, looking to see if his target was still pinned under the truck or on the run. Each time he appeared, he stayed in the window frame a little longer. Now, Emmet could see it was Liebert, the Nazi Colonel who somehow had made it unscathed from the cellar, and now, as most trained soldiers would do, he took the high ground.

Emmet rolled into a prone position and aimed his rifle toward the window using the shadow of the truck's tire to hide the glint of his own rifle and waited. Liebert appeared in the open window once more to see if Emmet was on the run again. Emmet had been a cavalry fighter, and had learned to shoot while in the saddle on a dead run, and if one can do that, one could shoot from a prone position easily enough. He pulled the trigger. He saw Liebert's head snap back and then he was gone from the frame.

Emmet waited for a few minutes then slid out from under the opposite side of the truck and retrieved the medical bag. He glanced back at the window once again, but Lieber was no longer peeking out. Emmet looked at all of the windows and the sides of the house before making a run back to it.

When he got back inside, he ran down to the basement, and into the wine cellar. Josephine had lit the candles again and was sitting on the floor next to Claude, his head in her lap. Her face shined with tears that poured from her eyes as if there was no end to them. Emmet raced over to them fearing what he would find. He dropped the now useless medical kit and felt for a pulse in Claude's neck. He found only stillness and cold flesh. Claude was gone.

SIXTY

Emmet said nothing but edged over and kneeled next to Josephine, noting the pistol he left her was still warm from firing a shot. He wrapped his arms around her and hugged her and began rocking her gently, side to side, like a father giving reassuring love to a daughter who has lost something most precious.

"He's gone, love," he said while trying to hold back his own tears for a lost fellow soldier. "But we are going to take care of him. Promise. Can you stay with Claude while I finish some things I have to do?"

Josephine wordlessly nodded her head, and Emmet kissed her cheek, tasting the salt of her tears on his lips.

When he got up, he went over to Heinz and held a candle over his face. There was a bullet hole between his eyes and what looked like pink pudding coming from one of his ears. Josephine had shot him when she saw Claude die. Emmet said nothing to her but turned and went up the stairs, taking the medical kit with him. He did not know who was left alive but brought it just in case someone needed it.

Hess was waiting for him in the sitting room where they had gone over the fake bomb plans, a gun in his hand. His face was pale, and his left pant leg was soaked with blood. He had taken off his belt and tied a tourniquet around the wound to slow the bleeding. Ford, Bennett, and Liebold were sitting next to him, quietly.

"Let me look at your wound," said Emmet, dropping the med kit on the floor next to Hess.

Hess shook his head. "No. I want the wound to appear as if I had to field dress it."

"Why would you want to do that?"

"Because it will be part of a plan I have concocted. I will need your help."

Hemingway appeared at the top of the stairs, his sons, Patrick and Gregory, standing next to him, tear tracks on their faces. "All clear up here," said Hemingway.

"Heinz is dead," said Emmet. "I think I got Lieber, too, but haven't gone up to check."

"He's dead as a doornail," Hemingway assured "Nice shooting for a Scotty pinned under a truck," he quipped.

Emmet nodded. "Good. Why don't you come down here? This man has a plan he would like to discuss and, unless I'm wrong, we need to hear it and act fast."

"You are correct," said Hess. "Time is short and there are other soldiers coming and I'm afraid Klaus Barbie might be with them. If he is, he will burn this house to the ground with everyone in it."

"We're listening," said Emmet. Hemingway came down the stairs with his sons and Gregory, "Gigi," came over and quietly took Emmet's hand and held it, like old friends, because they were.

"I will need your help loading up the dead soldiers into their truck. We will drive it up the road as far as I can get away from this house, and then we will shoot some holes in the truck and set it on fire. When Barbie and the *Schwarm* arrive, I will tell them we were attacked by a group of French resistance fighters. Barbie might want to look around, but I will order him to get me to a hospital."

"What if he doesn't want to listen and wants to come here?" Hemingway asked.

"I outrank him, and I will convince him that I have already inspected the Chateau and it is clear," said Hess.

Emmet nodded. "It could work."

"It will," said Hess. "Now, the sooner we get started, the better."

To Emmet's surprise, Bennett and even Liebold worked together picking up dead soldiers and placing them in the truck. Hemingway worked with Emmet, which he appreciated as his shoulder wound was throbbing as if it had a separate heart in it, though it had been cleaned and bandaged. Ford sat with Hess discussing the war, manufacturing, and their common hatred of Jews.

When the last of the dead *Wehrmacht* soldiers were loaded into the truck, Emmet and Hess got into the front seat. Emmet drove as Hess told him where to go. Hemingway and Bennett drove behind them to bring back Emmet, while Ford and Liebold began packing their luggage. Hess told Emmet where to park on a country road far from Josephine's chateau. While Emmet and Hemingway doused the vehicle with gasoline and lit it, Bennett drove the car around in the field to make it appear as if several units had been there, then escaped back to the hills after their attack on the German soldiers.

Hess found himself a shaded place under a tree and radioed the *Schwarm* that had been dispatched earlier. While waiting for them, Hess looked over the set of blueprints for a world-destroying bomb that would never work. Nevertheless, the Germans would spend lots of time, manpower, and money, which they were running through like water through a sieve. Their commitment to a doomed project was, in itself, a weapon for the allies in its own subtle way.

Before leaving him, Emmet gave Hess a canteen of water and some rations he found in the truck. "*Danke Schon*, said Hess, and he extended his hand to Emmet.

Emmet did not take it and said, "I can't do that, sir. We are still in a war that your country started. You and I just worked out something advantageous to both of us. But we sir, are not friends."

With that, he turned and went back to the car and climbed in with Bennett and Hemingway. They drove back to the chateau without saying a word.

A storm rolled in like panzer tanks. The sky was the color of gunpowder, and the lightning was just as explosive. The car's tires found potholes that splashed mud, the color of prisoner's stew, onto the windows.

When they arrived back at the chateau, Ford and Liebold were packed up, and ready to go. Bennett ran up to his room, grabbed his bags, and joined his entourage.

Before they left, Emmet took Ford to the side for a moment of privacy.

"Did you know the Nazis had placed the tube of gas in your mailbox, then had one of their own men dress up as the rabbi, to make it appear the Jews were trying to kill you?"

Ford chuckled. "Oh, Mr. MacWain, that could not be possible. I mean, who would even think of something so...outlandish? And why would they do that? What would they gain?"

Emmet gritted his teeth, trying to contain his anger. "No one gained anything. They did it to inflame other Americans to hate Jews as much as the Nazis do. As much as *you* do. To get them to believe one of America's success stories, a poor farmer who pulled himself up by his bootstraps and made himself the head of the largest-selling automobile in the United States, was almost killed by Jews who conspired against him."

Ford laughed though his blue eyes turned to ice. "This is what I hired you for? This crazy notion? Well, sir, thank you for your... efforts...and the laugh. I will send you a check, at least for your per diem, and you may enjoy the car I gave you. I believe that makes us even."

"We'll never be even," said Emmet.

With that, Ford shrugged, then turned to gather Liebold and Bennett. They escorted themselves out—without expressing gratitude to Josephine—to a car that was waiting for them, knowing they did not have to worry about encounters with Nazis, knowing they were guests of a country ruled by a madman who wanted to own the world, and they were safe and welcome.

EPILOGUE

KEY WEST, FLORIDA

MONTHS LATER

E mmet sat in his boat, some baited lines in the water, the gentle rocking of the boat, like a mother's hand on a cradle, finally allowing him to rest and feel at home.

He had stayed in France with Josephine, to help her grieve and bury Claude Durand. They made love a few times but managed to not fall in love. When they parted, both made promises to each other that they would see each other again, but with Josephine beginning another tour, neither would commit to a timeline for when they might reconnect. With the war in Europe escalating into the Pacific, who knew what tomorrow might bring, if anything? While touring, Josephine Baker continued to spy for the French.

Ford, Liebold, and Bennett returned to Florida briefly then back to Michigan, where Bennett's role as an advisor was increased and a man named Frank Campsall assumed the role of Assistant Manager, while Liebold's responsibilities diminished.

Rudolph Hess got into his Messerschmitt Bf 110, a small bomber-fighter plane, and flew to Scotland to meet the Duke of Hamilton and broker peace with Britain. He ran out of fuel and parachuted onto a farmer's field, identifying himself as Captain Alfred Horn, with the false identity obtained from Josephine. The identity did not last long, and he was arrested and taken to the Tower of London initially before being jailed in Spandau prison.

Hemingway brought his sons back to Key West where he caught hell from Pauline, then went back to Cuba to reunite with Martha Gellhorn.

Serey arranged a flight for Emmet back to the U.S. on an international Red Cross flight that took him to New York. While he waited for another flight to Florida, he stayed in the Ansonia Hotel on Broadway. He was looking out the window at the city that never sleeps, a chilly rain splattering the busy street below, when there was a knock on the door. He went to answer it, already knowing who it was.

Serey was wearing a trench coat under a floppy, soaked hat. Emmet let him in and handed him a towel. After some grumbling about the weather, Serey opened the bag and withdrew a bottle of scotch. He found two glasses, set them on a table, and poured Emmet and himself some shots. They drank them and sat down to talk, and Emmet poured two more.

"Will you be going back to Ft. Myers to collect the car that Ford gave you?" Serey asked, as though struggling for conversation.

Emmet shrugged and said, "Why not? At least I will have earned something from this...experience." His jaw muscles flexed.

Serey nodded, then said, "Agent Jason Abram was killed. We had good reason to believe Sheriff Ross was involved with the murder. My deputy, Agent Holly, went down there to investigate and found that Ross was a member of the Silver Shirts, a Nazi-inspired group very much like the KKK. Holly went to question Ross and found him dead in his office from a self-inflicted gunshot."

"That's convenient," said Emmet, his teeth grinding.

"Yes, it is," said Serey, then switched to a different subject. "I've already received news that the Germans have plans for an atomic bomb and they are rushing to get its construction underway." He smiled a little.

"Do you know if it was based on the plans we gave to Hess?"

Serey nodded. "Because we had not heard this intelligence until recently, we believe it is ours. By the time the Nazis figure out that it will not work, we'll have a real one that does."

"Somehow, I can't think of that as a win."

"It is," said Serey, enthusiastically, then softened his pitch with, "Time will tell." He finished his scotch and stood up, retrieving his damp hat and coat. "I'll have a taxi pick you up in the morning. It will take you to the airport and the plane will take you to Tampa, Florida. Get a ride down to Ford's house in Ft. Myers and drive your new car back to Key West. I'll get in touch with you there."

"Don't," said Emmet.

Serey stared at Emmet for a couple of deep breaths, dropped an envelope on the table, and gave Emmet a quick nod. He stood and walked to the door quietly, then left without saying another word.

Emmet opened the envelope and found ten thousand dollars in it. He put it inside his jacket pocket, as one might with a used handkerchief.

Emmet had not heard back from Bessie Murphy, the scarlet-haired young lady with whom he thought he had fallen in love, since the telegraph he received from her in Rio De Janeiro. She had talked about the Ringmaster Tommy Mandet with whom she had gone to dinner and that was the last he had heard from her. But when he went back to Ft. Myer's to fetch the car that Ford had given to him, he stopped by the Royal Palm Hotel where he had met the beautiful, flame-haired bartender. When he inquired about Bessie, the manager, a man named Ketchner, told him what he knew.

"Yes, I remember Bessie," he said. "Everyone loved Bessie, but she wanted to join the circus and travel the world and she finally did." That was information Emmet knew but there was more that he did not know.

Ketchner continued. "I think she was becoming a popular act with the circus for a while, jumping through rings of fire with her horse. Then something happened to her."

"What do you mean, 'something happened to her?'" Emmet asked, his heart suddenly beginning to pound.

"I don't know," said the manager. "She disappeared. It was in the newspaper. They were doing a show, somewhere, in New York, maybe? Chicago? I can't recall exactly. Some big city, and she disappeared. I believe the police investigated but they never found her."

By the time Ketchner had finished talking, Emmet thought he'd be sick to his stomach. He thanked the manager, got in his car, and drove back to Key West, using Victor Hugo Green's Travel Guide to find some nice places to stop along the way.

Now, as he sat on his boat, still recovering from the trip that took him to Brazil, then to France, and left him with more blood on his hands, and more chunks of flesh and bone from his own body, he needed to think, and believe in something good. He thought of Bessie Murphy. Their time together had only been a one-night stand, but it had been something more to him and, he believed, it had been more for Bessie, too.

Now, she had just disappeared. It was a mystery, and the more Emmet thought about it, the more he knew what he had to do. Mysteries are things that need to be solved, especially when you love someone. He reeled in his lines and began to pack a bag.

END

A WORD FROM THE AUTHOR

This book is a work of fiction. Many of the characters and some of the plots are based on real people and events. Henry Ford and Charles Lindberg were antisemites as were many people in America, indeed, even the world.

Rudolph Hess, once Adolf Hitler's second in command as Deputy Fuhrer, did flee to the United Kingdom in an attempt to bring the war to an end. He flew until his plane ran out of fuel and parachuted out, and landed on a farm south of Glasgow, his foot injured from his exit from the plane. He was discovered by one of the farmers and gave them a false identity while announcing he had an extremely important message for the Duke of Hamilton. He was detained and questioned by local police, his identity finally discovered, and he was sent to prison where he tried to kill himself several times. He was not successful until 1987 when he was found dead in his cell.

Ernest Liebold worked with Ford until 1944 but his role was greatly diminished. He was investigated by the United States Department of War's Military Intelligence Branch. An internal investigation into the Ford Motor Company found Liebold to have ties to the infamous Duquesne Spy Ring, a group of Nazi spies in America who were eventually captured in 1941. Liebold managed to stay out of prison and eventually retired from the Ford Motor Company.

Harry Bennett and Frank Campsall took over running the company before Edsel Ford took over. Edsel died of stomach cancer and Henry Ford resumed running the company until he was forced to vacate his position and ceded control of the company to his grandson, Henry Ford II, who fired Harry Bennett as his first order of business. Henry Ford suffered several strokes through the years and eventually died in April of 1947.

Josephine Baker continued to work with the French Resistance until the end of WWII. Though she had international success and was one of the biggest stars in the world, her performance career was never well managed. Married and divorced several times, she had countless affairs with men and women. But she was often taken advantage of, and she fell on financial hard times, losing the Chateau in France in 1968. Princess Grace helped her out and set up some performances for her. Her career rallied for a while until 1975 when she did a show in Paris to celebrate her 50th year in show business. After her performance, she went back to her hotel, suffered a massive stroke, and died. In November 2021, a memorial was inaugurated in honor of Josephine at the Pantheon in Paris following her election to the mausoleum by French President Emmanuel Macron in August 2021. She is the first Black woman to enter the Panthéon, and only the sixth woman, alongside Marie Curie, French legislator Simone Veil, and a handful of others.

There were many characters in this book that were either real people or based on real people.

Victor Hugo Green, who was briefly mentioned in the book, published The Negro Motorist Green Book, a guide for African American travelers, from 1933-1966.

Captain Alves (fictional name) was a British M16 spy codenamed "Cheese." He was a double agent working undercover with the Germans feeding their information to M16 for some six years. His real name was Renato Levi, an Italian Jew who was born in Genoa. When the Germans began to suspect he was a spy, but Hiter himself vouched for him. As in *Edison's Last Breath*, Levi fed the Germans false information.

The idea for *Edison's Last Breath* came from a true story. Edison's last breath was collected in several sealed tubes after his death. Stories of how and why this occurred vary. One story says that Henry Ford requested Edison's son Charles to collect them. Another story maintains that Edison saved his breath in honor of his very good friend, Henry Ford. Another story suggests the test tubes were simply in the room of his death bed, and when he breathed his last breath, the tubes were sealed with the assumption that they must have Edison's last breath in them. The fact is, there were many tubes said to contain his last breath, some still in existence, though many have been lost. One tube is in the Henry Ford Museum in Dearborn, Michigan and one is in the Ford and Edison winter homes in Ft. Myers, Florida.

Glossary of Languages

German:

Leichendiener: corpse servant

Diener: Servant

Weisskreuz: White Cross

Haupsturnfuhrer: Head Storm Leader

Untermensch: an inferior person

Schwarzer Teufel: Black Devil

Schwach: Weak

Armeezug: Army Platoon

Negresmac: offensive word for African Woman

Hast Duein Licht: Have you a light?

Ich Habt Keinen Taback Mehr: I don't have tobacco anymore.

French:

Leche cul: Ass licker

D'acord?: Understand?

Je lève mon verre à la libération: I raise my glass to liberty

Je Comprends: I understand

Bon nuit: Good night

  Qu'est-ce que c'est que ça ?: What the hell?

  Qu'est-ce que j'ai à perdre ? What have I got to lose?

Boches: Krauts

Patrick Kendrick worked a dual career as a firefighter and freelance journalist before turning to writing fiction full-time. As a freelance writer, he published articles and short stories in numerous newspapers and magazines. He was recently published in Punk Noir and the anthology, Unspeakable. He has had documentaries made about his work as a firefighter (*Behind the Smoke*) and about his non-fiction book, *American Ripper: The True Story of America's Serial Killer Cop, a biography of Gerard Schaefer*, a cop who was a prolific serial killer operating in Florida in the 1970's.

Patrick Kendrick

Kendrick was knighted by the Fraternal Order of Police for his articles on crime. He's won honorable mentions from the Mystery Writers of America and the Beverly Hills Film Festival. He won the Opus Magnum Discovery Award from the Hollywood Film Festival and the Florida Book Award for his first novel, *Papa's Problem*. He won a second Florida Book Award for his young adult novel, *The Savants*. He won the Florida Writer's Association's Royal Palm Literary Gold Award for Best Biography, for *American Ripper: The True Story of America's Serial Killer Cop*.

He lives in South Florida and when he is not writing, he spends as much time as possible in, on, or under the ocean.

We hope you have enjoyed Patrick Kendrick's tale of mystery, *Edison's Last Breath*. If you have not had the chance to read his other titles, we invite you to visit bluewaterpress.com to peruse his other works, as well as some of the other offerings by BluewaterPress LLC.